Sweet Union

"*Amo te*," Stuart whispered against her cheek. "I love you."

"Then show me," Anna whispered back.

He needed no further urging. Gently he guided Anna to lie down on her side and stretched out beside her. Holding her close, he kissed her forehead and her cheeks, her eyelids, and the tip of her nose. She shivered when he nibbled her earlobe, and her head fell back almost reflexively as his tongue probed the hollow of her neck and traced her collarbone. His hands moved lower, pressing in slow circles against her breasts, teasing her nipples to become pebble-hard. She strained against him, longing to feel his hands against her bare flesh.

Knowing her need, he plucked at the drawstring on her shift until it fell open, freeing her full breasts. His mouth covered one erect nipple, and his tongue first circled, then sucked the sweetness there before repeating his movements on the other breast.

He eased her shift the rest of the way off, then quickly removed his own clothing. She didn't have enough time to take in all the wonder of his naked body before he lowered it to cover hers. She felt as if every bit of her flesh strained toward every fiber of his body, seeking union.

Twin Willows

Kay Cornelius

HarperPaperbacks
A Division of HarperCollins*Publishers*

🏰 HarperPaperbacks
A Division of HarperCollins*Publishers*
10 East 53rd Street, New York, NY 10022-5299

This is a work of fiction. The characters, incidents, and
dialogues are products of the author's imagination and are
not to be construed as real. Any resemblance to actual events or
persons, living or dead, is entirely coincidental.

HarperCollins®, 🏰®, and HarperPaperbacks™ are trademarks of
HarperCollins Publishers Inc.

ISBN 0-06-101376-5

Cover illustration © 1999 by Jon Paul

First printing: February 1999

Printed in the United States of America

Visit HarperPaperbacks on the World Wide Web at
http://www.harpercollins.com

❖ 10 9 8 7 6 5 4 3 2 1

*To the memory of
William Moore, Sr. (1758–1844),
Revolutionary soldier and Kentucky pioneer,
and his wife, Olivia Ferree Moore*

prologue

The first time Ian McKnight saw the beautiful young Delaware woman, she sat beneath a weeping willow tree, framed by its slender, silver leaves. She turned her head in a gesture as graceful as the stirring of the tree's long limbs and regarded him with her great, dark eyes. From that very moment, Ian knew he loved her.

"You are my Silverwillow," he said, and by that odd *Yengwes* name she had since been known. Now, in a lodge far removed from the rest of the village, the young Delaware woman known as Silverwillow had been in labor for many more hours than usual, even for a first child. The two women attending her, one not much older than Silverwillow, the other twice her age, looked at each other and shook their heads, both aware that if the child she carried was not soon born, Silverwillow would surely die.

The older woman, Bear's Daughter, was the leading midwife of the sept of the Clan of the Turtle now living on the banks of the Muskingum River. She had felt uneasy when Silverwillow's belly began to grow huge early in her pregnancy. Bear's Daughter knew for a certainty that the trader Ian McKnight hadn't taken her to wife until the Moon When the Deer Turns Red, less than eight moons ago; before then, Silverwillow had lived chaste in Bear's Daughter's lodge.

"The spirit of a witch has entered that one," Blue Deer had muttered when all could see how much Silverwillow's body had swelled by the new Moon of the First Snow, which the white trader called "December."

Bear's Daughter had frowned and told the woman to stop her words, lest such talk mark the babe. But privately she was also concerned about Silverwillow, whom she had brought to live in her own lodge when the girl's parents had died from the white man's red spots.

As Bear's Daughter wiped the sweat from the young woman's brow, she remembered that some had said the girl was bewitched even then, because she had survived the illness that had killed her grandparents, parents, and her four brothers and sisters. The disease had quickly spread through the village and taken a heavy toll. There were those who thought that Bear's Daughter had been foolish to allow Silverwillow to stay with her when the half-starved girl came back to the village, so weak from the disease that had taken all her family that only Bear's Daughter's constant care had saved her life.

Silverwillow clamped down on the piece of rawhide between her teeth and moaned. Delaware women who cried out in childbirth were looked down upon, and at first she had made a conscious effort not to show how much pain she felt. Now, when she was past caring, she had no strength to scream.

"Where is my husband?" she whispered.

"I do not know," Bear's Daughter replied, half-truthfully. Like all men facing imminent fatherhood, Ian McKnight had been ordered to leave the village for a time. He said he would go check the traps he had set along the Paint River, but Bear's Daughter doubted that the burly, redhaired Scotsman would actually return with any pelts.

Silverwillow moaned softly. "I would see him again before I die."

"There will be no talk of dying," Bear's Daughter said sharply. "Take courage, my child. It cannot be much longer now."

Even as Bear's Daughter spoke, another racking pain seized Silverwillow, and her belly visibly heaved.

"The babe comes," Blue Deer said, and the women moved in concert, each to do her job in bringing forth the new life.

"A female child," Bear's Daughter announced with satisfaction moments later. Quickly she tied the cord and anointed the wriggling, screaming body with bear grease. But when she turned to place the babe in her mother's arms, Bear's Daughter saw that Silverwillow's agony had not ended. Her still-distended belly heaved once, then again.

"Ayee! There must be another babe in her womb,"

Blue Deer said in fearful tones. Only a few minutes later, her words were proven true when Silverwillow's labor produced a second child.

"Does it live?" Bear's Daughter whispered, seeing the unnatural stillness of the tiny form in Blue Deer's arms.

Blue Deer shook her head and gently set the baby down on a thick bearskin. "It is as well," she said. "A twin girl-child. It is a bad omen."

Tears welled in Bear's Daughter's eyes. "Such a beautiful child could never be a bad omen." She picked up the still form and patted the tiny girl's back. The baby gasped, her face contorted in rage, and she let out a lusty cry.

"They both live!" Blue Deer exclaimed almost fearfully.

"Let me see my babies," Silverwillow said weakly.

The woman knelt beside her. "This is your first-born," Blue Deer said, "a fine, well-formed daughter."

"And here is a second girl-child," Bear's Daughter said. "Your husband will be much surprised."

Tears formed in Silverwillow's eyes. Her cracked lips moved, but the women couldn't hear what she said.

Bear's Daughter bent her head close to Silverwillow's. "What is it, my daughter?"

"I wanted to give my man a son," she whispered.

"He will not care," Bear's Daughter said.

Silverwillow closed her eyes and seemed to be gathering strength to speak again. "Tell my husband he must not sorrow."

Bear's Daughter straightened, then laid Silverwillow's younger daughter by her side. "Rest now and you can tell him yourself. He will be here soon," she said.

Feebly Silverwillow shook her head. "No. I will not see him again in this life."

"Ayee," Blue Deer muttered. "The girl prophesies her death. Did I not say this one has been bewitched?"

Bear's Daughter wanted to tell her to stop, that Silverwillow wasn't dying, but she knew that denying the obvious wouldn't change it. "Your man and I will see that your babies are cared for," she said instead.

"It is good," Silverwillow said weakly. She turned her head and bent to kiss each baby's forehead, then closed her eyes and sighed. She drew a final, shuddering breath, then lay still.

Blue Deer leaned over and closed Silverwillow's eyes. "Her spirit is gone now," she said.

Bear's Daughter put a hand to her mouth and stifled the impulse to scream and throw herself on Silverwillow's body. The girl had been like a daughter to her for half of her young life, but even though Silverwillow's death grieved Bear's Daughter as nothing else ever had, it would not be the Delaware way to give in to it.

Instead, she rocked back on her heels and looked at the babies, who both now lay quietly with their eyes closed in sleep. "A nurse must be found for them, or they will die," she said.

"No one in our village can nurse two more in these hard times," Blue Deer said. "It would be better to smother them and tell the trader that they never breathed."

Bear's Daughter glanced sharply at Blue Deer. "No! I will never allow harm to come to Silverwillow's babies. There is another way."

"Would you suckle them yourself? You are old and have no milk," Blue Deer said scornfully.

"It is time you weaned your Little Faun," Bear's Daughter said. "You will have enough milk."

"Not for two babies," Blue Deer protested.

"Newborns do not take much. I will keep the second girl-child and leave the trader the firstborn."

Blue Deer made a derisive noise. "Whites are greedy. The man will want them both."

Bear's Daughter looked meaningfully at Blue Deer. "He will not know about the second one," she said.

Blue Deer shook her head. "Ayee, I like it not. How can he not know? Does he not live among us?"

"I have been planning to visit my kin among the *Shawonese* for many moons. I will take the second girl-child and find her a suckling-nurse there. We will not return to this place."

"It is not good," Blue Deer murmured. "Everyone knows that girl twins are likely to be bewitched. They are better off to die now than to cause us all grief later."

Bear's Daughter leaned forward and spoke earnestly. "Will you kill the babies yourself, woman? I promise that the moment you move to harm either of them will be your last on earth."

Blue Deer had always been half-afraid of Bear's Daughter. Now as the older woman riveted her with her dark, brooding eyes, Blue Deer could only reluctantly nod her assent.

"It will be as you say, then. But if the trader learns of this—"

Bear's Daughter made the cutoff sign. "If ever I find that you have told of this, it will not go well with you and yours, either in this place or any other that you might go to live. Know this."

"I will say nothing," Blue Deer promised.

"Go out now and show the village the daughter that Silverwillow died birthing. As you do, I will hide the other babe in my lodge."

"What about the trader?" Blue Deer asked.

"Send after him—he cannot be far away now. I will speak to him."

"I hope this thing will not bring trouble to us," Blue Deer said.

Bear's Daughter looked down at Silverwillow's still form and shook her head. "No. All will be done as I have said. Now go."

Casting a nervous glance at the second baby, Blue Deer took the firstborn twin and left the lodge.

Carefully Bear's Daughter wrapped the girl-child in a deerskin and concealed it beneath her buffalo-skin cloak. As a small group gathered outside around Blue Deer, Bear's Daughter made her way unnoticed to her lodge, where she quickly made a bed of soft bearskin for the child she already thought of as hers. Although traditionally a Delaware baby would not be named until it was about ten days old, Bear's Daughter already knew what she would call this child. Bending over the small form, she whispered the name into the child's tiny ear.

As if she heard and understood, the baby opened

her eyes and stared gravely at her new mother.

"Yes, Littlewillow—you already know who you are!" Bear's Daughter exclaimed. "Sleep now. I will be back soon."

As she left her lodge, Bear's Daughter heard the first keening notes of the Death Song, and pulled her cloak over her face as a sign of her grief.

No one in this village loved Silverwillow as I did, she thought. *And no one, anywhere, could ever love Silverwillow's daughter more.*

The chanting had been underway for about half an hour when Ian McKnight returned to the village. Over six feet tall, with curly, dark auburn hair and intense blue eyes, he normally cut an imposing figure. But this day, burdened with the news of his beloved wife's death, the trader's bearded face wore a stunned expression, and he looked far older than his thirty years.

"What happened?" he asked Bear's Daughter in the Delaware language.

She shrugged. "I do not know. Silverwillow lost much blood."

Tears glistened in the big man's eyes and he dug at them with the palm of his hand. "I should have stayed here," he said. "I should na' have let ye send me away."

"It would change nothing, trader. She said to tell you that you must not be sorry."

"Not be sorry!" Ian McKnight spoke rapidly in English, then recovered himself and set his jaw. "There is a girl-child?" he asked.

"Yes. Will you go to her now?"

The trader nodded. "Did Silverwillow live to see her?"

Bear's Daughter nodded. "Yes. Come, the child is in Blue Deer's lodge."

Ian McKnight clenched his fists and blinked his eyes furiously to keep back the tears as he looked for the first time at his dark-haired daughter's tiny features.

Bear's Daughter placed the child in her father's arms. Unconsciously repeating his wife's actions, the trader bent to kiss the child's forehead, then gazed down at the baby, who gravely looked back at her father.

"Welcome to this sad world," he said softly in English.

"Do you name her?" asked Bear's Daughter, who knew only a few words in the *Yengwes* tongue.

Ian McKnight looked over at her and nodded. "When the time comes, she will be called Anna Willow McKnight."

Everyone in the lodge exchanged glances and murmured about the strange *Yengwes* name that the trader had given his daughter.

"I will take her now," Blue Deer said. "I will keep the babe in my lodge until she is weaned."

Ian McKnight looked at Blue Deer in surprise. "My daughter will not stay here at all," he said.

"Then how will the child live? She will die if she is not suckled."

Ian McKnight looked back at his daughter. "There are those among my people who can nurse her. I will take her to them."

Bear's Daughter tried to sound distressed. "She is all I have of my Silverwillow. The Lenni-Lenape are her people, too. Surely you must let her stay here, where she belongs."

"You speak true, Bear's Daughter. But Silverwillow knew that I planned to take her and the baby back to my people in the time of the Pawpawing Moon. I will go there now instead."

Bear's Daughter nodded meekly. "It will be as you say. But Anna Willow should also learn the ways of her mother's people."

"I will tell her of these things. Someday perhaps she will come back here."

"May it be so, then." Bear's Daughter lowered her head and turned away from the trader, more satisfied than she could let anyone know. She didn't believe for a moment that the daughter Ian McKnight called Anna Willow would ever return to the land of her mother.

It is just as well that he takes her to his people, Bear's Daughter thought. Sometimes twins grew up to look almost exactly alike. If that should happen and Ian McKnight ever saw this other, he would know at once that he had been deceived.

It will never happen, Bear's Daughter vowed. Littlewillow would be raised as hers, and hers alone. The white man would never know she existed.

1

PHILADELPHIA, 1781

Since its founding in 1772, Miss Martin's School for Young Ladies had occupied a narrow red brick house in a fashionable lane just off Philadelphia's Market Street. Miss Martin's was neither the most expensive nor the most exclusive school in Philadelphia, but its director prided herself on serving a select clientele and upholding certain standards. Miss Matilda Martin, although a strict headmistress, made sure her girls got thorough instruction in how to be fine, proper, intelligent young ladies suitable to become wives in high society. Of course, being a spinster, Miss Martin taught by the book and not from personal experience.

Most of the young ladies were quartered in the bedchambers on the third floor. Anna Willow McKnight and her best friend Felicia Darby shared a small attic room a half flight above the fourth-floor servants' quarters. Although in hot weather it was undeniably the least desirable location in the house, in the winter its proximity to the kitchen chimney usually made it almost bearable.

On this raw December day, however, Anna McKnight shivered as she put on all three of her petticoats under her warmest wool dress. Because the other pupils were gone for the holidays, the amount of cooking had been greatly reduced, and along with it, the fires that produced the heat to warm the attic.

"You really ought to go home for the holidays," Miss Martin had told Anna, more from a desire to get rid of her than from any concern that she might be lonely.

"No, ma'am. I shall stay here and begin to catch up on all the work I missed when I was ill," Anna had replied.

"Very well, but don't expect to be catered to."

Anna had to bite her tongue to keep from saying that she'd never been catered to and knew better than to expect anything extra from the parsimonious headmistress. "I shan't, Miss Martin," she had said.

In any case, Anna had no desire to return to the place that she no longer regarded as her home. She had been fourteen, all long legs and big, dark eyes, when her father Ian McKnight insisted that his daughter should leave her aunt's western Pennsylvania farm to be educated like a lady.

Anna recalled Miss Martin's look of disdain when she arrived in Philadelphia, as if the muck of the pigpen still clung to her homespun dress. Anna had no doubt that she would have been turned away from the school's door without a second thought if it hadn't been for Miss Martin's nephew, Stuart Martin, who had served with Ian McKnight in the Pennsylvania Line during the War for American Independence. Despite the difference in their ages and backgrounds, the two men had become friends. Ian's concern that his daughter receive a proper education prompted Stuart Martin to urge his aunt to admit her. Daughters of rich men were seldom turned away, providing their bloodlines were sufficiently pure. Occasionally the daughter of a minister or some other poor man was allowed to enroll if she was willing to work hard for her keep, as Felicia Darby did. However, no one with Anna's background had ever dared to be presented for entrance to Miss Martin's school—and no father had ever been more insistent that his daughter should be admitted.

"I will pay the girl's tuition and board for all three years in one sum if ye wish," Ian McKnight had offered. That alone would have gone a long way toward changing Miss Martin's negative opinion, but she had been fully swayed by the letter he carried from Stuart Martin, who stated that he owed his life to the older man. So Anna had been grudgingly admitted, and so she had lived for two and a half years.

Her aunt, Agnes Barfield, the only mother Anna had ever known, had died the year before. Soon after, her eldest cousin Henry had married a local girl who had never liked Anna; and in a letter, Henry had made it clear that the Barfields didn't need another mouth to feed. Like it or not, Miss Martin's school had become Anna's only home.

The headmistress agreed that Anna had much

work to make up. "I would also remind you that my nephew has many matters to attend to on his holiday. You must not expect Mr. Martin to help you."

"No, ma'am, I shan't."

"Humph," Miss Martin had said, looking at Anna as if she doubted it.

In fact, Anna secretly hoped to spend some time with Stuart Martin. She recalled the first time she had seen him, soon after he had returned from the army to resume his studies at Princeton. His tall figure dominating the room was the object of many admiring female stares. Ignoring the others, he had sought out Anna and approached her with a smile of welcome.

"You must be Anna Willow. Colonel McKnight talked about you so much, I already feel that I know you."

Too shy to speak, she could only nod and curtsy, fearing she couldn't say a word to him without stammering. Since then, as his own schedule allowed, Stuart had taught enough Latin and Greek to his aunt's pupils to justify Miss Martin's claim that her young ladies were instructed in both scholarly and artistic subjects. Not a few of Miss Martin's pupils were interested in Stuart Martin, but so far, he had gone out of his way to avoid even the slightest personal contact with them.

"I think Stuart Martin likes me, though," Anna said aloud to the empty room, and her breath made a cloud in the cold room. Quickly she laced the bodice of her plain blue wool dress and peered critically into the shadowy piece of broken glass that passed for a mirror. As a child, Anna had hoped that her dark hair and eyes and complexion might miraculously lighten, making her look more like her cousins and everyone else she knew. The hurt of knowing that she was different remained even after Anna's father had explained that she looked very much like her Delaware Indian mother, who had died giving birth to her.

"Ye're beautiful, lass, and ye should never be ashamed of your mother," Ian McKnight had told her.

Her father had told her many times how he had met the beautiful Silverwillow when she brought her baskets to his trading post, and how only weeks later he had taken her down the river to find a white minister to marry them. His oft-repeated account made Anna even more curious.

"I want to see the village where you lived," Anna had insisted. "My mother's relatives still live there, don't they?"

"Nay, lass. Your mother had no relatives. She was an orphan, taken in and raised by a kind old woman no kin to her at all. When ye're older, I'll take ye there."

But long before that time had come, her father had gone off to war.

Anna sighed and pinched her cheeks for color, as she'd seen other girls do. She couldn't help but envy the light complexions of Miss Martin's other girls. Even Rose Smythe, with hair even darker than Anna's, had creamy white skin, strikingly set off by her rosy cheeks.

"I imagine that color comes from a rouge pot she's got hidden away somewhere," Felicia once told Anna, but that knowledge was small consolation.

"Stuart Martin will have to accept me as I am or not at all," Anna told the mirror as she pinned up her thick chestnut hair, covered it with a mob cap, and left her chilly room.

She found Miss Martin and her nephew seated at the round wood table in the family dining room, where Stuart conducted his infrequent lessons. Anna couldn't help but notice the contrast in the appearance of aunt and nephew. Both had wavy, thick hair of the same sandy shade, and startling, almost violet, eyes; but otherwise the two bore no other resemblance. Miss Martin's face was long and mournful, her mouth perennially drooping as if she had just heard bad news, and the tilt of her nose suggested she disapproved of everything that came her way. On the other hand, Stuart Martin's face was almost square, and the corners of his mouth turned up as if he knew some delightful secret.

As Anna approached the table, Stuart rose in greeting and pulled out a chair for her. Miss Martin scowled and rang for the servant.

"Miss McKnight has finally decided to join us," she told the elderly cook, Nancy, who shuffled into the room. Then she fixed her legendary stare on Anna. "I'm afraid late risers must make do with cold porridge."

"I don't mind, Miss Martin. I didn't realize the hour was so late." Anna attempted a slight smile, but as usual, the headmistress didn't return it.

"Even if her breakfast is cold, it'll still be warmer than the attic," Stuart said to his aunt. "I was up there yesterday when you and Miss McKnight were at the market, and my hands were numb with cold before I found my old Latin texts."

"You should have left your books here in our library in case any of my pupils wanted to use them," Miss Martin said.

Stuart waved at the wall where some fifty volumes resided on three shelves of a somewhat rickety old cabinet. "Calling that paltry collection of books a library is something of an exaggeration, Aunt Matilda. Anyhow, I doubt that any of your young ladies would ever voluntarily choose to peruse Caesar's *Gallic Wars* on their own."

"I should like to try it," Anna said.

Stuart nodded, unsurprised. "I just told Aunt that you are her only pupil with any facility for language at all. However, I suspect that the book may be too elementary for you."

"I know that Gaul was divided into three parts, but not much else," Anna said.

Stuart's look of pleasure was balanced by his aunt's opposite expression, which neither he nor Anna heeded. "Then we shall start a bit further into the book and see how you do with it."

Miss Martin's tone was frosty. "Perhaps I should remind you that Miss McKnight's father did not pay extra for private tutoring."

Stuart's lips compressed into a thin line and his face colored briefly. "Miss McKnight and I are scholars discussing a mutual interest. Such a conversation is not tutoring."

His aunt flushed, but she said no more until after

the cook had set Anna's breakfast before her and once more returned to the kitchen.

"I should think that your studies at Princeton would demand all of your time. Perhaps if you are to be unduly distracted here, it would be better for you to return at once to your lodgings at the college."

Stuart looked levelly at his aunt, something that few others ever dared to do. "Are you asking me to leave this house, ma'am?"

Miss Martin's cheeks flamed even redder. "You well know that this is your home, Stuart. But I would remind you that your poor departed father meant the funds he left you to be used for your education. I am sure he would not want you to abuse the privileges that you have been given in this household."

With fascination Anna watched the battle of wills being played out before her. Miss Martin's pupils knew that the building that housed the school had been owned by Stuart Martin's father, who had died the previous year. John Martin had broken convention by bequeathing the house to his unmarried sister instead of to his only surviving son.

Miss Martin shouldn't be angry with her nephew, Anna thought. She returned her attention to Stuart as he spoke, breaking the tense silence between him and his aunt.

"I am fully aware of your generosity, Aunt Matilda."

"I should hope your studies have taught you that generosity is due to be returned in like kind."

A slight smile played at the corners of Stuart's mouth, but whatever words he might have said were left unspoken. "And so shall it be. After the twenty-fifth of this month, I shall return to Princeton and bother you no more."

Miss Martin lowered her eyes and sipped tea from a bone china cup. "You may stay as long as you like," she murmured halfheartedly.

Stuart returned his attention to Anna, who had been quietly trying to appear oblivious to the scene she had just witnessed. In the past few days, Stuart had become fully aware that the coltish, gawky girl child he'd persuaded his aunt to admit to her school had become a beautiful young woman. Everything about her, from her obvious intelligence to her unusual complexion and the easy grace with which she moved, stirred him in a way he had never felt before. Lately Stuart had found it hard to sound businesslike when speaking to Anna.

"I have some errands to attend to this morning, Miss McKnight, but perhaps later today we can see where you stand with Mr. Caesar."

Anna glanced at Miss Martin, who apparently was completely absorbed in pouring more tea into her cup, then looked back at Stuart. The new way in which he seemed to be regarding her sent a thrill of hope through her body. "That is most kind of you, sir," she managed to say.

"My pleasure." Stuart sounded as if he meant it. He rose from his chair and bowed slightly, first to his aunt and then to Anna. "Please excuse me, ladies." His eyes held Anna's, seeming to hold a breath-stopping message that his words had not.

It's no wonder that half the girls at Miss Martin's are in love with him, Anna thought. His face was more rugged than handsome, true, and perhaps he was slender almost to the point of thinness, but Stuart Martin's warm and genuine smile and passion for life and learning had endeared him to her from the start. Never before had Anna met any man who attracted her the way Stuart Martin did.

I'm glad I'll see him again today, she thought happily.

"Well, Miss McKnight, I recommend that you use the morning hours to work on our wall hanging," Miss Martin said.

"I'll get my embroidery supplies." Anna rose to leave the table.

Miss Martin angrily smacked her palm against the polished rosewood. "Just a moment, young lady! Have you quite forgotten your manners?"

Her face warm, Anna sat back down. "I'm sorry, Miss Martin. May I please be excused?"

The headmistress compressed her lips. "In a moment. Perhaps it is time that I remind you, Miss McKnight, that I do not expect and will not tolerate any familiarity between you and my nephew. Is that clear?"

Anna nodded, aware that protest would be futile.

"Very well, then. You may leave the table. Next time, do not forget to ask permission to do so."

On her way back to her attic room for her scissors and embroidery hoop, Anna chastised herself for giving Miss Martin an excuse to remind her of how poor she considered Anna's manners to be.

"Were you reared with animals, Miss McKnight?" Miss Martin had asked Anna during the first meal she had taken at the school.

"Well, ma'am, my aunt and uncle have some hogs and cows and a yoke of oxen on the place," she had replied, setting off titters of ill-concealed laughter from the other young ladies at the table and making Miss Martin scowl at her.

"I will not be mocked by a half-breed, Miss Mc-Knight," Miss Martin had replied. The gasp that had gone up from the other girls had been followed by dead silence as Miss Martin's face turned from scarlet to ashen. Her mouth had opened and closed a few times before the headmistress recovered her composure and riveted her gaze on Anna.

"We will discuss this matter later," she said, but never again had Miss Martin directly referred to Anna's heritage. Anna had continued to be the object of sly glances and whispered conversation among Miss Martin's other pupils, however, which the headmistress had done little or nothing to stop.

"Half-breed," the other girls called Anna behind her back, and "squaw." Sometimes they made gestures of raising tomahawks and uttering their versions of war whoops. Anna tried to ignore them, but it was difficult.

Only two people in Philadelphia had ever seemed to accept Anna McKnight for herself. One was her roommate and only friend, Felicia Darby. The other person was Stuart Martin. Since he knew her father so well, Stuart was certainly aware of her mixed blood, but he had never mentioned it.

Until now, in fact, most of the time Anna had seen Stuart Martin with the ten or so other girls who crowded into the small dining room for his Latin and

Greek classes. Other than that he had been her father's friend, Anna knew little about Miss Martin's nephew.

I don't even know what he's studying at Princeton, Anna thought as she returned to the sitting room and unrolled the giant tapestry on which all Miss Martin's young ladies had been working for several months. She had fallen behind on her part during a recent bad cold that had confined her to her room for over a week. Since Anna had never done fancy-work before coming to Miss Martin's and was judged to lack skill in it, she had been relegated to filling in the dark background of a grandiose mural depicting some sort of triumphal procession. Once when Alice Daniels complained that Anna had spoiled her fleur-de-lis, Miss Martin had given Anna five blows with the ruler she called the Corrector. Twice afterwards, Miss Martin had delivered Anna two more blows, not for any specific error, but because she had failed to fill in the background as rapidly as the others had the designs.

Today, as Anna stretched the fabric taut around her hoop and threaded her fine-pointed tapestry needle, it was hard not to think about her forthcoming meeting with Stuart Martin. As she monotonously pushed the needle through the fabric, pulled the thread taut, then reinserted the needle as close as she could get it to the last stitch without splitting the thread, Anna found herself daydreaming about the way Stuart Martin had looked at her that morning. Did she dare hope that he was beginning to return her interest, or had she merely imagined what she wanted to see in his eyes?

Anna was so absorbed in her thoughts that she

didn't notice when Stuart entered the room. He stood beside her for several moments before he quietly spoke her name. Startled, Anna jabbed her finger with the needle. With horror she watched a drop of blood fall onto and stain some fancy golden-threaded scrollwork.

"Oh!" Anna exclaimed. She grabbed the fabric of her skirt between two fingers, aiming to blot the spot with it, but Stuart stayed her hand. Since he had just come inside, his own hand was still cold. Yet his touch made her feel strangely warm.

"Don't do that—you'll only make it worse." Quickly Stuart applied the corner of his lawn handkerchief to the globule of blood. Like a wick, it absorbed most of it. He dampened another corner of the cloth and pressed it against the remaining stain for a moment. When he took it away, Anna could see that most of the pinkness was gone.

"When it dries, it will be almost invisible," Stuart assured her.

"Miss Martin will see it," Anna said.

Stuart smiled. "Aunt Matilda doesn't miss much," he agreed. "But if you move your hoop to a fresh place and start over, I don't think even she will notice."

"I must finish this section first—she'll know if I don't."

"Will it distract you if I join you?" Stuart Martin asked. "I won't look at your stitches," he added, seeing Anna's hesitation.

"Of course not," she said.

Stuart Martin pulled up a Windsor chair and sat

near enough to Anna for his presence to have an odd effect. She had looked forward to being alone with him, yet now that she was, Anna felt awkward and tongue-tied.

"I went out to buy a mathematics text I need for my studies, but no one in Philadelphia seems to have it," he said.

"What will you do, then?" Anna asked.

He shrugged. "Go to New York, I suppose, although it will be a hard trip in this weather."

The easy manner in which Stuart Martin spoke to her, not as schoolmaster and pupil but as if they were friends, gave Anna courage to address him the same way. "I suppose you must have become accustomed to traveling in all kinds of weather in the army," she said.

"Colonel McKnight taught me how to be as comfortable as possible, no matter what the circumstances. I will always be in his debt for that."

Anna looked up briefly from her embroidery. It seemed strange to realize that Stuart Martin not only had seen her father more recently than she had, but also knew Ian McKnight perhaps even better than she did. Anna was also reminded of how long it had been since she had heard from him. "Do you know where my father went after your troop disbanded?" she asked.

Stuart returned her look and shook his head. "No, I don't. Several months before the war ended, he volunteered to scout in the Western territory, and I haven't seen him since. But Colonel McKnight often spoke about returning to the site of his first post. He said that when the war ended, the British wouldn't be continually stirring up the Indians, and it'd be a good time to branch out and establish new business."

Anna lowered her head and stilled her needle. "My father always promised to take me back to my mother's village, but he never did," she said wistfully. "I wish I knew for certain that he is still all right."

Stuart leaned forward and took Anna's left hand as if he meant to comfort her. "Don't worry. Your father is a man of action, not words. He knows your schooling will be finished in a few months. I wouldn't be surprised if he turned up on the doorstep quite unannounced."

Anna's hand tingled in Stuart's, and she pressed it lightly against his, happy that he continued to hold her hand as if it were natural to do so. "Do you really think he'll come for me?"

Stuart nodded. "Your father spoke about you many times. He regretted that he's had to be away from you so much, and that the frontier hasn't been safe enough for him to take you with him. Wherever he is, you can be sure that Ian McKnight will never forget his daughter."

It was the longest, most personal conversation Anna had ever had with any man, and she could only nod in response. She feared that if she attempted to say even a word, the tears that she had so far managed to suppress would surely spill onto her cheeks.

All opportunity for private conversation ended abruptly when the front door opened and Matilda Martin swept into the room. She registered immediate surprise at seeing her nephew, who had hastily dropped Anna's hand and stood, just in the nick of time.

"I thought you went out," she said accusingly.

"I did, and now I'm back again. It appears I must travel to New York City to find the book I need."

Anna thought that Miss Martin looked almost relieved. "When will you leave?" she asked.

Stuart half smiled at his aunt. "Don't sound so eager to get rid of me, Aunt Matilda. I'll make an early return to Princeton after Christmas Day and go on to New York from there."

"As you wish." Miss Martin turned her attention from her nephew to Anna. "You may work on the tapestry until luncheon, then help me mend the table linens."

"You forget that Miss McKnight has a previous engagement with Mr. Caesar and his wars," Stuart said smoothly.

His aunt looked annoyed, then shrugged and turned away. "Go ahead, for all the good it will do," she murmured.

What did she mean by that? Anna thought. Then she realized that she already knew. Miss Martin expected that when Anna completed her schooling, she would return either to the farm or to the frontier where Ian McKnight had always conducted his business. In neither place would a polished education be an advantage.

When his aunt was well out of earshot, Stuart leaned forward and spoke earnestly. "I hope you pay her no mind, Miss McKnight. My aunt and I often disagree, and I can assure you that I don't share some of her views about the value of education to a young lady."

Surprised by his tone, Anna raised her eyebrows. "And just what are your views about the education of young ladies?"

Stuart flushed. "That was a bit pompous, I suppose. I don't mean to sound as if I know it all, because I certainly do not. But my studies have led me to believe that true education is never wasted if any individual—male or female—uses it to realize his or her highest potential." He half bowed. "I apologize for interrupting your work. I'll go now and attend to some studying of my own."

"There's no need to apologize," Anna said quickly. She wanted to tell Stuart she could listen to him talk all day, but such an admission would only embarrass them both.

"I am glad you think so, Miss McKnight. Caesar and I will see you later."

Luncheon passed quietly, without the spirited discussions that had marked breakfast. However, Miss Martin's disapproval of her nephew's determination to spend the afternoon tutoring Anna hung in the air like a dark cloud. When the headmistress finally excused herself and left the table, Anna had to restrain herself from breathing an audible sigh of relief.

Neither Anna nor Stuart spoke as the cook cleared away the luncheon dishes and crumbed the table, but when they were alone, he smiled at Anna as if they were co-conspirators. "Well, shall we begin now?"

"Yes, sir," Anna replied.

Stuart moved his chair so close to Anna's that their

knees touched—too close for propriety. *I should move away*, she thought, but did not.

Without seeming to notice their nearness, Stuart opened the book on top of the stack of texts he had brought from the attic and pushed it toward Anna. "Translate, please."

She looked at him questioningly. "You have already taught us this."

"I know. I want to see how much you recall."

He was so near that Anna could hear his even breathing and feel the warmth of his body. With difficulty she forced herself to concentrate on the strangely marked words, and began to read, sliding her finger along the line. "All Gaul is divided into three parts."

Stuart moved even closer and used his left hand to remove Anna's right hand from the book. "Don't ever use your finger as a place mark," he said.

Anna's cheeks warmed, more because Stuart held her hand than from his gentle reprimand. "Why not?" she asked. "It's the way I learned to read."

"It slows you down, for one thing, and it wears the pages out as well. Books are too dear-bought to be ill treated."

"I'm sorry. I didn't know."

Stuart released Anna's hand and smiled slightly. "Don't look so distressed," he said. "That's not the worst thing you could ever do. Read on."

After Anna had translated another page, Stuart stopped her and turned to the next section. "Can you read this?"

With Stuart pressed close to her side, Anna

thought it was a wonder she could read anything at all. She made a halting start, but many of the words were unfamiliar, and she soon had to stop.

"This is where we shall begin," he said. "See that word you didn't know? If you will note, its root is the same as one you had no trouble with earlier."

Stuart's head bent close to hers and their shoulders met as he pointed out the line of text. Anna was so conscious of his nearness that she found it hard to concentrate on what he was saying about the ablative and genitive. For some strange reason, Anna found herself wondering how Stuart Martin's arms would feel around her, how his lips might feel on hers . . .

She swallowed hard and tried to make her voice firm, despite the fluttering she felt inside. "I'm not sure I understand," she finally managed.

As if he, too, had become aware of their closeness and found it uncomfortable, Stuart leaned back and moved his chair away. Even though their bodies no longer touched, Stuart's violet eyes looked into hers with an intensity that almost took away Anna's breath.

"You will."

His expression indicated that he had more in mind than Latin.

Aware that their conversation ought to be brought back to a safer level, Anna said the first thing that came into her mind. "I have never heard what you are studying at Princeton. Some of the girls think you plan to come back and take over this school yourself."

Stuart's laughter was quick and hearty. "No, I can assure you that I will never do that. As for what I am studying, just now it is a little of everything."

"Perhaps the girls said it because you really are a good teacher."

Unlike your aunt, Anna refrained from saying, but she thought that Stuart was well aware that Miss Martin's instruction was long on social graces and artistic pursuits, but rather short on the finer points of mathematics and rhetoric.

"You think so because you have never known better," Stuart said, confirming her belief that he knew all of his aunt's academic deficiencies.

"Then what do you plan to do, Mr. Martin?" It was a bold question, but Anna had grown up speaking plainly, and Stuart Martin's frankness had encouraged her to respond the same way.

"I am not certain, Miss McKnight," he replied, using her name as formally as she had his, "but I want nothing more to do with fighting and ill feeling amongst people. I have no desire to return to the army life, nor to read law. And I most certainly don't want become a physician."

"That doesn't leave much," Anna said.

Again Stuart Martin laughed. "You sound like Aunt Matilda," he said. "She wants me to make a great deal of money, without engaging in vulgar trade or commerce."

"How do you feel about that? You must know that my father has been a trader all his life."

"Yes, and unlike some who deal with the Indians, Ian McKnight not only made money, but also seems to have conducted himself honorably. Not all such men can say that."

"You are a good teacher. I can't imagine anything

you could ever do that would be any more suited to your talents."

Stuart looked away from Anna, then stood and walked over to the window, where a fine sleet rattled against the pane. After a moment he returned and sat down again, avoiding looking directly into her eyes. "If I tell you what I might do, will you agree to keep it to yourself?"

A shiver completely unrelated to the cold moved down Anna's spine as she realized that Stuart Martin was about to tell her something that he would probably not even discuss with his aunt. "Of course," she said faintly.

With fascination, Anna noticed for the first time the steady pulse beating in Stuart's temple. Had it always been so visible, or was she just now seeing it because of the heightened sensations she felt in his presence?

When he continued to be silent, Anna laid her hand lightly on his coat sleeve. "It's all right if you'd rather not tell me—I understand."

Stuart covered her hand with his and stared intently into Anna's eyes as if testing the truth of her words. "I believe you do, at that," he said. "So many do not."

"It is the same with me," Anna said quietly. "Many people don't understand my existence. Sometimes I think they wonder why I should be living at all."

A look of anger passed over Stuart's features, and he shook his head slightly. "The world is full of ignorant people, Miss McKnight. Sometimes I think I'm being presumptuous to assume that I can teach them better, but perhaps that may be my call."

"I thought you didn't want to be a teacher," Anna said.

"I said I would never teach here. Your father first put an idea into my mind that has stayed."

Anna looked puzzled. "My father? What did he say?"

"As you know, your father and I became very good friends. Sharing rations and quarters, we had many opportunities to speak frankly, as men are apt to do before battles they're not sure they'll survive. At such a time he told me about your mother, and how some members of his own family—he didn't name them—had cut him off when he married her because they thought of Silverwillow as a subhuman savage."

At Anna's sharp intake of breath, Stuart stopped, concern apparent in his expression. "I feared my words would be hurtful," he said.

"No," Anna managed to say. "It's nothing I haven't heard before about—savages."

"Of course, your father said that the aunt who brought you up didn't feel that way," Stuart hastened to add.

Anna nodded. "Yes, Aunt Agnes never differentiated between me and her own children. But I've heard such things from others, even my own cousins, all my life. I try not to let it bother me, but I do feel sad that people can be so cruel."

Stuart took her hand in his and gently pressed it. "Exactly what I thought when your father told me about it. Then he suggested I should consider living on the frontier, as he has done."

"Your aunt would not approve," Anna said.

Stuart pulled the corners of his mouth down in an

imitation of Miss Martin's perpetual expression. "Aunt Matilda hasn't liked anything I've ever done—she's unlikely to start now. Anyway, she cannot control my future."

"What would you do if you went West?" For a moment, Anna allowed herself to imagine Stuart Martin in buckskins. She liked the picture.

Stuart took his hand from hers again. "I would like to start my own school, but that will take more money than I have now. I might stay on at Princeton and tutor for a time when my own studies are completed. Then I'd like to cross the mountains and see the Northwest Territory," he said.

Where I was born? Anna's thought answered her unspoken question and finished what his own words had not. "It's still wilderness out there," she said, more distantly than she intended.

"It will grow less so in time. Anyway, all that's still far in the future. That's one reason nothing must be said about it now."

Anna's eyes silently reinforced her spoken words. "I understand. You can trust me."

For a moment Anna and Stuart gazed into each other's eyes, aware that something important had passed between them, but not quite understanding its true nature.

Then Stuart gestured toward the forgotten Latin book. "We seem to have strayed from the subject at hand. Shall we continue? I believe I can show you how to continue to study Caesar on your own after I leave."

"I wish you could stay here longer," Anna dared to say.

The way Stuart looked at her made Anna know that he shared the sentiment. "It is probably just as well that I must leave soon," he said, and Anna thought she knew what he meant.

Stuart Martin had his whole future ahead of him. Despite their apparently mutual attraction, she thought, having a half-breed wife would be a disadvantage to him. Immediately Anna chided herself for the presumption that marrying her could ever enter Stuart Martin's mind.

"Very well, sir. I will do my best to study on my own," Anna said.

Moments later Miss Martin entered the room, looking almost disappointed to see her nephew standing on the opposite side of the table from where Anna sat, listening as the young woman haltingly read aloud in Latin.

"I should think you've both had enough of that for one day," said the headmistress with some asperity. "Clear off the table and we'll take some tea."

2

The girl the Shawnee knew as Willow sat at the entrance of the lodge she shared with Bear's Daughter and gazed at their village without really seeing it. *Something unusual will soon happen.* Willow knew it in the same way that she knew that rain would come, even when the sky was blue. Furthermore, Willow sensed that Bear's Daughter shared her belief that some important change awaited them both.

We've had much change lately, and not for good, Willow thought as she recalled the source of their recent hardships. The red-coated *Shemanese*, who not many years past had fought the French and some of the O-hio tribes, now warred with Shemanese settlers. They brought fine gifts, rifles and powder, and iron cooking pots to any Shawnee, Delaware, Mingo, or Wyandot who would raid the *Shemanese* settlements to the west and south. Sometimes the red-coats even led the warriors themselves. Some of the septs had refused to take part, only to have their corn burned in the field by *Shemanese* who blamed all Indians for the work of a few.

The general unrest and persistent shortage of food forced Chief Black Snake to move his people from one place to another in a vain search for the security they had once taken for granted. They had wandered far to the north, visiting with their brothers along the way, but no one had much to share with them. A few moons back they had returned to Waccachalla. Once more they repaired their *wegiwas* and planted crops they knew they might never harvest.

Since their return, nothing seemed out of the ordinary, at least on the surface. Willow did not have to be told, however, that all was not well. Vague rumors spread through the village almost daily, and the lines between friend and foe, once so clear, were now less certain. Some said that the *Shemanese* settlers would spill from their farms to the east and make the Shawnee leave their villages. Others said that the redcoats and the other *Shemanese* would soon quit fighting each other. Then all would return to the faraway land from which they had come, and the Shawnee could continue the life that the *Shemanese* had so disrupted.

In the meantime, Black Snake's warriors spent a great deal of time away from Waccachalla, raiding with first one group and then another. Sometimes they came back with bounty from *Shemanese* settlements or from the strange flat boats the *Shemanese* rode on down the O-hio-se-pe. Even when they stayed in the village, the men spent more time readying their weapons than using them to hunt food. Often the warriors put on war paint and preened for no reason. With fierce war whoops, they'd shake their tomahawks at imaginary enemies while the old men, women, and children laughed and shouted their approval.

Willow had watched these rites from afar. While she wore a long, fringed deerskin shift identical to those of the other village women, Willow looked nothing like them. The Shawnee women were generally short and sturdily built, with high-bridged noses and coarse black hair. In contrast, the tall and slender Willow had lighter skin and more delicate features. Most strikingly different was her waist-length chestnut hair, which Bear's Daughter took great pride in adorning. This morning, the old woman knelt behind Willow as she braided thin rawhide strips into its soft, lustrous strands.

Willow grew weary of sitting still and turned to address Bear's Daughter, her tone carefully polite. "Is something wrong that you spend so much time dressing my hair this day, my mother?"

"The stiffness that holds my hands makes them slow, Littlewillow," Bear's Daughter replied.

"You are not well, my mother. The medicine man—"

"Sits-in-Shadow has no medicine for me," Bear's Daughter said scornfully, and Willow feared she spoke the truth. Her mother hadn't fully recovered from the terrible cold of last winter when even the O-hio-se-pe had frozen solid and they'd all hungered. Bear's Daughter touched Willow lightly on the shoulder. "Turn around. I will put this fine blue jay feather over your ear. Then I will be done."

Willow sighed. "No one else calls me Littlewillow. Am I not already even taller than the chief of Waccachalla village? I am no longer 'little,' my mother. The others smile behind their hands that you still call me so."

Bear's Daughter grunted in disapproval. "Do I not always tell you not to care what others say? Their laughter means nothing. I call my daughter what I like."

Willow well knew the futility of attempting to change her mother's mind. "It is so," she murmured.

Bear's Daughter leaned over Willow's shoulder and pointed toward a young warrior who had just returned to the village with a brace of rabbits. "What of Short Elk, Littlewillow? Perhaps he will yet bring you a deer."

Willow glanced at the Shawnee, a lad she had beaten in foot races as a child; then she looked away lest he should see her watching him and think she meant to invite his attention. "Short Elk is well named, my mother. I would not look down on my man."

"It is not good to say such things." Bear's Daughter tried to sound reproving, but her tone told Willow that she agreed. "My daughter must soon take a husband. Black Snake says it is a disgrace before the village that she does not already do so."

Willow's mouth tightened. "Why should this be true? There is not one warrior in Waccachalla you would want me to wed, nor any who would have me."

Bear's Daughter did not try to deny Willow's statement. "You are feared because you are different, but my kin the chief knows better. For many years Black Snake has cared for us both. It is right that someone else should now share his burden."

Willow regarded her mother with suspicion. "Does the chief himself say these words?"

"Black Snake does not have to speak. The women whisper that the great warrior Otter wishes to take you into his lodge."

Willow drew in a sharp breath and her eyes widened. Much older than she, Otter had been married for several years until his wife died of a fever. Willow had never thought of Otter as a possible suitor, nor did she wish to now. "Otter has not said this thing to me."

"Ayee, but his eyes speak it when he looks at you."

Willow shook her head in disbelief and raised her chin, half in defiance, half in appeal. "Does my mother think the chief will make this match?"

Bear's Daughter stood and looked at the beautiful young girl she'd reared from birth. She recalled how, years ago, Littlewillow's mother had said almost the same words. *I cannot choose from these warriors of the Clan of the Turtle*, Silverwillow had told Bear's Daughter. *There is not one I would have*. Scarcely a week later, she had met the redheaded white trader Ian McKnight. From the moment each had set eyes on the other, Bear's Daughter had known that Silverwillow would have no other man.

"The chief will know your wishes," Bear's Daughter said.

"My wish is not to take a husband from Waccachalla," Willow said.

"'That is bold talk," Bear's Daughter said. Her tone was reproving, but the suddenly relaxed lines around her mouth indicated she was not displeased by her daughter's words.

"You will know how to make it less so," Willow said.

Bear's Daughter lowered her head and sighed. "I will try, my child."

Black Snake has always listened to Bear's Daughter, Willow thought. *She will see that I do not have to take this man Otter.*

"It is good, my mother," Willow said aloud.

Yet after Bear's Daughter left, wearing her best white deerskin robe and ornamented as befitted an audience with the chief, Willow had to consider the possibility that her mother's mission might fail. Black Snake had shown a great deal of kindness to one so obviously different from the rest of his people, and to dispute his wishes would be unthinkable.

If only I looked like everyone else, perhaps I would be more content among them, Willow thought. From a very young age she had realized that she wasn't like the others in Waccachalla, even including the woman she called mother. At first Willow accepted without curiosity Bear's Daughter's explanation that she looked different because she'd been fathered by a white man, long since dead. When Willow asked Bear's Daughter what her father had been like, she would say only that he was a good man, for a *Shemanese*. Over the years, whenever Willow saw any *Shemanese*, she always wondered if her father might have looked like them. Lately, seeing men like Simon

Girty and Alexander McKee, who worked for the red-coats and seemed ready to turn on their own kind, Willow hoped that her father had not been like them.

As Willow grew older, the other village girls near her age began to take husbands and have babies, but no suitors sought her out in the forest or brought deer to her lodge door. She had always expected to marry someday, as was the custom, but she had seen no man who interested her, nor was she in haste to exchange the gentle care of her mother for the hard life of a Shawnee wife and mother. Without Willow's having to tell of her feelings, Bear's Daughter had seemed not only to understand, but also to sympathize with her.

Now, however, Willow knew that as a properly dutiful daughter, she was expected to marry, and thus provide for herself and Bear's Daughter in her mother's old age. Black Snake, both as her chief and her guardian, had the power to make her accept Otter, should he wish to do so. In that case, Willow would have no choice but to enter Otter's lodge.

I will do what I have to do for the sake of my mother, Willow resolved, but the thought of having to accept the touch of a man she cared nothing for made her cringe.

I could provide my mother with meat as well as any man in the village, she told herself. *It is not fair that I am not allowed to hunt.*

As a child, Willow had learned to set snares, to make arrows fly true, and to fear neither man nor beast. Yet from her twelfth year, she had no longer been allowed to go into the forest to do those things.

The other girls who had learned the ways of the woods with Willow now seemed content merely to plant and tend their corn, tan and sew the skins of the animals their men brought in, and bear and raise their babies.

Is it so with Shemanese women? Willow wondered. Her only knowledge of white women came from brief glimpses of some captives she'd seen during their wanderings, and of one blue-eyed woman with hair the color of corn-tassels who stayed in Waccachalla only a few days before being taken somewhere else. Without offering any reason, Bear's Daughter had made Willow stay inside their lodge until the woman left, and she never got to see the light-haired woman up close.

Willow sighed. A feeling of vague restlessness, always there just beneath the surface, had lately grown inside her. Bear's Daughter had taught Willow to honor and obey her elders, but she had also set an example that had led the girl to be independent.

Whatever Black Snake decides will change my life forever, Willow thought uneasily. *Why is it that my mother stays so long?*

When at last Bear's Daughter slowly made her way toward their lodge, Willow rose and forced herself to walk, rather than run, to meet her.

"What says Black Snake, my mother?"

Bear's Daughter glanced at Willow, but remained silent as she reached the lodge and exchanged her best robe for her everyday deerskin shift.

Willow longed to repeat the question, but she knew from experience that it would avail her nothing;

Bear's Daughter would speak only when she was ready. Willow sat cross-legged in the center of the lodge and tried to curb her impatience while she waited for her mother to join her.

When Bear's Daughter finally sat opposite Willow, she did not at first speak of her meeting with the chief.

"You know that you were not born in Waccachalla," she began, then paused for Willow to confirm her statement.

Willow nodded. "Yes, my mother. You say I was birthed near the forks of the Muskingum in the village of your Delaware cousins."

Bear's Daughter nodded. "Ayee, it is so. You have no blood kin among the warriors in Waccachalla. Since you do not have to look elsewhere for a husband, Black Snake would have you accept a deer from one of his own warriors."

Willow allowed her disappointment to show for a moment, then raised her chin and nodded assent. "I understand. How much time do I have?"

"The chief says only what he wants, not when. Do not concern yourself about this thing yet, my daughter."

My mother will not allow me to be forced into marriage, Willow told herself. Somehow Bear's Daughter would find a way to give Willow what she wanted. Had it not always been so?

"It will be as you say," Willow murmured, then hugged Bear's Daughter.

If Otter brings me a deer, my mother will deal with him herself, Willow assured herself. For now, that hope would sustain her.

3

PHILADELPHIA

Several more times, always in the presence of his aunt, Stuart Martin helped Anna with her Latin studies. They seldom had the opportunity to speak privately, and Anna thought that Stuart must prefer it that way.

As was the custom in most Philadelphia households, Christmas Day was quietly observed. Greenery garlands hung at the front door and over the fireplace in the sitting room, filling the room with a pleasant fragrance that reminded Anna of the woods around her former home. In honor of the day, Cook Nancy prepared a feast of roast duckling for their noon meal. After the plates had been removed, Miss Martin invited her to join them as she presided at a brief gift-exchanging ceremony.

Following a long-standing tradition, Miss Martin gave the cook a pair of mittens, and Stuart and Anna both received linen handkerchiefs, his boasting his initials, and hers with an edging of tatted lace.

In anticipation of the occasion, Anna had fashioned

felt pen wipers for Miss Martin and her nephew, and knitted woolen stockings for the cook, whose basement quarters were cold and dank. Anna had also made a mohair muffler for Stuart from yarn laboriously unraveled from a shawl that she seldom wore, but Anna thought she should wait to give it to him when his aunt wasn't present.

"Thank you, Miss McKnight," Stuart said when he received the felt pen wiper. "I seem to use a great many of these." Then he handed her a small, string-tied parcel. "I thought you might like to have this."

Anna didn't look at Miss Martin, but she felt certain that the schoolmistress was regarding her nephew with disapproval. Anna's hands trembled slightly as she untied the string and the paper slipped away to reveal a dog-eared copy of Caesar's *Commentaries on the Gallic Wars*.

"I cannot accept this," she said quickly. "It should stay here for all of Miss Martin's students to use."

"This is my personal copy, not the school's, Miss McKnight. I hope that it will encourage you to continue your studies."

"In that case, I thank you, Mr. Martin," Anna murmured.

"As well she should," Matilda Martin said shortly.

"I count it a privilege to be able to give gifts. Last year at this time, Colonel McKnight and I weren't certain we'd be alive to see another Christmas," Stuart said.

He looked at Anna and wished he could say more about that time, but his aunt's presence prevented him from doing so. More than once in the past few days, he had wondered what Ian McKnight would say if he knew how Stuart was beginning to feel about Anna. They had been the closest possible friends, but Ian probably still thought of his daughter as the child she had been the last time he'd seen her. He'd no doubt be pleasantly surprised to see how beautiful Anna was becoming—

His aunt's voice put a quick end to Stuart's wool-gathering. "We must prepare to leave now for our holiday gathering, nephew. Miss McKnight, I trust that you will take this opportunity to retire to your studies."

"Yes, Miss Martin," Anna said.

When his aunt went to get her cloak, Stuart turned to Anna. "I wish you could go with us. You shouldn't have to stay here alone today."

"I don't mind—I'm used to being by myself," Anna assured him. She could have added that even if she had been invited, she had no wish to endure the stares of his relatives—the mixture of curiosity and disapproval she knew so well.

"Nevertheless—"

Whatever Stuart might have said was cut short by Miss Martin's reappearance. With a curt nod to Anna, he took his aunt's arm and escorted her from the room.

"Will you be needin' anything else, Miss McKnight?" Cook Nancy's question startled Anna, who was still thinking about Stuart.

"No, thank you. I believe I'll sit by the fire and read for a while."

"Then if you don't mind, I'm off to me friend

Molly's. Her folks give her the day off and she asked me to come by, had I the chance."

"Go along, and don't worry about getting back for supper. I can make do with leftovers from the larder."

The servant's weathered face creased in a grateful smile. "Thank you, missy. Mayhap I can bring you a sweetmeat back from her mistress's house. They be fine folks, an' keep a good table."

Unlike your stingy mistress, Anna thought. She knew Nancy was too loyal to utter such a thing.

A few minutes later Anna heard the cook leave. She put down the book she had been only half reading and went to the front window. The fair and sunny day had brought out many people in their holiday satin and velvet finery to walk in the narrow street past Miss Martin's.

"Where are they all going, I wonder?" Anna asked aloud. The ticking of Miss Martin's stately old grandfather clock was the only reply she heard. For a fleeting moment she wished that she, too, had somewhere to go, and someone like Stuart—no, Stuart himself—to take her there. The notion passed, and Anna turned from the window and mounted the stairs to her attic room.

From its hiding place she took the scarf that she had knitted for Stuart, and wrapped it in the same paper that had covered her book. She went back down the stairs to the second floor, where Miss Martin and Stuart occupied adjoining rooms.

Feeling like an intruder, Anna entered Stuart's room. She winced and started guiltily when the door groaned on its hinges; then she smiled at her own foolishness. "No one else is in this house," she said aloud. Her voice sounded strange and hollow as it echoed against the walls of the sparsely furnished chamber.

Stuart had neatly spread the counterpane atop his bed, and the clothing he apparently meant to take back to Princeton was carefully stacked on top of his plain chest of drawers. Anna first put her package underneath two of his linen shirts, then decided to put a note on the package, and withdrew it.

Dipping one of Stuart's quills into his inkstand, she wrote, "From Anna Willow McKnight, with thanks, Christmas, 1781." She waited for the ink to dry, then rewrapped the mohair scarf and put it inside one of the shirts in the middle of the stack, where Stuart wouldn't likely notice it until he unpacked his things at Princeton. Anna had just turned to leave when she heard heavy footsteps coming up the stairs.

Her heart stopped. *I didn't lock the door after the cook left,* was her first thought. Yet the steady tread on the stairs didn't sound like that of a furtive burglar, but rather of someone who was perfectly at ease with being there and who knew exactly where he was going. For an instant Anna stood frozen where she stood, but as the steps grew closer, she started toward the door, intending to close it.

Just as she reached the door, Anna saw a man's figure mount the final stair and stride toward Miss Martin's room. When he raised his head, Anna found herself staring into Stuart Martin's violet eyes, now opened wide in surprise.

For an instant neither spoke. Then Anna recovered and walked into the hall toward him, leaving the door to his room open. "You frightened me."

Stuart folded his arms across his chest and stared at her, his face a dull red. "I could say the same thing, Miss McKnight. Might I ask what you were doing in my room?"

Anna looked at the floor, and wished that it would open and swallow her up and thus relieve her of the warm tide of embarrassment that engulfed her entire body. "I'm sorry, Mr. Martin," she managed to say. "I feared I wouldn't see you before you left tomorrow. I put a package for you with your things," she added, half turning to gesture toward the stack of clothing where she had placed the scarf. "I was just about to leave when I heard footsteps. I thought you must be a burglar."

"Well, I could have been, at that," Stuart said. "Did you know that the back door was all but standing wide open?"

Stuart's mild tone encouraged Anna to look at him. "No, Mr. Martin. I didn't check it when the cook left."

"Cook Nancy's gone to her friend Molly's, I suppose," Stuart said.

"Yes, Mr. Martin." Then another thought struck Anna. "Why did you come back? Has something happened to Miss Martin?"

"Not unless you count a spell of forgetfulness. Aunt Matilda had gifts to take to our relatives, but she left them in her room. I've returned with orders to fetch them."

"Oh," Anna said. She stood where she was, feeling awkward, while Stuart Martin regarded her with obvious amusement.

"You wouldn't make a very good criminal," he told her. "Anyone who can look as guilty as you do over nothing would surely give herself away if she ever tried anything really underhanded."

"If I look guilty, I am sure I deserve to," Anna said stiffly. "I shouldn't have entered your room without permission."

"Granted, but in this case, the cause was just. May I open the package?"

Anna nodded, and Stuart walked past her into his room. He looked around but saw nothing, and turned back to her with a puzzled expression.

"It's inside the third shirt from the top," she explained. "I thought if I put it there, you wouldn't see it until you were well away from here."

Stuart withdrew the package and opened it. "Why would you ever want to hide such a useful gift?" he asked, admiring her handiwork. "Its warmth will come in quite handy on my trip to New York."

Anna stood in the doorway and watched with pleasure as Stuart looped the muffler around his neck. "I didn't think Miss Martin would approve of my giving it to you," she said.

"*Honi soit qui mal y pense,*" Stuart murmured.

"I don't understand what you just said. Is it Latin?" Anna asked.

"No, but it's close. In French it means 'evil to him who evil thinks.' Sometimes Aunt Matilda seems to look for wrong where none exists."

"I see," said Anna, not knowing how else to respond to Stuart's criticism of his aunt.

"Anyway, I'm glad I had to come back, so I can

thank you properly for the muffler. A letter couldn't have told you half so well how much I like it."

"I made it with yarn from one of my old shawls—I hope you don't mind."

"It doesn't matter," Stuart said. "I assure you that I will get much good use from it—and think of you each time I wear it."

Although Stuart had spoken matter-of-factly, his words brought a flush of color to Anna's cheeks, and she turned away from him as he left his room and closed the door behind him.

"I was hoping I might see you when I came back," Stuart said. "I'll be leaving quite early in the morning, and it may be a long while before I'm free to return to Philadelphia."

Anna's face reflected her concern. "At least you'll be back for the Commencement exercises, won't you?"

Anna felt her heart lurch as Stuart took both of her hands in his and held them loosely. He looked steadily into her eyes. "I hope to, but I must make the money my father left me last a long time. If I can find suitable employment during the rest of the school term, I'll have to take it, even if it means I can't come back to Philadelphia as often as I'd like."

"I'll finish here in June," Anna said.

"I know. I'll be sorry to lose my best pupil."

Anna's eyes filled with tears as she realized the futility of any hope that this man might ever want her to share his life. Surely, she told herself, if Stuart Martin felt about her the way she was beginning to feel about him, he would vow to return to see her, no matter what the cost.

"And I'll be sorry to lose my best teacher," Anna managed to say.

Stuart released her hands and backed away with a sigh. "I'm afraid I must get back to Aunt Matilda before she sends the Watch after me."

Anna's voice wavered only slightly. "Yes, I know."

Stuart put his hand on his aunt's door, and Anna turned toward the stairs to her attic room, already thinking of how much she would miss him.

"Wait—" Stuart called.

Anna turned to face him, aware of the sudden pounding of her heart.

"Yes?"

Stuart regarded her intently. "I'll leave about six tomorrow morning."

Anna felt her face grow warm, and she wondered what he expected her to say. Fearful that she might misspeak, she merely nodded.

Once more he walked toward her. He took her into his arms and kissed her full on the lips almost before she had time to realize what was happening. Then he released her.

"Good-bye, Anna," he said, and with a farewell wave, Stuart turned and entered his aunt's room.

Almost as shocked that he had called her by her first name as that he had kissed her, Anna breathlessly turned and fled up the stairs to her attic room.

In the privacy of her own room, she wonderingly touched her fingertips to her lips. *I mustn't be foolish,* she told herself sternly. Stuart had kissed her, but what did it mean? However, he had all but invited her to see him off. Anna knew with certainty that Miss

Martin wouldn't approve. On the other hand, seeing Stuart again was worth incurring his aunt's wrath.

Elation and confusion warred within her as she sat alone in her room for the rest of the afternoon, thinking of Stuart's kiss, and of the time they had spent together in the past few days. But by the time she heard the Martins coming back from their visiting, Anna knew what she must do.

The sun had not risen when Anna, fully dressed and carrying her shoes, crept down the stairs in her stockinged feet. She stopped in the dining room to put on her slippers, and heard a floorboard creak behind her. She turned, ready to invent some excuse for being caught downstairs before daylight.

Even in the predawn dimness, Anna realized with relief that the approaching figure was far too tall to be Miss Martin. When Stuart came closer, he raised a finger to his lips to caution silence, then took Anna's arm and guided her through the back hallway to the rear door, where he stopped beside his luggage.

Without speaking, Stuart took Anna into his arms and drew her head down to rest on his shoulder. Heedless of the rough cloth of his cloak against her cheek, Anna felt a peace and contentment that she'd never before known.

After a long moment, Stuart spoke quietly. "I wasn't certain you'd come."

"I wasn't certain you wanted me to."

In reply Stuart tightened his embrace, and Anna raised her arms to circle his neck. Stuart kissed her again, this time with a great deal more feeling and for much longer than he had the evening before. He drew back briefly, then tightened his hold even further and kissed her again. This time, Anna kissed him back with equal passion. They stood thus for several long moments, their bodies pressed together, until Stuart put his hands on Anna's shoulders and took a half step away from her. "I should never have done that—forgive me."

Anna felt breathless and bewildered. "For what?"

"For a moment, I forgot myself. I would not for the world take advantage of you."

Anna wished for more light, so that Stuart could read in her face the yearning of her heart for him. "If that is what that was, then I hope you will keep doing it."

Stuart smiled as he bent his head to kiss her again, finally drawing back with a reluctance that matched hers. He remained silent for a moment, then sighed and spoke in a much firmer voice. "I must leave now."

"When will you be back?"

"I don't know. But believe me, I will come back to you as soon as I can. Good-bye, Anna Willow."

"Good-bye to you—Stuart." It was the first time Anna had spoken his first name, and she could only hope it would not be the last.

Then he picked up his luggage and left, admitting a blast of freezing air through the door that left Anna shivering in the cold darkness. Savoring the feelings that Stuart had aroused in her with his embrace, Anna longed for them to be repeated.

4

As winter faded into spring, Anna tried hard to accept the fact that Stuart Martin would probably never have a part in her life. She also became more concerned that she had heard nothing from her father. Miss Martin's Commencement tapestry was almost finished, and the other girls who would be completing their studies were discussing their future plans. Anna could no longer ignore the nagging possibility that something could have happened to Ian McKnight.

"What will you do after Commencement?" Felicia asked Anna late one March evening when they both lay sleepless in their attic room.

"I suppose I'll have to return to the farm. Even though I don't want to go there and they don't want me. I won't know what else to do until I hear from my father."

"What if he has met with some kind of accident?"

Anna had lately asked herself the same question. "I wouldn't stay with my kin, that's for certain. I would return to the city, I suppose. There must be hundreds of employers here in Philadelphia eager to take in skilled young ladies like us."

Anna's tone brought the intended laugh from Felicia. "Ah, Anna, you can always find something to be merry about. In your place, I'm not sure that I could."

"Well, it's not June, and I haven't given up yet," Anna said.

On Father or on Stuart Martin, either, she added to herself. Stuart had not been back since Christmas, but Miss Martin mentioned that he had become a private tutor, and his duties confined him to the Princeton area. In the meantime, Miss Martin had hired Mr. Fogelman, a half-deaf former headmaster who shouted Latin declensions and Greek stems at his pupils with an equal lack of success.

Stuart hadn't written to Anna, but she had not expected him to. Aside from the fact that he probably didn't have the time to write, Stuart knew that his aunt reviewed all the mail that came for her charges, and read most of it before she passed it on. However, Anna mentally composed many long letters in which she poured out her heart to him.

Finally, late one fine April Friday as they were gathered in the dining room for a cold supper, Anna heard a commotion at the back door. Shortly thereafter, Stuart Martin walked into the dining room as casually as if he had just left the room for a moment.

Unlike Anna, Miss Martin seemed almost disappointed to see him. "Stuart!" she exclaimed. "You could have let me know you were coming."

"I wasn't sure that I could get away until the last

moment," he said. Although Stuart's glance did not linger long on Anna, something in his eyes made her know that she was the only reason for his impromptu visit.

"Mr. Fogelman is using your room," Miss Martin said. "He went to sup with his sister, but he will be back in a while."

Stuart waved a hand in dismissal. "Give me a blanket and I'll sleep on the parlor floor. It certainly won't be the worst place I ever passed a night."

A night? Anna wondered, and hoped he would be there longer.

"Only one night?" Miss Martin asked, with an opposite concern.

Stuart nodded. "I'm afraid so."

Miss Martin looked at Anna and frowned, almost as if she had read the girl's mind. Then she addressed her nephew. "It surprises me that you would even bother to come for such a short time."

"I am glad to see you too, Aunt." Stuart spoke with such good humor that Rose Smythe giggled out loud, while several of the others found it hard to suppress their laughter.

Miss Martin glared at them. "That will do, young ladies." She turned back to Stuart. "I suppose you can join us for supper."

Without waiting to be told, the cook entered, bearing a pewter plate, cutlery, and a linen napkin. "Here you are, Master Martin," she said. She set the plate where Stuart had always taken his meals, between Miss Martin and Rose Smythe, and across the table from Anna.

Following the established rule, no one conversed during the meal, and as soon as it ended, Miss Martin dismissed the girls to their rooms, making it clear that they were not to linger in her nephew's presence.

Anna started to leave with the others, until Stuart called to her. "Miss McKnight, I would have a word with you."

Miss Martin watched closely, looking from one to the other as Anna returned to stand before Stuart.

"Yes, Mr. Martin?" She tried to look past his ear, afraid of what her face might reveal if she looked him in the eye.

"I wondered if you might have heard anything from your father." When Anna shook her head, Stuart continued. "I recently spoke to a former soldier in our company who saw Colonel McKnight not long ago. When your father learned the man was coming to Pennsylvania, he told him he should look me up at Princeton."

"Did my father say anything about me?" Anna asked.

"Only that you would soon finish school and return to Bedford."

"Oh." Anna didn't try to hide her disappointment that her father hadn't said more.

"Our friend assured me that Colonel McKnight looked fit. I thought you would want to know."

"I am sure Miss McKnight welcomes that news, but it could well have been put into a letter," Miss Martin said.

"Thank you for telling me, Mr. Martin," Anna said aloud. Silently her eyes asked, *How are we going to see one another alone?*

"Not at all. I think often of your father and the dangers we faced together."

"You may go now, Miss McKnight," Miss Martin said pointedly.

With her eyes modestly lowered, Anna curtsied. "Good evening, Mr. Martin, Miss Martin," she murmured before she left the room.

"Her father will be glad to see what a fine young woman Anna has turned out to be," Stuart said, loudly enough for Anna to hear.

She also heard Miss Martin's reply. "Nonetheless, she'll always be a half-breed."

Stuart doesn't think of me that way, Anna told herself, but her face still burned when she reached her attic room.

Felicia immediately peppered her with questions. "What did Mr. Martin want? Did you notice the way he looked at you? Did you see Rose Smythe? She was positively green with envy."

Anna shrugged as if the encounter was of no consequence. "Someone Mr. Martin knows saw my father not long ago and said he looked fit. He just passed on that news."

"Well, don't tell Rose that. Let her think the worst—it would serve her right."

That night Anna made her usual preparations for bed, although it would be next to impossible to sleep, knowing Stuart shared the same roof. *He is in the parlor,* she thought. *If I can just get past the creaking floorboards in front of Miss Martin's room, I can see him, at least for a little while.*

Anna made herself stay in bed long after Felicia's

even breathing told her that her friend was asleep. Finally she got out of bed and put a robe on over her long nightdress. Hardly the proper attire to pay a visit to a gentleman, but she didn't want to risk making any noise that would awaken Felicia. Anyway, Anna told herself, except for her feet, her body was more completely covered than if she had on her daytime attire.

Carefully she crept down the stairs, stepping around the spots likely to squeak. When she reached the second floor, the loud snores coming from their respective rooms told her that Miss Martin and Mr. Fogelman did not hear her. Anna's heart hammered as she groped her way down the dark staircase to the first floor.

Following the faint light that shone from the parlor, she found Stuart, still fully dressed and sitting at a small table, writing by the light of a lone candle. His eyes widened when he looked up and saw her.

"Don't worry, I'm not a ghost," Anna whispered.

Hastily Stuart stood and came to her, holding out a piece of paper. "I was just going to ask Cook Nancy to give you this."

Anna read the words aloud. "'Join me in the parlor. S. M.' Now you won't have to bother her."

"I'm glad. I feared Cook's heavy step might awaken my aunt. I presume you did not?"

"No. She was snoring." Anna drew her robe about her, suddenly embarrassed that, while Stuart was fully clothed, she was not.

"Are you cold?" he asked. "I have a blanket."

Anna shook her head. "I'm fine. I can't believe Miss Martin would make you sleep on the floor."

"I don't mind." Stuart took another step forward, and Anna raised her face and waited, instinctively knowing he would kiss her.

"Oh, Anna," he exclaimed, placing his hands on her shoulders. "I've missed you so much these past months."

"I've missed you, as well." She stepped into his embrace, and wordlessly they clung together for a long moment before he put his lips on hers. His kiss was even more wonderful than she remembered, and she responded with all her pent-up longing. She felt herself leaning toward him, almost melting into his body, until he unwound her arms from around his neck and helped her down beside him on the blanket. Loosely embracing, they lay facing one another, attempting to regain their breath.

"I have never known anyone like you, Anna Willow." Tenderly Stuart's hand traced her straight forehead and outlined her straight nose and full lips before he once more bent his face to hers.

Her head fell back as his tongue gently parted her lips. The hand that had outlined her face now stroked her neck and shoulders and paused to probe the pulse in her throat before moving down to the curve of her breasts.

No one had ever touched her there before, and she started in surprise.

He pulled back and looked at her with concern. "I didn't mean to hurt you."

Anna took his hand in both of hers and returned it to her breast. "You're not. But I—I'm not used to this sort of thing."

"I know. And as a matter of fact, neither am I."

"Really?"

He smiled ruefully at the challenge in Anna's voice. "I have never felt about anyone the way I feel about you." He looked deeply into her eyes. "I know now that I never really loved anyone before."

Stuart Martin loves me. Tears welled in her eyes, and her voice, which would have affirmed her own love, failed her. She leaned closer, intending to kiss him, but Stuart suddenly pulled away and reached for the candle, which he quickly extinguished.

"What?—"

"Shh!" Stuart warned.

At almost the same moment, Anna heard the approaching footsteps that had alerted him. She hurried toward the carved screen in one corner, reaching its cover just as Miss Martin entered the parlor, carrying a candlestick.

"I thought I heard someone talking down here," she said accusingly.

Stuart yawned noisily. "Sometimes I talk in my sleep. I'm sorry if I did so loudly enough to wake you."

"Never mind. Bring your blanket and come upstairs. You can pass the rest of the night on the floor of your old room. Mr. Fogelman won't mind."

"There's no need to disturb him, Aunt. I'm fine here."

"Don't argue with me. Come along, now."

Anna waited for a long time before she dared to return to her room. Her pulse returned slowly to normal, but her heart raced when she thought of Stuart's declaration of love.

What else would have happened if Miss Martin hadn't interrupted?

Anna sighed. As she crept up the stairs and went back to her own bed, she wondered how long it might be before she could find out.

The next day, Miss Martin made doubly sure that Stuart never had an opportunity to be alone with any of her pupils, especially Anna. She sent Anna and Felicia to the market with the cook, and by the time they returned, Stuart had left.

Again he did not write, but Anna was almost certain that he would come back for her at Commencement. He had said he loved her. Surely, he could not let her go away without even saying good-bye.

In mid-May Miss Martin took Anna aside and handed her a letter. For a brief moment, she dared to hope that Stuart had written her after all; then she recognized the scrawling handwriting.

"It's from your father, I believe," Miss Martin said. "It seems to contain some kind of parcel."

Eagerly Anna took the packet. Although the wrapping was creased and dirty, the crude wax seal still remained intact. Resisting the urge to tear it open on the spot, Anna managed to get as far as the third floor landing before she broke the seal. After putting the small parcel that had been enclosed with it in her apron pocket, Anna read the single sheet of parchment.

"My dear daughter," Ian McKnight had written,

> I had hoped to fetch ye from Miss Martin's
> when ye are done there, which I reckon to be

early in June. I am near Lexington, in Kentucky
County, where I have made a land claim.
Should I leave it overlong, others will get it, so I
cannot come there. It's best that ye go to
Bedford if ye don't already have plans to stay in
the city. I herein send ye something fine I got
from a Spanish trader. May it remind ye of the
love of your father.

Anna gasped as she unwrapped a square of linen to
reveal a finely wrought slender chain of gold links.
Anna, who had never owned any jewelry, had seen
nothing to compare with this gold necklace, and she
knew it must be worth a great deal. But more important than its monetary value was what it represented.

*My father still loves me and he hasn't forgotten me, even
if he can't come for me now.* Anna's eyes filled with tears
as she slipped the chain over her head. Apparently,
Ian McKnight did not know that his sister had died—
and she had not been able to write him, not knowing
where he was. Now that she had an address, Anna
could write him the sad news.

I'll keep this necklace always, she silently vowed, and
wished she could show it to Stuart.

He has to come back before I must leave—he just has to,
she thought.

5

WACCACHALLA

Willow moved almost soundlessly in the forest beyond her village, searching for the plants whose tender leaves might tempt her mother's appetite. Eight moons had waxed and waned since Bear's Daughter's interview with Black Snake about Willow's future, and for most of that time, Bear's Daughter had been ill. First she took a fever and for many days lay in a stupor from which Sits-in-Shadow's best medicine and loudest chants had failed to rouse her. When she came to herself, she was so weakened that Willow feared her mother might never walk again. Slowly, with Willow's good nursing and the generosity of Black Snake's wife in providing food for them, Bear's Daughter began to get better. As the weather warmed, Willow helped her mother to sit outside their lodge on clear days in the hope that the powers of the sun would restore her mother's strength. But Bear's Daughter had little appetite, and her uncharacteristically gaunt appearance frightened Willow.

If I can get my mother to enjoy food again, all will be well with her, Willow thought.

She left the hunter's trail and pressed on toward a stream that she knew to be lined with all manner of plants and herbs. She lifted her head to the newly green canopy overhead and breathed in the rich scents of a woodland spring. She had always enjoyed being among the trees, with only her thoughts for company. Lately that pleasure that had been denied to her.

She had asked the Great Spirit to make her mother well, and now it seemed that would come to pass. Willow realized that was not all she had to be grateful for, either. Black Snake had said nothing to her about taking a husband. The warriors, including Otter, had kept their distance from the lodge, lest the evil spirits that caused Bear's Daughter's sickness should enter their bodies, as well.

"It is good," Willow murmured aloud.

"I did not think you saw me, Littlewillow."

Startled, Willow looked toward the sound and saw Otter emerge from the cane around the creek. She had not seen him for some time, but his absence had done nothing to endear him to her. Otter was sturdily built, about her height, with thin lips in an almost-round face. A battle scar ran along his jaw from chin to ear, pale against his bronze skin, except when he filled it with war paint. *An imposing man,* Willow thought. Not one she would want to be her enemy—but certainly not one she wanted to wed.

"I saw no one," Willow said.

"You talk to yourself? Maybe what is said about you is true."

Willow didn't have to ask Otter what he meant. She knew the things many villagers said about her, things that Bear's Daughter had told her not to mind.

"Were they able, they would look like you, my daughter," her mother said to her often.

"If I could, I would look like them," Willow replied, but her mother scolded her so for saying it that she never again voiced the words.

"It does not matter," Willow finally said to Otter. She resumed walking, and he fell in step beside her.

"The old woman still lives. They say you have great powers to make her come back from being nearly dead."

"I have no such powers," Willow said.

"You are wrong, Littlewillow." Otter stopped and seized Willow's arm.

"You have much power here." He touched his chest with his free hand.

"My name is Willow," she said. "Let me go." She did not raise her voice, but something in her eyes made Otter drop her arm and move away.

"Yes, you are no longer a child. It is time you take a husband. Everyone else might be afraid of you, but Otter is not."

Willow looked at him blankly, then modestly lowered her head. "My mother has not recovered. I must stay with her."

Otter's thin-lipped smile made him look strangely sinister. "For now, it is so. But my time will come."

In one quick movement, Otter grabbed both Willow's hands and pulled her toward him. His lips stifled the protest on hers as he kissed her roughly, then let her go so abruptly, she almost fell.

"You'll see," he said. "Black Snake wants you to take a husband. I want a woman to lie with and give me sons. This thing will be done."

When he walked away, Willow wiped her mouth with the back of her hand and wished that Otter shared the others' fear of her. Their encounter proved what she had long suspected—that Otter would not use her well. Willow feared what he might do the next time they met. She most certainly would not walk alone in the woods again.

And I will never marry Otter, she vowed.

6

PHILADELPHIA

Despite her high hopes, Anna had no word from Stuart as her time remaining at Miss Martin's dwindled to a fortnight, and then a week. All too soon, the day came for Miss Martin to hang the new tapestry and say farewell to her six graduates.

Anna had no choice but to go to the farm where Helen, her cousin Henry's wife, now ran the household, and await her father's instructions.

Her roommate, knowing that the Barfield farm was located near Bedford, some distance west of Felicia's home in Lancaster, quickly invited Anna to travel that far with her.

"I really thought I'd feel happier to be leaving this place," Felicia said to Anna on the morning they took their last breakfast together at the scarred table. The Commencement ceremonies were scheduled for mid-afternoon, after which the town girls would go home with their parents. The others would depart the next morning.

"Good-byes are always hard," Anna said through the growing lump in her throat.

Anna knew that in all probability, she and Felicia would never meet again. A cousin of Felicia's who lived in York had told her parents that he wanted to marry her, and the match had all but been made only a few weeks ago, before anyone had bothered to mention it to Felicia.

The arrangement shocked Anna. Privately she thought she would willingly die a spinster before she would agree to spend even a small part of the rest of her life with any of the cousins with whom she had been reared.

After breakfast the girls went upstairs to the room they had shared for the past three years, to begin packing their belongings.

They worked silently for a time, each absorbed in her own thoughts. Finally Felicia turned to her friend and sighed.

"I wish you could stay in Lancaster until after my wedding," she said.

"So do I," Anna said, turning to face her friend. "But your mother will have quite enough people in the house without adding one more."

Anna knew, however, that wasn't the only reason she shouldn't stay there. Felicia's mother would welcome any of the other young ladies from Miss Martin's, but not Anna. Not the one who looked different because her father had committed the sin of falling in love with and marrying an Indian.

Stop it! Anna told herself as self-pity threatened to overwhelm her. Her father had often declared that she shouldn't care what others thought about her.

But it does matter, and it always will, Anna admitted to herself, sitting down dejectedly on her bed. If her skin were as white as Felicia's, Stuart Martin might have been bold enough to court her openly, despite his aunt. Miss Martin would no doubt approve if he'd taken a liking to one of the rich girls . . .

"Are you all right, Anna? You look peculiar."

Anna managed a wobbly smile. "I suppose I was woolgathering. I was just thinking what a beautiful bride you'll make."

"And so will you, someday. You must let me know when you plan to marry—if there's any way I can come to your wedding, I will."

Anna laughed. "You may be too old and infirm to travel by then."

Felicia put down a petticoat she had just folded, and reached for Anna's hand. "No, I really mean it. I'll never have another friend like you. I hope that you'll find a good husband."

"'And they married and lived happily ever after,'" Anna quoted. "Don't you think I could be a happy spinster?"

Felicia pulled the corners of her mouth down in an approximation of their headmistress's perennial expression. "If Miss Martin is an example of unwedded bliss, then I would say you'd be better off marrying a warty toad than staying single and becoming like her."

Anna made a face. "Ugh! What a choice!"

"Well, since warty toads often turn into handsome princes, you just might consider it."

"I will," said Anna, but the only man she wanted to wed was neither toad nor prince—and since he had not come back for her Commencement, it appeared that he didn't return her love. Anna knew she ought not waste her time thinking about Stuart Martin.

The sound of chimes interrupted the girls' conversation.

"Oh, is it the luncheon bell already?" Felicia exclaimed. "This day is passing faster than any I've known."

"I agree," Anna said. "Isn't it strange that everything we've done all day is for the last time as Miss Martin's pupils? The last breakfast, the last luncheon—and tonight, the last dinner."

"And if we don't hurry, perhaps our last scolding," Felicia said.

When luncheon ended, Miss Martin formally dismissed the girls and reminded them to be in the hallway promptly at a quarter 'til two o'clock.

"Miss McKnight, stay here. I would have a word with you."

She knows something she hasn't told me, Anna thought as the others filed silently from the room. Felicia smiled encouragingly, while some of the others cast her curious glances as if wondering what kind of trouble the half-breed had gotten herself into this time.

"Your father knew when he left you here that your term would be up today," Miss Martin began. "Am I correct in assuming that you do not expect him to come for you?"

"Yes, ma'am, I don't." Anna replied to the confusing question.

"Then I must ask what you intend to do. You know, of course, that you cannot remain here."

Anna flushed, but she did not look away. "Yes, ma'am. I plan to travel to Lancaster with Felicia Darby, then go on to my cousins' home."

Miss Martin's expression did not change, but Anna thought she detected a slight note of relief. "That seems a wise course of action. I feared that you might try to stay in Philadelphia."

"Feared?" Anna repeated the word and raised her eyebrow slightly.

Miss Martin shrugged. "For your own good, of course, Miss McKnight. It is quite unlikely that you could find employment in the city, and I feel obliged to Colonel McKnight to see that you return safely to your family."

You needn't worry that I plan to stay here and lay a trap for your nephew. And even though I dread going back to the farm, it's far better than staying another day under your roof. Even on her last day, Anna wouldn't express her thoughts aloud.

The headmistress reached into her waist pocket and handed Anna a square of linen into which some coins had been tied. "This should be adequate to pay your way home."

"Thank you, Miss Martin. I know that my father will repay you as soon as it is possible."

Miss Martin's cheeks reddened briefly. "That won't be necessary," she said gruffly. "He left this sum for just such a purpose. You may be excused, Miss Mc-Knight. The hour grows late."

Yes, it does, Anna thought. She passed the clock and

noted with a trace of sadness that it was already after one. Stuart Martin would already have arrived if he were coming for the ceremonies. Although Anna's mind had accepted that he wouldn't be there, her heart still hoped that he might. When she knew without any doubt that he wasn't coming, her accumulated disappointment combined to bring rare tears to her eyes. Anna did not cry easily or often, but this afternoon as she watched the other girls with their proud parents and admiring beaux, she allowed herself a brief moment of self-pity before she wiped away her tears and squared her shoulders.

I'm not like those other girls, and I don't even want to be, Anna told herself as she stood apart at the reception in the parlor following the Commencement ceremony. Now that she was truly on her own with no one to look after her interests, Anna had no time to feel sorry for herself.

So absorbed was she with her thoughts that she didn't see Cook Nancy hurrying toward her until she had almost reached Anna's side.

The cook glanced around warily as if to make sure that Miss Martin wasn't watching. "Miss Anna, this just came for you," she whispered.

Anna looked at the folded page the cook handed her, too small to be a letter, and felt her mouth go dry. "What is this?" she asked.

"I don't know, Miss Anna. A messenger boy brought it to the back door."

"Thank you, Nancy," Anna managed to say.

Although no one was paying her any heed, she

turned away and started up the stairs toward her room before she unfolded the paper.

Anna recognized the handwriting instantly and stopped halfway up the stairs. Her heart raced, then all but stopped, as she read Stuart Martin's brief message:

Meet me in the carriage house as soon as you can. S. M.

Anna read the note again and wondered if she dared trust her eyes. Stuart had apparently come back to Philadelphia in secret and now waited to see her. After weeks without so much as a note from him, it seemed almost too good to be true, and her heart began to beat rapidly in anticipation.

With all the calm she could muster, Anna walked back down the stairs, past knots of conversing graduates and their families in the parlor, where Stuart had told her he loved her, and into the back hallway, where she and Stuart had shared their first embrace. She had been unable to forget those precious moments, so often reliving the way she had felt in Stuart's arms. That memory remained fresh as she went out the back door and hastened to Miss Martin's carriage house.

Anna had just put a hand on the latch of the carriage house's side door when it suddenly opened, and to her relief, she faced Stuart Martin. He was real, all right, and even more handsome than she remembered. They looked at each other for a moment in silence before Stuart spoke.

"I see you got my message."

Anna nodded and tried to keep her voice level against the rising tide of her pleasure in seeing him again. "I kept hoping you would come for another visit, if not to Commencement."

"So did I. Last week I wrote Aunt Matilda that between my own studies and preparing my thick-headed charges for their examinations, I couldn't leave Princeton. I thought she might share that news with you."

Of course she wouldn't tell me anything about you, Anna thought. Instead, she shook her head. "No, she didn't, but I am glad to see you now." Anna clasped her hands together to stop their trembling, but the gesture did nothing to stay the sudden emotion that roughened her voice.

"And I am glad to see you, as well."

In the dim light that filtered through the dirty panes of the single window, Anna searched Stuart's eyes for a brief moment as if to gauge the feelings reflected there. Reading the desire in his eyes, she took a step toward him. He opened his arms, and eagerly she entered his embrace. All the longing locked deep inside her flared in Stuart's fierce hold, and she returned his kiss with all the ardor of his own.

After a long moment Anna snuggled her head into his chest. "I feared I might not see you again," she whispered.

"You know I couldn't let my best pupil leave without saying good-bye," Stuart said against Anna's hair. His hand stroked lightly along her cheek. "Ah, Anna, my love, you are even more beautiful than I remembered."

Her heart thudded to a stop. He thought she was beautiful? Her heart resumed beating, with a vengeance. "Oh, Stuart—"

"Shh." He put his fingers to her lips and kissed her forehead, then her cheeks and chin. Finally he returned his lips to hers in a long, tender kiss, which she returned with growing passion.

He nuzzled her neck, and a delicious thrill coursed through her body and awakened strange new sensations deep in the core of her being. They were even more intense than the feelings she had had that night in the parlor when they had been interrupted. Time seemed to stop now as their lips met again and again and then once more, until Anna's head swam dizzily. She sagged against him, was grateful for his strong encircling arms.

"Let's sit down," Stuart said. Keeping one arm around her waist, he opened the door to Miss Martin's boxlike cabriolet and helped her climb inside. "No one will see us here."

I wouldn't care if they did. Anna almost said the words, but they weren't quite true. For Stuart's sake, Miss Martin mustn't know that he had come back just to be with Anna.

Stuart closed the carriage's side curtains, creating a dark, private place, then turned back to take Anna into his arms. She drew a long, shuddering sigh and rested her head on Stuart's shoulder.

"How did you manage to get away?"

"I said I had pressing business in Philadelphia." He

suited action to his words and pressed her body to his, and Anna shivered in delight. He kissed her once again, at first gently, and then with a rising urgency that she felt herself matching. She had dreamed of the moment when Stuart would once more hold her so close, she could feel his heart beating. Now he was here, and being with him was even more wonderful than she had imagined.

As they embraced, Anna's body yearned toward him. She couldn't get close enough to Stuart, couldn't get enough of his mouth moving on hers, of his hands caressing her face, her neck, then pressing against the swell of her bodice. She moaned with pleasure, enjoying each new sensation. She felt herself sliding sideways on the carriage seat, until finally she and Stuart lay side by side, close together in a way that Anna hadn't known to be possible. Nothing else mattered but that she was here in this place and at this time with this man she loved, moving together with him toward some new emotional and physical intimacy that she was breathlessly eager to explore.

Suddenly Stuart pulled away from her and sat up. "No, Anna," he said.

With difficulty, Anna struggled to a sitting position beside him and tried to comprehend what he was telling her. Both were breathing hard, and Anna's carefully dressed hair had fallen loose. Absently she brushed it from her face.

"Did I do something wrong?"

Stuart touched her face with a tender hand and sighed. "No, my darling, but I was about to."

"But I—" Anna began; then she realized what he

had called her, and repeated it uncertainly. "Darling? No one has ever said that to me before."

"I am glad of it. But as much as I care for you, I have no right to claim all your love now."

"Why not, when I am more than ready to give it?" Anna lifted her chin and strained in the dimness to see Stuart's face, hoping that his expression might belie his words.

Stuart raised Anna's hands to his lips and kissed each finger in turn before he spoke again. "Your father is my friend, but apart from that, I love you too much to take advantage of your youth and innocence."

Even as tears of joy gathered behind her eyelids, Anna sought confirmation for what she had heard. "You do love me?"

Stuart put a hand on each of her shoulders and lightly brushed her lips with his. "What has passed between us should prove it."

"Why do you pull away from me, then?"

"Because I have no right to claim your love yet. At the moment, I have neither prospects nor money."

"I don't care about money."

Stuart smiled slightly. "Maybe not, but unfortunately, a certain amount of it is necessary."

"Maybe you have no sure prospects now, but undoubtedly you will when you finish your studies."

He opened the side curtains, admitting enough light to reveal the set of his features, then turned back to her. "I hope so, but for now, we must live apart. Do you understand that, Anna?"

The tears she shed now were in sorrow, and

speech again failed her. Anna nodded, and Stuart took her into his arms and kissed her, thoroughly but without his previous passion, then leaned back to look at her as if memorizing each line and curve of her features.

"What will happen now?" Anna asked when she found her voice.

"Have you had further word from your father?"

Anna pointed to her necklace. "Father sent this as a Commencement gift. He's near Lexington, in Kentucky, and says he can't leave his claim to come for me. He told me to go to my cousins' farm."

"It's pretty," Stuart said of the necklace, then sighed. "Oh, Anna, how I wish I could take you back to Princeton with me this very day."

Anna's heart ached with the knowledge that they were about to part again, but she felt sad joy in what she saw in Stuart's violet eyes. *When he says he loves me, Stuart surely speaks the truth. How can I let him go now?*

"Stay here tonight," she urged. "I'll come back to the carriage house after Miss Martin goes to bed."

He shook his head. "No, that would be dangerous for us both. You should go back inside before you're missed, and I must return to Princeton."

Anna put her arms around Stuart's neck and raised her face to be kissed. "I am willing to face the danger. After all, what could Miss Martin do to me now?"

"My aunt is not the risk that concerns me." Stuart brushed her lips lightly, then opened the carriage door. "Don't worry, Anna. We will yet be together— I swear it. Until then, you must write to me at Princeton College."

"And you will write back?" Anna asked.

Stuart took her into his arms one last time. "Yes, my love, if you will tell me where. For now, all I have to offer are my words—and my love."

As Stuart kissed her, Anna wanted with all her heart to believe him.

At Anna's request, the cook summoned Felicia to the kitchen to help restore Anna's coiffure before she went back to the parlor.

"You look different," Felicia said, but Anna was reluctant to tell even her best friend that she had been with Stuart.

"I went for a walk, and the wind blew my hair. It wasn't anchored very well," she said. Felicia looked dubious, but she let the matter drop.

With her friend's help, Anna managed to look normal enough to escape Miss Martin's notice for the rest of the afternoon. The headmistress, tired from the long day of Commencement, merely nodded when Anna asked to be excused from supper, pleading a headache.

Anna barely slept that night, instead reliving every word, every kiss, that she and Stuart had shared. She and Felicia arose at dawn, and it seemed no time at all before their luggage had been carried down the stairs and loaded onto the wagon that would take them to Lancaster.

Miss Martin came out to see them off. Standing stiffly on the doorstep, she offered her hand to Felicia, then to Anna.

"I trust that you will have safe journeys," she said.

"Thank you, Miss Martin." *And by the way, your nephew and I are in love.* Anna longed to say the words, but she did not.

Anna climbed up onto the wagon seat beside Felicia. The drayman slapped his reins across the horses' backs, and the wagon creaked away from Miss Martin's door, each turn of the wheel taking her away from Stuart Martin and toward an uncertain future.

7

The warmth of the sun, along with the medicine and herbs Willow gave her, combined to help Bear's Daughter shake off the lingering effects of her near-fatal fever. She gradually grew stronger, until the day came when Bear's Daughter walked without help, then went about her normal activities.

Willow watched her mother's improvement with mixed feelings. Of course, she was happy over Bear's Daughter recovery, but she also knew that Otter was a man of his word. He had stayed away from Willow while she cared for her mother. Now that Bear's Daughter no longer needed her constant attention, Willow feared he would soon insist on wedding her.

As if she knew Willow's mind, one warm day when they sat grinding corn outside their lodge, Bear's Daughter asked what had become of Otter.

"I do not know, my mother. I suppose he is still raiding."

Bear's Daughter looked closely at Willow. "You

know more about this thing. Does Otter speak to you again?"

Willow nodded. "He still wants to take me into his lodge. He knows I do not want it."

"Ah. What says Otter about that?"

Willow shrugged. "Only that he will ask again."

"Ayee, it is that way with a man. He will want most what he cannot have."

"Or take it by force," Willow added.

Bear's Daughter compressed her lips. "Has this Otter dared to put his hands on you? He should know that Black Snake will not allow such a thing to happen in his village."

"Calm yourself, my mother. Otter has not harmed me. He thinks I should be glad that he offers to take me off Black Snake's hands."

Bear's Daughter made a derisive sound and spat into the grass. "I will see Black Snake about this thing before Otter comes back."

"I will go to the chief with you," Willow said.

"No, I go alone. Help me get dressed."

Willow watched Bear's Daughter make her way to the chief's lodge. She marveled at how straight her mother still held her back, how sure her steps, even after being so ill, and felt a wave of tenderness for her. *My mother is old,* Willow realized sadly. *But none of her fighting spirit has left her.*

Bear's Daughter was gone so long that Willow feared she might have had some mishap. "Are you all right, my mother?" she asked when she finally returned.

"Yes. Black Snake spoke long about Chief Netawa-tawees."

"Who is that?" Willow asked.

"The chief of the Delaware village on the Muskingum where you were born. Black Snake hears that some trouble has come to his old friend."

"What has that to do with us?" Willow asked, bewildered.

"Black Snake says it would be a good thing for us to go to this place and find out for him what happens there."

Willow's heart began to beat faster in anticipation of the possibility of leaving Waccachalla, even if only for a short while, but she spoke cautiously. "It is a long journey to the Delaware villages. Why does Black Snake not send a warrior to do this thing?"

"I do not ask the chief his reasons. Black Snake has asked it, and it will be done. My old village lies to the northeast on a well-marked trail. I would see it once again."

Her mother's melancholy tone frightened Willow. "I fear that my mother lacks the strength for such a journey."

"You are my strength, Littlewillow. We can no longer stay here."

Willow sat in silence for a moment, beginning to understand the real reason Black Snake was sending them away. "What about Otter?"

The creases around Bear's Daughter's mouth bent in a fleeting smile. "Otter has duties here. When he returns from the O-hio-se-pe, he will not be allowed to follow us. It is likely that he will finally weary of waiting for you and choose himself another wife."

Willow knew an almost overwhelming sense of

relief that she might yet escape a forced marriage to Otter, but as she had been taught from birth, she made no open show of her feelings. "It is good. When do we begin this journey?"

Her expression equally impassive, Bear's Daughter glanced around the lodge at their few possessions. "Black Snake would have us go when the signs show such a journey will be good, perhaps in another waxing of the moon."

Willow nodded. As much as she wanted to be out of Otter's sight, Willow knew the delay would help her mother gain strength. "We need time to ready ourselves for this journey."

Bear's Daughter nodded. She closed her eyes and rocked back and forth as she did when she communicated with the Great Spirit. Willow couldn't make out the words her mother mumbled, but she knew their intention, which she also shared.

Make smooth our path and direct us there in safety.

Although Willow knew that the way that lay ahead would not be easy, her heart sang a silent song of hope.

As difficult as this journey might be, almost anything would be better than living in Otter's lodge.

8

The journey that took Felicia and Anna from Philadelphia to Lancaster went as well as might be hoped, with a few long delays caused by wagon wheels that broke or came loose, and had to be repaired on the spot. Such things were to be expected.

Although they were both tired when they arrived, Anna and Felicia talked far into the night, promising never to forget their friendship. The next morning, each tried unsuccessfully not to cry when Felicia's younger brother Davy loaded Anna's luggage into the family buggy and took her into Lancaster to board a westbound wagon.

As the wagon carried her still farther from Philadelphia, Anna felt a pang knowing that each turn of the wheels put more distance between herself and Stuart Martin; but for now she had no choice.

And the following day, when the wagon finally left the Bedford road and entered the land to which she had been brought as an infant, despite everything,

Anna felt a sense of homecoming. The property had remained in the Barfield family for many years. Fresh from Scotland, Agnes McKnight had come there at fifteen as the bride of William Barfield. At the time, her brother Ian, her only living relative, was presumed dead, having been taken in an Indian raid several years earlier. Agnes and William's marriage spanned twenty years until William's death, and produced six children, only two of whom had lived to maturity.

Anna knew the story by heart: Agnes and William had been married almost two years when Ian McKnight finally returned home. At once William Barfield offered to deed him the McKnight land, which Agnes had brought as her marriage dower, but Ian had refused it. By then he'd made a life for himself among the Delaware Indians with whom he traded, and he declared he had no desire to live in Pennsylvania.

Agnes had always felt indebted to her brother for his generosity, and always welcomed his visits.

Aunt Agnes paid that debt many times over when she took me in, Anna thought, and tears came to her eyes.

"Looks like some folks are to home," the driver said.

Anna saw the arrow-straight plume of smoke rising from the stone chimneys that flanked either end of the sturdy frame house. In this place she had early come to know that she was Anna Willow McKnight, not Barfield.

Quickly she wiped her eyes, determined not to give her cousins the pleasure of seeing her tears. In their childhood days they had sometimes played a cruel game they called "Indian Captive," in which her cousins chased her. When they caught her, they tied her to a tree and made as if to burn her alive. Anna had heard that Indians never showed any emotion, but the harder she tried to keep from crying, the worse her cousins' tortures became. Once they tied the bonds so tightly that she fainted. Thinking they had killed her, her cousins ran away. Aunt Agnes finally came upon her while herb-gathering and quickly revived her. No lasting harm had been done, but that had marked the end of her cousins' Indian Captive game.

"At least the dogs are home," Anna said as a half-dozen lop-eared hounds emerged from their resting places to raise a barking chorus.

The driver handed Anna down from the seat and put her luggage on the ground near the doorstone. He climbed back on his wagon, but when no one immediately emerged from the house, he hesitated a moment after gathering the reins and letting off the wheel-brake. "Are y' sure—"

He was interrupted by a voice from inside the house. "What's all the commotion?"

"It's just me—Anna Willow," she called back, as if it had been hours instead of months since she last stood at the Barfields' doorstone. "It's all right—you can go now," she said to the driver, who nodded and slapped the reins across his team's sturdy backs.

As the wagon jolted out of the yard, Anna had a momentary impulse to call after him to wait, that she had changed her mind about staying here, after all. But it quickly faded. For now, although it might not be what either she or her cousins preferred, Anna had nowhere else to go.

Her cousin Henry's unsmiling face when he saw her confirmed that he probably wouldn't make things easy for her. Henry had inherited his mother's red hair and fair coloring, but his eyes were as dark as Anna's, and he had the Barfield's jerky spareness of figure.

"Anna Willow—I'm surprised to see you. You should have let us know you were coming."

Anna was grateful that Henry stayed in the doorway, a safe distance away, thus sparing her the indignity of a forced cousinly kiss of greeting.

"I thought Father might have written you," she said.

"No. We've heard nothing from Uncle Ian for many months. Everyone thought you'd probably stay on in Philadelphia."

You mean you all hoped I would, Anna thought. "Father wrote me to come back to the farm, so here I am."

"What is, it, Henry?—Oh!"

Helen Thayer—now Helen Barfield, having married Henry a few weeks after his mother's death—appeared in the doorway behind her husband.

Although she and Anna were almost the same age and had known each other for most of their lives, they'd never been friends. Anna always thought there was something hard about Helen, something in her character that matched her sharp features and shrill voice. With hair so blond it was nearly white, and light gray, almost transparent eyes, Helen enjoyed the local gossip that she could put a spell on anyone at will. Anna had never believed it, but from the way Helen looked at her at that moment, Anna thought her cousin's wife would gladly hex her if she could.

"As you can see," Henry said, "our cousin Anna Willow is back from the big city."

Helen crossed her arms over her chest and gave Anna a searching glance. "I never expected to see you in these parts again—we thought you'd a-caught yourself a fine gentleman an' be wed by this time."

Anna returned Helen's glance and spoke calmly. "Father didn't send me to Miss Martin's to find a husband."

"Humph! Anyway, I hope you didn't come back with so many city notions that you've forgot the way common folk live," Helen said. "We don't put on no airs around here."

Anna thought of the way she had lived at Miss Martin's, and smiled faintly. "Neither do I. And I don't intend to cause you extra work—I'll do my fair share and keep to my room the rest of the time."

Helen and Henry exchanged glances, then Helen looked back to Anna.

"We're using that room now ourselves—it's better for the baby. You can have the attic."

"Baby? You didn't write me about a baby."

"There's hardly been time," Henry said. "Little Henry came on April twentieth, several weeks early."

"Congratulations," Anna murmured. "What about James? Is he also married?"

Henry shook his head. "No, and with his lack of prospects, it's not likely."

A thin wail came from within the house, and Henry and Helen turned toward it in unison. Anna swallowed hard against the growing lump in her throat, picked up her smallest bag, and followed them inside.

Anna had known coming back to Bedford wouldn't be easy, but she'd also harbored the hope that marriage might have mellowed Henry and Helen. Obviously, if anything, they seemed to resent her even more.

When Henry's brother James came in for supper that evening, he seemed almost glad to see her again. Anna could scarcely believe it. Two years younger than his brother Henry and two years older than Anna, James Barfield looked more like his mother and now seemed to have inherited some of her pleasant disposition, as well. In the last few years before Anna left home, he had simply ignored her rather than antagonizing her, as Henry had continued to do.

"I thought you'd stay in Philadelphia City for good," James said, repeating his brother's words.

"No. I don't think I'd like to live in a big city," Anna said.

"Then what are your plans?" James asked.

"I'm not sure. Father told me I should return here. I suppose something will come along for me to do until he can come for me."

"It had better," Helen said sharply. "Ian McKnight hasn't sent us anything toward your room and board, and now with the baby—"

James ignored his sister-in-law and stared at Anna. "You've done some growin' up since the last time you were here," he told her.

Helen frowned and spoke as if Anna weren't present. "If anything, I'd say Anna looks even more like an Indian squaw the older she gets. She'd better not braid her hair around these parts, for a fact."

Anna bit her lower lip and looked down at the table, struggling against the hurt in Helen's words.

"She shouldn't wear buckskin, neither," Henry contributed.

To Anna's relief, the baby chose that moment to begin crying, and as both parents rose at once to see to him, James looked across the table at Anna.

"I reckon my nephew's bound to be the spoiledest brat in all of Pennsylvania," he said.

"Henry surprises me—I didn't think he'd make such an attentive father."

"The newness will wear off soon, I'm sure," James said. "At any rate, becomin' a father hasn't softened Henry up any."

"So I noticed," Anna said. "He and Helen—and perhaps you, as well—probably wish I'd stayed on in Philadelphia."

James shook his head, but his expression told Anna that she wasn't far from the mark. "If Mother was still with us, she'd be remindin' us we ought to be kind to you. I reckon we heard that just about every day."

The unspoken sadness that Anna had felt all day threatened to overwhelm her, and she knotted her hands in her lap and struggled to maintain control. "I miss Aunt Agnes so much," she said softly. "I keep looking around, expecting to see her come in the door any moment with her herb basket . . ."

"I know. I still feel the same way myself. But Mother suffered so much there at the end, it was almost a relief to let her go. She just wasted away."

"Who took care of her?" Anna asked.

"Helen—she brought her things over here and moved into Mother's room when she took to her bed."

"I don't think of Helen as being a nurse," Anna said. Although James said nothing, his face confirmed what she suspected; Helen had probably come to nurse his mother in order to catch Henry Barfield, and not from any charitable impulse.

Henry emerged from the bedroom carrying his son. "Little Henry was just wet," he said.

"He's always wet," James muttered, too low for Henry to hear, and Anna smiled.

As long as there's one person I can talk to in this household, I can stand it, she thought.

The next day, Anna unpacked and wrote several letters, the first to Stuart telling him that she had arrived safely. She paused, debating how she should address him. "Dear Mr. Martin" seemed too formal, yet "My darling Stuart" sounded too familiar, even to her.

What if someone else reads this? The worry was not unfounded, but Anna decided she had to take that chance. Until she could be with Stuart in person, her letters would have to speak for her. She wanted to confirm the feelings she had for him, while letting him know where she was. But this first letter she would make brief and to the point. Anna hesitated, then began to write.

My dearest Stuart,

I am safe at my cousins' house. Many things have changed since I was last here. It could be that I will no longer be in Bedford by the time you finish your studies. Should I leave this place, I will write you with the particulars.

Wherever I am, I hope you can be also. You are often in my thoughts.

Anna Willow McKnight

After sealing Stuart's letter with a generous amount of wax, Anna began a letter to her father. She gave him the family news, but made no comment about how unwelcome her cousins had made her feel.

She was more candid in her note to Felicia. "You wouldn't believe how much like Miss Martin's I find the way I am living here," she wrote. "I am not sure how long I can stay here, under these circumstances."

That night at supper, Anna told James she wanted to go with him when he went to the Bedford market the next day.

Helen directed a sharp glance at Anna. "What business do you have in Bedford?"

"I have letters to post," Anna said.

"We can all go," Helen declared, as if Anna couldn't be trusted in town.

The next day brought sunny weather. James left the wagon at a Bedford livery stable and helped Helen and Anna down. Saying that she would meet them there later, Helen Barfield walked away, holding the baby in her arms, and soon disappeared down a side street.

Anna and James exchanged amused glances. "That's not the way to the market," James said. "Helen must be aimin' to visit someone."

"I'm sure she has her own errands," Anna replied absently, dismissing Helen as she took in the familiar market scene.

Bedford's center teemed with people who had come from miles around to barter their goods at the monthly market. The kaleidoscopic scene provided a variety of competing sensations. Bleating sheep, mooing cows, and hawkers crying out the virtues of their wares reminded Anna of her childhood, when the Bedford market had seemed an almost magical place.

"Not much like the Philadelphia market, is it?" James asked.

Anna shrugged. "Actually, it's very much like it, except in Philadelphia it's much bigger, of course. And there aren't any Indians around there."

Anna looked at a group of Indians who occupied the same area they'd claimed for years. The men squatted beside stacks of hides and pelts, seldom talking. The women sat cross-legged on their trade blankets, speaking occasionally as they worked. Some wove baskets, while others applied beads to soft deerskin, stitched moccasins, or cared for the children who had come along with them.

In her childhood, Anna had watched the Indians from a safe distance and tried to imagine if her mother had really looked like any of them. But many of the squaws that came to Bedford were old and wrinkled, and none of the younger ones remotely resembled Anna's mental image of Silverwillow.

Your mother was beautiful, my Anna Willow, the most beautiful of all the daughters of the Delaware tribe. Tall she was, taller than many men, and so graceful she could balance a pitcher of water on her head and walk up a hill without spillin' a single drop, Ian McKnight had told Anna.

She never once doubted that her father had truly loved Silverwillow, or that her mother was every bit as beautiful as he described her.

Since leaving Philadelphia, Anna had worn the necklace her father sent her under her bodice, near her heart. Now, thinking of him, she drew it out and fingered the delicate chain, seeking comfort from this reminder of her father.

"They're still mostly Shawnee," James said when he saw Anna staring intently at the group of Indians. "Except on market day, they pretty much keep to themselves."

"I'm sure that suits everyone around here just fine," Anna said.

"Yes, it does. That hasn't changed since you went away."

Anna untied the pocket around her waist and produced her letters. "I need to post these."

"Have you any hard money? The post hardly ever barters its fees."

Anna smiled faintly. "I have no barter, but I've still got a few bits left from my travel money."

James pointed to Anna's neck. "That gold necklace would fetch a great deal, in cash or barter either. I don't recall seein' it before."

Anna stroked it lightly. "My father sent it to me for

a graduation gift. It's worth far more than gold to me—I'd never willingly part with it."

"Then you'd best not show it around here," James advised. "There's a bad lot of men around the market these days. One of them might just try to relieve you of it."

Anna tucked the chain inside her bodice without question. "I understand. Is the post still in Tom Gray's tavern?"

"Yes. I'll walk along with you—I have business with his son."

Anna paid for her letters to be posted, then went back to the market for a while before she returned to the livery stable where they had agreed to meet. At the door, Anna heard her name being called and looked back to see Helen Barfield coming toward her, holding her wailing baby.

"Where on earth have you been?" Helen asked, obviously irritated. "I've been lookin' high and low for you for the last quarter hour."

"I was walking through the market," Anna replied.

Helen spoke quickly, all but shouting over her child's cries. "Silas Duward wants to see you—he's probably one of richest men in these parts. After his wife died last year, he brought his family out here and took up the Elliotts' old tract. He's been lookin' for someone to teach his five young ones ever since. He's agreed to talk to you about it."

Helen must really want to get rid of me to go to this much trouble, Anna thought.

"What makes you think I'd be interested in doing that?" she asked.

A strange look came over Helen's face. "Seems to me like you don't have much choice, missy. That fancy school oughter at least given you a way to make a livin' for yourself."

"I'm sure that my father intends to provide for me," Anna said stiffly.

"Then let him do it, but in the meantime you're gettin' your bread an' board from us for free. I'd think you'd at least want to pay your way."

Anna felt her anger rising , but decided not to speak her mind. "Where is this man?"

Helen shifted the baby from one hip to the other, momentarily quieting him. "Master Duward's at Tom Gray's tavern. Hurry—don't keep the man waitin' any longer."

Anna stood motionless for a moment, considering what she should do. Although it galled her that Helen Barfield had taken it on herself to find her a position, Anna knew she'd be foolish to cut off her own nose to spite her face. She would hear the man out. If Mr. Duward had a place for Anna, it would not only serve to get her out of a house where she wasn't wanted, but might also allow her to acquire enough money to pay her way elsewhere.

All right, I'll talk to him, Anna decided, and for the second time that day she made her way to Tom Gray's tavern.

The interior of the building was so poorly lighted that Anna had to go all the way inside and wait for her eyes to adjust the smoky dimness before she could make out the shadowy figures seated around the rough-hewn plank tables. When a male voice called her name, she turned and saw a dark-haired, middle-aged man an inch or so shorter than herself.

"Miss McKnight? I'm Silas Duward. Your cousin said you might be interested in teaching my children."

"Perhaps," Anna replied.

"We can discuss the matter outside."

Anna blinked in the daylight and tried not to stare at Mr. Duward's pockmarked face. His clothes were obviously made from expensive material, but he did not wear them well. His waistcoat gapped over his ample stomach, and his carelessly knotted stock revealed that he'd probably dressed in haste when Helen Barfield summoned him to meet her.

Mr. Duward stopped a few paces from the tavern and abruptly reached out to pull off the white mobcap covering Anna's hair.

Anna gasped, too surprised to protest.

"Your skin is dark, and you've the hair and eyes to match it," he said. "You don't look much like any of the Barfields, either. How do you come to be related to them, Mistress McKnight?"

"We are first cousins," Anna said with as much civility as she could muster. "My father and their mother were brother and sister."

Silas Duward folded his arms across his chest and riveted her with his gaze. "What about your mother? From the looks of it, I'd wager your dam's no white woman."

Anna held her chin a little higher and looked down on him. "My mother was a Delaware, Mr. Duward. She died at my birth."

Mr. Duward unfolded his arms and thrust Anna's

cap into her right hand. "Mistress Barfield neglected to tell me that."

"Does my Indian blood concern you?" Although the answer was already obvious, Anna felt the need to make him admit it.

Silas Duward's face darkened. "My children will never be taught by a savage, Miss McKnight. We have nothing further to discuss. Good day."

He turned to walk away, but Anna held the sleeve of his frock coat, forcing him turn back and face her again.

"Look at me, sir. Do I really appear so savage that you would deny your children access to the knowledge I could pass on to them?"

Mr. Duward pursed his lips, then jerked his sleeve away from her and brushed the fabric as if her touch had soiled it. "Perhaps Mrs. Barfield neglected to tell you that my children have no mother because raiding savages scalped her and left her dying on our doorstone. They'd have done the same to the children, had they not hidden themselves as they'd been taught to do. Since then, they've been in perfect terror of all Indians."

"I can understand how you feel, sir, but surely if the children and I could just meet—"

"They'll stay ignorant of all but what I can teach them before I'd subject them to the likes of you. Good day, miss."

As Silas Duward strode away, Anna shook her head at the man's blind prejudice and wondered what Stuart Martin would say to him.

Oh, Stuart, if only you were here, Anna thought forlornly. Slowly she walked back to the livery stable, not eager to deliver her bad news.

The next day, Helen Barfield's sour mood encouraged Anna to stay out of her way. Telling Helen that she was going for walk, Anna crossed the creek that had divided the McKnight and Barfield land. Through a path that had all but grown over, she reached the cabin, abandoned many years past, where her father and Aunt Agnes had lived as children. Its roof sagged and its rock chimneys were crumbling, but the cabin still stood on a rise in the middle of the land that Agnes had brought to William Barfield as her dower. The old cabin was crude compared to the Barfield house, yet in her childhood it had offered her peace and a place of refuge from her cousins. Anna always liked to pretend that the cabin belonged to her, even though she knew better.

This day, Anna looked at the cabin with a critical eye. A few basic repairs would make it habitable, she decided. She'd ask Henry about fixing it up for her to live in. He and James might grumble about doing the work, but Anna suspected that for once Helen would be her ally in the matter.

Her inspection completed, Anna sat sideways on the doorstone and leaned back against the still-sturdy doorframe. She had brought along the book that Stuart Martin had given her, not so much to read as to have a tangible reminder of him. She traced the lettering on the cover with her forefinger and pictured Stuart in her mind's eye. At first, she had almost been afraid of him. Now she could scarcely believe how bold her love for Stuart Martin had made her become.

Does he think of me as often as I think of him? Anna wondered. With the slowness of the post, it would probably be at least another week before her letter would reach him, and an equal or longer amount of time before she could expect a reply. At any rate, letters were a poor substitute for the manner in which she wanted to express her feelings to Stuart. She would much rather feel his arms around her and hear again his whispered pledge of love, which she would answer. Then, without interruptions or postponements, their love could truly be consummated.

Anna stroked the cover of Stuart's book and remembered when he gave it to her on Christmas Day, the same day he kissed her for the first time. She pressed her fingertips to her lips and sighed.

"Oh, Stuart, how I wish you were here," she murmured.

"I thought I might find you over here."

Anna looked up, startled to see James standing only a few feet away. She didn't like to think that he had been watching her; perhaps he had even heard her speak Stuart's name. Hastily she pulled at her skirts and stood. "Am I wanted in the house?"

"No, no—sit down. Do you mind if I stay here awhile?"

Anna shrugged. "If you like."

In response to Anna's somewhat grudging tone, James opened his arms wide, as if to show that he had no hidden weapons. "See? I'm not carryin' any pine cones."

"Ah, yes, I recall that you and Henry often pelted

me with them when I came to the cabin, knowing Aunt Agnes couldn't see what you were up to."

James sat down beside Anna. "I reckon we weren't very nice to you in those days," he said.

What do you mean, 'in those days'? Since when have the Barfields ever gone out of their way to be nice to me? Anna forced herself not to voice the words.

"You weren't," she agreed.

"We might've acted pretty bad sometimes, all right, but a lot of it was due to bein' jealous."

Anna stared at James in surprise. "You and Henry jealous of me! You must be joking."

"No, I'm not. Look at it this way—bein' as you're younger and a girl, we both thought that Momma favored you over us. I guess it sort of stuck in our craws."

"At least you admit it," Anna said. "I don't think Henry would."

James idly picked at splinters in the doorframe. "I know you've not been happy since you got back, Anna. What would it please you to do?"

Marry Stuart Martin, she thought immediately, but James had no power to grant that wish, in any case.

Anna thought for a moment. "If I had the money for passage, I'd go to Kentucky and ask Father to take me to the place where my mother lived. He promised to, but then the war came along, and now he can't leave his claim."

James looked oddly at Anna and took one of her hands in both of his. "If that's what you really want, I'll take you there."

Once more, James had surprised Anna, and she

said the first thing that came into her head. "I didn't know you had any money."

"Momma left me a stake—not much, but enough to get us to Kentucky."

Anna's mind whirled. Going to Kentucky appealed to her, but doing so with James did not. "'Tis a long, hard trip, I'm told. If you'd just give me loan of the passage money—"

"No!" he exclaimed, then his face reddened. "You don't understand, Anna. I'm thinkin' you an' me— we'd—we could get married first."

Anna's mouth fell open in amazement, and it took a moment for her to recover enough to speak.

"Married? You and me?"

James released Anna's hand and leaned back against the doorframe. "Is the thought so bad as all of that? You'd think I'd said I intended to burn you at the stake."

"I'm sorry, James—I don't mean to hurt your feelings, but you must know that I never thought of you in that way. We're too close kin."

"'Tis not against the law," James said. "I know a dozen families where first cousins have married—"

"Other families aren't my concern," Anna said quickly. "I appreciate the way you've treated me since I came back, but we're much too near the same branch on the McKnight family tree to wed."

James pulled the corners of his mouth tight and made a gesture that took in the cabin and the area around it. "You can't fool me, Anna Willow. I know you're worried about this land, but I swear that it'll always be yours if you marry me."

Anna stood and tucked Stuart's book under her arm, then addressed James in a firm voice. "I'm going to the house now, and there will be no mention of what has passed between us."

She turned on her heel and walked away, her mind busy. What had really possessed James to propose marriage to her? And what did he mean about seeing to it that she'd never lose the land?

My cousins must know something about my father's old property that they haven't told me, Anna thought to herself. "I must get to the bottom of this," she said aloud.

When a noisy, mocking blue jay answered her, Anna laughed and threw a pine cone in its direction. Then she quickened her step. If she hurried, she'd have time to confront Henry before James came back home.

Anna found Henry in the barn, sitting on an upturned keg as he used an awl to repair some bridle tack.

"Henry, I must speak with you."

He put down the awl and regarded Anna without curiosity. "About what? If you and Helen have had a fuss, I don't want to hear of it."

"No, it's not about Helen. It's about Aunt Agnes."

Henry frowned. "What about her?"

Anna forced herself to speak with more authority than she felt. "Why didn't you write my father that she had died? And why didn't you tell me the terms of her will?"

The color in Henry's face deepened. "Why do you bring up the subject now? 'Tis a long time now since my poor mother was laid to her rest."

"Yes, and all the more reason that those who had need to know about her wishes should already have been told."

Henry picked up the awl and bridle again and made as if to resume his work, but the slight tremor in his hands assured Anna that her words had hit their mark. He glanced at her with mingled annoyance and concern. "We sent a letter to Uncle Ian, all black-bordered as is fittin'. If he never got it, it's because he moved around too much for any letter to catch up with him."

"That may be true, but you certainly knew where I was, and all you wrote me was that Aunt Agnes had died—with no details of her illness, much less any mention of her will."

"When I first wrote, I didn't know she'd made a will. When it was found, the news of it went to your father, as is proper since he's your guardian until you marry. It was up to Uncle Ian to tell you about it, not us."

I don't believe that, Anna thought. Aloud she said, "Legally, perhaps, but don't you agree that I had a right to know about it? Aunt Agnes would certainly have wanted me to be informed."

"That's your opinion," Henry said stiffly. "Anyway, you know now, so no harm is done."

Know what? Anna's bluff had worked too well; she had convinced Henry that she had knowledge that she didn't possess, and now she had no idea how to get him to tell her more without betraying her ignorance.

"That's also a matter of opinion," she said calmly.

"I don't think your mother would be at all pleased at the way you've handled this matter."

"Oh, really? And just what do you think would please her?"

Anna ignored the heavy sarcasm in Henry's voice. "Do you have a copy of Aunt Agnes's will?"

Henry shook his head. "Nay. 'Twas filed in the county court."

"Then it seems I'll be making another journey to Bedford. Good day, Cousin Henry."

Anna half expected Henry to call after her in protest, but he didn't. She was almost certain that an important part of the document concerned her, but without first verifying it, she dared not make any comment about it to her cousins.

"I could be wrong," Anna said aloud, but she didn't really think so. If her suspicions were correct, Aunt Agnes had left the McKnight's land to her—not out-right, maybe, but for use as her dower.

That must be why James proposed to me, Anna thought. Then a further possibility occurred to her: Henry and Helen might have put James up to asking her to marry him to keep the land in the Barfield family. Should Anna marry anyone else, the Barfield holding would have considerably less value. And now that Henry had a son, he'd want to make sure that his property wouldn't have to be shared with James.

"So here you are, finally," Helen said when Anna came in. "The stew needs stirrin', if you've time to spare."

Unable to trust herself to look directly at Helen,

Anna started toward the attic stairs. "I'll just get my apron," she said.

Anna wasn't sure how she'd be able to use the advantage she sensed she held, but for the moment, it was enough merely to know that she, too, had some resources.

9

The same Bedford court clerk who had first been employed by the British to record land claims in the years before the Revolution still guarded the ponderous ledger books in which all transactions were recorded.

In a clipped Yorkshire dialect virtually unchanged in the fifty years since he'd left the land of his birth, Master Heath asked Anna what she wanted.

"Here's the date of death of my aunt, Agnes McKnight Barfield. I wish to see her Last Will and Testament, please."

The old man squinted and held the scrap of paper at arm's length, then nodded and turned to a high shelf on which a dozen dusty volumes rested. "Should be about 'ere," he mumbled to himself.

He climbed on a three-legged stool and pulled down one of the books and brought it to the counter.

"The scrivener that copied these had a fair 'and," he commented. "The lad went on West just this month past, nothin' will do these young folk but to move on an' take their chances in the wilderness. I tole 'im there'd be precious little copyin' done there for a time, but he said 'e'd 'ad 'is fill o' quills an' parchment."

As the clerk talked, he turned pages and squinted to see the headings. Anna tried to make out the writing, but it was upside down to her and she caught only a few of the words—Articles of Indenture—Cattle Marks—Inventory of Goods and Chattels—before he stopped at one page.

"This be what y' seek, young miss." The clerk swiveled the book toward Anna, and instantly she saw that it was, indeed, the Last Will and Testament of Agnes McKnight Barfield, Deceased. It had been witnessed by Judge Winton Waverly and Thomas Gray, Esquire, and bore an official-looking seal. Apparently the document had been executed some four months before her aunt's death.

"Yes, sir, I think this is it," Anna said. Her eyes suddenly filled with tears, and she had to apply her handkerchief to her eyes.

Dear Aunt Agnes, she thought. *No doubt you had some notion that your days on this earth might be numbered when you did this. If only I'd known you were so ill, I'd have come back to see you. You were always so good to me—*

The clerk noisily cleared his throat and Anna looked up at him. "Y' can skip all that first part, young miss. Th' bequests will all be on th' next page."

Anna turned the page and skimmed a list of items that Henry and James were to have, including separate sums of money for each. Then Anna saw her own name, and sucked in her breath as she read the words that followed it.

To my beloved niece Anna Willow McKnight I bequeath the property known as the McKnight holding, said property to be given on her marriage as her dower. In the event that said Anna Willow McKnight should predecease me or should never marry, the property shall then pass unhindered to my brother, Ian McKnight, or to his heirs or assigns.

In addition, it is my wish that Anna Willow McKnight should have the following items now in my possession: the bedstead, mattress, linens, and coverlet in my niece's room, the rugs she wove, my velvet-lined jewelry box and the contents thereof, namely a set of jade earrings, a silver bracelet, a cameo pin, and two gold rings, for her to employ as she sees fit.

Anna finished reading and looked at the clerk, who had been watching her with interest. "Master Heath, who sees that the terms of a will are carried out?" she asked.

He blinked at her in surprise. "Why, th' executor, of course. He's t' make sartain that the bequests in the will is all met."

Anna looked at the end of the document and noted, as she expected, that Henry Barfield had been named as the executor. "And what if he doesn't?"

The clerk shrugged and pulled at one ear. "Well,

young miss, I'd say if that's th' case, y' mought need a lawyer."

"I think I can settle this on my own," Anna said.

"Mebbe so, but if y' ha'e need o' one later, let me know."

Anna nodded. "All right. Can I get a copy of this if I need it?"

"Aye, young miss, for a fee. But it might take some while t' find a willin' scrivener."

"Never mind—I doubt if it'll be necessary."

The clerk winked at her as if they were conspirators. "Jus' in case, I'll leave the book out."

"Thank you for your help, Master Heath. Good day, sir."

Anna's mind whirled as she left the clerk's office. In the light of her cousins' failure to carry out their mother's wishes on her behalf, Anna knew she must act quickly and decisively. She would be their Indian captive no longer—Anna intended to fight back. And this time, she intended to win.

James was working in the barn when Anna rode back in later that afternoon. From the way he looked at her when he helped her from her horse, she was sure that he'd been sent there to find out what Anna intended to do about her inheritance.

"How was your trip?" he asked.

Anna stripped off her gloves. "Very interesting," she said. "I can scarcely wait to tell Henry all about it."

James removed the saddle and bridle and began to brush the horse he'd let Anna ride into town. "Tell me now," he said.

"No—you'll both hear this together. And Helen,

too, of course. I'm sure she's been part of every plan you and Henry made."

James compressed his lips and looked uncomfortable. "Anna, you mustn't think too harshly of Henry. He really took Momma's death hard—you might say he hasn't been himself since. And now that he and Helen have the baby—"

"I'm going to the house now," Anna interrupted. We'll speak no more of this until after supper."

Helen's face told Anna that she, too, feared what Anna might say. For a moment Anna felt pity for her, but her sympathy evaporated when she recalled that this woman would have allowed Anna's rights to be taken away without a word of protest.

No evening had ever seemed to pass more slowly. For once, the baby went quietly to sleep before the evening meal and allowed the rest of the household to eat without interruption. The meal proceeded in silence, and finally the moment that Anna both dreaded and welcomed arrived. She rose from the table.

"I would have some words with you," Anna said in a voice that sounded unlike her own.

Glancing uneasily at one another, James, Henry, and Helen took seats in a rough semicircle around Anna, who stood before the mantelpiece. Anna knotted her hands behind her back and forced herself to look into her cousins' eyes as she spoke.

"I know you've never had much use for me," she began quietly. "I was an intrusion in your lives and you resented me, perhaps with some cause—but that's not important now. Your mother loved both of you with all her heart. Surely you must know there's nothing that she wouldn't do for you when she was on this earth. I'd hope that you loved her enough in return to want to see that her last wishes were respected."

Henry's face had grown increasingly red, and when Anna paused for breath, he tried to interrupt her. "Anna Willow—"

"No, Henry, let me finish." Although her voice was steady, Anna's nails dug into her clenched fists, and silently she sought the strength to finish what she had to say. "I know all about the McKnight property. I have no use for the land just now, but I reserve the right to claim it later under the terms of Aunt Agnes's will. She also wanted me to have certain of her things, and those I do have immediate need of. In return for seeing that I get them, I promise to leave this house and never bother any of you again unless it is absolutely necessary."

"We never meant for you not to have them, Anna Willow," James said earnestly.

"Oh, really?" Skewered by Anna's angry stare, James looked down at the floor. "And just when were you planning to tell me about them?"

"We thought you knew and were just bein' polite because you knew we needed the things ourselves," Henry said.

Anna felt a momentary urge to laugh and call him the liar she knew him to be, but she had no wish to prolong this painful interview. Her gesture took in the house and its furnishings. "You have much here, Henry. I don't covet your goods, but I intend to take what Aunt Agnes meant me to have."

Helen had been silent, but now she glared at Anna before addressing her husband. "Since she'll be takin' the very bed from under us, I reckon you'd best be makin' a pallet on the floor."

"And don't forget that the beddin' is hers, too," James said.

Henry's face was a study in frustration as he looked from Helen to Anna. "Surely you can wait a few more days, Cousin Anna. We must have time to get another bedstead, at least."

Anna hadn't thought of the necessity to place a time limit on receiving the goods, but now she pulled one from the air. "A week," she said firmly. "I will have what is mine by this time next week."

"'Tis a good thing Momma isn't here to see this sad day," Henry muttered.

"What did you say, Cousin Henry?"

Henry made his mouth a straight line and looked Anna in the eye. "I don't believe Momma would approve of the way you're ridin' roughshod over your own kin. But if that's the way it is to be, you'll have the goods, and that in two or three days rather than seven."

Anna nodded. "Very well. That is all I have to say. It's been a long day and I intend to go to bed now. You may keep your bedstead for the present," she added, seeing the alarm that crossed Helen's face when she realized that Anna might have asked for it immediately.

Henry and Helen turned away without another word, but James followed Anna to the loft stairs, his eyes wary.

"What do you aim to do now, Anna?"

"You needn't worry—I'll not stay here and continue to make life miserable for us all."

"You'll go to Kentucky?" It was more a statement than a question, and Anna nodded.

"I've not seen Father for some time. I trust my welcome there will be a bit warmer than what I got here."

"I suppose you'll be wantin' to sell the goods to pay your way?"

"Yes. I have no choice."

"I'll help you get a good price, then."

Anna looked at James closely and decided that his offer was sincere. "Thank you, James. I wish it hadn't come to this."

James shrugged. "So do I. I've been thinkin' of what you said about Momma. She's gone, but she'd want you to be treated right. I reckon it's the last thing I can ever do for her on this earth."

Seeing how speaking of his mother had affected James, Anna gave his shoulder a light touch of sympathy. "Aunt Agnes would be proud of you," she said softly.

James raised troubled eyes to Anna's. "Oh, Anna Willow, I wish—"

But Anna cut him off. "Too much has already been said. Good night, James."

She turned away without another word and quickly climbed the stairs to her close attic room. She went to the window and leaned out, taking a deep breath of the night air, sweet now with the distant scent of honeysuckle. Overhead, the cloudless sky revealed a magnificent display of twinkling stars. Anna turned her head to look to the east. In that direction lay Lancaster and Felicia; farther on were Philadelphia and Miss Martin; and even farther, New Jersey and Stuart Martin.

Stuart.

Amo te. I love you. Anna whispered the words on the wind and wished he could somehow hear the silent cry of her heart.

It was true. Anna loved Stuart with an intensity that almost frightened her, a fierceness which their days apart had done nothing to diminish.

Do you feel the same way about me? Anna murmured, but the silence of the night gave no reply.

She hugged her arms to her body and recalled the strength of his arms as he had held her, so close that they had almost been the same person. Closing her eyes, she imagined she could feel his touch in the faint breeze that caressed her eyelids and teased her parted lips. Her head fell back and she trailed her fingertips over the curve of her throat as he had done. Her hand brushed across the bodice of her dress. Her nipples stiffened, but her own touch did nothing to pleasure her breasts, which longed for the caresses his hands had once given.

Anna breathed raggedly as she relived every moment, every detail of their all-too-brief time together. She still sorrowed that he had pulled away from her in the carriage house without giving her the fullness of his love. Yet, although she could imagine him as plainly as if he stood beside her, she could not make her absent lover become flesh and blood. He did not appear by her side to take her into his arms. Until they could physically be together again, her almost palpable yearning would continue, a constant and bittersweet presence in her life.

She shivered, then once more opened her eyes to the night skies. It would still be a few months before she and Stuart Martin could again be together. For the present, the East held nothing for her. The evening star, now advanced halfway up the western horizon, marked the direction in which her life must now turn.

Somewhere to the west is Kentucky, and my father, Anna thought. And just to the north, on the other side of the Ohio River, lay the land of her birth. Anna was determined to go to Kentucky. There, she would see her father, and this time persuade him to take her across the river. From what Anna could tell, he must now live relatively near her mother's village. She knew she might never again have such an opportunity to go there.

By the time she had made that journey, Anna hoped that Stuart Martin would be able to join her in Kentucky. He should have no trouble finding employment there as a schoolmaster. They would marry, take full pleasure in each other's love, and never again have to part . . .

Anna turned away from the window and sighed. Before those dreams could come true, however, she would have to get to Kentucky.

James was as good as his word, serving as go-between to see that his brother and Helen turned over to Anna the things that Agnes Barfield had willed her, then loading them on a wagon and taking them to Bedford to negotiate a good price.

Anna went into town with James, and while he found potential buyers, she visited the clerk who had let her examine Agnes Barfield's will. He sat on a high stool with his back to the wall, apparently dozing until her footstep brought him to attention.

"Good day, Master Heath," Anna greeted him when he shuffled over to the counter.

The old man squinted, then nodded. "Mistress McKnight, is it? What can I do for y'?"

"Master Heath, you said something the other day about a scrivener who went to Kentucky. Do you know how he got there?"

The clerk frowned and scratched his head. "Why, he rid 'is 'orse, ma'am. He left out a 'ere with all 'e 'ad in th' world in two saddlebags."

"Oh. Do you know of any other way to get there from here?"

"Why do y' ask, young missy?"

"My father lives there. I'd like to join him, but I don't know how to go about it."

"Well, a young miss like y' can't go by y'rself all that way on an 'orse, that's for sure. But if y' can get to Pittsburgh, y' can likely find a flatboat t' take y' west."

"Thank you, Master Heath. I'll see about that."

When Anna neared the livery stable where James had left the wagon, she saw that many of the goods had apparently already been sold. James stood in earnest conversation with a bearded man, who, with many gestures and much head-shaking, finally bought the remainder of the household effects.

"It looks as if you've done well," Anna told James after he'd helped load the items onto the man's Conestoga.

James handed Anna a handful of coins, a jumble of Spanish pieces of eights and Portuguese gold pieces. "I didn't get as much for the bedstead as it'd be worth in barter, but the other things brought more, and that made up for it."

Anna closed her hand around the coins, still warm from James's hands, and enjoyed their hefty weight. "I thank you for doing this for me, James."

Her cousin looked away in embarrassment. "I wish it hadn't had to come to this. If you'd marry me, I'd fix up the old place for us—"

"That subject is closed," Anna interrupted. "Anyway, I've found out the best way to get to Kentucky is by flatboat from Pittsburgh."

James looked dubious. "I dunno about flatboats, Anna Willow. Give me a horse any old time and I'll get to where I want to go. Travelin' by water—that's a different story."

"Well, I can't ride a horse through the wilderness, so I don't have much other choice. Master Heath says flatboats leave for Kentucky all the time. All I have to do now is find one."

"No—first you got to get to Pittsburgh, and that's still a lot of hard goin'," James said. "How do you aim to get there?"

"I'll use some of my hard money to buy a horse— you can pick one out for me. I can sell it when I get there."

"If you're not robbed by then." James shook his

head. "You can't go to Pittsburgh alone, Anna Willow."

"I got here from Lancaster by myself, didn't I? If I don't buy a horse, then I'll find myself a ride. Lots of Conestogas go through Bedford to the West. I'm sure that many of them would welcome a paying passenger."

James tightened his mouth in the gesture of disapproval that he and his brother shared, and which Anna knew only too well. "Henry says it's your Indian blood that makes you so stubborn, but I recall that Uncle Ian's the same way. He'd not want you goin' off alone, and I'll not let you do it, neither."

"Neither you nor Henry nor anyone in Bedford can keep me from going to Kentucky," Anna said firmly.

"No, but I can have some say in how you get there. I'll go to Pittsburgh with you to see the flatboats. If you still want to go on after that, you'll be on your own."

What James proposed made sense, and Anna decided that she might as well give in gracefully. "All right, if you must, you can travel to Pittsburgh with me. But for now, take me to Gray's tavern. I want to send a message to my father to let him know I'm coming."

The lone traveler in Tom Gray's tavern was a merchant of indeterminate years, on his way back to Pittsburgh after a visit East.

Anna explained what she sought. "I need someone to see that a message gets to my father in Kentucky. He lives near a place called Lexington."

The man nodded. "For a bit of hard money, it can be done."

After giving the tavern owner a penny for a sheet of paper and the loan of a scratchy quill, Anna wrote her father a hasty message, sealed with wax from a greasy tavern candle. On the outer fold she wrote in a bold hand: Colonel Ian McKnight, Lexington, Kentucky County, Virginia, and handed it to the merchant, along with a bit coin.

"My father will probably add another for its safe delivery," Anna said.

The man nodded and stuck the letter into a well-worn fringed pouch. "Consider it done, missy."

For a while after they left the tavern, neither James nor Anna spoke. As they rode out of Bedford, Anna broke the silence.

"Henry and Helen won't like it that you're going to Pittsburgh with me."

"They don't like much I do. In fact—" James fell silent for a moment, then spoke rapidly, as if he might otherwise lose his nerve. "Anna Willow, this might not be a good time to bring this up, but since you won't be usin' the McKnight cabin anytime soon, will you let me fix it up and use it—just 'til you need it, of course?"

"I wondered how you've stayed under the same roof with Henry and Helen this long," Anna said. "Since you're going out of your way to help me, I suppose that the least I can do is return the favor. Yes, you can use the cabin until such time as I need it myself."

James looked relieved. "I'm much obliged," he said.

As Anna expected, Henry and Helen Barfield thought she had lost her mind even to consider trying to join her father in Kentucky, but when James added that he planned to go with her as far as Pittsburgh, they were really concerned.

"You can't leave now, when the crops all need seein' to! Anna must bide here a while longer, at least 'til the corn's laid by."

"No, I don't intend to wait any longer," Anna told him. "You might as well find someone to help you with some of the chores, anyway. When James returns, he'll be busy fixing up the old cabin to live in."

Henry and Helen exchanged startled glances. "Does that mean you'll marry James?" Henry asked hopefully.

"No, and I'm not giving him the land, either. You can continue to farm it until such time as I need it. But in the meantime, James can live in the cabin."

Henry scowled. "Well, now I see why you've got to go with her. 'Tis a hard trip—I hope that cabin's worth it."

James opened his mouth as if to protest, but Anna laid a finger to her lips in warning. *Let it be,* her eyes told him, and James turned and left the room.

"When will you be leavin'?" Helen asked.

"As soon as I can decide what to take and what to store. I do expect to come back after I've seen my father," Anna added, lest Helen think she'd seen the last of her.

"Humph," Helen said. "I just hope James knows what he's gettin' himself into."

* * *

Anna might have said the same thing herself a few days later. James had found and outfitted a horse for her, and they had chosen and packed what would be needed for the journey. She and James hadn't ridden more than a few miles west on the old Forbes Road before Anna realized that this trip over the mountains would be much more difficult than she had expected.

Once they passed Somerset, a town similar to Bedford, facilities for travelers were few and far between. For long stretches, the trail was barely a wagon-rut wide, alternately muddy and dusty. Streams swollen from recent rains had to be forded with caution, and more than once Anna and James were forced to ride through dense woods to get around a broken-down wagon. As long as the weather held fair, Anna didn't mind sleeping in the open, but she gratefully accepted shelter underneath another traveler's Conestoga when a heavy thunderstorm swept through the meadow where they had stopped for the night. Still, she never once considered turning back. Not for anything would Anna give Helen Barfield the satisfaction of saying "I told you so."

10

PITTSBURGH

The afternoon sun sparkled on the waters of the Monongahela when they finally reached Pittsburgh, and Anna marveled at the size and beauty of the river.

After asking directions, they found a rough camp hard by the flatboat construction site at Redstone Old Fort, from which a man in his middle years came out to meet them.

"What is it?" he asked James.

"I'm lookin' for a boat to go to Kentucky. You have one?" James asked.

"Aye. She's 'most finished, wantin' just the pens."

Anna looked at the water, puzzled that she saw no vessel. "Where is it?"

The builder pointed to what Anna had taken to be some logs lying on the ground. "Over there. I reckon you never seen a flatboat before."

"I thought it'd already be in the water," James said.

"Come along, take a look."

James and Anna followed the boatman and stood in silence as he proclaimed the craft's virtues.

"What you see now is the bottom. She'll be turned over tomorrow and the pens put in place. That's hewed and whipsawed hardwood, with ever' crack filled with oakum and rope—not a drop of water will ever come up from the bottom."

Anna looked at it in disappointment, having expected the vessel to resemble the sailing ships she'd seen in Philadelphia. "It looks like a raft," she said.

"'Tis a flatboat—made to travel downstream with the current, steered by an aft rudder and guided by poles. Fifteen foot wide and nigh unto fifty foot long—you never saw no raft that size."

James looked at Anna. "Do you really mean to travel all the way to Kentucky on this thing?"

Anna tried to imagine life aboard this flatboat and decided it would be quite uncomfortable. However, that did not diminish her resolve to go to Kentucky. Rather than answering James, she spoke to the builder. "Do you still have space on this boat?"

As if he hadn't heard Anna, the man addressed James. "How much household goods do you have?"

"None, and the lady has one saddlebag."

The builder frowned at James. "You ain't a-comin' with her?"

"No."

"I'm sorry to hear that—we can allus use an extra hand with a rifle."

"I'm a pretty good shot, myself," Anna said.

James had detected something in the man's tone that Anna had not, something that made him frown and look anxious. "Just what'll y' be shootin'?" James asked.

The flatboat owner shrugged. "The usual varmints, like on every run. We tie up at night and use our rifles to get our meat. 'Coons, squirrel, rabbits, turkeys— ever' now and then, a boar. We eat pretty good."

"What about Indians?" James said.

"We sometimes see a few along the way, but nothin' we can't handle. I've took a dozen parties to Kentucky with nary a life lost, man nor beast. Anyhow, if the young lady wants a place and has hard money to pay for it, she had best say so now."

"I do want to go, sir. What is your charge?" Anna asked.

"Will you be bringin' your horse?"

Anna glanced uncertainly at James. "I haven't thought about it—I didn't know I could."

James shook his head. "'Tisn't wise, Anna Willow. You won't need to be burdened with the care of an animal."

Anna turned back to the flatboat owner. "I'll sell my horse before we leave—it'll just be me."

The man looked at Anna's plain homespun gown as if trying to decide how much he could get away with charging her. After a moment he named a figure, which James instantly rejected.

"That would be robbery and you know it," he said. "I'll not let her be taken advantage of that way."

"It takes a great deal of coin to build and supply these boats," the owner said defensively. "I've got a family what has to be took care of whilst I'm away—"

"Others will be headin' downriver. Come, Anna, let's go."

James turned as if to leave and Anna opened her mouth to protest. Before she said a word, however, the man threw his hands over his head and quoted a price that was half of what he'd originally asked.

"Still high, but if you'll agree to give her a rifle and shot for the trip, we'll take it. Payment in hard coin, half now, half when you make land in Kentucky."

"I need it all now—the supplies—" the shipmaster began, but the set of James's mouth persuaded him that further protest would be futile.

Anna turned her back to retrieve the necessary coins from the pocket hidden in her bodice. The man inspected the money carefully before nodding his approval. "We'll leave as soon after first light on Wednesday as we can manage. Look to see that you're here then," he told Anna.

"She will be." James turned to Anna. "We'd better be on our way now if we're to get back to Pittsburgh before dark."

When they had ridden out of the boatman's hearing, James spoke without looking directly at Anna. "Now that we're here and I see how things are, I'm thinkin' I might ought to come along and see this Kentucky for myself."

Anna gasped in surprise. "James Barfield! You can't do that—what would Cousin Henry think?"

James smiled ruefully. "More important, I guess, is what you'd think. Anna Willow, I've truly enjoyed your company these last few days, and even though you say you won't marry me, I believe you've felt the same way."

Anna nodded. "Yes, despite everything, the trip

from Bedford wasn't bad, and I know I could never have made it without your help. But we share the bond of kinship, and that's all it can ever be. That won't change, even if you come to Kentucky with me. Besides, what would you do there? You can't take up land without so much as a plow to break it, and lacking the money to buy one."

A shadow passed over James's face and his lips tightened. "Thanks for remindin' me how poor I am," he said bitterly.

Without further conversation, they rode the rest of the way into town to find lodging.

Anna sighed and wished that her relationship with James could be different. Although he been nicer to her in the past few days than he had in the rest of their lives put together, James hadn't really changed. He still tended to behave like a spoiled child when he didn't get his way, all but thrusting out his lower lip in a pout. From long experience, Anna knew it could take a while for her cousin's mood to change for the better.

When they reached an inn that looked like a likely place to stay, James dismounted and said shortly, "Take your saddlebag inside—I'll see to the horses."

Without replying, Anna went inside and sat at a table in the tavern. Now that her cousin wasn't looking over her shoulder, she would write another letter to Stuart Martin. She hadn't had time to hear from him before leaving Bedford, but she wanted him to know where she was going.

Anna opened her saddlebag and removed a quill pen and paper. Rather than mix some of her precious ink powder, she bargained with the inn owner for the use of his inkwell in exchange for copying one of his documents.

When she finished that task, Anna smoothed out her own paper and began to compose her second letter to Stuart Martin, this one inviting him to join her and her father in Kentucky.

My dearest Stuart,

I write this in Pittsburgh, where I am about to journey by flatboat to visit Father in Kentucky. I expect to stay there for several months. I have long wanted to see where my mother lived. It is my hope that my father can at last take me to that place.

I hope you are well and that your studies are progressing on schedule. Do you recall that afternoon in the carriage house as often as I do? I treasure each of those precious moments, and I think of them—and you—each day. It already seems a lifetime since we were last together.

You can write me care of Col. Ian McKnight, near Lexington, Kentucky County. I am sure my father will be almost as glad to see you as I will, should you be able to come to us in Kentucky. In the meantime, I am eager to know how you fare.

Anna sighed, not satisfied with the way the letter had turned out, but even if she had known any way to improve it, she had no more paper. She signed her first name, then folded the page, sealed it well with thick candle wax, and tucked it inside her pocket. She would ask James to post the letter when he got back to Bedford.

By the time Stuart gets my letter, I should already be in Kentucky, Anna thought. Then she would send him more specific directions on how he could find her. Imagining their reunion, she smiled.

Parting is such sweet sorrow, Mr. Shakespeare once said. But meeting again—that would be pure pleasure.

Anna was so weary that night that not even the snoring women around her in the room where she slept and the considerable noise from the tavern below kept her awake very long.

James, in a better mood after a good night's sleep, reported the same experience when they took breakfast together the next morning.

"What do you think we should do first today?" he asked her.

"I need to sell my horse—let's find a livery stable and see what kind of price we can get."

The first stabler offered less than Anna had paid, but at the second, James struck a deal for her horse and arranged for the buyer to pick it up at Redstone Old Fort the next morning. There he would pay Anna and bring the animal back to Pittsburgh.

Their business in town concluded, the two cousins started back towards Redstone Old Fort and the site where the flatboat would set out the next day.

"You should have a part of the price for coming with me," Anna told James. "I'd not have gotten here nearly so soon without your help."

He shook his head. "You bought the horse with your own money—anyway, you know I didn't come with you expectin' any pay."

"Yes, but you sold it for more than I paid. At least let me give you the difference—it can be part of your stake."

James pulled down the corners of his mouth. "I'd need a sum a hundred times greater than that to be my own man."

"I'm sure that with hard work, that day will soon come," Anna said.

James laughed without humor. "Hard work for someone else won't help much. Henry says I ought to marry me a rich widow. Maybe if I stay around Pittsburgh long enough, I'll find myself one."

Anna didn't doubt for a moment that Henry would have suggested that his brother should find a rich wife, nor that James might even take the idea seriously himself, but she had little regard for the idea herself. "If so, you'd probably deserve each other," she said.

As soon as they had left the noise of Pittsburgh behind and could speak without raising their voices, Anna handed him the letter she'd written to Stuart.

"Will you post it for me in Bedford?"

James nodded. "For a fee." His expression was serious, but Anna knew that in his own way, James was teasing her. He glanced at the address, then at Anna. "Stuart Martin—is he that lieutenant that Uncle Ian soldiered with, the one who got you into the fancy school?"

Anna nodded. "Yes. He was always kind to me when I was at Miss Martin's."

James opened the flap of his saddlebag and dropped the letter inside. "You don't have to explain. No wonder you wouldn't marry me."

Anna sighed. "Oh, James, we're cousins. Stuart Martin has nothing to do with that."

"I said I'll mail your letter, and I will, and that's the end of it."

Anna said nothing, but privately she wondered. Just about the time she thought that James had given up any notion of marrying her, he'd do or say something that showed how much her refusal still stung him.

When they reached Redstone Old Fort, they found a flurry of activity around the flatboat launch site. Many of the passengers had already arrived and were making preparations to camp there overnight.

Anna looked in awe at the assembled jumble of running children, harried mothers, busy fathers, and bawling livestock. "How can one flatboat hold all this?" she wondered out loud.

The boatmaster overheard Anna and came over to where she and James stood. "A flatboat's the sturdiest craft that man ever made," he declared. "There's room and plenty for all that you see about you here today."

James looked equally dubious. "I hope so. This lady's father is Colonel Ian McKnight, a man of some note in the wilderness. He'd not take it kindly should any harm come to her in your care."

At the mention of Ian McKnight's name, the man narrowed his eyes and stared hard at Anna. "Colonel McKnight, is it? We hunted together, many years past. I recall that he took an Indian wife—you must be hers, all right."

You look Indian enough to be daughter of a savage, Anna knew he meant. She raised her chin slightly and looked him in the eye.

"My mother was Delaware."

"Graceful people they are, for savages," the boatman murmured. He nodded brusquely and left them to greet some other new arrivals.

James turned to Anna. "Now that you're in safe hands, I'd best start on back. I can be down the road quite a ways by nightfall if I go now."

Anna felt a moment of panic at being left alone with all these strangers. "What about my horse?"

"The livery man will come for him tomorrow and pay you then. If not, you can prob'ly find someone else to buy it—or even change your mind and take it to Kentucky. You don't need me anymore, Anna Willow—if you ever did."

Seeing the expression on his face, Anna felt her heart constrict. Saying good-bye to James wouldn't be as easy as she had imagined, but he must never know it.

Anna forced her voice to be steady. "In that case, I thank you for bringing me this far, James. I know Father will appreciate your kindness to me when he hears of it."

"Tell Uncle Ian I send the family's greetings," he said stiffly. "Since you're such a scribe, you might write an' let me know you got there."

Anna nodded. "I will. And James—should a letter come for me from Mr. Martin—"

James interrupted her. "I'll send it on, in the care of Ian McKnight, near Lexington."

"Thank you. And remember—I expect you to use the old cabin."

James nodded. "Good-bye, Anna Willow. 'Tis a wild trip that you're undertakin'. Be careful."

"I will. And don't look so worried. I'll be all right."

Mutually they moved toward each other for a brief embrace, but did not kiss good-bye. Then James turned and mounted his horse.

Shading her eyes against the afternoon sun, Anna watched James give her a final wave, then ride away, bound for the familiar life of Bedford.

She felt a strange sense of isolation as she realized that her last contact with her old life was gone. From now on, she'd truly be on her own.

11

OHIO RIVER

After James rode out of sight, Anna turned back to the camp, where she noticed that a plump, motherly-looking woman regarded her with a blend of curiosity and sympathy.

"Looks like your man ain't comin' with you," she observed. "Will you be travelin' alone, then?"

Instinctively Anna raised her chin. "The boatman will look after me."

The woman's laugh showed that she still had strong, white teeth. "I'd not depend on Master Perkins for that if I was you, lass. He'll have all he can do to pilot the boat. I'm Mary McIntosh, and that big fellow yonder helpin' build the pens is my man, David. You're welcome to join up with us."

Anna looked in the direction the woman indicated, to see a Goliath of a man whose beard all but obscured his face. *He'd be a fine champion to have in a fight,* Anna thought. She turned back to the woman and nodded. "That's very kind of you, Mrs. McIntosh.

"I'm Anna McKnight. I'm going to visit my father in Lexington."

"Glad to know you, Anna. All the folks at Harrodsburg call me Mary, and so should you." She glanced at Anna's hand. "Do you not have a ring?"

"A ring?" Anna repeated, not understanding the purpose of Mary McIntosh's question.

Mary gestured toward the half-dozen other men working alongside her husband to secure the boat's superstructure to its base. "If those young bloods know you're spoken for, they'll leave you alone."

"I do have a ring," Anna said, truthfully enough. For a moment she considered letting Mary McIntosh continue to believe that James was her husband, but she didn't think she could sustain the falsehood all the way to Kentucky. "However, I'm not married—the man you saw me with is my cousin."

"Well, if you ain't lookin' for a husband, you might better put on the ring anyhow and let the bachelors b'lieve you're spoken for. Otherwise, they could get mighty pestiferous around a pretty thing like you."

Anna glanced at the men and fervently wished one of them were Stuart Martin. "I'm going to Kentucky to see my father, not to find a husband," Anna said aloud.

Mary McIntosh laughed, a merry sound that started as a chuckle and ended in a near-whoop. "Aye, but the men'll find *you*, I can tell you that. You'd best do as I say. Bring your things over to yonder tree—that's where we're camped. David will see to your horse."

"It's been sold. Someone's to come for it tomorrow," Anna said.

"Did you sell the saddle with it?" Mary asked.

"I don't think so, just the bridle and halter."

"Take the saddle off right now, and put it with your things—saddles fetch a fair price in Kentucky."

"I hadn't thought of that," Anna said.

Mary inclined her head. "There's much you haven't thought of, lass."

True, Anna thought, but without fear as she walked into the woods to screen herself from view while she retrieved her aunt's ring from its hiding place inside her bodice. The trip hadn't yet begun, but Anna felt a strange blend of excitement and contentment.

Edward Perkins might have intended to get under way at first light, but by the time the animals and supplies had been loaded onto the flatboat, the sun stood more than halfway up in the morning sky.

Anna watched the Pittsburgh road in vain for the man from the livery stable to appear. When she knew that he wasn't going to get there in time, she reluctantly gave up another coin so her horse could join the rest of the livestock making the trip.

"'Tis probably for the best, lass," David McIntosh told her. "You might need it, and if you don't, you can sell the animal there for a lot better price than you'd a-got in Pittsburgh."

The boatmaster had assured all the passengers that it would take the flatboat no more than eight or ten days to reach Limestone, where Anna, the McIntoshes, and a few others would leave it.

"That's if nothin' out of the ordinary happens otherwise," Mary McIntosh added under her breath.

"Indians don't raid boats as much now as they did there for a while, but when we get to the narrows, every man, woman, or child what can fire a piece will have some kind of rifle at the ready. Sometimes just seein' that we're ready seems to scare them off."

"What kind of Indians?" Anna asked, not wanting to think her mother's tribe could do such things.

Mary shrugged. "Who knows? They're all the same to me."

That is not so. Not wishing to argue with this kind, though misguided, woman, Anna kept the thought to herself.

The first few days of their voyage passed so peacefully that Anna began to think that Mary had exaggerated the dangers. The steady motion of the craft soothed her by day, and at night when they'd made camp along the shore, Anna enjoyed sleeping under the stars. When she was a small child, her father had told her wonderful stories about the constellations, the Hunter and the Bear. His formal education in Scotland had been scanty, but to Anna, her father was about the closest to perfection that any human could be, and her only regret was that they had been apart so much in recent years.

That would soon change, however, and they would be together again when she got to Kentucky. In the meantime, travel aboard the flatboat had been far more enjoyable than Anna had expected.

Inevitably, the pleasant days came to an end. They encountered their first, quite frightening, stretch of shoals. Although Edward Perkins kept assuring his passengers that the broad-beamed craft was in no real danger of being swamped, the strained faces of the polemen testified that even they had their doubts. Finally, though, the shoals were successfully run.

Then rain fell in a deluge for two days. It was nearly impossible to keep a fire going on shore at night, so everyone had to endure the discomfort of wet clothes until the sun and a warm south wind combined to dry them.

A new challenge appeared the next afternoon when the flatboat reached a narrow stretch of the Ohio River where it would be forced to pass much too close by the wooded north shore for comfort.

"Over yonder's home to thousands of savages," David McIntosh said. "They like nothing better than to get their hands on a boat like this, loaded down with goods and livestock."

My mother's home was somewhere over there too, Anna thought. From everything her father had told her about Silverwillow and her people, Anna couldn't believe that they could be the bloodthirsty murderers that everyone seemed to make Indians out to be.

"The Delaware are gentle people unless they are provoked," her father had told her. "Never forget that they were always kind to me, Anna Willow. They would have kept you and raised you as their own had I not taken you away. Remember that, if you hear ill said of your mother's people."

So Anna grew up thinking that, no matter what other kinds of Indians might do to whites, her mother's tribe was different. The thought that she might well have been brought up as one of them had made her even more eager to see how the Delaware lived. Ian McKnight had promised that when she was older, he'd take her there.

At that thought, Anna felt a wave of uneasiness. For the first time, it occurred to her that circumstances could have changed since then. Her father might not be able to take her to her mother's village, after all, thus removing a major reason for making this journey.

Don't borrow trouble, Anna reminded herself. With the others, she stared across the narrow channel at the opposite shore. Edward Perkins cautioned the passengers to be ready to fight, if necessary.

"Fresh prime your guns, and keep them to hand," he ordered.

True to his word, the shipmaster provided Anna with a sturdy old flintlock rifle, along with powder, ball, and flint. Anna knew how to fire it, but she couldn't imagine aiming it at any human being, and hoped that such an action would never be necessary.

All conversation ceased as the channel narrowed even more, putting them in easy reach of rifle fire from the northern shore.

"They're over there, just watchin' us," David McIntosh said quietly.

"Who lives there?" Anna asked, almost afraid to hear his answer.

"This part's 'most all Shawnee."

Anna strained her eyes, expecting top-knotted and war-painted Shawnee braves to erupt from the dense woods at the water's edge at any moment. In addition to their rifles, they'd probably all have tomahawks raised in readiness to scalp all the passengers . . .

Anna held her breath and listened. Were those faint cries only from the usual shore birds? Or Shawnee signals that would soon change to loud war whoops?

Anna turned to David McIntosh and whispered as if she feared the Indians could overhear her. "I don't see anything."

"If they're there, they don't aim for you to see them 'til they're ready," he replied.

Everyone continued to watch in tense silence. When the flatboat finally reached a wider part of the river without incident, a collective sigh of relief rippled throughout the passengers. Edward Perkins circulated among them, saying that the worst danger had passed, and Anna gladly put down her borrowed flintlock.

Before they had time to fully relax, however, another incident again brought the passengers to attention. One of the lookouts pointed to a cleared area on the far shore, a few hundred yards downstream. When the boat got closer, they saw a white man, naked to the waist. Frantically he waved a tattered shirt over his head. When the flatboat came within hailing distance, he fell to his knees and clasped his hands before him and cried out.

"Help! Save me!" he said, over and over.

Anna stood to get a better look at him and her heart skipped several beats. Like Ian McKnight, this man was tall; and also like her father, his faded red hair seemed streaked with gray. Although the man's heavy beard and the distance between them obscured his facial features, Anna had no doubt that this poor man could actually be her father—or someone eerily like him. She expected the flatboat would be poled to a stop and a party sent to the man's aid.

But to her horror, the boatman kept an impassive and steady hand on the rudder and ordered the men at the flatboat's corners to pole even faster. In moments the current had swept them past the man, and his pleading cries gradually receded in the distance.

Her eyes wide in shocked disbelief, Anna turned to David McIntosh. "Why didn't we stop and help that poor man?"

David McIntosh looked at Anna, his dark eyes soft in his grizzled face. "Ah, lass, don't take on so. He's probably only a decoy, sent out by the savages to trick us into stoppin' to help. Once we did, we'd be overrun and scalped afore we'd have time to prime our rifles, much less to fire them."

"How do you know it's a trick? Surely, as many as there are of us, we could cover anyone willing to take the canoe to him."

"It cannot be risked, Anna," Mary McIntosh said. "Too many travelers have died just that way because they were taken in by such ruses."

Anna shook her head impatiently. "You don't understand—that man could be my father—he looked just like him!"

David McIntosh regarded her with pity. "They allus look like someone's father, lass, but they almost never are."

"Likely he's a renegade white, or maybe a prisoner who's bargained for his life in return for ours. Don't think any more about it," Mary added.

Her heart heavy, Anna looked back at the man,

who appeared smaller and smaller as the flatboat moved farther and farther downstream. Just as the boat was almost out of sight, the man turned and walked back toward the woods, and the passengers went back about their business as if nothing unusual had happened.

I won't forget about this, Anna vowed. *I'm going to ask Father what he'd have done if he were in the boatmaster's place.*

She felt a chill run down her spine. If that man really was her father, she'd never again have the chance to ask him anything. For the first time, Anna realized that she ought to have some alternate plan ready if, for any reason, she couldn't find her father when she got to Kentucky.

Anna sighed as she recalled how she'd chastised James Barfield for even considering going to Kentucky without money or land or the means of getting either. *I'm not really much better off,* she admitted to herself.

Although she had a modest amount of money, it wouldn't last long. She'd have to find someone willing to take her in until she could find a way to get back to Pennsylvania. She already knew that she couldn't return by flatboat, even if she wanted to— the boatmaster had confirmed that this vessel, like all the others he'd brought downriver, would be broken up and its timbers sold after it reached Louisville.

Anna would have to find someone traveling east who'd be willing to take her along. She didn't know what she'd do then, but one thing was certain—she would never go back to the Barfields.

12

KENTUCKY

The rest of the journey passed in relative calm, apart from some unpleasant weather that forced them to tie up to the shore for almost a full day, thus delaying their landing at Limestone.

"Will your father be meetin' you?" David McIntosh asked Anna when the Limestone landing came into sight.

"I don't think so. I doubt that he's had time to get the letter saying I was coming."

"Then you can ride with us—Lexington's on our way and still several days' travel from there."

Anna's heart sank. With no clear idea of where Lexington was, she'd expected that when the flatboat reached Limestone, her journey would be over. *It's a good thing I kept the horse,* she thought.

The road from Limestone to Lexington passed through land that both closely resembled Pennsylvania and was quite different from it. The forests were thick, but honeycombed with deer paths and buffalo trails, which David McIntosh told Anna were also used by the Indians who crossed the Ohio to raid Kentucky settlements. Near creeks and in other places stood thickets of nearly impenetrable cane, some twenty and even thirty feet tall, which the McIntoshes told her Indians used to ambush white travelers.

"Do many Indians live in Kentucky?" she asked.

"Nay, lass, Indians never lived here—they just use the land for hunting."

"First they hunted buffalo and deer, and now they stalk whites," Mary McIntosh said grimly. "That's the way of it. You won't come and go in Kentucky as free and easy as you did back home."

After passing near to a few small settlements, the small party that had left the flatboat at Limestone reached the walled town of Lexington. Anna had expected something on the order and size of Fort Bedford, and she was disappointed.

"'Tis a great deal smaller than I thought," she remarked.

The McIntoshes pointed out the cabin of an old man who could direct her to the place where her father lived. With mutual expressions of hope that they would soon meet again, they and Anna said their farewells.

Half an hour later, Anna rode out of Lexington in the company of Hezekiah McCanless, who had the longest, whitest beard she had ever seen.

"This here's an old buffalo trace," the old man explained. "It wanders some, but it'll get us there."

"I thank you for taking the time to come with me, Mr. McCanless," Anna said.

Her companion grinned, revealing gaps where he had lost several teeth. "Just call me Hezzy, like everyone else. You don't need to thank me for nothin'. I've knowed your pa a long time. We was both hunters in the old days, y' know. Now I'm seized up with the rheumatics, an' your pa sees that I'm kept in meat, even salts it down fer me. They's not much I wouldn't do to help out Ian McKnight or his kin."

"Does my father ever talk about me?" Anna asked.

Hezzy made a noise deep in his throat that she took to be a chuckle, then he turned his head and spat before speaking. "All the time, missy—'Yer oughter to see my Anner Willer, she's pretty as a pitcher,' he allus says. Why, I reckon he'll be purely tickled to have y' come in like this, and him not a-knowin' a thing in the world about it."

They reached a stretch of cleared land on which corn grew, and Anna recalled that her father had written that he had to grow a crop of corn in order to claim more acreage.

"Whose corn is that?" Anna asked.

Hezzy shook his head. "I don't rightly know, but it b'longs to someone what's livin' at the Station. There's the trace to it yonder."

Her guide pulled his horse to the left and motioned for Anna to follow him across a shallow creek. On the other side, a rectangular palisade occupied the highest ground in the area.

"Hallo, there!" Hezzy called out.

Someone called back, and after a moment a man in a long buckskin hunting shirt opened the gate and waved them through.

Inside, in an area slightly more than two hundred yards long and some fifty yards wide, forty cabins faced one another in parallel lines, protected by twelve-foot-high palisades and firing towers at each corner. In the large open area between the cabins, men worked at various tasks, several women tended cooking fires, and a blur of children chased after one other in a game of tag. All activity soon halted, however, as everyone in Bryan's Station regarded the newcomers with interest.

"Don't tell me you've done gone an' wed yerself a young squaw," one of the men said to Hezzy.

No one had referred to Anna in that way for some time, and her face warmed in surprise and anger.

"I'd be proud t' tell y' such, but I can't—this here's Ian McKnight's daughter."

A spare woman wiped her hands on her apron and squinted up at Anna. "You don't say! Welcome to Bryan's Station, missy. I'm the Widow Stucker, and this here's my boy Jacob. Don't just stand there like a dead stump, son. Holp her off'n her horse."

Immediately several other residents surrounded Anna, telling her their names and adding their welcome to the widow's.

"Go fetch Master McKnight," the widow directed yet another son, but someone else had apparently already thought to do so.

A tall man in buckskins hurried toward them, his mouth open wide in astonished surprise. "Anna Willow! Is it really ye?"

Anna's relief and joy rendered her temporarily mute as she slid down from her horse and threw her arms around her father's neck. The people who at first had crowded around them returned to their occupations, thus giving them a measure of privacy for their reunion.

"Praise the Lord that ye got here safe," her father said at last. "But what are ye doin' in Kentucky, lass? I thought ye'd bide a time in Bedford."

"I wanted to see you." Anna stepped out of her father's embrace and looked closely at him. As she had anticipated, his red hair had faded somewhat, but nothing about Ian McKnight looked frail. If anything, the eyes that searched her face were even bluer and keener than she remembered.

"I see ye got the necklace I sent ye," he said. A look of wonder crossed his face as he stared at her. "Why, ye're a woman grown now. How is it that no man has yet claimed ye?"

Stuart Martin wants to, Anna almost said, but she wanted to wait before she spoke of Stuart to her father. "Did you send me to Miss Martin's only to wed me off so soon?" Anna asked instead.

"Ah, Anna Willow—" Ian began, but before he finished the thought, they were joined by a slender woman whose mobcap didn't entirely conceal the straw-colored hair beneath it. She stopped just short of Anna and stood with her arms on her hips as she regarded her. "I suppose you must be Ian's girl."

"Yes, I am," Anna said. She smiled and waited for the woman to identify herself, but her father spoke first.

"Anna, this is Rebecca—my wife."

If she had been physically slapped, Anna could not

have been more surprised. Her mouth fell open, and a weak "Oh" was all she could manage.

Her father stepped between them and put his right arm around his wife, with his left arm circling his daughter's waist. "I reckon ye didn't get the letter I sent about weddin' Rebecca, but now that ye're here, ye can get to know one another right well."

Anna felt numb. "The only letter I got had this necklace in it," she said.

Rebecca gently disengaged herself and adjusted her cap. "I'll go see to makin' up some kind of place for you in the lean-to. We're not much used to company here."

"I'm not company," Anna said, but Rebecca had already turned away, and made no reply.

Ian McKnight continued to hold his daughter in a loose embrace. "How fares the family in Bedford? When did ye leave there, and how did ye manage to get here alone? 'Tis a long, hard journey."

Anna smiled at her father's earnest puzzlement. "All in good time, Father. Right now, my horse needs seeing to, and I could use a bit of rest myself."

"Of course," Ian said. "I'll tend to the animal whilst ye wash up. Rebecca'll be glad to show ye where everything is."

I'm sure she will. Anna tried to stifle the uneasy feeling that she was an intruder in her father's home. Rebecca seemed civil enough, but Anna was quite aware that a newly married couple didn't need anyone else around.

I'll stay out of their way. Anyway, this can't be any worse than living with Helen Barfield, Anna thought wryly.

*   *   *

Later that day, as they worked to make a bed for Anna, Rebecca explained that her first husband, Richard Engler, had been killed by Indians a few months ago, soon after the death of their two children from a fever. She spoke matter-of-factly, but Anna could imagine how hard this woman's life must have been. Her father's new wife didn't want to talk much about herself, however, and asked many questions about Anna's childhood and upbringing.

"I thought Father would have told you all about me," Anna said after briefly tracing her life's history—less her love of Stuart Martin—for Rebecca.

"Ian said he'd married a Delaware woman and had a girl-child by her that his sister raised. He said you'd had a lot of fancy schoolin'. The way he talked, I thought you'd stay East."

Perhaps I should have—had I known that Father had taken himself a wife, I'm not sure I'd be here now, Anna thought.

"I don't intend to stay in Kentucky. I'll be going back as soon as I do what I came for," she said aloud.

"And what is that?" Rebecca asked.

"I want to see where my mother's people lived. Father promised to take me when I was old enough."

Rebecca raised her eyebrows. "He never told me that. With things like they are now and the Indians raidin' across the river every chance they get, it's too dangerous to travel up that way."

Anna tried not to show anger at the way Rebecca so quickly dismissed her cherished dream. "I'll leave it up to Father."

"Of course. But don't be surprised if he says no."

*   *   *

Anna's first chance to broach the subject came that night after supper, when Rebecca made an excuse to visit a neighbor, and left them alone.

"I still can scarce believe that my nephews would let ye come all this way by yourself," he said when Anna finished the account of her journey.

"Don't blame them, Father. They both tried to talk me out of it at first. When James saw that I was bound to come, he offered to travel with me, but I wouldn't let him. Besides, as I've said, good people saw to me on the boat."

Ian McKnight narrowed his eyes and regarded Anna closely. "Ye were never good at dissembling. Every word may be true, yet there's something ye've left unsaid, lass."

Anna looked down at the logs that made up the cabin's puncheon floor, then back at her father. "The last I heard from you, you didn't know that Aunt Agnes had died. Did you ever get a letter from Henry about her will?"

Ian's mournful expression made his denial unnecessary. "Aye, lass, your news was a bitter blow. I've had no letters from the Barfields."

Holding her father's hand, Anna told him how Anges had died and what her aunt had written in her will. "Aunt Agnes wanted me to have the old farm for a dowry."

Ian sighed heavily. "Aye, Agnes was a good woman, and from the first she loved ye as her own. I wanted no part of the farm myself, but it pleased me that she wanted ye to have it."

Anna glanced at her father in surprise. "You knew

all along that she'd leave me the property? Why didn't you tell me?"

"I didn't know for certain—it was a matter about which we always disagreed. I sent ye to Miss Martin's so ye wouldn't have to marry a poor farmer, but she always hoped ye'd come back to Bedford."

Anna sat silent for a moment, debating if she should tell her father about James Barfield's marriage proposal. She decided against it.

"Be assured, I have no intention of living in Bedford, nor do I want the property. I do want something else, though, something that only you can give me."

"Oh? And what is that, lass?"

Anna leaned forward and spoke with quiet sincerity. "Many times over the years you promised to show me where my mother and her people lived. You said that when I was old enough, you'd take me. I want to go there now, Father."

Ian McKnight began shaking his head even before Anna finished speaking. "Ah, Anna Willow, I've ever been a man of my word, but in this case, I canna grant what ye ask. I doubt that Silverwillow's village still stands, and 'tis far too dangerous to chance finding out. Some weeks past we heard that the British had massacred over two hundred Delaware under their chief Netawatawees, who had taken the name of Abraham. All through the Ohio the Redcoats have stirred up the Indians so much that even I'd not feel free to walk among them in peace."

Anna had anticipated her father's reaction, but she had hoped he might change his mind when he saw how much it meant to her. However, the set of his jaw told her that no amount of pleading would move him. So Ian McKnight had always been, and so he was still. Once he made up his mind, there was no changing it.

Anna made no attempt to disguise her disappointment. "I still want to go there. Maybe things will change soon," she said.

"I doubt it. Besides, I have responsibilities here now. I canna traipse off into the wilderness on a whim. I'm sorry. I know how much it meant to you, but please forget about it, lass." Ian McKnight stood. "I'm going to find my wife."

Too late, Anna realized that her words had somehow hurt her father's feelings. She followed him to the door and called after him to return, but Ian McKnight strode away without looking back.

Anna was still considering how she could smooth her father's feelings when he returned. He crossed the room and embraced her.

"Ah, Anna Willow, forgive me. Ye can stay here as long as ye like and if ye decide ye want to go back East, I'll see ye safely there as soon as I'm free to go. But I will not take ye beyond the Ohio."

"I understand," Anna replied, her spirits rising. "It's all right."

Yet Anna's heart silently denied her words. *Someday it will be as I have always dreamed,* she told herself. *I will yet see my mother's land.*

13

WACCACHALLA

To Willow, the waxing and waning of the moon had never seemed to take so long as when she waited for the time that she and Bear's Daughter would journey to the land of her birth. She felt glad that Otter was absent from the village with a war party, but she worried that Bear's Daughter had not gained as much strength as Willow had hoped.

"This journey will be hard, my mother," Willow said the morning they were to leave, when simply preparing the last of the food for their backpacks seemed to have exhausted Bear's Daughter. "I fear that you should not go."

Bear's Daughter looked steadily at Willow. "I have not taught you to fear. I will hear no more such talk."

Dawn had not yet broken when Willow and Bear's Daughter walked out of the village. Each carried only a backpack with a blanket, a spare pair of moccasins, and a small amount of food. Their journey would take them a few days, and they would need to gather more food on their way.

The sky gradually lightened, and eventually the sun rose in a bright pink sky. After walking for a while, they left behind all familiar landmarks and took a fork that led to an eastern trail.

"I have not seen you so content in many moons, my mother," Willow remarked.

"Not all will know contentment this day, Littlewillow. Not Otter, who will bring a fine deer to an empty lodge."

"You know that he does this?" Willow asked.

"Ayee, Black Snake told me that it will be so. That is why we left on this day."

Instead of taking satisfaction in imagining Otter's displeasure, Willow feared its consequences. "What if Otter should follow us?"

"He will not. Otter is a warrior and he must serve his chief. He will not track us."

"So may it be," Willow said, unconvinced.

More than once that day Willow looked back uneasily, half expecting to see Otter coming after her on his black horse. One did not safely cross such a man. There were tales about how warriors waited for many cycles of the moon to surprise their enemies, and then, when they no longer expected it, took their revenge.

Bear's Daughter glanced at Willow as if she knew her thoughts. "You must not think of Otter. He can disturb you only if you allow him into your mind."

"It is a wise saying."

Bear's Daughter nodded. "You will see, Littlewillow. A good man will take you into his lodge and you will be glad of it."

Will I? Willow didn't want to think about such a time. For the moment, it was enough that the man wouldn't be Otter.

The sun was just past the middle of its journey across the sky when Willow's keen hearing alerted her to the sound of horses, still at some distance to the north.

"Someone rides this way, my mother."

Bear's Daughter stopped and raised her head like an animal taking a scent. "Step behind those bushes and watch. Tell me what your young eyes see."

A band of warriors rode into view, and from the colors and patterns of their war paint, Willow told Bear's Daughter they were Shawnee, but not from Waccachalla.

"Show yourself," her mother said. "I would know where they are bound."

Just before the riders reached the women's hiding place, Willow stood to her full height and took a step toward the trail. The lead warrior sharply reined in his horse and stared at her in surprise. While his attention was thus diverted, Bear's Daughter calmly stepped forward and seized his horse's bridle.

"Greetings, warrior. What is your village? Where go you in this war paint?"

Some of the Shawnee behind him laughed, and one or two made remarks that Willow couldn't hear. She guessed they were making fun of her mother, and she watched to see how the young lead warrior would handle the situation.

Signaling for the others to be quiet, he slid off his horse. He faced Bear's Daughter and nodded as a gesture of respect. To Willow's surprise, the warrior matched her height almost exactly, and she wondered if he really could be Shawnee.

If this warrior brought a deer to our lodge, I would not turn him away. Willow dismissed the thought almost as soon as it formed, but from the way Bear's Daughter looked at him, there was no denying that she had also noticed and admired the young warrior's appearance.

"Greetings, old woman. I am White Eagle. We come from Shawnee Town and go to raid the *Shemanese*. Where are your men, that you travel alone?"

White Eagle. The name suits him very well, Willow thought. His skin was lighter than that of the Shawnee in Waccachalla—still darker than hers, but of a similar hue. The warrior had a firm jaw and dark, expressive eyes under heavy, straight brows. His long hair fell in a braid down his back, adorned with a single white feather. In preparation for battle, his bare, heavily muscled chest and arms had been rubbed with with oil, and they gleamed in the sun. Altogether, White Eagle's looks pleased Willow as no other man's ever had, and she stared at him with more boldness than modesty.

Such a one as this must surely already have taken a wife, Willow told herself. She judged him to be about year or so older than she, the age when most warriors chose to take wives. His closeness almost dizzied her, and Willow hoped he was too occupied with her mother to notice how rudely she stared at him.

"I am Bear's Daughter. My daughter *Match-squa-thi* Willow and I have no men. We go to the Muskingum, where once we lived among the Lenni-Lenape Clan of the Turtle."

Her words brought murmurs from some of the other men in White Eagle's party, and he raised his hand for silence. "Once I see you and this girl on the Scioto Trail with Black Snake. Why do Shawnee now seek out Delaware?"

Although Bear's Daughter drew herself up to her full height, the top of her head still didn't quite reach White Eagle's collarbone. "Ayee, young warrior, I am Bear's Daughter, true cousin to the Shawnee chief Black Snake and also kin of the old Delaware chief Bright Horn. We travel to his village."

White Eagle frowned. "Do you not know that there is much trouble in the Delaware Nation, old woman? This thing you cannot do."

"Black Snake hears that the chief Netawatawees has taken a new Great Spirit and now calls himself A-braham," Bear's Daughter said. "Black Snake would have us see what passes with his friend."

White Eagle spoke with urgency. "Listen well, old woman. In these sad days you will find no Delaware villages the length of the Muskingum, or on the Tuscarawas or the Walhonding, either."

Bear's Daughter frowned. "Black Snake does not know this thing. Why would it be so?"

White Eagle shrugged expressively. "Some Delaware raid in the east, in the places where they lived before the *Shemanese* drove them away. Some go to the Upper Sandusky to get away from the *Shemanese*.

But of that chief Netawatawees and all of his people—they no longer live."

Greatly affected by his words, Bear's Daughter fell silent, and Willow turned to address White Eagle. "Why is this so? Did the red spots or the pox of the *Shemanese* take them?"

Willow felt her face warm as White Eagle directed the full power of his gaze toward her. He spoke bluntly, as if he wanted to shock her and Bear's Daughter into realizing the danger in the path they walked. "No. They gave up their *Wishemenetoo* for the *Shemanese* Great Spirit. Then the *Shemanese* killed them all."

Bear's Daughter spoke again. "You do not see this thing with your own eyes?"

"I know from one who saw and lived to tell it. Turn back to your village, before you and your daughter come to harm."

"Why do we waste this time idling with women?" one of the men with White Eagle called out. "Our brothers wait for us."

White Eagle raised his hand to acknowledge his companion's words, then nodded to Bear's Daughter and glanced at Willow. "Will you give your word to go home?" he asked.

Bear's Daughter nodded stiffly. "We go to Waccachalla, young warrior."

White Eagle mounted his horse. "Tell Black Snake what I have said. It may be that he and his warriors will raid with us."

Willow and Bear's Daughter stood where they were until the men had ridden out of sight; then

Bear's Daughter resumed walking in the direction of the Muskingum.

"The path to Waccachalla lies behind us, my mother," Willow said. "The warrior said we must not go on this way."

Bear's Daughter stared resolutely ahead. "I know not this White Eagle or of his people. I would see with my own eyes if he speaks the truth."

Willow tried again. "White Eagle would have no reason to tell us of danger unless it is there. You told him that we would return to Waccachalla."

"Yes, but I do not say when. Now we go on to the Muskingum."

Willow considered threatening to return to Waccachalla on her own, but the set of her mother's jaw told her that nothing would keep Bear's Daughter from finishing this journey, no matter what the danger. Willow could not leave her mother alone.

She nodded, resigned. "Yes, my mother," she murmured.

As they walked on in silence, Willow puzzled over her mother's odd behavior. *There is something strange about this journey,* she thought. Bear's Daughter had never before knowingly put Willow in danger, yet now she seemed determined to ignore White Eagle's warning and press on to the village on the Muskingum.

My mother must have a strong reason to go there, Willow decided. Whatever it was, Bear's Daughter would tell it when she was ready, and not a moment before. Willow sighed and shifted her backpack to a more comfortable position.

As she walked, the image of the warrior White Eagle came into her mind and would not go away. She tried to tell herself it was only because it might be a long time before they saw another friendly face, but she knew that was not the only reason.

I would like to see this warrior when he is not wearing war paint, Willow thought. Warriors were forbidden to have any physical contact with women once they had readied themselves for the path of war. Had he not been so garbed, Willow wondered if the young Shawnee warrior might have looked at her with more interest.

With such thoughts did Willow pass the time as she walked beside Bear's Daughter, not allowing herself to feel concern about what awaited.

The red sky that had greeted them at dawning had at first turned fair, but soon after White Eagle's band rode away, it began to darken with clouds. Despite their best efforts to find cover, a heavy shower soaked Willow and Bear's Daughter to the skin. Then the rain stopped as suddenly as it began. Willow used the inner part of her blanket to dry them both as well as she could, then wrapped the blanket around Bear's Daughter's shoulders.

"You are chilled, my mother. We must find shelter where we can make a fire and dry out."

Bear's Daughter shook her head. "We have far to go yet. It is too soon to stop."

Doggedly they walked on until late afternoon, when Willow found a likely place to make camp just off the main trail, yet screened from view.

"We must have no fire," Bear's Daughter warned.

Willow understood the need for caution. They did not need to attract attention to themselves.

Willow ate sparingly, giving Bear's Daughter more than her portion of the venison jerky and pemmican they had brought, the first food they had eaten since leaving their village. Water from a nearby creek slaked their thirst. Willow could find no ripe berries, but she gathered an armful of honeysuckle vines whose flowers were sweet to chew. When they had eaten, Willow used her belt-ax to cut hemlock branches. Piled on the ground and topped with a blanket, the limbs made a soft bed.

"Lie down now, Littlewillow. I will keep watch over you," Bear's Daughter said.

"No. You are tired, my mother. You sleep first."

Somewhat to Willow's surprise, Bear's Daughter did not protest. It was a further indication to Willow that her mother was not fully herself. Wrapped in her blanket, Bear's Daughter fell almost immediately into a deep sleep.

Willow stayed awake as long as she could, but the stars that nightly circled the heavens had not made half their course when she, too, slept. Willow came to her senses in the half light of the new day, when some forest creature skittered across her moccasins.

"You did not keep watch," Bear's Daughter said accusingly, awakening at the same moment.

"There was no need," Willow said. "*Wishemenetoo* looked after us as we slept."

Bear's Daughter tried to rise, and Willow held out a hand to help her up. "The Great Spirit must do so this day, as well," she murmured. "I fear what lies ahead at the Muskingum."

"Then let us go back to Waccachalla, my mother."

Bear's Daughter shook her head. "No. We must do this thing."

As that day and the next passed, Willow watched Bear's Daughter with growing alarm. Her mother's usual color drained away, and Willow had never before seen such a tightness about her mother's mouth or such a strange look in her eyes. Yet, though at times she seemed near collapse, the old woman would neither turn back nor slow down.

"My mother, we must stop now," Willow said in the late afternoon of the third day. "We both are weary, and this seems a likely place to make a camp."

Bear's Daughter shook her head and raised a trembling finger to a massive oak tree a hundred yards away. "There stands the council tree where the *She-manese* once treatied with the Delaware. The village cannot be far. Listen, and you can hear the rushing waters of the Muskingum."

"Stay here. I will go ahead and find someone to help you get the rest of the way," Willow said.

"I can walk," Bear's Daughter insisted, but long before they reached the water, Willow was supporting much of her mother's weight.

Bear's Daughter signaled for Willow to stop. She looked around, then sank to the ground with a sharp cry and began to wail.

The sound, unlike anything Willow had ever heard, chilled every fiber of her being. "What is it, my mother? What ails you?" Willow asked, but Bear's Daughter did not cease keening for some time. At length she lifted her head and gestured toward a blackened circle several feet away.

"That is the village firestone," she said. "No lodges now circle it."

Glancing around, Willow noticed the small piles of debris and ashes, all that remained of the lodges that had once stood in this place. She had seen many burned villages, and with sadness Willow knew that whatever Bear's Daughter sought here, she would probably never find.

"Is this the village of Netawatawees?" Willow asked.

Bear's Daughter wiped her eyes. "Once, Bright Horn was chief here. There were many lodges then. The chief lived in the middle. By the water was a fine steam house. My own lodge stood there."

Willow looked where her mother pointed and wished she could share the vision of her mother's memories. "Is that where I was born?"

Bear's Daughter shook her head. "Help me up. I would go past those trees."

Willow did as she was told, once more supporting most of Bear's Daughter's weight as they slowly made their way to the ruins of a lodge set well apart from the rest of the village.

"Here. This is the place of the birthing lodge," Bear's Daughter whispered.

Willow looked around, expecting the spot to stir some emotions in her. But she felt nothing more than the chill of the light evening breeze on her bare arms.

She shivered and tried to imagine the scene in the birthing lodge as Bear's Daughter held her for the first time and the shadowy figure of the *Shemanese* who had fathered her looked on.

"Let me sit against the oak," Bear's Daughter said, and Willow eased her down in front of a huge old oak tree. She saw something in her mother's face that she had never seen before, and it frightened her.

"What is it, my mother?" she asked gently.

Bear's Daughter stared at the place where the birthing lodge had stood and began to rock back and forth, chanting a part of the Death Song. After a moment she stopped and turned to look full into Willow's eyes. "Your father never came to this lodge," she said. "The day of your birth, he walked out to check his traps."

Sensing that in this place Bear's Daughter might speak more freely, Willow asked the question that had always been on her mind. "Tell me about my father."

Bear's Daughter stared at the ruined lodge as if seeing some vision from the past. "He was a good man for a *Shemanese*," she said.

Disappointed, Willow leaned her forehead against the tree's rough bark and sighed. "You have said this before. I would know more."

"Ee-an M'night," Bear's Daughter said slowly. At first Willow thought her mother was making up another chant, but when she repeated it, Willow understood that Bear's Daughter must be naming her father.

"What did you know of him?" Willow asked.

Bear's Daughter looked back at Willow and

frowned as if trying to remember. "It is a long time ago. Tall, with wild red hair on his head and face the color of the maple leaf before it falls. A good hunter, a fair trader. A good man."

Willow sat in silence for a moment, trying to construct a full image from Bear's Daughter's description. "Why tell me this now, when you never would before?"

"It is to keep you safe. The *Shemanese* can see that you have their blood. The name of Ee-an M'night is honored among them. You must say this if any *Shemanese* ever seek to harm you: Ee-an M'night fath-er."

"Ee-an M'night fath-er," Willow repeated. "A strange name."

"Not among the *Shemanese*. He is called Ee-an M'night. 'Fath-er' is how *Shemanese* say *notha*."

"You have said that my father died many years ago. It may be that the *Shemanese* do not know this name."

Bear's Daughter raised her head and gazed into Willow's eyes. "His name is all your father could ever give you. You must say it with pride."

"Ee-an M'night. I will not forget it, my mother."

"There is something more," Bear's Daughter said haltingly. "Before I die, you should know that I am not—"

She stopped suddenly and closed her eyes. Willow waited expectantly. "Yes, my mother?" she prompted.

Bear's Daughter opened her eyes and Willow sensed that she had changed her mind about what she had intended to say. "I am not young now, nor was I when you were born."

"I know," said Willow. She'd often wondered how it happened that her mother had so long been childless, but it was not the kind of question that she would dare to ask.

Bear's Daughter closed her eyes again and spoke quietly. "I will not live to see your children. They should know the name of their *Shemanese* grandfather. It could help them one day. Remember it."

Willow nodded and tried not to show how disturbed she was at Bear's Daughter's strange behavior. "Rest here, my mother. I will make camp by the Muskingum. The sound of the water will soothe you."

Willow lay awake for a long while that night, alternately worrying about her mother's labored breathing and wondering about the tall man with bright red hair who had fathered her. Had he and her mother been of an age? Or had he perhaps been older—or even younger? *Even if my father's name has no power to keep me and mine safe,* she thought, *yet I am glad to know it. If only my father could be here to help us.*

Willow sought a more comfortable position and considered what her life might have been like if her father had lived. Perhaps Ee-an M'night would have taken them to live among the *Shemanese,* but even if he had not, he would have been there to help them, and she and Bear's Daughter wouldn't have had to depend on Black Snake to take care of them.

Willow sighed. Her mother grew weaker every day, despite the good herbs that Willow had gathered for her, and their food was all but gone. Willow didn't need the Shawnee warrior White Eagle to tell her that they needed protection. The only question was, who would provide it?

Willow closed her eyes and made up a chant-song, which she hummed softly to herself, over and over.

Great Spirit, help us safely back to Waccachalla.

The next morning Willow and Bear's Daughter returned to the Kanawha Trail that would eventually lead them back to their village. Willow walked more slowly than when they had first started out, not only because of Bear's Daughter condition, but also because she too was becoming weak from lack of food. Also, Willow dreaded what awaited on their return to Waccachalla.

Bear's Daughter had planned to stay many weeks in her Delaware village, had it not been deserted. By then Otter would certainly have grown tired of waiting for Willow and taken another to be his wife. However, if the women returned sooner, it was more than likely that Willow would be forced to accept Otter, especially if Bear's Daughter did not recover from her illness.

At midmorning Willow broke her worried silence. "Let us rest now, my mother," Willow said.

"We have not come far enough. We must go on," Bear's Daughter murmured.

"We must have water. I will go to the creek over there," Willow said.

Bear's Daughter sank down onto the soft grass beside the trail and closed her eyes. "As you say."

The sound of running water at the creek masked all others, but as Willow returned to the trail, she heard approaching hoofbeats. *Shemanese,* she feared. Alarmed, Willow ran to Bear's Daughter, whose eyes were still closed, and shook her.

"Wake up, my mother. Someone comes this way."

Slowly Bear's Daughter opened her eyes and looked around as if surprised to see where she was. "What?" she asked thickly.

Willow reached with both hands to pull her mother to her feet. No nearby shrubs offered protection; they would have to seek the cover of the forest. "We must leave this trail," Willow said. "Hurry."

Willow's efforts were useless. Bear's Daughter rose with great difficulty, but before they could reach cover, a lone warrior rode into view.

Willow stopped and stared at the familiar figure. *Is this really White Eagle, or in my hunger does my mind call up what I wish to see?*

Then he spoke, and when Bear's Daughter also turned toward him, Willow felt relief that she hadn't imagined his presence.

White Eagle swung down from his horse and spoke to Bear's Daughter reprovingly. "You did not do as I told you, old woman."

Bear's Daughter held her head high. "We go to Waccachalla now. What of you? Why does this warrior ride alone?"

"I feared some harm might come to you." White Eagle looked closely at Bear's Daughter, then turned to Willow. "This old woman cannot walk so far."

Without the red war paint that had somewhat disguised his features, White Eagle looked even more handsome, Willow thought, and she struggled to steady her voice. "We found everything in the old village as you said. My mother is sad and weary."

White Eagle looked back at Bear's Daughter. "You must go on my horse to my village. Then I will take you to Waccachalla."

Willow half expected Bear's Daughter to refuse his offer, but she merely nodded. "It is good. We have little food and my care is a heavy burden for my daughter."

"It is not so," Willow began, but White Eagle drew his hand, palm down, against his throat in the cutoff sign, and motioned for her to help him get Bear's Daughter onto his horse. When that had been done, he put his hands around Willow's waist to lift her onto the horse as well.

Immediately Willow backed away, completely unnerved by White Eagle's touch. "I will walk," she said, more shortly than she intended.

"Mishewa is strong. He can carry you both."

"I will walk. I have said it," Willow repeated.

"Then let us go."

With White Eagle leading his horse on the left and Willow walking on the right to occasionally steady her mother, they made their way south on the Kanawha Trail. Without mentioning that she had been born there, Willow told White Eagle what they had found in the old Delaware village.

"Those places are not safe," White Eagle said when Willow finished her account.

"Speak to me of your Shawnee Town," Bear's Daughter said, surprising them with her sudden entry into the conversation. "Is it safe?"

"For now. We raid the *Shemanese* who might come to us."

Bear's Daughter was silent for a moment. "I would know if White Eagle has a wife," she said.

Willow's breath caught in a gasp at her mother's bold question, and she felt grateful that White Eagle couldn't see her reaction.

White Eagle's answer was quick. "No. I have been too much in war paint. I do not have time to think of such a thing."

Willow's relief at his answer immediately changed to further embarrassment as Bear's Daughter spoke again. "A warrior has need of a wife. My daughter has need of a man. There is none in Waccachalla that she will have."

What makes you think I will have this man, either? Willow knew that she should say the words for the sake of her pride, but they stuck in her throat.

"Your daughter is old to be yet a maiden," White Eagle said matter-of-factly, further shaming Willow. Even though it wasn't her place to do so, Willow would have spoken on her own behalf, had any sensible words come to her mind.

In the meantime, Bear's Daughter kept on talking as if Willow weren't there. "Her father was a *Shemanese,* well known among the Delaware of Bright Horn's village. She has not taken a man, and I can no longer care for her."

Although Willow couldn't see White Eagle's face, his tone reassured her. "In that case, I would welcome you both to my *wegiwa,*" he said.

Bear's Daughter chuckled. "I do not think White

Eagle would want to take this old woman to wife," she said.

Shocked, Willow managed to find her voice. "My mother, you should not speak of such things." Willow hoped that Bear's Daughter's frank offer of Willow's hand hadn't offended White Eagle.

White Eagle turned so he could see Willow's face. "I do not mind, maiden. Among my people, the old say what they like. So be it."

"I would talk of this thing with your chief," Bear's Daughter said.

"Tall Oak will hear of it," White Eagle promised.

Satisfied, Bear's Daughter closed her eyes and remained silent the rest of that afternoon. As the evening sun began to cast long shadows, White Eagle led the horse off the trail to a camping place that evidently he and many others had used before. He helped Bear's Daughter from the horse, then unearthed a cache of food and fed her as a mother would a sick child.

Later, when Bear's Daughter shook with a sudden chill, White Eagle rubbed warmth into her limbs and made a fire whose flames seemed to comfort her.

"I like not the way my mother looks," Willow said quietly.

White Eagle laid his hand on her forehead and shook his head. "She feels chill, yet she burns with fever. It is not good."

Bear's Daughter slept for a time, then roused and looked around with wild eyes, as if she had forgotten where she was. "My daughter! Where are you?"

Quickly Willow bent over her and held her hands. "I am here, my mother. Calm yourself."

"What of the warrior?" she asked.

White Eagle knelt beside her. "White Eagle is here. What would you have, old woman?"

Bear's Daughter took a deep breath and gasped for air. "Your word. You must care for my daughter."

White Eagle leaned closer to Bear's Daughter and spoke clearly. "All will be done as you have said. It will be so."

Bear's Daughter's eyes remained closed, but she nodded slightly to indicate that she heard and understood what he said. "I can rest now," she whispered.

"She sleeps again," White Eagle said.

Willow pulled the blanket under her mother's chin and shook her head. "Her breathing is not right."

Bear's Daughter's chest lifted with each slow intake of air, followed by a pause that seemed longer each time. From somewhere deep in her chest came a hideous sound that Willow had heard far too often not to recognize.

"The spirits of the dead will soon come for her," Willow whispered.

White Eagle made no effort to deny Willow's words or to comfort her in any way. Instead, he drew apart from them; then, facing the east, he began the first low notes of the Death Song.

Does Bear's Daughter hear him? Willow wondered. She hesitated for a moment, then as the rattling of her mother's breath grew ever more pronounced, she gently withdrew her hand from her mother's grasp. Covering her head with her blanket, Willow turned in the same direction as White Eagle and began her own Death Song.

When she had finished the chant, Willow spread her blanket and lay beside her mother. Wide awake, she waited for the long night to end, for the Death Spirit to take her mother, or for *Wishemenetoo*, the Great Good Spirit, to restore her health.

Willow also waited to learn her own fate. Although White Eagle had made a promise to her mother, such vows were not always kept. *I will go with this man and be glad of it*, she thought, and wondered if he knew that it was so.

White Eagle sat beside the fire and kept it burning brightly until the darkness faded to gray.

Somewhere toward the dawn, Bear's Daughter's struggle for breath ended, and her chest no longer moved. At first light Willow found her lying as she had been the night before, yet with a stillness not of the living. A trace of sorrow lingered on her mother's face, along with an expression that was almost quiet satisfaction.

White Eagle watched silently as Willow performed her last service for Bear's Daughter. She placed flat pebbles over her mother's eyes, washed her face and limbs, and wrapped her as well as she could in her blanket.

When she had finished, Willow rocked back on her heels, her face taut with grief. "What more can be done? I will not leave my mother here alone."

White Eagle picked up his tomahawk. "This soil is light. Her grave will be here in this place."

White Eagle found a level spot beneath a massive

chestnut tree and with his tomahawk began to break the ground. Willow picked up her ax and joined him. In silence they dug a shallow depression. They laid Bear's Daughter in her last resting place, her feet facing east, the place of new beginnings, as was the custom. When they finished, the clouds that had brooded all morning began to produce a drizzling rain.

Still without speaking, White Eagle broke up their camp and removed all traces of the fire that had burned the night before. When all was ready, he turned to Willow and put his arms around her waist. She supposed he meant to help her onto his horse, but instead, he moved one hand to the middle of her back and drew her toward him. Willow laid her head on his shoulder. The salt of his sweat mingled with her tears, the first she had shed since her mother's death.

White Eagle stood quietly for several minutes, stroking her hair and allowing her to weep. His surprisingly gentle touch soothed her as nothing else ever had, and Willow closed her eyes, grateful for his presence. Then White Eagle touched her cheeks with his flattened palms, wiping away her tears. "Do not cry, Willow. We go now to Shawnee Town. There you will be safe."

White Eagle lifted Willow onto the horse, then swung into the saddle in front of her. With White Eagle's back to her, Willow took a deep breath and asked the most important question of her entire life. "What will be done with me in your village?"

White Eagle looked back at her, inadvertently jerking on the reins so that his horse suddenly side-stepped. Willow grabbed at White Eagle's arm to keep from falling off.

"Did you not hear? I have said that I will take care of you. Tall Oak will give us a *wegiwa*."

Apparently not expecting any further response from Willow, White Eagle turned around again and rode out of the camp. Willow held on with her arms loosely around his waist as the horse settled into a steady gait. She barely resisted the temptation to lay her head against his broad back.

Tall Oak will give us a wegiwa, White Eagle had said. Truly, he must mean that she would be his woman.

Never had Willow experienced such a strange mixture of grief and joy. Her heart ached for the mother she had just lost. But Willow also rejoiced that White Eagle would keep his promise to Bear's Daughter.

Now Willow could only pray to *Wishemenetoo* that White Eagle would come to feel the same love toward her as she already felt for him.

14

BRYAN'S STATION

Anna soon discovered that life in a forted settlement would be unlike anything she had known. The lean-to where she slept made Miss Martin's attic seem spacious. The only light and air came from a few small openings through which rifles could be fired. Because of their cramped quarters, everyone in the Station stayed outside most of the time.

Within a week, Anna learned the names of nearly all her new neighbors, although it was harder to sort out the many children always underfoot. Her father told her that sixty-four children, forty-eight men, and thirty-two women currently lived at Bryan's Station. Not one of them was named Bryan.

"Four Bryan brothers from North Carolina started the station," Ian explained, "but when the oldest was killed by Indians, the other three went back home."

"Plenty of others took their places soon enough," Rebecca added.

Anna was surprised to see that so many craftsmen

lived at the Station, including a cooper, cabinetmaker, and even a hatter. Most were married, but among the single men were older sons who'd come with their families and other men who ventured alone. Most of the bachelors lived in the blockhouses at the four corners of the Station. Among them was Richard Story, a portly ex-schoolmaster. Although he looked nothing like Stuart Martin, his occupation reminded Anna of Stuart—not that she needed any prompting. Anna had quickly written to let Stuart know she had safely reached Bryan's Station and hoped to see him soon. She wondered if he would read her longing for him between every line.

Ian regarded Anna curiously when she asked him to dispatch it on his next trip into Lexington. "So ye're writing my friend Martin, eh? Ye never said ye knew him all that well."

Anna tried to appear unconcerned. "He was kind to me when I was in his aunt's school. He holds you in such high regard, I'm sure he'd like to know where you live now."

Ian's eyes twinkled. "I'm not so sure Stuart's concerned about *my* whereabouts," he said.

Anna tried to feel hopeful when her father rode out of the Station with her letter. She'd done all she could—any further contact between them was now up to Stuart. Soon he would finish his studies—and her letter would tell him where to find her.

Bit by bit, Ian told Anna what he'd been doing since the war's end. Realizing that his old life of hunting and trading among the Indians was no longer practical, he'd joined many others to make a land claim when the Kentucky land opened up for settlement. He'd lived nearby on his own acreage until a few months ago, when the winter weather broke and bands of raiding Indians became a constant threat. In just such a raid had Rebecca been widowed and moved into Bryan's Station with her brother. When he decided to return to Virginia, he left her his land and cabin.

"I think your father really married me to get this cabin," Rebecca said one evening as they all sat on the doorstone in the deepening twilight.

Ian had made a small smudge fire to discourage the many biting night insects, and between its smoke and the dim light, Anna couldn't see Rebecca's face well enough to know if she jested. Even though her father's wife had a strong independent streak and often spoke more fiercely than tactfully, Rebecca also had a lighter side. More than once Anna had seen Rebecca coax a smile from her usually serious husband.

"Nay, wife—had I been looking for a home, I'd have wed that widow in Lexington."

"Then you'd not have the two Engler parcels of land to add to your own." Rebecca glanced at Anna. "Your father could be a wealthy man if the savages would just leave us in peace."

"Why don't they?" Anna asked.

Ian sighed heavily. "Before I left the Muskingum, I heard the British solemnly promise the Delaware that their big chief across the waters would let the Delaware keep their hunting grounds in Kan-tuck-e if they helped the Redcoats fight the white settlers. King George's orders kept settlers on the other side of the mountains, but once Cornwallis gave up the fight, no force on earth could stop them. Still, a few British and other whites who seek to gain from attacking settlers tell the Indians otherwise, and keep them on the warpath."

"Are my mother's people fighting whites too?" Anna feared his answer even before she heard it.

"Silverwillow's people are all scattered, from what I hear. However, I wouldn't be surprised if some Delaware are among the raiders."

Rebecca slapped at her forearm. "Whoever's to blame, the result is that the savages keep pestering us all, just like these mosquitoes. Each time we think they're finally goin' to leave us alone, back they come, killin' and stealin' stock."

"It seems you'd be afraid to stay here, then." Anna directed her words to Rebecca, but her father answered.

"Nay, lass. The raiders come in small groups. We don't leave the Station but to tend crops, and that in large parties with a guard. We're aware of the danger, but we aren't fearful. If I didn't think you were safe here, I would send you back East."

Anna said nothing, but once more she felt a sense of loss that she'd probably never see the place where Silverwillow had lived, or meet any of those who shared her mother's blood.

As July melted into August, Anna settled into the routine life of the Station, hoping each day to get a letter from Stuart Martin. Her presence caused quite a stir among the Station's bachelors, some of whom awkwardly set out to court her, only to be politely, but firmly, rebuffed. As a result, some in the Station said that Ian McKnight's half-breed daughter held herself to be better than they, and any other men who might have a notion to court her kept their distance.

One day when she rode into Lexington with her father, Anna's heart nearly stopped at the sight of a tall blond man who walked a few paces ahead of her. She had never seen Stuart Martin in buckskins, but this man's bearing and build were so familiar that Anna ran to catch up to him, certain that it was Stuart. She was about to call out his name when the man stopped and turned aside to enter a tavern. Her heart fell when she saw his beard and coarse features, so unlike what she remembered of Stuart.

That night Anna found it hard to fall asleep. Adding to her restlessness, the day's heat had concentrated in the windowless lean-to where she slept, making it even more sweltering than usual. Sometime after midnight, she took a blanket and slipped out of the cabin in search of a cool breeze. In the light of an almost full moon, she climbed the palisade nearest the McKnight cabin. Spreading her blanket on the rough-hewn timbers, she sat on it and leaned back against the wall.

Anna could barely make out the form of the lookout on the north palisade, his rifle barrel glinting in the moonlight. The men took turns nightly watching for marauding Indians. Since her arrival, none had come, but the very necessity of such caution dashed Anna's remaining hopes of ever getting to her mother's land.

Her father was obviously quite happy with his new

wife, and he didn't need his daughter's continued presence. Anna's only reason to stay in Kentucky now was to wait for Stuart to come to her.

He is probably on his way this very minute, Anna told herself. She closed her eyes and imagined their meeting. It would probably be in the daytime, and Stuart would wear the bucksins he had traveled in. She pictured him with a beard, then dismissed the image as not suiting a man of his refinement. Besides, her father's beard had always scratched Anna when he kissed her. On the other hand, Stuart's clean-shaven cheeks were just rough enough to be manly and exciting.

Stuart would take her into his arms immediately, of course. They would kiss a long time before Stuart told his former colonel that he wanted to marry his daughter. They would have to go to Lexington to be married, and perhaps they'd stay there for a time, at least until Stuart's future was decided. There was a cabin at Bryan's Station just vacated by some people who were planning to move to Danville; it might still be available when Anna and Stuart were ready to live in their own private place.

Thinking of the look that she would see in his eyes on their wedding night, Anna's body flushed with a rising warmth that had nothing to do with the heat of the summer night. Stuart was older and obviously more experienced in matters of love than Anna, but from what had already happened between them, she expected he would be both a considerate and a passionate lover. She longed to show him how ready she was to meet him more than halfway, to allow him to break down the last barrier that prevented them from truly being one flesh, now and forever more.

With a sigh, Anna lay on her side and caressed the rough bulk of the blanket beside her, pretending that Stuart slept there. She was all too painfully aware that he did not, but until the welcome day that Stuart actually arrived in Kentucky, her imagination would have to sustain her.

15

PRINCETON

On a warm August morning, Stuart Martin looked around the quarters he would soon be leaving, and thought how much his life had changed since he had come here. Compared to many Princeton students, he lived in luxury, quartered in the home of the brothers he tutored. His small private room opened onto the study where he spent several hours each evening preparing his charges to take their Princeton entrance examinations.

When Charles Hoagland, the elder son, had failed to be admitted to the freshman class, his father had hired Stuart to tutor both Charles and his younger brother.

At first, Stuart considered himself extremely fortunate to get the post. Not having to pay for his room and board enabled him to hold on to more of his small inheritance. Further, if and when Princeton accepted the boys, Stuart would also receive a sum of money. "An admirable arrangement," Mr. Hoagland had called it, and at the time, Stuart agreed.

But that was before he realized just how deeply he had fallen in love.

The stacks of shirts and smallclothes he started to pack reminded him of the past Christmas, when Anna Willow McKnight had entered his room at Miss Martin's and hidden her gift to him among his shirts. It was then that he had kissed her for the first time. The second time their lips met, she had kissed him back, and nothing in his life had been quite the same since.

Anna Willow.

Like an infatuated schoolboy, Stuart often spent late winter evenings writing her name on scraps of paper, then adding "Martin," as if she were already his wife. He liked to speak the name out loud, emphasizing the trochaic cadence of its syllables: *An*-na *Wil*-low *Mar*-tin. Many times when he should have been concentrating on Euclidean proofs or Horatian odes, he found himself seeing her dark eyes and hearing her sweet voice instead. He imagined his hands moving from her long chestnut hair to caress her body. He took pleasure in mentally kissing the palms of her hands, the tips of her fingers, each earlobe. In these pleasant dreams, she was always warm and pliant, instantly responding to his slightest touch. Not a poet himself, he nevertheless wished he had the ability to compose tender verses that would convince her of the depth of his love.

Stuart knew the reality was quite different, however. No amount of imagining how wonderful it would be when he and Anna were together could change the fact that, for the present, he and Anna were not only physically separated, but also unable to share their thoughts.

The territory where Anna had traveled to since her Commencement from his aunt's school was far away, and it took many weeks for letters to reach there. He had so much he wanted to tell Anna—and no way to do it. He hoped no harm had come to her. Most of all, he hoped the feelings for him she had expressed in her warm kisses had not changed.

Strange, Stuart thought, how Colonel McKnight's gangly girl-child had turned into the lovely young woman who now occupied the center of his life. None of the other young women he had held possessed even a faint glimmer of Anna's rare combination of insightful intellect, unusual beauty, and passionate innocence. Each time he saw her, each moment they shared, had made Stuart want her even more.

His mind returned to their brief April encounter, when their growing intimacy had been cut short by his aunt's unexpected appearance. It was no wonder that Stuart had felt compelled to return to her. He had finally done so on the day of Anna's graduation from Miss Martin's, even though it meant that he jeopardized his own studies by missing an important examination.

It was worth it, he thought. Since that day, time and time again he had relived each embrace, every word they had shared in the carriage house. His loins ached with desire at the memory of her touch, of the way she had so sweetly yielded to him, of the breathless eagerness to surrender herself completely that had made it even harder to leave her again.

Sometimes he allowed himself to imagine that he

had possessed her there when he had the chance, before reason stepped in and overruled his heart. At those times, filled anew with frustration and longing, Stuart immersed himself in his own studies and redoubled his efforts with his pupils.

How ironic, Stuart thought, that this tutoring post, which had once seemed so advantageous, had instead kept him and Anna apart. If he were not living with the Hoaglands, and if he were concerned only with his own education, Stuart could have brought Anna back to Princeton with him the very day of her Commencement. Stuart thought of his aunt's likely outrage at such an act, and smiled faintly.

But all of that was about to come to an end. Stuart had completed his baccalaureate degree, and had just learned that both Hoagland brothers had passed their entrance examinations. At last, he was free to leave Princeton, free to be with Anna. It was all he had thought about for months, but now that the time had come, Stuart wasn't sure where she was.

Anna's first letter had reached him not long after she left Philadelphia. It verified that she was at her cousins' home near Bedford, but she had said that she might not stay there long. He immediately wrote back that he would come to Bedford as soon as he could; even though he'd heard nothing further from Anna, he still planned to go there.

"Master Martin, are you in there?"

Stuart put down the shirt he'd been about to fold and opened the door to admit a smiling Mr. Hoagland. "I suppose you must have heard the news already," he said.

"Indeed! Charles ran all the way to the counting-house to tell me. He was so out of breath, he just handed me the dean's letter."

"You must be quite pleased at its contents."

"Yes. And I hope, Master Martin, that you will be equally as pleased with the contents of this bag."

Stuart took the leather pouch from Mr. Hoagland, pleasantly surprised by its unexpected weight. *Gold coins*, he thought. His heart beat faster as he realized that this might be enough to give him and Anna a start, at least. "Thank you, sir. You are most generous."

"No more than you deserve." Mr. Hoagland looked past Stuart to the evidence of his packing. "Are you leaving so soon? I had hoped we might persuade you to stay on a while longer. The boys have been admitted to Princeton, but it's more than likely that they will have even more need of a tutor when they commence their studies."

"If so, you can ask the dean to recommend someone. I must be on my way."

Mr. Hoagland nodded. "Then I wish you Godspeed." He started to go, then slapped at his pocket and turned back to Stuart. "Say, I almost forgot—the dean asked Charles to give you these letters." He squinted at the top one as he held them out to Stuart. "This one came all the way from Kentucky County— I never saw a letter from that far west before."

"I cannot believe that you would refuse such a fine opportunity, Stuart. My school needs a good teacher, and you need a position."

Stuart sat at his aunt's table in Philadelphia where he had often helped Anna McKnight with her studies, so reminded of her that he scarcely heard his aunt's words. Being back in this house where he and Anna had met and fallen in love only made him more impatient to see her and be with her again.

"Stuart! Are you listening to me?"

His aunt's face reflected her anger and bewilderment, and Stuart felt a moment of pity for the lonely woman. He knew that Matilda Martin cared for him as much as she could care for anyone, yet she had never quite known how to reconcile her affection for him with her own selfish ambition.

Stuart nodded and spoke matter-of-factly. "Yes, Aunt Matilda. Your offer is quite generous, but I cannot accept it."

"Then I must assume that you have a better prospect in mind."

Stuart patted his coat pocket, which contained his last letters from Anna. He could close his eyes and quote every word. The looping, somewhat uneven handwriting was as familiar to him now as his own. Although the first of the letters had been posted from Bedford, she had written that she was in Pittsburgh, on her way to Kentucky. Anna's latest letter told him she was in Kentucky with her father, where she waited for him to join her.

"I do, Aunt. I plan to start a school of my own in Kentucky."

If Stuart had told his aunt he was leaving for China in a rowboat, she could not have looked more stunned. "Why would a man with your education even consider going to that wild land?" she asked.

Because Anna is there, he could have said, but knowing how his aunt felt about her former student, he did not. "Perhaps because that's where I'm most needed."

Matilda Martin's face reflected her bewilderment. "Sometimes I wonder if being in the army all those years left you unbalanced. Kentucky, indeed!"

Less than a week later, Stuart felt growing excitement as he loaded his small store of possessions onto a Kentucky-bound flatboat. A hidden leather pouch held the coins left over from outfitting himself for life in the wilderness and paying his passage.

At the last moment, when she finally understood that her nephew meant to go to Kentucky if he had to walk, Matilda Martin had pressed a money pouch into his hands, saying she felt obliged to give it to him for his father's sake. When he opened it later, he found that it, like Mr. Hoagland's, contained a far greater amount than he had expected.

The money had allowed Stuart to travel in relative comfort to the mouth of the Greenbrier River. From there, he bargained for passage on a flatboat bound for Kentucky via the Kanawha and Ohio Rivers. If all went well, in less than two weeks, Stuart would be welcomed by his old army companion, Ian McKnight—and, even more important to Stuart, by his daughter.

Stuart hadn't written that he was coming, in part because he knew that he would likely get to Lexington before any letter could, but also because he wanted to see the expressions of surprise on their faces when he arrived, unannounced.

Despite the flatboat captain's general words of

warning, most of the passengers had no serious fears about the trip they were about to undertake, although they were all aware that they would pass uncomfortably close to land where several groups of hostile Indians still harassed settlers. They passed the first trouble spot without incident, but the worst would lie ahead, especially when they reached the waters of the Ohio. From then on, whenever they tied up to the shore for the night, the captain posted double and sometimes even triple guards.

One night, a week into the journey, Stuart stood watch with Davy Darby, the youngest of those who voyaged alone. He had introduced himself to Stuart as soon as he'd heard Stuart's name.

"My family's from Lancaster, but my sister Felicia went to a Miss Martin's School in Philadelphia," he said. "Might you know of it?"

Stuart stared at the boy, whose features were very like his sister's. "Yes, that is my aunt's school. I taught there some. I remember Miss Felicia Darby very well. As I recall, she had a friend there named Anna McKnight."

Davy had smiled widely at the coincidence. "Aye, that's so. She came home with my sister after they graduated. Felicia's married now."

"Have you heard anything more about Miss McKnight?"

"Not directly. She went on to some relative's house in Bedford, but she wrote she aimed to go to Kentucky. Maybe we'll meet up with her there."

All through the journey, Anna was never far from Stuart's mind, most especially when the flatboat briefly came under fire from Indians on the north side of the river. He knew that she had safely reached her father, but that didn't stop him from wondering if was she still all right.

Stuart would be uneasy until Anna was in his arms once more. And this time, he would not hold back; he would give her all his love.

16

WACCACHALLA

Otter sat under a tree near his lodge, applying red and yellow war paint in the pattern he'd used for the ten turnings of the seasons he'd been a warrior. Never had the prospect of a fight been more welcome. From the day that Bear's Daughter had taken Willow from Waccachalla, Otter's anger had grown hot inside his belly.

He recalled how long he had waited for the old woman to get better, until at last the time was right for him to claim Willow. All one night he had hunted to find a deer worthy as a wedding offering, only to find himself bringing it to an empty lodge. Otter had no doubt that Bear's Daughter had meant to keep him away from Willow, and had Black Snake allowed it, Otter would have gone after them immediately.

"Let the girl go. Full-blooded Shawnee maidens in a dozen villages can give Otter strong sons. You must look elsewhere for a wife," the chief told him.

Remembering that day, Otter grunted so loudly

that Bright Stone, his young warrior companion, looked to see what ailed him.

Noting how Otter's eyes smoldered, Bright Stone nodded. "Your eyes show you are ready to kill the *Shemanese*. You will make our village proud."

Otter considered the young man's words. "There is none my equal on the warpath," he said, more stating a fact than making a boast.

"So all Waccachalla knows." Bright Stone stood and looked back to the village, where the women made preparations for the Warriors' Dance. "Soon we prove it with the scalps of many *Shemanese*."

"You have not walked the warpath before, Bright Stone. Do not boast of scalps before you take them."

"I have gone with my brothers on many raids—I am ready. My wife will be proud."

Otter thought with envy of the maiden that Bright Stone had been joined to last year. Had she not been too near his own kin, Doe Eyes could have been the mother of Otter's sons. Already she had given Bright Stone a man-child. Otter frowned, not wanting to think of such things.

Instead, he imagined how he would be greeted with new respect when he returned to Waccachalla, victorious over the *Shemanese*.

Then I will find Willow, he vowed. Otter sensed that Black Snake thought that if Bear's Daughter had found a warm welcome in her old village, she'd likely stay there for some time. By now Willow could already share another man's lodge in that place. The thought made him even more angry.

I must know about this thing, Otter told himself.

Black Snake could not stop a man from going hunting. If on the way he happened across Willow and she came back with him, then Black Snake would have no choice but to join them in marriage.

For the first time in many days, Otter felt almost happy. Now that he had determined the solution to his problem, he was ready to take the path of war to far Penn-sylvania, where the *Shemanese* lived who had killed Chief Netawatawees. Now they must pay with their lives for their dark deeds.

A few days later, Otter and Bright Stone sat together, two of more than a thousand Delaware, Shawnee, Ottowa, Chippewa, Mohawk, and Wyandot warriors who had gathered near Chillicothe on the Ohio River to avenge the death of their brothers. All waited while their leaders talked to Simon Girty, one of the few white men the Indians trusted. Among the expedition heads, the Mohawk chief Thayendanega was the only Indian. The others included William Caldwell, a British captain; Alexander McKee, a trader with a Shawnee wife; and some fifty red-coats. The party had almost reached the Kanawha River when Girty had intercepted them, shouting that they must stop and hear his important news.

"This talking goes on too long," Otter complained.

Bright Stone looked up through the trees at the sun making its way from the land toward which they traveled. "We take no scalps sitting this place," he said.

Curious to know what was happening, Otter left his companions and moved as close as he dared to the parley site. Although still too far away to hear their words, he could tell from the leaders' faces that something important was under discussion.

When the parley ended, Otter approached a Shawnee from another village who had been close enough to hear some of what was said. "What news does this Girty bring that makes so much talk?"

"You know that the red-coat captain Crawford and many men from Penn-sylvania burned the villages of our brothers on the Upper Sandusky." The warrior waited for Otter's nod, then continued. "The man Girty saw the Delaware take Crawford and burn him at the stake."

"What has that to do with us?"

"Some of the *Shemanese* with Crawford got away. By now they will be back in Penn-sylvania, making strong their forts. They know we come."

"I do not fear the *Shemanese* forts," Otter said with scorn. Although he had never seen a large one, he had heard stories of ways warriors could break into a fort and take many scalps.

"Nor do I, brother, but you will see—we do not go there now."

Several more parleys followed until the matter was finally decided. Taking the advice of Simon Girty, the chiefs agreed not to continue toward Penn-sylvania. Instead, Girty proposed that the British William Caldwell should lead them against one of the newest and weakest of the Kentucky settlements, a small fort called Bryan's Station. From the account of a captured *Shemanese* who lived there, Girty believed the Station would quickly fall.

Several Shawnee warriors close enough to hear the discussion murmured among themselves, pleased both at the prospect of action and its location. Near that Station at the Blue Licks salt flats, the man called Sheltowee by the Shawnee and Daniel Boone by the *Shemanese* had once been captured. Even though the Shawnee chief Blackfish had made him a blood brother, the man had run away to his own people and now plotted against his former Shawnee friends.

Otter had heard many stories about this Sheltowee. "I would like to fight this man," he declared to Bright Stone. "It will be good to go to this place, better than Penn-sylvania."

"The Mohawk warriors do not think so," Bright Stone observed.

Indeed, in disagreement with the plan devised by the leaders, many of the Mohawks had already left the camp. So many other warriors followed them that the force soon numbered less than three hundred.

Bright Stone looked apprehensive as he told this to Otter. "We are much fewer now."

"Our warriors are brave and this station is small. We will take it easily," Otter predicted.

Not long after, the remaining warriors, led by William Caldwell and his Redcoats, and with Simon Girty scouting ahead, silently made their way southwest toward Bryan's Station.

The horseman who rode into Bryan's Station after dark one night in mid-August brought unwelcome news: a large band of Indians had been spotted, apparently bound for the neighboring Hoy's Station.

"You all know they'll need your help," the messenger concluded.

The men gathered in the center of the Station to discuss the news. Some wanted to ride out immediately, while others feared an Indian ambush, which was a common practice, particularly at night. When it became obvious that their noisy arguments would settle nothing, David Suggett, the oldest man in the Station, turned to Ian McKnight. Suggett's seventy years carried some authority, and when he held up his hand for silence, the others soon quieted.

"Someone must decide what's to be done. It seems fitting that a military man like Colonel McKnight ought to take charge. What say you, Ian?"

"I appreciate your confidence, Mr. Suggett, but I'm not the only military man in this place. I'll do naught without the word of the others."

"If any man thinks he can do a better job, let him come forward and declare so. Otherwise, I say we put our trust in Colonel McKnight."

When no one moved, William Tomlinson, who had two sons of fighting age, stepped forward and shook Ian's hand. "Seems like y' got yourself the job, Colonel. How do y' say—do we ride out or not?"

Ian searched the faces of the silent circle of men. "How many want to go to the aid of our neighbors?"

With one voice the men declared their readiness to do so, some even that very night.

"Very well, we'll go, but night travel's risky, and we need time to prepare. We'll leave with the dawn tomorrow."

"This is the first time I've ever seen my father as a

soldier," Anna remarked to Rebecca as the men parted.

Rebecca glanced appraisingly at Anna. "Everyone in Kentucky is a soldier of sorts, I reckon. I should've asked earlier how well you handle a rifle and powder horn."

"Well enough. From the time I could walk, my father saw to it that I learned the ways of the woods."

"Good. With most of the men gone, the women will have to defend the Station."

As she had done on the flatboat, Anna tried to imagine how she'd feel if they came under Indian attack. "Have you ever had to fire at Indians from the Station?"

"A few times. Sometimes when the men are off huntin', we put on men's hats and huntin' shirts and carry rifles when we have to go outside the gates. If they think there are many men in a station, more often than not they leave it alone."

"And if they don't?"

Rebecca shrugged. "In that case, everyone gets a rifle and finds a chink in the wall to fire it from. After a few rounds, the savages usually turn tail and run back across the river."

It was late when Ian returned to his cabin, reporting that all was ready for the men to depart at dawn. Anna bade Rebecca and her father good night and had started for the lean-to when Ian followed and took Anna's hand. "I'm sorry to leave ye and Rebecca here, lass, but I have no choice."

"I know, Father. Don't worry—we'll look after one another." Even as she assured her father, Anna only hoped she spoke the truth.

*   *   *

Skirting the southern shore of the O-hio-se-pe, the Indians scattered before camping that night, then came together for the final day's march. They forded the Licking River at their usual spot and encountered no one until they reached Blue Licks, where a party of white settlers worked at salt-making.

"Surely they must see us," Bright Stone murmured to Otter. At a signal from Simon Girty, the warriors took whatever cover they could find. Some hid in high grass or stands of cane, while Otter and Bright Stone crouched behind a wide-trunked sycamore tree. "Why do we not kill them before they can warn the *Shemanese*?" Bright Stone whispered.

The older and more experienced Otter explained the situation. "It would not be wise. Other *Shemanese* could be nearby. Our rifles will not talk except to answer theirs, else all will know we are here, and the surprise will be lost."

They waited for what seemed a very long time. Finally the white men left the area without showing any sign that they knew the warriors were watching them. After waiting a time to make sure the salt-makers had gone, the party moved on.

It was nearly dark when Bright Stone lifted his head and sniffed the air. "Smoke."

Otter wrinkled his nose as he detected other odors. "The stink of sheep and cattle. We must be very near the *Shemanese*."

The party skirted the livestock pens and stopped in the cover of the dense woods near a spring. They could tell little about Bryan's Station except that it stood on a hill and seemed fairly small. A creek ran beside it, and to the south, beside an old buffalo trace, lay a large field of corn. The size of the station disappointed Otter, who had hoped it would be more like the real French and British forts he had seen.

"We should go in now and take the place while they sleep," Bright Stone whispered.

"Even you must know that cannot be done," Otter said. They would wait for daylight to attack; attempting to take a palisaded Station in the dark would be foolhardy.

Otter's heart began to beat faster at the prospect that dawn would bring the chance to prove himself in battle. Then he would return to Waccachalla and claim Willow . . .

The sound of a single horse approaching the Station from the south at a gallop interrupted Otter's reverie, and he frowned.

"No one fires—why is this so?" Bright Stone asked when it became obvious that the horseman would be allowed to enter the fort. "He might tell them we are here."

"And shooting him would not?" Otter asked. "We are hidden, and this man does not see us. Take your rest now—it is yet a long while until dawn." *Then this place will be ours, and Willow will be mine.* Smiling at that pleasant thought, Otter spread his blanket and lay down to sleep.

The sky had not yet emptied of stars when he awakened. In his usual rite before a battle, he bathed in the icy stream that ran past the Station. He did not break his fast, nor did he feel hungry. In the first faint predawn light, Otter climbed a tree for a better look at the object of their attack.

Bryan's Station seemed to be only scarcely bigger than his own village of Waccachalla, crude in comparison to the grand forts of the French and British. Still, Otter hoped that his part in bringing it down would give him the honor he sought.

"This place may be small, but I will fight well here," he assured himself.

At least they would have the advantage of surprise, Otter thought. No one in the Station seemed to know what awaited outside their gates. A rooster crowed, and smoke from cooking fires rose lazily in the still air. Otter looked closely at the palisades, but saw no telltale rifle barrels. He put his hand on the hilt of his scalping knife, which he had honed to a sharp edge, and licked his lips in anticipation. Soon, perhaps, it would be put to good use.

The lookout's cry jolted Anna awake from an odd but pleasant dream in which she and Stuart had been making love. Still holding her close, he whispered that he would take her to see her mother's village.

"Indians!"

"Where?" Anna heard someone ask.

"Everywhere—we're surrounded."

Now wide awake, Anna opened her eyes and saw it was not yet fully light. She dressed with haste. Her father was nowhere to be seen, but Rebecca sat at the table, fully clothed and calmly eating breakfast.

"Ian's gone to see what the fuss is about. Take some of this johnnycake—it might be a while before you have another chance to eat."

Although Rebecca spoke matter-of-factly, the tightness in her voice suggested that she felt some concern over what lay ahead.

Anna wasn't hungry, but she crumbled some of last night's bread into a trencher of clabbered milk. "What will happen now?" she asked.

That depends on the savages. If they want a fight, we'll give them one." Rebecca pointed to several long-barreled rifles propped against the wall by the hearth. "The first one's mine, but you can take your pick of the others. All are primed and ready to fire."

A knock sounded on the cabin door, and Rebecca opened it to John Atkinson. "Everyone's to come outside now for muster," he said. "Don't bring the rifles yet," he added as Rebecca and Anna both moved toward them.

"What does this mean?" Anna asked, but Rebecca merely shook her head.

A few moments later, most of the Station's inhabitants formed a loose circle around Ian McKnight as he explained their situation.

"There's a great many Indians out there—more than usually come a-raiding. We think it might be the party we were warned about last night, come here in place of Hoy's Station. I reckon they don't know we've seen them."

"If we go out now, they'd surely catch us in an ambuscade, then try to overrun the Station while the gates are still open," James Craig said.

Anna shuddered to think how close to death her father and the other men had come.

"We've food and ammunition enough to withstand a siege, but as ye know, the spring lies outside the gates, and we cannot last long without water."

He paused for a moment, and James Craig spoke in the sudden silence. "I agree that we must have water, but how can we fetch it, with the savages watching our every move? 'Twould be suicide—"

"I think not," Ian said. "Every morning since there's been a Station here, the women have gone out for water. They can do so now, just as usual. The Indians won't risk firing at them—'twould only give them away."

Charles Beasley, who had been back only two days after escaping from Shawnee captivity, nodded in agreement. "Aye, the colonel speaks the truth. Some Shawnee ways I know all too well. No warrior would disgrace himself by firin' at women."

Some men agreed, while others murmured against the proposed plan.

"Seems like y' oughter ask us women what we think about it, seein' how it's us that'd be doin' the goin' out there," the Widow Stucker said.

All were silent for a moment. When several women began to speak at once, Ian McKnight held up his hand.

"Quiet! Ye might as well invite their chief in for a powwow," he admonished.

Rebecca McKnight took a step toward her husband. "Very well, sir. The more water we have, the better the chances we can hold out. I'm goin' after a bucket now. Any woman or girl willin' to join me, do the same and meet back here. We'll all go out together."

My father married a brave woman, Anna thought

with admiration. Whatever Rebecca's faults might be, cowardice was not among them.

Silently the women scattered to their own cabins, to return in a few minutes with a variety of buckets— one-handled piggins, upright-handled noggins, and a few sturdy copper-bound oaken buckets with rope handles.

"I reckon we're ready," the Widow Stucker declared.

Anna's heart pounded as her father gave the men a series of rapid orders.

"We must have several of ye posted at the palisades and firing stations. Take care not to show yourselves, and hold your fire unless the Indians shoot first."

When the men had taken their places, Ian nodded to the Widow Stucker and Rebecca, stationed in the front of the party. In silence the women moved toward the Station's front entrance, their usual route to the spring. David Herndon lifted the heavy bolt and let the gates swing open just enough to allow them to pass through in single file.

Anna had gone down the hill to the spring many times, but never had the trip seemed quite so long as it did on this morning. She feared that the Indians must surely hear the collective pounding of their hearts. At the head of the little column, the Widow Stucker seemed engaged in ordinary conversation with Rebecca, but few of the others had enough presence of mind to do much more than moan softly to themselves as they made their way down the hill.

The spring was too narrow for more than three or

four to bend over it at a time, and in their haste to fill their buckets and be gone, some of the women jostled one another as they reached it.

"Mind your manners," the Widow Stucker said sharply. Finding herself near the end of the column, Anna watched the others and waited her turn. She knew that the widow was right; undue haste on their part would surely arouse the Indians' suspicions and perhaps even draw their fire. At first Anna had to resist the urge to run, but as she finally reached the spring with her two oaken buckets, her legs weakened beneath her so much that she could scarcely walk. She knelt to fill her buckets, and when she stood, their heavy weight surprised her.

Well, at least I won't be tempted to run back up the hill, Anna through wryly.

She looked back toward the Station walls, which the Widow Stucker and Rebecca had almost reached. A few more yards, and the gate would swing open to them. Some of the women behind them started to run, and Anna saw Rebecca turn to them, frowning.

Surely the Indians will be suspicious of the way we're acting, Anna thought. At any moment she expected to hear the report of their rifles, or worse, to feel the painful thrust of an arrow in her back. She knew that most Indians had smoothbore rifles furnished by the British. According to her father and other men Anna had heard on the subject, these were far inferior to the Pennsylvania rifles, whose spiral bores fired a bullet longer and truer. However, the Indians had also retained their skill with the bow and arrow, and many preferred to use the old weapons for stealth and quiet.

Sometimes the arrows were tipped with poison . . .

Anna swallowed hard and looked toward the Station, which now seemed impossibly far away.

From his vantage point, Otter detected a movement. As he looked toward its source, the station's front gate opened. With every muscle tensed and ready for action, he waited to see what would happen next.

Perhaps the Shemanese know we are here and will be foolish enough to come out to fight us. That notion was short-lived, however, as he watched the two women with water buckets emerge from the Station and start down the hill to the spring.

Otter relaxed and let his breath puff out his cheeks. No doubt, bringing water was women's work everywhere. It would be natural for the *Shemanese* women to fetch water every morning, as did the Shawnee. As he watched, other women followed, and still more, all carrying buckets.

Otter had not seen many *Shemanese* women, and he studied them as closely as he could from his hiding place. They seemed to be of all ages, from grandmothers to mere girls who looked too weak to carry their heavy buckets back up the hill. All wore long dresses, and some kind of cloth covered their heads. He found the color of their skin repulsive, like the undersides of dead fish. The light color of some of their eyes made him uneasy.

Then another water carrier came from the gate, and Otter rubbed his eyes in disbelief. Had his sight somehow tricked his mind? But he looked again, and what he saw had not changed.

"This one is not *Shemanese*," he told himself. Although the girl's clothes were like the others', her appearance definitely was not. Her skin was far darker than theirs, and her features seemed more sharply defined.

Perhaps it was the grace of her carriage that convinced Otter that this water carrier was no stranger to him. The way she held her head, and every other thing about her was as familiar to him as the back of his own hand.

Willow. He said the name softly to himself, then repeated it. Willow-*neewa*, the one he would call wife. But how did she come to be in this *Shemanese* station, wearing their clothes and fetching their water?

The Shemanese *must have stolen her and brought her here. Black Snake should never have let Bear's Daughter take her from his protection.*

Otter watched the girl's progress all the way down the hill. His anger flared when he saw several of the women push her aside. When she reached the spring, Otter noted with approval that while the others bent awkwardly to fill their buckets, she was the only one who knelt, in the Indian way.

With hungry eyes, Otter watched the girl rise, being pushed several times in the process. *The Shemanese women must surely be jealous of her beauty,* he told himself. He rehearsed how he would spring from the tree to rescue her as all the other warriors looked on with envy and amazement, while the *Shemanese* women screamed in terror.

"Ah!" He all but smacked his lips in anticipation of Willow's gratitude when she realized that he was rescuing her and taking her back to her home. And if the old woman still lived, Bear's Daughter would be grateful, too. No doubt the story would be told around a hundred campfires, wherever and for as long as the Shawnee honored their own.

Yes, Otter thought with satisfaction. *When I bring Willow back to Waccachalla, there will be no doubt that she belongs in my lodge. Even Black Snake himself will be proud of this thing I do.*

With that thought firmly in his mind, Otter jumped down from the tree and moved quickly toward the spring.

Intent only on going back up the hill, Anna did not notice the dark figure that darted from the trees and ran toward her until he stood beside her. By then, it was too late. Her two buckets fell from her hands, the water sloshing onto the ground and over her feet.

A confusion of images simultaneously assailed Anna's senses. She smelled a strange, musky odor she recognized as bear grease, saw the flash of a red band around a painted face, and heard unintelligible words being rapidly spoken in a guttural tongue. She felt herself being picked up and lifted high by strong arms, briefly carried like a sack of meal slung over her captor's bare shoulder, and finally being thrown onto the back of a waiting horse.

Anna's captor was obviously pleased with himself. Keeping up a rapid stream of gibberish, he swung up behind her, spurred his horse, and headed away from Bryan's Station at a brisk gallop.

Desperately Anna tried to look back, but already

the Station was out of sight. And even if anyone there had seen what had happened, they didn't appear to be doing anything about it.

Of course no one can come after me now, Anna realized dully. *That could only lead to bloodshed.*

She briefly entertained the idea of trying to jump from the horse. She was tightly wedged between her captor and the elevated front of the saddle, however, and on either side the Indian's muscular arms formed a solid barrier as he held the reins. Since Anna knew that to fall from a galloping horse would most likely injure her badly, she held on with all her might.

Behind her, Anna's captor laughed, a sound that somehow chilled her even more than a growled threat would have. "*Willow-neewa!*" he cried in her ear. "*Willow-neewa!*"

Did he really speak her name, or did she imagine it? *Impossible,* Anna thought. *This savage doesn't know me. Surely he has nothing to do with me or my mother's people.*

Yet a strange prickling at the base of her scalp made Anna wonder if she could be so certain of that.

Always be careful what ye ask for, Anna Willow—ye might get it. The words her father had spoken to her many years before echoed in her mind like distant thunder before a storm.

I meant it when I said I wanted to see where my mother's people lived. But this isn't how I wanted to get there.

Anna's world now contained only the continuing near-chant of her captor's voice and the labored breathing of his horse. Every hoofbeat took her ever farther north, away from all that she knew, and all that she held dear.

17

BRYAN'S STATION

When Rebecca re-entered the Bryan's Station gates carrying her water buckets, Ian embraced her, relief written on his face. But just as he turned back in expectation of his daughter's safe return, a lookout high on the palisade cried out.

"An Injun just grabbed one of the women!"

The last of the water carriers surged inside the gate, which immediately closed behind them.

"I didn't see no Injuns," the Widow Stucker muttered.

"No wonder, since we were all just lookin' to get back to the Station," Rebecca said.

The women glanced around uneasily, soon discovering the truth of what Ian had immediately feared. Of them all, only Anna Willow McKnight had not returned from the spring.

Quickly Ian scaled the ladder and joined the lookout on his narrow ledge. Although no one was in sight, Ian's scalp prickled, aware that the deceptive calm could soon be broken. "What did you see?" he demanded.

The young lookout shook his head. "It all happened so quick, I don't rightly know, sir. One minute the women was all comin' back, with not an Injun in sight—an' the next thing I knew, one dropped out of a tree close to the spring and had ahold of someone afore she had any chance to get away."

"Where did he take her?" Ian asked.

"Into the woods, I reckon. He sure didn't waste no time haulin' her out o' sight."

"Stay here, and if you see anything else, let me know right away."

"Yes, sir. You think the Injuns might go away, now they've got them a hostage?"

A hostage. Was that why they had taken Anna Willow? Did they hope to get a ransom for her, or—? Ian passed a shaking hand over his brow, not willing to carry the thought further.

"Anna's not here," Rebecca said when Ian returned to her side.

"I know. I must go after her."

Overhearing, James Craig joined them. "Colonel, I know you're worried about your girl, but if you so much as set one foot outside these walls, you'll be a dead man."

"James is right," Rebecca said. "Don't do anything foolish—that won't help Anna or anyone else."

"We need you here at the Station," James added.

The words were no sooner said than two lookouts cried out at almost the same time. "Injuns!" said one, and "They're comin'!" yelled the other.

At once Ian McKnight, worried father, had to become Colonel McKnight, in charge of protecting the lives of those in the Station. "All right, everyone, you know what is to be done. Women and children, go to your cabins. Men, look to your weapons!"

After seizing the girl he thought was Willow, Otter had ridden as hard as he dared toward the O-hio-se-pe. Only when he had crossed it would he and Willow be safe. His initial elation at stealing his intended wife from her *Shemanese* captors had settled into keen anticipation as he continued to picture the stir when he brought his prize back to Waccachalla.

Anna rode before him, her first numbed shock replaced by a sober consideration of what might happen next. Undoubtedly, she had already been missed, and her father would come after her as soon as he could. Unless, of course, the Station had since come under Indian attack. In that case, no one would be able to come for her for some time. In the meantime, she would have to rely on her own wits.

The horse gradually slowed from a full gallop to a canter, then to a walk. Finally it halted in a deep, gloomy place, which no ray of sun penetrated. Water murmured nearby, and Anna's heart contracted as she realized that they must be near the Ohio River.

Her captor slid from the horse and let go of the reins as he reached his arms out to help her down. In the split second before she could weigh any possible consequences, Anna leaned forward and grabbed the reins. She slapped them hard against the horse's withers and dug her heels into its flanks. With a surprised snort, the animal reared back, then stretched out its neck and began to run.

Ducking tree limbs and branches, Anna managed to work her way backward to sit in the saddle, but she still felt far from secure as the horse raced forward. Unable to reach the stirrups, Anna pressed her legs tightly against the horse's sides. The animal's labored breathing and the steady tattoo of its hoofbeats muffled the shouts of her captor, which soon faded away.

I have escaped, Anna thought, with a mixture of relief and fright. She had no idea where she was, but at least she was free from her the man who had seized her.

She had little time for celebration, however. The horse half reared, took a few skittish steps to one side, then came to an abrupt halt as the trail descended into a clearing and stopped suddenly at the river. No side paths branched into the dense underbrush, and since she could ride no farther, Anna decided to abandon the horse. She slid off and turned the animal to face the direction from which she had come. Using a fallen tree branch, Anna hit the horse's rump. The horse reared and neighed its displeasure, then ran from her.

Perhaps when the Indian sees his horse, he'll presume I was thrown, and look for me on the trail. By that time, she planned to be well out of sight.

Anna plunged into the underbrush and started to work her way back south. She intended to stay parallel to the trail, but far enough from it so that the Indian would never find her.

Or at least, so she hoped.

★   ★   ★

Otter did not enjoy being tricked. He had been unhappy when he brought that prime deer to Willow's lodge, only to find her gone; but he'd believed that when he rescued the girl from the *Shemanese*, she would gladly accept his offer of marriage. Now, however, this girl Willow had caused Otter to be truly angry.

What evil spirit is in her, that she mocks me and steals my horse when I saved her from the Shemanese who made her their slave?

Absorbed in his anger, Otter walked on. He hadn't gotten far before he heard hoofbeats coming in his direction. His first thought was that Willow had meant only to tease him, to play a joke, and now she returned on his horse. Otter put on a stern face, ready to let her know that stealing a warrior's horse was not a jesting matter. When she came into his lodge, she could not behave as a silly maiden; the mother of his sons could not do such things.

The hoofbeats abruptly stopped. *The girl might have been thrown off,* Otter thought. He ran ahead until he came to the horse, foraging contentedly beside the trail. Willow was nowhere in sight.

Otter took the horse's reins and mounted. As he rode slowly back toward the river, his eyes searched the ground around the trail. When the path ended, he swung from the horse and looped the reins around a sapling. In the dappled half light of the clearing, Otter found the unmistakable evidence of her footprints. For some reason, Willow had entered the underbrush and headed south again.

He sighed in exasperation and annoyance. Why

would she do such a thing? Surely the girl couldn't want to return to the *Shemanese*. Perhaps she had fallen from the horse and addled her senses. He had heard of such a thing happening, even to warriors.

But no matter why Willow had run from him, Otter would soon find her. With almost every step, she had brushed against a small tree or bush, thus perfectly blazing her trail. It was only a matter of time—and not much time at that—before Otter would claim her.

The siege of Bryan's Station lasted throughout the rest of that day and night and all the next day. Rebecca kept busy supplying the men with bullets and tending to the wounded. Ian was everywhere, seeing that the women and children were as safe as possible, while taking his turn at the firing stations. In the night, the invading Indians sent flaming arrows onto the cabin roofs, starting many fires that burned some structures to the ground. When Ian climbed to the roof of one cabin in an attempt to beat out the flaming shingles, an arrow grazed his side. Ignoring the pain, he succeeded in saving the cabin before he sought out Rebecca to dress the wound. And through it all, his heart felt the constant dull ache of fear and dread that he did not know what had become of his daughter.

Although they were far outnumbered by the Indians, the settlers had superior weapons and were well protected by the Station walls. Guided by the skill and experience of Colonel Ian McKnight, the settlers were able to inflict heavy losses on their attackers, who finally gave up and fled.

Only a few hours later, Colonel Daniel Boone's small force from Boonesborough reached Bryan's Station. They were soon joined by Colonel John Todd, who headed a hundred and seventy men from Harrodsburg, Booneville, Danville, Lexington, and Stanford.

As soon as Ian McKnight heard they were there, he insisted on meeting with the leaders, despite his painful wound.

Daniel Boone looked imposing in his long brown hunting shirt and black hat, but his voice was characteristically and surprisingly soft. "I see that Simon Girty's up to his old tricks. What happened here, Colonel McKnight?"

Briefly Ian described the siege. "Before it started, a warrior kidnapped my daughter outside the Station. We lost two men killed and several others were hurt. The Indians slaughtered all the sheep and nearly a hundred head of cattle. I suspect they're probably riding for the Licking River now, but since they made off with most of the horses, we can't even pursue them."

John Todd and Daniel Boone exchanged glances, then Todd nodded. "We'll ride hard. Maybe we can still catch them."

Daniel Boone extended his hand to Ian. "You did good work here, Colonel. I'm sorry about your daughter."

Rebecca had stood by while Ian talked to the two men. When they left, she laid her hand on his arm. "There's naught you can do to help them, and it's past time you took some rest."

"I'm all right," Ian protested, but he allowed

Rebecca to link her arm in his and lead him to their cabin,

"Lie down and be quiet for a spell."

Reluctantly Ian lay down, but sat up again immediately, a motion that caused him to wince and hold his hurt side. "How can I rest, when I ought to be going after Anna Willow?"

"But Ian, be sensible—you've been wounded. You're not strong enough to do this."

Ian shook off his wife's protests. "There's no help for it—I maun find Anna Willow. Captain Craig, will ye join me?"

A wide smile lighted James Craig's craggy face. "Yes, sir! Ever since the Crutcher boys found those horses, I've been hopin' for a chance to get in this fight."

A quarter of an hour later Ian McKnight and James Craig rode out of Bryan's Station. Any of the other men would have gladly gone with them, but Ian decided to leave the other horse at the Station in case it was needed.

"We'll make for the Licking River. It may be that the men with Colonel Todd and Colonel Boone have already caught up with Girty's band."

"And whupped 'em too, I hope," James Craig said.

Yet the closer the men came to the place where the Indians would have forded the Licking River, the more uneasy each became.

"Something's not right here," Ian muttered.

They saw no one, nor did they hear any sounds of a battle. At the Blue Licks they halted their horses and gazed at the terrain beyond, a maze of ravines and underbrush that made an ideal place for an ambush. More than once, Indians had taken white settlers captive in this very spot, and only a few had escaped to tell about it.

After a long moment, John glanced questioningly at Ian. "I suppose we'd better take a look and see what we can find."

Almost as soon as he spoke, several militiamen staggered from the narrow defile. A few were obviously wounded, and they all seemed dazed. That they had been in a battle was abundantly and awfully clear.

Ian and James Craig dismounted when they saw an old acquaintance who lived in Boonesborough. "What happened here?" Ian asked.

The man's mouth twisted in a sardonic smile. "I reckon you can tell that pretty plain. Colonel Todd and Colonel Boone didn't want us to go after the savages, and we didn't, 'til Major McGary started off alone, hollerin' that he wasn't a-feared to go. Of course, ever'one followed him, not wantin' to be counted as cowards."

"The Indians made an ambuscade?" Ian asked.

"Aye. Trapped us back there in the narrows, with no place to hide. 'Tis a wonder that any of us lived to tell of it."

"What about the Indians? Where are they now?" James Craig asked.

McTavish laughed without humor. "Well, now, I didn't follow 'em, but I'd guess they're either already acrost the river or well on their way to Ohio by now."

"Did ye notice a captive girl with them?" Ian asked.

"No. The way they was actin', I'd say they didn't aim to take no prisoners."

He and Ian walked into the ravine with their rifles at the ready. They soon lowered them, however, as it became all too apparent that those who had caused the slaughter had already taken their scalps and left.

James Craig touched his hand to Ian's shoulder. "I'm sorry, Colonel. I reckon we got here too late."

Ian McKnight's jaw set in a stubborn line. "For this battle, maybe, but I'm not yet finished with Simon Girty's rabble. If it takes going to every village on the other side of the Ohio, I'll find Anna Willow."

Less than an hour after she had run away from him, Otter found the one he called Willow. But that had only been the start of his trouble. After trying to speak to her and find out why she had run from him, Otter discovered that this was not the girl he had known in Waccachalla, not the girl with whom he had hoped to share a marriage blanket.

Otter frowned and wondered what *matchemenetoo*, what trick of an evil spirit, could have made her look so much like Willow. Even in the full light of the afternoon sun, he had no doubt that anyone who'd ever seen Willow would mistake this girl for her. But this one spoke the *Shemanese* tongue, and she seemed not to understand him. Unless the *Shemanese* had somehow managed to possess her spirit, this was not the same Willow that Otter had thought to bring into his lodge.

"Who are you?" Otter asked her, but he hadn't understood her *Shemanese* answer. Stubbornly she had looked in the direction of the Station and signed that she wanted to go back to it. The girl pointed to herself and spoke slowly. "Anna Willow McKnight." Then she repeated the words, but Otter did not understand.

"You look like Willow."

The girl shook her head and touched her hand to her heart. "No! I am *Anna* Willow McKnight. My name is *Anna* Willow, not just Willow."

All Otter could grasp was that this girl looked like the Willow that he knew, but talked in the *Shemanese* tongue and pretended not to understand Shawnee words. Even though her strange behavior puzzled and confused him, Otter would not let her get away from him a second time. When she turned and made as if to run, Otter quickly caught her. With one hand he held her by her long hair, while with the other he brandished his belt knife.

Even then she did not cry or beg for mercy, but closed her eyes as if waiting for him to scalp her. A lesser man might fear her and set her free. But Otter was a strong and brave warrior, and now he had a way to prove it. Rather than taking this one's scalp, Otter would take her to Waccachalla. All the people there would see this strange thing for themselves, and Black Oak himself would say what to do with her.

Once more the girl with the strange Willow-name would ride with Otter, but this time she couldn't escape. He bound her hands with a long rawhide strip from his leggings. When she protested that the strip hurt her wrists, he removed his sweaty red headband and tied it around her mouth. She gagged on the rank odor of bear grease that seemed to permeate everything about the man, but her captor paid her discomfort no heed.

Otter lifted Anna onto his horse, where she rode in front of him, barricaded on either side by his muscular arms. When he urged the horse into the Ohio River current, Anna realized that if he had not so placed her, she surely would have been swept off the horse and drowned.

As Anna's captor bore her northward, she now knew his name—the only thing he'd said that she had understood. But she still had no clue why this Otter had taken her captive, why he had called her "Willow" from the first, where he was taking her, or what would happen to her when they got there.

This man has had several chances to kill me, Anna realized. Why hadn't he scalped her immediately? She had heard stories of some Indian captives who had been tortured and killed, and of others who had been well treated. A few had even been adopted into Indian families. A woman named Mary Jemison had eventually married an Indian warrior and refused to leave him, even when she had the opportunity.

Recalling the story, Anna felt even more uneasy. *I hope this Indian doesn't have anything like that in mind for me.*

18

KANAWHA TRAIL

Riding behind White Eagle, Willow automatically noted the direction in which they traveled and identified landmarks that would help her find her way again, should that ever be necessary. Although several other trails crossed theirs, the area seemed relatively deserted.

Something important must be going on, that no men hunt and no women gather berries and acorns along this way, Willow thought. She asked White Eagle nothing, however, content merely to enjoy his presence and her strange new feeling of peace and well-being.

Once they stopped in a small Shawnee village that to Willow's eyes seemed even poorer than Waccachalla. Its chief greeted them warmly, however, and insisted that Willow and White Eagle should partake of a meal of persimmons and acorn bread. Willow washed her food down with a bitter herbal tea the chief's wife assured would make her strong.

"Your woman is too pale," she told White Eagle.

"This one will always be so," he had replied. Beyond telling them that she was called Willow, White Eagle said nothing about her, but Willow took heart that he hadn't corrected the chief's wife when she called Willow his woman.

Late in the afternoon White Eagle stopped by a message tree, an ancient dead oak with many curious carvings on its bark. White Eagle barely glanced at it, though, as he helped her down from his horse.

"We walk into Shawnee Town from here," he said. "It is not far to the village now."

Willow smelled the settlement even before they reached its *wegiwas*. She closed her eyes briefly as her nose recorded each familiar aroma. Sun-drying hides, wood-tanned skins, bear grease, boiling herbs, cooking pots full of stew—rabbit or turkey or squirrel—and overall, the ever-present pungency of fragrant wood smoke. Comforting home smells.

A moment later the path widened into a large clearing. "We are here," White Eagle said unnecessarily.

Willow felt a bit overwhelmed as she saw the village spread before her. "This Shawnee Town is a fine place," she said.

Not only was it the largest village Willow had ever seen, it also reminded her of Waccachalla in the days of her youth, before the first burning of their *wegiwas* and the destruction of their crops in the fields.

As if he knew her thoughts, White Eagle's hand touched the small of Willow's back in a comforting gesture. "Tall Oak does much to keep his people safe. All around us is hidden food, should the *Shemanese* do with us as they have others. Here you will be safe."

With you I will feel safe anywhere. Willow wished for
the boldness to say the words as well as think them,
but she remained silent.

"There is my mother." White Eagle pointed
toward a matron who sat cross-legged before a large
wegiwa, intent on her task of grinding corn.

At the same moment White Eagle spoke, the
woman looked up and saw him. In one graceful movement, she rose and moved toward him.

Willow stopped and let White Eagle greet his
mother alone.

"Why do you come back so early, my son?"

White Eagle accepted his mother's embrace, then
half turned toward Willow. "This is Willow, a maiden
from Black Snake's village. She will stay here while I
parley with Tall Oak."

White Eagle's mother touched her hand to her
heart and then toward her *wegiwa* in a gesture of welcome. "Come, my child. You will have food and
drink."

"We will talk later this day, my mother." Without
looking at Willow, White Eagle strode off toward the
largest lodge in the village. Willow knew it must be
the *msi-kah-mi-qui*, the place where Chief Tall Oak
held council.

"I am called Shining Star," White Eagle's mother
told her. Then, seeing the way Willow looked back at
White Eagle, she frowned slightly. "My son will soon
return."

Ashamed that she had allowed her feelings to show
so plainly, Willow followed Shining Star into her
wegiwa, even though her heart and thoughts still

stayed with White Eagle. Willow wondered what his chief would say.

After Willow had eaten, Shining Star folded her arms across her chest in the Shawnee way of showing readiness to listen to a matter of importance. "Now I would hear how you come here with my son," she said.

"It is a hard thing. I do not know how to tell it all," Willow said.

"Make a beginning. The rest will come."

Haltingly at first, then speaking more surely, Willow traced what had happened the past few days. Only once, when she described how White Eagle had buried her mother, did her voice waver, and that only for a moment.

"So I am come to this place, as White Eagle promised Bear's Daughter," she finished.

Shining Star grunted softly, but did not comment on what she had heard. She pointed to a bed of skins. "Now you will rest there."

Willow lay down, but although she was tired, she waited, wide-eyed, for White Eagle to return. It seemed like a long time before she heard his voice.

"I am back, my mother."

"What says Tall Oak, my son?"

"It is decided. He will do as I wish."

"I do not understand this thing. Did Tall Oak not promise you his own daughter, Fair Moon? This girl Willow does not even look Shawnee."

"Her mother was kin to the Lenni-Lenape and her father was a *Shemanese* trader. But the girl Willow is all Shawnee."

"Take her back to her village, my son. You must have our chief's daughter to wife."

"Fair Moon is just a child. My mother surely knows she is too young to marry," White Eagle said.

"I well know her age. Were not she and your brother Gray Shadow born in the same moon? In one more turn of the seasons, Fair Moon will be ripe to marry."

Willow couldn't see White Eagle, but she guessed that he must have made the cutoff sign. When he spoke again, it was with a warrior's authority.

"I have told you this thing is decided. Tall Oak has said it."

"So let it be, then."

Willow heard the note of resignation in his mother's voice, and knew that even though Shining Star might never mention the subject, she would not likely forget that Willow wasn't her choice as her son's bride.

I will be such a good wife to White Eagle that Shining Star will come to love me, too, Willow vowed.

"I will see Willow now," White Eagle said.

"The girl sleeps inside."

"Leave us, my mother."

As White Eagle entered the *wegiwa,* Willow sat up and made an effort to smooth her hair, which had not been properly dressed since her mother's illness.

White Eagle knelt beside her and reached for her right hand. "My chief asks to see you. He would welcome you to Shawnee Town."

"Is that all?" asked Willow, who knew it was not.

"He gives us a fine *wegiwa,* as well."

"Then you will be my man?" she asked.

The corners of White Eagle's mouth lifted in a brief smile. "It is already so, since my first sight of you."

Willow wanted to throw her arms around White Eagle and cry out with joy, but a sadness in her heart stilled her. "There is one thing I would ask of your chief."

"Tall Oak is your chief now. What is this thing?"

Willow withdrew her hand from White Eagle's and crossed her hands with her palms over her heart to show the importance of what she was about to say.

"Black Snake does not know to mourn for Bear's Daughter. I would go to Waccachalla to tell the chief that his kinswoman no longer lives."

He nodded. "I will say this thing to Tall Oak. We go together."

Willow squeezed his hand. "It is good, my husband."

She had not dared to call him that before, and surprise briefly marked White Eagle's face. He pulled Willow so close to his body that she felt the steady throb of his heart. She found herself holding her breath as his lips pressed against hers for the space of several heartbeats.

"Willow-*keewa*," he whispered against her hair. Willow, you are my wife.

"*Niwy sheena*," she replied. You are my husband.

Then White Eagle left the *wegiwa*. Willow lay back on the bed of skins and touched her lips with her fingertips, cherishing the memory of his kiss and wondering what would happen that night, the first they would spend together as man and wife.

She had not properly mourned Bear's Daughter, but at least her mother's last desire was going to be fulfilled.

My mother, all will be as you wished. You will be honored.

19

SHAWNEE TOWN

Willow spent most of her first day in Shawnee Town with White Eagle's mother. Shining Star candidly told Willow that she wanted her son to marry Fair Moon. "It is not a small thing for the chief to give his only daughter to White Eagle."

"That is so. But I will be a good wife for your son."

Shining Star laid her forearm beside Willow's. Willow's skin was several shades lighter than the older woman's. "You are not like us. I would not have you bring my son trouble."

Willow spoke earnestly. "I cannot help the way I look." She touched her hand to her heart. "In here, we are the same."

Shining Star turned away without replying, but later that day she took the girl to the creek and helped her wash her traveling dress. She stood watching while Willow waded into the water and washed her body and her hair.

When Shining Star offered to dress Willow's hair,

she misread Willow's look of distress, and sat back on her heels, obviously displeased. "It is true that I have no daughters and my hands are not skilled in such work. I will call another to do this thing."

Realizing that she had hurt Shining Star's feelings, Willow spoke quickly. "No, Shining Star. Your offer honors me. I thank you for it. I only thought how my mother used to dress my hair. It took a long time because her hands were stiff with age."

Shining Star's tone was matter-of-fact. "What have we to do with that now? Come, sit in the light."

Shining Star lifted the back of Willow's hair with one hand and pulled a wide-toothed comb through it with the other, murmuring in surprise at its softness. "This must feel like the hair of the *Shemanese*. White Eagle found this comb on a *Shemanese* boat on the O-hio-se-pe. He took it to give to Fair Moon. Now it is yours."

Willow felt brief jealousy that White Eagle had already been saving gifts for Fair Moon before her common sense checked it. *White Eagle did only what custom said he should. And that was before he knew me.*

When Shining Star was satisfied with Willow's appearance, she took her outside, where White Eagle waited.

With pleasure, Willow briefly noticed the look of admiration in his eyes before she looked away, as befitted her station.

"You have cared well for Willow, my mother. Come, Willow. Tall Oak would speak with you now."

As they walked to the council lodge, she said to White Eagle, "Perhaps your chief will not like me."

He glanced at her and shook his head. "Tall Oak will like my woman because I do."

Willow felt her heart lift at his words. With White Eagle beside her, Willow held her head high as they entered the council lodge.

Soon Willow realized she had nothing to fear from Tall Oak. She thought he was more than kind to her, particularly since her sudden appearance had spoiled the plan for his daughter to marry White Eagle. Tall Oak told Willow that he knew of her mother, Bear's Daughter; he agreed that all of Waccachalla should know of her death and mourn her. Then he picked up a blanket and beckoned Willow and White Eagle to come and stand before him.

"White Eagle, is it your wish to have this woman?" he asked.

Willow lowered her head and dared not look at him. She felt great relief when he answered.

"Yes, my chief."

Tall Oak turned to Willow. "Will you share White Eagle's blanket?"

Although her heart exulted, she spoke quietly. "Yes, my chief."

The chief unfolded the blanket and came behind them to lay it across their shoulders, thus giving his approval to their wish to join their lives.

White Eagle kissed her forehead, and the thing was done—Willow and White Eagle were married. She folded their marriage blanket and waited quietly for Tall Oak and White Eagle to finish their parley.

"I would also send a gift to my Shawnee brother Black Snake," said the chief. He pointed to a magnificent buffalo-skin robe, hand-cleaned by Tall Oak's wife with white sand and the finest of quill brushes.

"Chief Black Snake will be much pleased with this gift."

Tall Oak nodded. "He is a worthy chief. Say to him we would have his warriors help us against the *Shemanese*."

"I will tell Black Snake this thing." White Eagle paused, then glanced at Willow before he spoke again. "My chief knows that my wife has no horse."

Tall Oak understood what the warrior wanted and shook his head. "She came to Shawnee Town on White Eagle's horse. She must leave the same way. I have no horses to spare."

If the reply disappointed White Eagle, he gave no sign of it. Willow smiled to herself as they left the chief. Mishewa was a strong animal. He could carry them both with ease, and riding double, she could keep her arms around White Eagle the whole way.

"This night you will stay in my mother's lodge," White Eagle said when they had walked a few paces from the council lodge. "We ride out at dawn." Then, almost as if he knew her thoughts, he put his hand under her chin and raised her face to his. "Then we will be together."

Willow nodded. "It will be as you say."

That night, Shining Star gave Willow a pair of fringed leggings to wear under her doeskin shift. They would make riding more comfortable and protect her legs from briers and brambles if she had to walk through underbrush. Willow thanked Shining Star, but she was even more grateful that White Eagle's mother seemed to have accepted Willow as her son's wife, no matter how reluctantly.

Just before dawn she stood at the lodge door with Shining Star and watched White Eagle approach, outlined in the morning light. Willow's heart swelled. It thrilled her to know that this handsome young warrior had promised to be her man for as long as the seasons turned for them both.

No longer in war paint, White Eagle wore a long cloth hunting shirt over his fringed leggings and breechclout. His hair was held out of his face by a scarlet headband, but hung loose about his shoulders.

"Are you ready?" he asked Willow.

"Yes." She stepped from the *wegiwa*, then turned to bow to Shining Star. "I thank White Eagle's mother."

The woman nodded. "May you journey safe."

White Eagle embraced his mother, then helped boost Willow onto the seat he'd fashioned from two folded blankets. Riding out of Shawnee Town behind White Eagle, Willow felt a surge of happiness. She imagined the look on Otter's face when he saw her fine husband, and smiled.

When they reached the trail, White Eagle turned to look at Willow as if to reassure himself that she was still there. "My father would like you," he said.

Other than his name and that he had been a warrior, Willow knew nothing about White Eagle's father. "Did the *Shemanese* kill Red Hawk?"

"Not with their rifles. A *Shemanese* trader gave him sickness that no medicine man could cure. My mother and I watched him die."

Willow was silent for a moment. Her own father

had been such a *Shemanese* trader. Even though her father had been dead for many years and could not have been the one who caused Red Hawk's death, White Eagle could have rejected Willow because of her white blood. Yet he had not.

She tightened the pressure of her arms around his waist and pressed her cheek against his back. "You knew your father. I did not know mine."

White Eagle glanced over his shoulder at her. "You never saw the *Shemanese* who fathered you?"

"No. My mother did not talk of him. Only lately have I known his name—Ee-an M'night."

"That *Shemanese* does not matter. You do not need him now."

Her heart lifted in exulation, but she spoke quietly. "I know. I am glad for it, my husband."

Truly, Willow thought, *White Eagle is the only man I will ever want.*

20

WACCACHALLA

Otter reached his village late in the afternoon, when most of the people were gathered around their lodges before the evening meal. Long before he saw anyone, the aroma of roasting meat wafted out to greet him. Anna smelled it, too, and realized that she hadn't eaten in a very long time. She hoped that Otter would at last allow her food and drink. He stopped on the edge of the village and dismounted, then lifted her from the horse. His gestures explained that he was going to remove her gag, but she must remain quiet.

When he looked at her questioningly, Anna nodded that she understood. *I don't know who he thinks I'd talk to or what I would say,* she thought. Unless someone in the village spoke better English than she did Shawnee, it wouldn't matter what she said—no one would understand her.

Anna gestured that she wanted her hands untied, but Otter shook his head and gave her a push on the shoulder to make her start walking. Along with her fear, Anna also felt a certain amount of anticipation. Despite the unfortunate circumstances that had brought her there, her lifelong desire to see an Indian village was about to be realized.

She didn't have much time to observe, however. As soon as the first villager spotted them, she and Otter became the center of attention. A large group thronged close to them—it seemed to Anna that it must be every man, woman, and child in the place. The women chattered in animated excitement, and many called her "Willow," as Otter had. With his hand on her shoulder he continued to nudge her forward, as he waved away the crowd. He was silent, although Anna thought he looked very much as if he wanted to make a speech. The crowd began to step back, giving them room to proceed.

Soon Anna realized that they were heading toward the largest building in the village, which she guessed belonged to the chief. *I will soon find out what is to be done with me.* Her throat suddenly felt dry.

Anna had tried to remain calm as her captor had led her through the woods, so as not to rile him, and to think of any means of escape. Now that she was truly a captive in an Indian village, the full terror of her situation hit her. Would she be tortured and killed? Would she be held captive, or married to this man, or another Indian warrior? Would she ever see her father again— or Stuart? Her heart lurched at this last thought, but she did not allow herself to cry. She was determined to maintain her dignity, despite her desperate circumstances.

The lodge was a shaky-looking building with a

wooden frame, partially covered with skins. Otter stopped at the entrance and said something to the others that caused them to turn away in obvious disappointment.

Otter must be fairly important, Anna thought, and as she stepped into the dim, smoky interior, she straightened her spine and tried to keep a calm expression on her face. She hoped to make as good an impression as possible.

Otter bowed to an older man who sat in a chair that appeared to have been carved in one piece from a single huge tree trunk. The man stared at Anna for a long moment before he gestured to her to come forward.

"Black Snake," Otter said.

Anna didn't know what she was supposed to do, so she merely stood before the chief. Miss Martin hadn't instructed her charges in the proper etiquette of being an Indian captive. *Stuart's aunt would swoon dead away if she could see me now.* The ludicrous thought momentarily lifted Anna's spirits.

Black Snake addressed her in the same guttural language that Otter had used. Again, the only word she understood was "Willow." When she made no response to him, the chief looked bewildered. He turned to Otter, and the two spoke at length. Anna presumed that her captor was telling the chief how he had caught her, probably also making himself appear brave and heroic.

Finally the chief stood and approached Anna. He put out his hand and touched her hair, then he fingered the material of her skirt.

I must look terrible, Anna thought. The dress that she had put on that morning had been torn in several places during her escape attempt. The briers that had ripped her dress had also scratched her face and arms. She had long since lost her bonnet, and her uncombed hair fell into her face. With her hands tied behind her, Anna was powerless to brush it back.

The chief's silent inspection continued for a few moments before he beckoned to a young girl Anna hadn't noticed before, who appeared to be twelve or thirteen. He spoke to her briefly, and she nodded and left the lodge.

Black Snake resumed his seat and spoke sharply to Otter. From his tone, Anna guessed that the chief was upbraiding him. *Because he brought me here?* she wondered.

Otter pointed to Anna, to himself and Black Snake, then back to her as he seemed to defend himself from some charge. When he finished, Otter folded his arms across his chest and stood with his head slightly inclined, as if waiting for the chief to make some sort of decision.

The girl Black Snake had sent out returned, carefully holding a plain doeskin shift over her outstretched arms. She handed it to the chief, who with great ceremony stepped down from his chair and held it out, seemingly as an offering to Anna.

Anna found her situation so ludicrous that she almost laughed. She gathered that the chief meant for to accept the robe, but how could she, with her hands still tied?

Quickly Otter realized the situation and unbound

Anna. She rubbed her chafed wrists, then attempted to extend her arms to take the robe from Chief Black Snake. But her cramped muscles trembled from the slight exertion. She lacked the strength to hold even such a light burden.

Black Snake said something else Otter didn't seem to like, then he handed the robe back to the young girl who had brought it. From his gestures, Anna guessed he meant she should take Anna with her and leave.

The chief's fierce scowl immediately quieted Otter. Chastened, he could only stand and watch the young girl take Anna's hand and lead her from the lodge.

Anna felt an overwhelming sense of relief to be away from her captor. From the way the chief looked at him, Anna doubted that bringing her there had earned him any reward.

Maybe the chief will just let me go back home, she thought. The prospect, however unlikely, gave Anna at least some glimmer of hope.

Many of the villagers had remained near the lodge, waiting to see what would happen when Black Snake met this girl who could be Willow. When they saw her leave the lodge accompanied by his daughter, Blossom, and gifted with a doeskin robe, they looked at one another in wonder.

"How comes this Willow back, alone and in a *She-manese* dress?" one asked.

"That girl looks something like Willow, but she is not," another said.

"Perhaps Black Snake gives her to Otter," murmured Little Turtle.

While they spoke, everyone watched to see where Blossom would take this strangely dressed girl. The whole village knew that Otter had brought a deer to Willow's lodge, only to find that the girl and her old mother had left Waccachalla on some mysterious errand. Many thought that Bear's Daughter had deliberately taken Willow away because she thought her too good to be Otter's wife. Others believed that Bear's Daughter had long planned that journey and meant no offense to Otter in making it when she did. In any case, the situation had furnished the women with much to discuss. Now all waited to see what would happen.

Among the most interested was Gray Fawn, Otter's sister. She did not blame her brother for wanting to have sons, nor for seeking out a likely young girl to bear them for him. However, Gray Fawn never trusted the one called Willow, who did not look or act like the other village girls. Her heart had been glad when Otter's effort to bring Willow into his lodge had failed.

Gray Fawn had been almost relieved when Otter went raiding with the other warriors. She hoped that when he came back, he would have forgotten Willow. Then he could marry someone like Green Briar, the plain daughter of a respected warrior in a nearby village.

Gray Fawn sighed. Now she scarcely knew what to think. It was hard to stand in the door of her *wegiwa* and wait with her daughters to see if Blossom would bring this girl to her. She turned away, unable to watch any longer.

Stretching Cat, the eldest daughter, took her mother's place in the doorway. "They still come this way," she reported.

Gray Fawn put her hands to her ears. "I do not want to hear it."

"No, look—now they turn aside."

Gray Fawn looked up in time to see Blossom take the girl into the chief's *wegiwa*.

"Ayee, such a thing as this has not happened before," Gray Fawn murmured. "Surely Black Snake does not mean to take her as another wife."

"Bear's Daughter and Willow have not returned. Perhaps the chief means for this girl to take the other one's place."

Without comment, Gray Fawn looked toward the *msi-kah-mi-qui*, and saw Otter and Chief Black Snake emerge from the lodge. The two men stopped at the firestone in the center of the village, where the chief raised his hands to signal to the villagers that he was about to speak.

"Let us go hear his words, my mother," said Stretching Cat.

Gray Fawn shook her head. "Take your sisters with you if you like. I stay here."

"Come see your uncle, little ones," Stretching Cat said, and the two younger girls followed her.

Gray Fawn listened from her doorway.

"People of Waccachalla, this is a strange day," Black Snake began. "Otter tells of a great battle with the *Shemanese*. Soon the warriors that crossed the O-hio-se-pe return." A murmur ran through the crowd, then stopped when the chief spoke again. "All your eyes saw the girl that Otter brings from the Kan-tuck-e. She looks much like our Willow who went away with my kinswoman, Bear's Daughter. Yet this one does not speak our tongue or understand us." Another murmur rippled among the villagers, until Black Snake raised his arms for quiet. "For now, she stays in my lodge. Know this—none will harm her."

When the chief finished speaking, he beckoned to Sits-in-Shadow, the medicine man. Clearly enjoying the attention, the medicine man noisily cleared his throat before he spoke.

"People of Waccachalla, much is to be done. When our warriors return, we will make a feast of rejoicing. Prepare for these things."

Gray Fawn hadn't caught every word, but she understood at least one thing. Even though Otter had brought both this girl who looked like Willow, and the first news of the other warriors, Black Snake hadn't let him speak of those things himself. That was not a good sign.

Anna lay on a bed of fragrant hemlock branches in what seemed to be the chief's home, called a *wegiwa*. She had eaten some stew, not unlike what her stepmother made at Bryan's Station, and had been given some sort of herbal tea to drink. Now, weary but comfortable under the cover of a soft blanket, Anna tried to sort out her feelings.

Everyone in the village, including the chief, had seemed almost afraid of her, especially when they realized that she did not speak or understand their language. Anna didn't think she resembled these people at all, especially the way she was dressed. Yet even her captor, who knew she lived in a white settlement, had seemed surprised that Anna didn't speak his language.

Still, she had been treated well, at least so far. As soon as Anna reached the chief's *wegiwa*, a woman Anna presumed to be his wife and the girl's mother had removed Anna's torn dress and replaced it with the soft shift the chief gave her.

As its folds settled around her, Anna's skin had tingled with a strange sensation. Never before had she touched an Indian garment, yet the moment this shift touched her, Anna experienced something like a sense of rightness, of homecoming.

My mother wore clothing like this. The conflicting emotions Anna often experienced when she thought of the mother she'd never known had overcome her.

Indians don't show their emotions, but that doesn't mean they don't feel deeply. Her father had told Anna so, but at least in that respect, Anna had never been like her mother. More often than not, her face betrayed her feelings even before she acknowledged them herself.

In the chief's *wegiwa*, Anna knew she must do nothing to make it appear that his gift had displeased her, so she had blinked back her tears. She stroked her new doeskin dress and smiled. The girl had smiled back, while her mother had merely inclined her head slightly.

Later the chief's wife showed Anna where she would sleep. She was thankful that Black Snake had allowed her to stay in his own lodge with his wife and daughter, instead of giving her to the man who had brought her there. Anna did not feel so frightened as she pondered what might happen to her. So far no harm had come to her. Once she had been separated from Otter, these Indian villagers had treated her well—almost like an honored guest, Anna thought. The realization filled her with hope that she would be allowed to return to Bryan's Station.

I wish I understood their language. That thought reminded Anna of her Latin teacher—Stuart, from whom she had learned much more than Latin. Although she was separated physically from him, Stuart Martin was never absent from her mind and heart for very long. He might be arriving in Bryan's Station even now, she thought. She imagined his surprise and dismay that she wasn't there to greet him. But he would be there when she returned, she thought with confidence, ready to be with and protect her the rest of their lives.

Anna sighed. As bright as that prospect seemed, for the foreseeable future, at least, she had only herself to depend upon.

21

Kanawha Trail

"We stop here," White Eagle said at midafternoon.

Willow had expected to travel until sunset, but made no reply as he turned from the trail, through dense underbrush into a hidden clearing beside a quiet stream.

She spread their wedding blanket on the ground while White Eagle unsaddled Mishewa and tied him a few yards away, between the glen and the trail.

"If anyone comes near, Mishewa will let us know."

Suddenly shy, Willow ducked her head and turned away. "I will gather firewood."

White Eagle put out a staying hand. "We have no need of a fire."

From the intense look he gave her, Willow didn't have to ask what he meant. She knew that when a man took a wife, certain things passed between them. Unfortunately, she had no clear idea of exactly what those things included. Willow remembered what Bear's Daughter had said to her when her moon-cycles began.

"Your body will be ready to bear children when you take a husband."

"How does this thing happen?" Willow had asked.

"Your man will lie with you. His seed will fill your belly."

Willow had felt more puzzled than enlightened. "Where does this seed come from, my mother?"

"A man carries it inside himself."

"How does it get out to fill his wife's belly?"

Bear's Daughter sighed. "I have already said too much. When it is time, you will know of it."

Bear's Daughter had never again spoken of the matter, but since then, Willow had learned a few things for herself. She knew that a man kept his seed-planter under his breechclout. She had felt a hardness there in the young warriors who had pressed their bodies against hers during the last Corn Dance. Sometimes, although she was careful not to show it, Willow had felt a strange stirring, a desire to press back, to prolong and deepen the contact between herself and them. Then, some weeks ago while gathering herbs deep in the forest at dawn, she had almost stumbled over a naked couple, twined together in sleep on a bed of pine needles. Although she immediately averted her eyes, Willow had seen enough to make her wonder even more.

Yet Willow sensed that nothing she had previously seen or heard or experienced could have prepared her for this moment, when her husband's arms closed around her and his mouth fastened hungrily on hers. She wanted to respond in the same way, but when she thought she heard a twig snap, she pulled away, wary lest someone should come upon them.

"The sun is yet high," she said against his shoulder.

Although she had been unsure what would actually happen between them, Willow had presumed that their first coupling would take place in the dark privacy of their own lodge, not outside in the open sunlight.

White Eagle drew back and looked at her intently. "Its light helps me see you better. You have beautiful hair," he murmured, stroking it. "Your eyes are like a doe's." He kissed both her eyelids, then framed her face in his hands. "Your skin is the color of ripe grain." His voice seemed hoarse, his breathing more rapid. "Your lips are sweeter than berries," he said, and once more tasted them.

Willow stood still, uncertain of what White Eagle expected of her. Even as he spoke words of praise, she could not be sure he meant them. Men often uttered extravagant compliments during Corn Dances; but even then, the warriors who had pressed their bodies close to hers had never said such things of her. She had thought it was because her hair was not as black nor her skin as tawny as the other maidens. Now, as her husband embraced her again, Willow tried to remember some of the words the maidens spoke to their men, but she could not. Instead, she spoke what was in her heart.

"You are a brave warrior," she said against his chest. "Your body is strong. Inside your arms, I feel safe." She lifted her head and looked boldly into his eyes. "Your touch pleases me, my husband."

"So do your words please me." He touched his fingertips to his mouth, then laid them on her lips. "I am your man. I will keep you safe."

He took a step back and pulled off his hunting shirt, revealing his muscular bare torso. Slowly but deliberately he unlaced the top of her shift, which began to slip from her shoulders. She shivered, although the day was warm. Instinctively she put her hands on the garment, arresting its further slide down.

He pressed close to her, his bare chest radiating a heat not born of the summer day. "I would see your body," he whispered.

His words expressed his yearning, and in this, she would do his will. With her eyes fastened on his face, she slowly lowered the shift until it dropped to the ground. She stood before him, naked save for her knee-high buckskin leggings, anxious only that her body might not displease him.

The late afternoon sun slanted into the glade, gilding their bodies and outlining each line and curve. For the space of a heartbeat, White Eagle stared at Willow. She read the admiration and hunger in his eyes and realized the growing need she felt for her body to press against his.

He made a noise low in his throat, and she thought he was about to speak. Instead, White Eagle took her hands and pressed them briefly against the swell of his breechclout, then he swept her into his arms again. She felt a warm glow where their bare flesh met, and shivered in surprise when he parted her lips with his tongue. While one arm still circled her waist, half supporting her, his free hand began to explore her body. She closed her eyes and rested her head against his shoulder. She gave herself over to the pleasurable prickling of her skin where he touched her face, her arms, her neck. When his hand found her breasts, she felt a thrill of surprise that his light touch could so harden her nipples. They tingled and strained against his hand, and her whole body ached to be caressed. Palm down, his hand stroked her flat belly, then cupped the softness of the mound between her legs. She gasped and pushed herself into the unexpected hardness of his hand as he continued to fondle her. Savoring his touch and feeling a need to return it, she put one hand around his neck to steady herself. With the other, she rubbed his chest and taut stomach.

He wrapped his hands around Willow's buttocks and pulled her against the center of his growing hardness. His mouth moved over her breasts, and his tongue circled her taut nipples, dropping to lave her belly, until her head fell back and she sighed with pleasure. His touch traveled over her entire body and produced sensations she had never even imagined, much less known.

"Come, my love," he whispered. Effortlessly he picked her up and carried her to the waiting wedding blanket. Gently he laid her down, then knelt beside her. His hands stroked her face, and he buried his face in her breasts, murmuring endearments.

When he touched her inner thighs, she opened her eyes and gazed into her husband's face as if seeking reassurance. "I have not been with a man before."

"I am glad of it."

His hair brushed her face. She shut her eyes as he leaned down to kiss her, then she felt him move away. She opened her eyes again just as he reached down to remove his breechclout. She caught only a fleeting glimpse of the naked hardness she had only felt before as he lowered his body to hers.

"I will be careful. It will not hurt long."

Her ears heard but her mind did not understand his words. What hurt could there be in this pleasure, when her whole body vibrated with love for him and longed for his caresses?

Gently his knee urged her legs apart while his fingers found the tender wetness of her womanhood. He lowered his body to hers and slowly began to enter her. She gasped and stiffened involuntarily at the unexpected stab of pain. He pulled back for a moment, his eyes searching hers.

"Do you want me to stop?"

Willow shook her head, ashamed she had cried out. Her pain had already faded; it was far less important than the need she felt to finish what they had begun. She put her arms around him and pulled him close. Her body strained upward to meet his, then began to pulse with a rhythm she felt in her blood.

Feeling alternately numb and vitally alive, she forgot her discomfort as he swelled inside her. Every part of her body longed for the release that she sensed his body could give her. Nothing else existed except the two of them, working together to express their shared love. Breathlessly they moved, slowly at first, then faster and faster until, hearts beating as one, they both found that sweet agony their bodies sought.

"I love you," she whispered at the moment of her man's jubilant cry.

"Now you are truly mine," White Eagle said when his breath returned.

"And I am yours, my husband," she whispered.

They lay together side by side, drowsily content. As if from a long way off, Willow heard the sound of the nearby stream, and somewhere a mourning dove called to its mate.

Even though it could bring bad luck to say such a thing, Willow wanted to tell her husband that never had she felt so complete or happy. When, unaccountably, she shivered in the cooling evening breeze, White Eagle held her even closer and kissed her cheek. She looked up at him and laughed.

"What do you find funny?" he asked.

Willow smiled. "I did not know what a fine thing this seed-planting could be."

22

KANAWHA TRAIL

"The sun is already high. We must be on our way," White Eagle said the next morning.

They had bathed in the stream, at first playing like children, then coupling again in the shallow water. Willow looked around the peaceful glen where they had shared their love, and sighed.

"I do not want to go."

Her husband put a comforting arm around her waist and pressed his hand to her heart. "This place will always be with us here."

"I would have you to myself a while longer, my husband."

"It cannot be so. I go to saddle Mishewa."

Willow's heart already ached with the burden of their parting. He would take her to Waccachalla, as he had promised. But once the mourning and feasting were done, Willow knew that her man would put on war paint once more. In these troubled times, his people—who were now hers as well—needed all their warriors.

Reluctantly Willow folded the still-damp wedding blanket on which they had coupled, first in the afternoon and again sometime in the night. Their second was better than the first, and when they had joined in the water this morning, she could imagine no greater ecstasy. Dipping the blanket in the creek had removed the pink stain that proved she was no longer a maiden. The not unpleasant ache in her loins was another such proof.

Bear's Daughter did not tell me these things about this seed-planting, she thought. Was it possible that her mother could have felt about the *Shemanese* man who had fathered her as Willow did about White Eagle? She knew a sudden stab of sorrow that she could not speak with her mother about her new joy. She wished Bear's Daughter could know how deeply she already loved her new husband. *You did well in choosing White Eagle for me, my mother.*

White Eagle returned with Mishewa, and Willow raised her face for another kiss. As they left, Willow took a long, last look at the glen in which she and White Eagle had truly become one. *I will never forget this place,* she vowed.

They traveled on as before. Willow rode behind White Eagle with her arms lightly circling his narrow waist and her head resting on his broad back. They had not been on the trail long when Willow felt her husband suddenly tense.

"Listen—riders come this way."

He slowed his horse, and from a small rise in the trail, Willow saw two *Shemanese* approaching from the south, so close that she could tell they held rifles at the ready.

"Stop!" one of the men cried. It was one of the few English words Willow understood, but either White Eagle didn't know its meaning, or he chose not to obey. He kicked Mishewa's flanks and jerked the reins sharply to the right in an effort to gain cover. Almost immediately one of the *Shemanese* fired his rifle, and Mishewa reared at the unexpected sound.

White Eagle's horse is used to the noise of battle. He shouldn't do this, Willow thought, even as she felt herself losing her balance. Desperately she grabbed at White Eagle, but it was too late. Seeing that she would fall, Willow went limp, protected her head with her arms, and rolled as she hit the ground.

White Eagle called to her over the shouts and gunfire. "Run and hide! Hurry!"

Without looking back, Willow struggled to her feet and plunged through the underbrush next to the trail. As she ran, she heard gunfire for a time, then nothing except her own labored breathing. She kept on for a few hundred more paces, but finally exhaustion forced her to drop to the ground behind a fallen tree. She strained to hear what might be happening on the trail. Warily she watched for a sign that she had been followed, but saw none. Still, she concealed herself until she judged that sufficient time had passed, then left her hiding place and started back to the trail, not retracing her steps but walking at some distance parallel to them.

The nearer Willow got to the place where she had last seen White Eagle, the more apprehensive she became. She wanted to call out his name, but she feared that the *Shemanese* might be lying in ambush. Just before she reached the spot where Mishewa had thrown her, Willow stopped and listened again. Hearing nothing more than the usual forest sounds, she stepped back onto the trail.

She and the white man saw each other at almost the same moment, and each reacted immediately. Willow turned and fled back into the underbrush, and the man jumped down from his horse and pursued her.

"Anna! Stop!"

Closer and closer the man came. Breathless, in desperation, Willow turned back toward the trail, then ran north, paralleling it. She thought she had lost her pursuer until she felt the ground shake beneath his running feet and heard his harsh breathing as he rapidly closed the distance between them. Soon the *Shemanese* would reach her, and she was helpless to defend herself. When he found her, surely he would kill her. *How will he do it?* she wondered. Perhaps he would shoot her. Or, more likely, he'd save his shot and powder and use his rifle butt on her skull.

He grew closer, and she gasped for air. She plunged into the underbrush, hoping the briers that tore at her leggings and scratched her hands would slow her pursuer. Willow thought of White Eagle. *No matter what happens to me, may the Great Spirit protect my husband.*

She turned her head to see if the *Shemanese* still followed, and her moccasin caught in a trailing vine. She lost her balance and pitched forward, unable to avoid the fallen log and rock outcropping that rushed up to meet her.

Willow's head hit something hard. She heard a dull thud and knew a sudden jolt of pain. She felt her senses grow faint.

"Anna Willow! Why do ye run from me, child?"

Dimly hearing her name amidst the strange *She-manese* words, Willow tried to open her eyes. Through a thick haze she saw that the white man who knelt beside her had fierce blue eyes and a strange red beard, grizzled, like an old bear's, and wiry white hair.

He spoke again, but his voice seemed to come from far away. Her ears roared, and her head ached. She shut her eyes, and strange lights flashed behind her closed lids. *I do not want to die here in this place, with none to sing the Death Song for me.*

It was her last conscious thought for a long time.

When James Craig and Ian McKnight had crossed the Ohio River in search of Anna Willow, they knew the danger of their mission. They were bound for a Delaware village where Ian had often enlisted the chief's aid. Word of a white captive would spread from village to village, and once Ian and his friends knew where Anna Willow was, they could devise a plan to get her back, perhaps by paying a ransom. They sought no confrontation, but rode with rifles primed and ready to fire should the need arise.

They had traveled a long way without encountering anyone else, but shortly before midday, Ian had signaled James to stop.

"Someone is riding this way," he said.

"I don't hear nothin'—" James Craig started to say, then stopped as a Shawnee topped a slight rise and came into view.

"He's not in war paint, and there's a woman with

him," James said. "Likely he'll leave us alone."

"Maybe he can tell us something. We'll parley with him," Ian said, and called out for the man to stop.

Instead, the Indian jerked his horse's reins, and when the animal wheeled to one side, Ian had a clear view of the woman who rode with him. Her braided hair and garb were Indian, but there was no mistaking her features, as familiar as his own.

"Stop him! He's got Anna Willow!" Ian cried out.

In the confusion that followed, James Craig fired his rifle, the Indian's horse reared and ran into the underbrush, and Ian lost sight of his daughter after she tumbled from the horse's back.

James Craig rode after the Shawnee, while Ian hastily secured his horse and went in search of Anna Willow. He entered the underbrush at the point where he had last seen her, and called her name repeatedly, but there was no answer.

Had she been knocked unconscious in the fall, he would have come upon her by now. Perhaps the Indian had somehow managed to recapture her. *She must have panicked*, Ian thought. Otherwise, why would she not answer him?

He returned to the trail, thinking that Anna would soon realize it was safe to come out of the under-brush. Finally she did, and his heart swelled with relief when he spotted her. Yet as soon as she saw him she turned and fled into the wilderness. Even as he called to her to stop, Ian resumed the chase. Winded and doubled in pain from the wound in his side, he pressed on. When she entered a thicket, he followed. She turned her head and looked at Ian as if she didn't recognize him. With her attention thus diverted, she tripped and fell heavily, landing against a rock outcropping.

"Anna Willow! Why do ye run from me, child?"

She had opened her eyes briefly and looked at him. He thought she wanted to speak, but lacked the breath. Then she lost consciousness.

Ian had stood and whistled through his fingers to signal James Craig, who joined him a moment later. "The Indian got away, but I see you found your daughter."

"Yes, but she's hurt."

James peered closely at the limp young woman. "I wouldn't a-known the girl in that Indian garb. What happened to her?"

"She fell off the Indian's horse, and then she tripped and hit her head against that rock. The skin's not broken. The lass will soon come to herself."

"We can't stay here, Colonel. Likely the savage that took her has already gone for help."

"Aye. We must go now and ride fast."

With the girl they called Anna secured to the saddle behind Ian, he and James Craig rode away at a gallop, every hoofbeat taking them farther south, away from all that the one named Willow knew, and the man she held dear.

Thanks to his quick reaction and his fast horse, White Eagle had escaped death at the hands of the *Shemanese,* but one of their bullets had passed through his thigh. When he dismounted to tie off the bleeding, as he knew he must, White Eagle hadn't taken time to secure Mishewa's reins. When the *Shemanese* sent another volley of rifle fire thundering into the woods, the horse had bolted and run away. By the time White Eagle had tended his wound, found Mishewa, and returned to the place of the *Shemanese* ambuscade, the white men—and Willow—had vanished.

Clinging desperately to the hope that she had come to no harm at the hands of the white men, White Eagle thought that perhaps she was hiding nearby. He called out Willow's name, but the raucous screeching of a blue jay was his only answer. Returning to where Willow had fallen from his horse, White Eagle found her footprints and followed them. He saw a place where she had stopped, then stretched out behind a log before taking another direction back toward the trail. *She did the right thing,* White Eagle thought, but when her footprints crossed those made by a *Shemanese* boot, he knew it had not been enough.

With growing trepidation, White Eagle noted the evidence that the *Shemanese* had put Willow on one of their horses and turned back south. No blood stained the earth, and for that White Eagle felt relief. So far, it appeared that the *Shemanese* had not harmed Willow.

Grimacing with pain from his leg wound, White Eagle mounted his horse and followed the fresh tracks of two horses making for the O-hio-se-pe. The depth of the hoof prints told him they rode fast. Near Raven Rock they had left the trail and veered off to the right onto an old deer trace. It was what White Eagle expected: *Shemanese* would not risk crossing the river at Raven Rock, where the Shawnee kept an almost constant lookout.

White Eagle reined in his horse and considered what he should do. His heart wanted to continue to trail them, but he knew it would be a foolish gesture. The *Shemanese* had such a head start that they were likely already on the other side. Even a warrior in top condition would hesitate to cross the river in lone pursuit of armed *Shemanese*. For him, light-headed from pain and loss of blood, it would be suicide.

Reluctantly White Eagle turned his horse to the northwest. He would stop at Chillicothe, the nearest village. The medicine man could bind his wounds. Then he would go on to Waccachalla, now much nearer than his own home village. Black Snake would be told what had happened to his kinswomen.

Many willing warriors will cross the O-hio-se-pe with me, he thought. He would find Willow, even if he had to go to every *Shemanese* station in the Kan-tuck-e.

23

BRYAN'S STATION

By riding hard and stopping infrequently, Ian Mc-Knight and James Craig reached Bryan's Station late that night. Most of the Station's residents slept, and it took several hails to raise the lookout.

The man who opened the gate smiled widely when he saw the girl with Ian. "I'm right glad to see you, Colonel. Everybody in the Station was some worried about you."

"Has aught happened since we left?" Ian asked.

"Nay, Colonel. Perhaps the savages will leave us be for a spell."

"Aye, but I doubt that we've seen the last of them."

Ian dismounted and turned to help the girl. She had opened her eyes from time to time during the journey, but she had not spoken and still seemed dazed. When he set her on the ground, her knees buckled. Ignoring the pain in his side, he picked her up.

"I'll see to your horse, Colonel," offered James Craig.

"Thank ye—and thanks for going with me," Ian said.

The commotion of their homecoming awakened many of the Station's residents, still on edge from the recent siege. Faces peered from several open doors as Ian walked past, carrying what appeared to be an Indian woman.

"What's goin' on?" a sleepy voice inquired.

"Go back to your beds. 'Tis only Ian McKnight, safely back from across the river."

Ian's own door was barred shut from the inside. He had to knock loudly several times to rouse Rebecca.

Finally she slid back the wooden bar and opened the door. "Oh, you found Anna! God be praised!" she cried.

"The girl's been hurt," he said.

"I'll make a light and get her pallet."

Rebecca thrust a long twig into the fireplace coals and touched it to a stubby candle-end, then pulled Anna's bedding from the lean-to. In the wavering candlelight, the girl's features certainly looked like Anna's. The way she was dressed, however, made her appear more Indian than white.

"I see that the savages wasted no time putting their garb on her," Rebecca said. Quickly she examined the knot on the girl's head and noted that other than a few scratches, she had no injuries. Rebecca put her hand to the pulse in the girl's neck and was pleased by its steady throb. "That's a bad lick she took on her head, but otherwise she seems well."

Ian described how she received her injury. "I'm most worried that Anna Willow doesn't seem to know who I am."

The girl's eyes opened, and she moaned. Immediately Ian knelt beside the pallet and took her hand. "Ye're safe at home now," he told her. "Ye maun rest."

"'Tis good to have you back, Anna Willow," said Rebecca.

The girl slipped her hand from Ian's and looked puzzled. "Willow?" she repeated.

Rebecca and Ian exchanged a worried glance. "'Tis your name—Anna Willow McKnight," Ian said.

The girl raised her chin in a familiar gesture, but the strange words she uttered and the voice that spoke them were not Anna's. The only thing she said that Rebecca understood was "Willow."

"What did she say?" Rebecca asked.

Ian looked bewildered. "I'm not sure, but it was Shawnee talk." A faint uneasiness began to prickle him. How could this be his daughter—but how could it not?

His suspicion grew when the girl spoke again—this girl was not Anna. Ian thought that she asked him about the man she had been with. Being more fluent in Delaware, he replied in that tongue. He told her he knew nothing about her companion, then he asked her name. *"Auween khackev?"*

She frowned slightly, then said, *"N'hackney Willow."*

"Her name is Willow," Ian said.

"How strange! Ask her where she comes from," Rebecca said.

"Takoom?"

"Otennink noom Scioto-se-pe."

"She says she lives near the Scioto River," Ian translated.

The girl who called herself Willow looked at Ian and spoke slowly, as if reciting from rote. "My fath-er Ee-an M'night."

Rebecca gasped. "This girl thinks you are her father!"

"I don't understand it myself." Ian turned to the girl and pointed to his chest. "*N'hackney* Ian McKnight."

Her eyes darkened and she shook her head. "Ee-an M'night *nepwa*."

"She says I am dead." Ian again said he was "Ee-an M'night," but her eyes told him she didn't believe it. "What is your mother called?" he asked in Delaware.

"Bear's Daughter—*nepwa*."

"I know that name, but Bear's Daughter cannot be this one's mother."

The girl who called herself Willow moaned softly, and her eyes closed.

"She's just fainted again," Rebecca said at Ian's look of concern. "Leave her be. She needs to sleep. By mornin', she should be much better."

Ian passed a shaking hand over his brow and sighed. "This Willow is a puzzle."

Rebecca looked thoughtful. "Anna Willow's mother was a Delaware named Silverwillow, wasn't she?"

"Aye."

"Since this girl claims you're her father, perhaps you forgot to mention you had another Indian wife named Bear's Daughter?"

Ian smiled faintly at his wife's tone. "Nay, Silverwillow was my only wife before ye. Bear's Daughter raised Silverwillow after her parents died. She was also the midwife who put Anna Willow into my arms after my wife died birthing her." His thoughts went back to that time, and his face turned ashen as he began to realize the truth.

Rebecca looked questioningly at Ian. "Then how could you be this girl's father, too?"

"Silverwillow's belly grew large. I did not suspect that she carried more than one babe, but in those days I understood nothing of such things. Bear's Daughter loved Silverwillow like her own flesh—" Ian stopped, overcome with emotion.

Rebecca nodded. "I think I understand what happened. Silverwillow probably gave birth to twin girls. Bear's Daughter must have kept one of them—and named her Willow after her mother."

Ian nodded. "Aye, that could be the way of it. I took Anna Willow to my sister when she was only days old. I never saw Bear's Daughter again. Some time later I heard that she had gone to live with some of her Shawnee kin near the Scioto."

His expression grew grim. "If I had sought out Bear's Daughter then, I'd have seen that Anna Willow had a twin sister."

Rebecca touched her fingertips to his lips. "Hush. You can't blame yourself for what happened. We'll talk more about this tomorrow. The girl is asleep, and you must rest yourself."

When Rebecca put out the candle, Ian took her into his arms and kissed her. "I thank ye, ma'am," he said huskily.

Rebecca half smiled in the darkness. "For what?"

"For marryin' me. And for lettin' me go and do what I must."

Rebecca said nothing, but she knew that Ian Mc-Knight would never be satisfied until his Anna Willow was safely back at Bryan's Station. She had no doubt that her husband would once more cross the Ohio and put himself in harm's way to find the girl.

Don't go, Ian. Soon you'll have another child to think about, perhaps a son to carry on your name. Stay here and take care of your wife.

Rebecca had rehearsed the words she would say in case Ian returned without Anna. Now that it had happened, however, the speech stuck in her throat. She would not pit Ian's unborn child against his missing daughter.

Her husband would do what he must, and she must allow it.

Anna awoke after her first night in Waccachalla to find Blossom sitting cross-legged beside her, apparently waiting for her to awaken. Anna's muscles protested as she stretched, then sat up.

The girl pointed to a wooden bowl filled with dew-dampened berries, then to Anna. She put out her hand and pretended to bring berries to her mouth. *"Oui-then-eluh."*

"Eat?" Anna asked.

The girl nodded, pleased. *"Oui-sah."* She handed Anna a gourd filled with cool spring water. *"Nipe."*

Obediently Anna repeated the word, then added "water."

"Wat-eh?" Blossom repeated, and seemed pleased when Anna nodded.

As long as I'm here, I might as well learn their language, Anna thought.

Blossom seemed to understand Anna's intention. While Anna ate, she patiently repeated the Shawnee names for the various objects that Anna pointed out. In return, Blossom signaled that she wanted to know Anna's names for everything, beginning with herself. Anna decided to drop the "Willow," which only confused everyone, and the "McKnight," which they had trouble saying.

As a result, Blossom told the steady stream of visitors who came to the chief's *wegiwa* that their strange visitor was named "An-na." Most stared at her in wonder, as if they had never seen anything like her. A few attempted to converse with Anna, first in one language and then another. Some knew a few English words, but no one knew enough to conduct a meaningful conversation.

By midafternoon, Anna's effort to communicate had taken its toll, and she felt relieved when Blossom closed the skin door of the *wegiwa* to further visitors. Anna had just settled down to rest when she heard distant shouts.

Obviously excited, Blossom looked outside, then turned to Anna. *"Nenothtu,"* she said.

The warriors must be coming back, Anna thought. Her captor had been alone when he took her from Bryan's Station, but undoubtedly he hadn't gone there by himself.

Curious, Anna stood at the door and looked at the

half-dozen men who rode into the clearing. Time, sweat, and their exertions had taken a toll on their war paint, and they were obviously tired. However, they circled the village in a show of energy, yelling and brandishing tomahawks, war clubs, and rifles.

Blossom signed to Anna that the warriors would first go to the *msi-kah-mi-qui,* and she watched them head in the direction of the chief's lodge. They stayed inside briefly; and then, instead of joining their waiting families as Anna expected, the men came from the *msi-kah-mi-qui* and went toward the creek and the steam house.

There they will be ritually cleansed, Anna thought, then immediately wondered why she had known so. Something her father had said, perhaps; Ian McKnight had told Anna many things about Indian life. Even in the brief time she had been in Waccachalla, Anna had already seen much to remind her of the stories she'd heard, from him and others, about Indian ways.

For years she had wondered about her mother's life as a Delaware Indian. Even though her captor had made it clear to Anna that he was Shawnee, and Waccachalla was a Shawnee village, she thought their lives and customs must be similar. However, Anna would certainly not have chosen this captivity as a means to learn about Indian ways.

By signs and gestures, Blossom made Anna understand that, since one warrior had not returned from across the river, there would be a general mourning. But even if she hadn't been forewarned, when she heard the first notes of the Death Song, Anna would have recognized its purpose.

Those sounds of grief come from their very hearts, she thought. In that regard, at least, Indians and whites were the same.

Willow struggled awake, at first aware only that it was still dark and that her head throbbed painfully. Every sense told her she was in an unfamiliar place. Instead of the buffalo robes and animal skins that had made her bed in the lodge of Bear's Daughter, or the wedding blanket she had shared with White Eagle, Willow now lay on a too soft feather-stuffed pallet.

White Eagle. Was it only a sleep ago that they had loved and slept under the open sky, waking only to love again?

Through the hurt and confusion in her head, Willow tried to sort out all that had occurred. She remembered riding with White Eagle until they were stopped by the *Shemanese*. Then the one who called himself Ee'an M'night had taken her away from White Eagle and brought her to this place. Bear's Daughter had told her that her father was dead, and Willow had no reason to doubt it. Could her mother have been mistaken? Or could two *Shemanese* have the same name?

Willow put that puzzle from her mind to consider a more important one. *What has happened to White Eagle?* They had shared their love for a pitifully short time. Now Willow feared that her husband might be dead, killed by the same *Shemanese* who had brought her to this awful place, or lying hurt and alone. No warrior should die unmourned. Tears of sorrow stung her eyes and ran down her cheeks. Willow allowed herself to weep for a few moments before she drew a deep breath and wiped her eyes on her sleeve.

I must be strong. She had to believe that her man still lived and that they would be together again. *White Eagle lives and he will seek me. He is a brave and strong warrior, and he will do what he must so we can again lie together in peace.* Once more, they would take pleasure in their love, just as they had in the glen. She would think of that time. She would shed no more tears.

The next morning, the girl Ian had brought to the Station seemed to be recovering well from her head injury. Although she ate little of the mush Rebecca offered for her breakfast, she seemed more alert, and her eyes were clear. She seemed to like being called "Willow," and dutifully she repeated their names, "Ee-an" and "R'becca."

Willow seemed more comfortable seated on the floor, and there Ian spent several hours talking to her. Their only common language was Delaware, which Willow knew only slightly and Ian had to dredge from deep memory. They could exchange only the most basic information, and Willow seemed particularly unwilling to tell him any more about herself than he already knew. Ian believed that Willow finally accepted the fact that he was her father, but when he tried to explain that Bear's Daughter hadn't been her mother, the girl shook her head in stubborn disbelief.

"I've done all I can to set things straight with her for now," Ian told Rebecca that night. "Maybe in time the lass will come to believe me."

"When will you let her go back to her home?" Rebecca asked.

From the way Ian's mouth twisted, Rebecca knew her words hurt him. Ian might be ready to acknowledge this girl as his daughter, but he must be aware that she might never accept him as her father.

"This Willow is as much my daughter as Anna is. I only want what's best for the lass. When I return with her sister, perhaps she'll want to bide here with us."

"What if she still wants to leave?"

Ian shrugged. "Then I maun take the lass back. But I owe it to the memory of her mother to do what I can to help her first."

With as much grace as she could muster, Rebecca accepted Ian's promise not to hold Willow indefinitely against her will. Reluctantly she agreed that he should go back north the next day, this time by himself.

"Traveling alone is really safer. I'll stay off the main trails. My old friends among the Delaware will help me find Anna Willow."

"I hope that you're right."

Ian had already kissed Rebecca good-bye and turned to leave when she called him back, her expression serious. "One thing more—"

"Aye? What is it?"

"Promise you won't come back here with any more young'uns you claim not to know you had."

Chuckling, Ian kissed her again. He still smiled as he rode from the Station.

24

"I reckon y' must a-thought we'd never git here, Mr. Martin," the flatboat captain said cheerfully. With the end of their long voyage in sight, he shared the jovial mood of his passengers.

Stuart nodded in agreement. "Yes, sir, I will confess there were times that I wondered about it. But it has been a most interesting journey."

The captain cupped his hands to his mouth to call out an order. "Look sharp, men—a few more feet of polin' and y'll reach the bank."

Stuart leaned on his pole and pushed it in rhythm with the other men. It hadn't rained in some time, and the river was so shallow that the poles soon found mud even though they were still far from the shore.

The master kept up his running instructions until the flatboat stopped with a jolt that knocked the feet from under several of the standing passengers.

Stuart moved his books and other possessions

ashore, and surveyed the small store that occupied the landing. He would need to buy a few provisions for the journey ahead of him. As he contemplated how far he had to go on foot, he groaned.

Lexington lay some thirty-nine miles to the south. There he planned to buy a horse and ride to Bryan's Station, where he would once more be with Anna Willow. And this time, he wouldn't ever let her go.

It was a long, tiring walk in the August weather, but Stuart didn't mind his physical discomfort. He would gladly walk twice the distance for the opportunity to see Anna Willow McKnight. It had been too long since she had been in his arms. He would hold her again and tell her that he wanted to marry her. As he walked, Stuart pictured the scene over and over in his imagination, the details changing only slightly as he saw more of Kentucky. He realized that this Bryan's Station where Anna now lived was bound to be both beautiful and wild. And from rumors he'd heard, it might also be dangerous.

Aunt Matilda wouldn't like this place a bit, Stuart thought. He imagined her look of horror if she could hear the stories of Indian atrocities. The flatboat passengers had delighted in recounting, in vivid detail, every scalping story they had ever heard. His aunt would have even more reason to tell Stuart that he should have stayed with her in civilized Philadelphia.

But his love was here, in Kentucky, and soon he and Anna would be together.

As she talked with the man who claimed to be her father, Willow discovered that Bear's Daughter spoke the truth when she said he was good, for a *Shemanese*. Haltingly Ian told her about her sister, who was called Anna Willow.

"You were twin-born. You both look the same," he said.

Willow knew that such a thing was possible. Tecumseh, the Shawnee warrior who sometimes rode with White Eagle, had three brothers who were born at the same time. It was a great gift for a woman to give her man more than one man-child at a time. She did not understand why Ee-an did not know about her, until he explained that Bear's Daughter had midwifed the birth.

"She was like a mother to Silverwillow. She wanted you to take her place."

Willow nodded her understanding, but not her acceptance. *I do not care what anyone says of her. Bear's Daughter was my mother. I will always think of her as such.*

As if satisfied that her parentage had been explained, Ian changed the subject. "I saw you with a warrior. Is he your man?"

Willow lowered her head, fearful that her eyes would give her away. She was reluctant to tell him that White Eagle was her husband, lest it put him in danger. "We were bound for Waccachalla. There I would tell my chief that my mother Bear's Daughter was dead. He still does not know this thing."

"He will," Ian said.

Willow raised her head and looked into her father's eyes. "I want to go home."

"I know," he said.

But he would not tell Willow when or how she would be returned to her village.

The next day, when Willow realized that Ee-an had gone north without her, she lost all hope. She knew, even more than R'becca, what a dangerous thing he did. Even if he found his Anna-daughter— which would not be easy—he could well die if he tried to free her.

He can never take me to White Eagle then, she thought. Willow's heart was heavy, and for several days she fasted. R'becca continued to put the strange *Shemanese* food before her, only to remove it later, untouched.

On the fourth day, Willow knew even more sadness. White Eagle's seed-planting had not put a babe in her belly, after all. The evidence so badly stained her doeskin shift that R'becca gave her a printed calico dress of Anna's to wear in its place. She brought water in a large wooden bucket and motioned for Willow to bathe, and Willow realized that the *Shemanese* must not have a women's lodge where she could stay until the end of her bleeding.

It is just as well, Willow thought. The curious eyes of the *Shemanese* women would only make her more uneasy.

"I'll help you comb your hair," R'becca said, matching gestures to her words. She always spoke English to Willow, who was gradually beginning to understand a few words.

When that was done, Willow sat at the table and took the full trencher of cornmeal mush R'becca offered.

I will be with you yet, White Eagle. But for this time, I will do what I must.

Rebecca watched Willow struggle to eat with a spoon, as Rebecca had shown her. In Anna's dress, with her hair loose as Anna wore it, Willow looked so much like Anna that Rebecca sorrowed for the missing girl.

She and her father will both come home to us. They have to. Rebecca told herself that often, but she also knew times of doubt.

Rebecca knew that Willow was the center of gossip in Bryan's Station, and for all she knew, maybe even in Lexington and the other settlements as well. She didn't particularly like it, but at least talking about the strange turn of events with Ian McKnight's daughters served to distract people from their own troubles in the aftermath of the Station's siege.

As she went about her daily chores, Rebecca tried not to count the days her husband had been gone or to think about the horrible things that could be happening to him. She had enough to do around the Station to occupy her, not the least of which was keeping an eye on Willow, who she feared might try to run away. She knew Ian would never forgive her if she allowed that.

To keep an eye on her, Rebecca took Willow along when she went out to hackle flax. By now everyone in Bryan's Station knew that the girl Ian McKnight had brought back had turned out to be not only his long-lost daughter, but Anna's identical twin. In Anna's dress, Willow's resemblance to her sister was even more pronounced.

Hannah Drake, Anna's favorite companion, and her mother were among the women gathered for the task of combing the long flax fibers. Hannah tried to be friendly with Willow, but Willow, not understanding, only stared at Hannah blankly.

Hannah turned to her mother. "Wouldn't you just give a pretty penny to know where that girl's been all her life?" she said.

"We already know that she lived in a Shawnee village," Rebecca said tartly. For her husband's sake, she wanted to protect Willow. Those who hadn't fully accepted Anna's Indian blood would feel even less charitable toward her sister, since Indians had so recently laid siege to their Station.

"I wonder what she must think of us," Hannah said.

"I'm sure bein' here can't be easy for her," Rebecca had responded.

Even the women who might have misgivings about Willow didn't object to letting her work alongside them, particularly at a hard task like preparing flax to be made into linen yarn.

After working for a time, Rebecca left Willow with the other women and went back to the cabin to check on the bread dough she had set out to rise. When she emerged from the cabin, Rebecca could scarcely believe the scene before her.

Willow stood wrapped in the arms of a strange white man who appeared to be kissing her rather thoroughly. Apparently, the man had just ridden into the Station, gotten down from his horse, and immediately embraced Willow.

Several of the women gaped at them, unable to speak. However, when Betsy Craig saw Rebecca, she called out, "Come quick, Miz McKnight. Some man has got ahold of Willow!"

Even as Betsy spoke, the words were no longer true. Willow had managed to pull away from him and now shouted incoherently while she flailed at his chest with both fists.

Willow's face showed anger and outrage, while the man's was a study in bewilderment. He backed away from Willow's blows, only to have his arms pinned behind him by several of the men who had heard the commotion.

James Craig turned to Rebecca as she approached. "Ma'am, do you know this man? He claims to be a friend of the colonel's."

Rebecca studied the intruder for a long moment. He was younger than Ian McKnight, with comely features and unusual, almost violet, eyes. Even though garbed in a common linen hunting shirt and buckskin trousers, the man didn't look to be a hunter or a homesteader.

"No, Mr. Craig. He is a stranger to me."

Although his face was flushed in agitation, the man's deep blue eyes regarded Rebecca without guile. "Ma'am, my name is Stuart Martin. Ian Mc-Knight and I served together in the war. Is the colonel here?"

"No, he's not." Rebecca turned to James Craig. "I've heard my husband praise Lieutenant Martin many times. You can let him go."

Mrs. Drake finally found her voice. "You'd best

watch him, though. You didn't see how he attacked that girl!"

Stuart's face reddened even more. "Begging your pardon, ma'am, I never meant any harm. Miss Mc-Knight and I—" He paused and looked over to where Willow stood glaring at him, her fists still clenched. "She was a student at my aunt's school in Philadelphia. We were—uh—friends."

James Craig and Edward Clements exchanged glances and made no attempt to suppress their laughter. The ladies seemed less amused, although Hannah Drake smiled.

"I'm sure you were," Rebecca said dryly. "However, that girl you were just kissin' isn't Anna."

Stuart looked in confusion from Rebecca to Willow and then back again. "Then who is she? Where is Anna?"

Rebecca held out her hand. "I'm Rebecca McKnight, the colonel's wife. Come to the cabin and I'll try to explain."

James Craig pointed to Willow. "What about her?"

"She'll come with us, of course." With a reassuring smile, Rebecca beckoned to Willow.

"I'm terribly sorry if I offended you, miss," Stuart said when Willow joined them, but Mrs. Drake cut short his apology.

"Yer wastin' yer breath—the girl's a savage. She don't speak English."

Rebecca's eyes flashed as she turned to Mrs. Drake. "Willow may not speak English, but she's no savage. And even without knowin' the meanin' of your words, the girl understands the feelin' behind them."

Mrs. Drake opened and closed her mouth a few times, then apparently decided against answering Rebecca. "Come, Hannah," she called to her daughter. "I don't know what this world's comin' to, when decent people get yelled at for tryin' to be helpful."

James Craig spoke quickly. "I'll unsaddle your horse and pen him with the others, Mr. Martin."

Stuart looked questioningly at Rebecca. "Will I be here that long?"

"Of course," Rebecca assured him. "My husband would never forgive me if I let his friend leave now."

"All right, then," Stuart said uncertainly.

James Craig removed the saddlebags from Stuart's horse. "What about these, Miz McKnight?"

She considered for a moment, then pointed to the blockhouse. "That's where some of the bachelors stay," she told Stuart. "From the way you were kissin' Willow, I do presume that you're not married."

For the first time since his arrival at Bryan's Station, Stuart smiled.

"Not yet, ma'am. But I came here to ask Anna Willow to be my wife."

Rebecca's momentary lightness vanished. "I'm not sure when you'll have the chance."

Stuart looked alarmed. "Has something happened to Anna?"

"I'll tell you about it when we get to the cabin."

As soon as they crossed the threshold, Rebecca released Willow's hand. With a last puzzled glance at Stuart, the girl disappeared into the lean-to and closed the door behind her.

Rebecca gestured for Stuart to sit at the table.

"I must say that I am quite at a loss to understand all of this," he said.

Rebecca sat across the table from Stuart and drew a deep breath. "No more than we were, I can assure you. But I'll try to tell you all that's happened since Anna Willow came to Bryan's Station."

25

WACCACHALLA

Anna tried to note the passing days by making a crude calendar from sticks, but when Blossom accidentally disturbed it, she lost count of the time she had been at Waccachalla. Here, people didn't seem to mark time by the day, nor did they count weeks, except by the phases of the moon. Anna figured that the warriors had been back in Waccachalla for about a week when the medicine man, Sits-in-Shadow, appeared at the chief's *wegiwa* one afternoon and beckoned to her.

As he had done at the feast to welcome the warriors, the medicine man wore his ceremonial regalia, complete with a somewhat soiled buffalo robe around his shoulders, a towering headdress, and ankle bracelets made of brass, bones, and feathers. With his face painted in the lines of a fierce scowl, he looked altogether menacing. Anna glanced uneasily at the chief's wife.

"*Wepetheh.*" Standing Crane gestured to let Anna know that she should go with him.

Anna turned to Blossom, expecting that the girl who had been her constant companion would accompany her. But when Blossom took a step forward, Sits-in-Shadow immediately stopped her. *"Mat-tah! Squithetha wepetheh."*

No! The girl alone must go with me. Her interpretation might not have been a word-for-word translation, but Anna understood his meaning well enough. For the first time since she had been brought to the chief's *wegiwa*, Anna knew a faint prickle of fear for her safety. However, she was determined not to show it.

Anna thrust out her chin and nodded. *"Oui-sah,"* she said, even though "it is good" was quite the opposite of the way she felt about going anywhere with this wild-looking medicine man. When he turned and walked away, Anna followed.

Sits-in-Shadow stayed a few paces ahead of her until he reached the medicine lodge, a *wegiwa* that Blossom had pointed out and let Anna know that she must never enter without permission. He lifted the skins covering the entrance and motioned for Anna to go inside.

Her first impression was of darkness and an oppressive mixture of heat, and strange, pungent odors. Outside, the weather was still pleasantly warm, but the heat radiating from the small fire that glowed in the center of the medicine man's *wegiwa* made Anna feel momentarily faint. As her eyes grew accustomed to the dimness, Anna saw a variety of strange objects. Bundles of dried herbs and sticks hung from the sides of the *wegiwa*, alongside a jumble of masks and antlers and what appeared to be bears' paws, deer hooves, and other animal parts. She regarded the strange collection with interest and curiosity, but when she raised her eyes to the ceiling and saw what appeared to be strips of hair, her stomach lurched in revulsion. Most were matted with dried blood, and they looked unmistakably like human scalps. From the light color of much of the hair, Anna guessed that most, if not all, of the scalps had been lifted from the heads of whites.

Imagining how it might feel to be scalped, Anna shuddered.

While Anna surveyed the medicine lodge, Sits-in-Shadow removed a buffalo-hide pouch from a white oak basket near the door. With a great deal of ceremony he took out a few dried leaves and sprinkled them into the coals of the fire. They flamed briefly and released a billow of acrid smoke that stung Anna's eyes and made her gasp for breath.

Sits-in-Shadow didn't seem to notice her discomfort. He stood before the fire with his eyes closed and his arms outstretched, unmoving as a statue. After a moment he began a low chant, which gradually grew louder and faster. With his eyes still closed, he withdrew two gourd rattles from beneath the folds of his robe. Holding one in each hand, he shook them while raising and lowering his arms in a series of jerky movements. Then he opened his eyes and moved slowly toward Anna.

It took all of Anna's willpower to force herself to stand still when Sits-in-Shadow touched the top of her head with both the gourds, then slowly moved them across her shoulders and down her arms and legs as if tracing the outline of her body. Then the medicine man tossed another handful of the dried leaves on the fire and began to chant and sway back and forth. Shaking the gourd rattles in time with his deliberate steps, Sits-in-Shadow moved around Anna in a slow ritual dance that was unlike the dances she had seen in honor of the returning warriors.

After circling Anna for what seemed a very long time, Sits-in-Shadow stood before her and shouted a chant, emphasized by shaking the gourd rattles. Then he turned slightly to his right, then turned again, repeating the chanting and gourd-rattling until he had faced all four directions of the compass. Without looking at her again, Sits-in-Shadow sat cross-legged before the fire and stared in silence into its scarlet coals.

What happens now? Anna wondered. She had been standing long enough for her legs to be tired, but she dared not sit. When Sits-in-Shadow closed his eyes and seemed to be asleep, Anna shifted her weight uneasily and thought about trying to slip out of the medicine lodge. Before she could do so, however, the medicine man's eyes flew open, and he directed a piercing gaze at Anna and began to speak.

Anna had no idea what he said, but from time to time he paused and looked at her expectantly, as if waiting for her answer to a question. The third time, Anna spoke.

"I'm sorry, but I don't understand."

Sits-in-Shadow rose and stood so close to her, their eyes were only inches apart. *I am taller than he is,* Anna thought with a fine irrelevance. He stared at her for a moment longer, then shook his head violently and gestured toward the entrance.

"*Wepeteh*," he ordered. Anna hesitated, uncertain that she was really being dismissed, until the medicine man grunted and pushed her toward the entrance. Resisting the impulse to run, Anna made herself walk sedately, her head held high, all the way back to the chief's *wegiwa*.

When Otter saw Sits-in-Shadow and Anna enter the medicine lodge, he dropped the arrowhead he was knapping and squatted outside his *wegiwa*, waiting to see what would happen. From the first moment he'd realized that this girl really didn't understand what he said to her, Otter had known no peace. His desire to have the girl in his lodge had made him beg, not ask with pride as a warrior should, for the chief to give her to him.

"I brought her back from the *Shemanese*. By our custom, she is mine."

Black Snake shook his head. "It is possible that the *Shemanese* used some evil magic on Willow when they captured her."

If somehow the *Shemanese* had caused a *matche-menetoo* to steal away the girl's wits, then Sits-in-Shadow must confront that evil spirit and try to drive it away. Only then would Black Snake decide what was to be done with her.

Otter had spoken openly of these things to his sister. "It is with the girl as I told you," he said to Gray Fawn.

"No man will risk taking a woman bewitched with

an evil spirit. The chief himself will be in danger if she remains here."

Otter said nothing, but the words had secretly pleased him. *If no one else will have the girl, the chief must either give her to me or dispose of her elsewhere. He will not keep such a girl in his own* wegiwa.

"Look, the strange *squithetha* leaves the medicine lodge," Otter heard someone say. It was true; Otter watched the one he called Willow walk to the chief's *wegiwa* with her head held high. Her proud and disdainful expression was so much like Willow's that at first Otter thought the medicine man had restored her wits. Yet Sits-in-Shadow was nowhere to be seen. If he had, indeed, brought the girl Willow back into her right mind, would he not take her to Black Snake with a great deal of ceremony?

What would happen next, Otter did not know.

But as she walked out of his sight, he smiled with satisfaction at the thought of the fine sons this proud girl could bear him. *This matter is not over. She will yet be my woman.*

As soon as Anna left the medicine lodge, Sits-in-Shadow removed his ceremonial trappings and went to the *msi-kah-mi-qui.*

Black Snake frowned. "Why is the girl not with you?"

"My chief, I sent her back to your lodge."

"You could not rid her of the *matchemenetoo?*"

Sits-in-Shadow shrugged. "I cannot take away what is not there. This girl has no evil spirit."

"Then what is wrong with her?"

"This girl the warrior Otter brought back from the *Shemanese* is not the same Littlewillow that lived in this place with Bear's Daughter."

"How do you know this?"

"Hear me, Chief. The *kinnickkinnick* smoke gave me this vision. In it I saw two babies, born of the same father to the same mother at the same time. One lives here, one does not."

Black Snake looked skeptical. "Can such a thing be true?"

Sits-in-Shadow nodded solemnly. "Yes, my chief. After the vision, my eyes were opened. This girl is not the same. She stands taller than Willow."

Black Snake considered his words. "Even when Bear's Daughter first brought Littlewillow here, she kept some truth from me. I thought it must be from shame that she had borne a child to a *Shemanese*."

Sits-in-Shadow nodded. "There is this other thing. I do not think that Bear's Daughter still lives."

"Is this also in your vision?"

"No, my chief." Sits-in-Shadow touched his forehead. "It is here. Bear's Daughter will not be back."

Black Snake made a gesture of dismissal. "Go now. I would think about these things."

Sits-in-Shadow turned to leave, then stopped and spoke again. "Whatever you decide, I tell you this: You cannot break this girl's spirit."

"I know," Black Snake replied, so softly that the medicine man barely heard the words.

When Anna returned to the chief's *wegiwa*, neither Standing Crane nor Blossom acted as if her summons had been out of the ordinary. Anna tried to dismiss the entire episode from her own mind. Yet from time to time that day, she caught them looking at her strangely, and Anna knew that her visit to the medicine lodge had in some way been important to her fate. But what that might be, Anna had no idea.

26

Each day that he passed at Bryan's Station brought Stuart Martin new challenges and revelations, but he still felt a mixture of shame and chagrin over his near-disastrous arrival, when he had mistaken the girl Willow for Anna.

"'Twas an honest mistake. You shouldn't keep botherin' yourself about it," Rebecca McKnight told him. But that was easier said than done.

The girl was the first person Stuart had seen the moment he arrived at Bryan's Station. She had been working with her back to him and hadn't noticed when he rode in. But Stuart had recognized her dress as the one that Anna Willow wore the first time he kissed her. He had quickly dismounted and gone to her. When he called her name, she turned toward him, obviously startled.

Seeing her after so long a time and with so much expectation overwhelmed Stuart, and he had immediately swept the girl into his arms and kissed her with the pent-up passion of several months. He had come a long and dangerous way with the express intention of marrying Anna Willow, and he had every reason to think that she would be as pleased to see him as he was to see her.

It hadn't taken him long to find out out how mistaken he was.

"Someday you'll look back on this time and laugh," Rebecca predicted, but Stuart doubted it.

"Even if I can, I don't think Willow ever will," he said. The girl had avoided him during his first few days at the Station. When she finally realized that he meant her no harm, she gradually spent more time in his company. As Rebecca had done, he pointed to an object and named it in English, and Willow told him the Shawnee word.

"The colonel would be surprised at how much Willow's learned already," he told Rebecca one evening as they sat on the doorstone after Willow went to bed.

At the mention of her husband's name, Rebecca turned away to hide the sudden tears that came into her eyes. In the last few days it had become obvious to Stuart that she was expecting a child. He made an awkward, oblique reference to the fact, saying that Ian McKnight must be quite excited at the prospect of becoming a father again after so many years, but Rebecca surprised him by saying that Ian didn't yet know it.

"Had I told him, it would've made it harder for him to go after Anna Willow," she had explained.

"You're a brave woman, Rebecca. I hope Ian appreciates you."

Stuart had spoken seriously, but to his surprise, she laughed. "Be sure to tell him so when he comes back. A man sometimes needs some remindin' about such matters."

Unspoken between Stuart and Rebecca was the knowledge that every day that passed without news of Ian or Anna Willow made it less likely that they would ever see either again.

Rebecca regained her composure and turned back to Stuart with a question he knew that she must eventually ask. "How long do you plan to stay here, Stuart?"

Forever and a day, if that's how long it takes for Ian to bring Anna Willow home, he wanted to say. Under the present circumstances, with the fate of Ian and Anna Willow still uncertain, he didn't want to leave Bryan's Station. But he didn't want to impose on the McKnight's hospitality, knowing that resources were scarce here in the wilderness. And he knew he ought to be making some sort of plans for his future.

Stuart returned her steady gaze. "I came here to marry Anna Willow. If it's not too much of an imposition, I'd like to stay until she and the colonel come back. I'm sure he'd want me to look after you and Willow."

Rebecca smiled sadly. "Ah, Stuart, of course you're welcome to stay as long as you like. You're more than earnin' your keep, workin' around the Station and helpin' the men bring in what crops the Indians didn't ruin. But when you feel you need to move on, you're not beholden to us in any way."

He nodded. "I appreciate your kindness."

Rebecca stood and stretched, pressing both her palms into the small of her back. "Hacklin' flax wears me out. I'd best turn in now."

Stuart helped her over the doorstone. "I'll come to see Willow after breakfast. We must keep trying to communicate with her."

"Yes, but I'm afraid that the only thing on the girl's mind is gettin' back across the river as soon as she can. Ian said she was with a Shawnee warrior when he found her. My guess is, that Indian's still on her mind."

"If he's alive, he must still think of her, too. Anyway, maybe we'll hear something from the colonel tomorrow."

White Eagle opened his eyes and saw the old woman bending over him, and he had a moment of panic. He didn't recognize her, nor did he know where he was or even how he had gotten there. He raised his head in an attempt to sit up, but pain convulsed his thigh and brought a wave of nausea.

"Lie still, *nenothtu*, else you undo my medicine."

"I do not feel like a warrior," White Eagle said weakly.

The old woman chuckled. "It is no wonder. Had my son Red Pole not seen you fall from your horse on the Scioto Trail, you would feel nothing by now."

White Eagle looked around the *wegiwa* in which he lay. It was obvious that the woman tending him was a *chobeka s'squaw-o-wah*, a village medicine woman. Often their practical remedies were preferred over the rituals of a tribe's official medicine man.

"What is this place?" he asked.

"The Chillicothe on the Scioto Trail," she replied.

Pain shot through his leg, and White Eagle gritted his teeth and moaned as he remembered all that had happened—how the *Shemanese* had shot him and taken Willow away—how he'd tracked them almost to the river and then realized, too late, that he might not be able to make it to the nearest village.

"Willow," he murmured, and the woman chuckled.

"This Willow again! From sunup to sundown, that has been the only word your lips have said."

White Eagle's eyes flew open. "How long have I been here?"

The woman put a soothing hand on his brow. "*Sehe*," she cautioned. "If you are ever to leave this place, you must rest."

White Eagle put out his hand and gingerly touched his throbbing thigh. "Does this flesh die?" he asked.

"Not yet. You are spared to some purpose, perhaps."

Once more White Eagle attempted to raise his head. "I must go—gather warriors—find Willow—"

The old woman offered White Eagle a drink of something bitter from a wooden cup, then gently but firmly made him lie flat on his back again. "*Wuhk-ernekah*," she said.

"Tomorrow is not soon enough," White Eagle wanted to say, but his tongue was suddenly heavy. He tried to keep his eyes open, but he soon wearied with the effort.

I will sleep now, White Eagle told himself. After he woke, he would feel better. Then he would get on Mishewa and go after Willow.

27

WACCACHALLA

It was the time of harvest, and the men and women of Waccachalla had much to do. The men hunted and fished daily, while the women sun-dried corn, beans, and apples, and ground meal from corn and a variety of seeds. The fish and game the men brought in had to be smoked or dried for the coming winter. Anna worked, too, not only because it was expected, but also because having her hands occupied kept her mind from dwelling on her situation.

Several days after her strange interview with the medicine man, Anna was spreading apples out to dry when she noticed that the villagers seemed excited. A woman was going from group to group, apparently telling them something that caused an animated discussion. In the way they had worked out to communicate, Blossom indicated to Anna that there would be *psai-wi oui-then-eluh*, great feasting that evening.

Thinking it would be a dinner in honor of the harvest, much as she'd known in her childhood in Pennsylvania, Anna pointed at the food around them and made eating motions.

Blossom shook her head and touched Anna's arm. *"Mat-tah,* An-na. An-na *psai-wi oui-then-eluh,"* she said. Her solemn expression was so uncharacteristic that Anna thought that the girl must be teasing her. Once again, she felt frustrated at her inability to talk with these people with whom she now lived.

I wish I had my father's ability to understand Indian tongues, Anna thought. As a small child she had watched him use sign language with Shawnee and Mingo Indians at the Bedford market, then talk fluently to a group of Delaware. When Anna asked him how he'd learned their languages, he'd shrugged as if it had been nothing. "I just listen to them, lass. Never forget that ye always learn a deal more listening than ye do talking."

Anna had remembered the advice, but so far it hadn't served her very well in Waccachalla. From her first hours in captivity, Anna had closely observed everything the people did, and carefully listened to the words they spoke, yet rarely did she understand the full meaning of what she heard.

Later that day, however, when Blossom took her hand and led her to the creek, Anna readily understood that she was to bathe herself. Even though the shallow water was always cold, Anna enjoyed the opportunity to wash in it. She waded into the water and sat down, shivering. Standing beside her, Blossom brought up sand from the creek bed and scrubbed Anna's face and arms until her skin felt raw. Then Blossom applied the underside of a strip of slippery elm bark to cleanse Anna's long hair, and helped her rinse it.

When a shivering Anna came out of the water, Blossom handed her a plain linen shift in place of the doeskin robe that she'd been wearing. The garment was so identical to the summer shirts that her father and most of the other men at Bryan's Station wore that Anna had no doubt it had been plundered from some white settlement. Worse, it might have been taken from a settler killed by Waccachalla warriors. Reminded again of her father, Anna's heart ached with fear that she might never see him again.

I won't allow myself even to think of such a thing, she told herself.

Trying to think only in terms of the present, Anna leaned back against a warm rock by the creek bank to let the sun dry her heavy hair. Anna's hair fascinated Blossom, who liked to touch it. When she had invited Anna to touch her hair, Anna had been surprised at how much coarser it felt than her own. Now Blossom lifted and spread Anna's hair until it was dry.

"*Oui-sah,*" Blossom said, which Anna had learned to be the Shawnee equivalent of "it is good." Taking Anna's hand in her usual way, Blossom led her back to the *wegiwa,* where Standing Crane was waiting for them. The chief's wife motioned for Anna to sit down, then worked a pleasantly fragrant ointment into Anna's hair before she plaited part of it into a tight braid.

"Why do you do this?" Anna asked. From her first days in the *wegiwa,* the chief's wife manner toward her had reflected mere resigned acceptance of Anna's presence. This day, however, a subtle change seemed to have come over Standing Crane, and she smiled faintly as she made a dramatic gesture of opening a small wooden chest and taking from it an elaborate hair decoration.

Like other such ornaments worn by Indian men and women alike, this one was made of feathers placed inside a round bone and bound with a rawhide strip. But its one unusually large, pure white feather, and smaller, iridescent blue-black feather made the ornament far more elaborate than any Anna had seen. In addition, intricate sky blue and red beading, worked in the same geometric pattern that Anna had admired on the chief's vest, covered a large part of the rawhide strip that bound the feathers to the bone.

"It is beautiful," Anna murmured, then added, "*Oui-sah*," Although "good" and "beautiful" didn't mean the same thing, both Blossom and her mother understood and seemed pleased that Anna liked the ornament.

Standing Crane took a long time to weave the decoration into a strip of Anna's hair. Its blue-black feather followed the contour of Anna's right cheekbone and moved as she turned her head. *I wish I had a mirror*, she thought. Even without seeing herself, Anna knew she must look more Indian than ever. *More like my mother, perhaps*, she thought. She wondered what her father would think if only he could see her.

When Standing Crane finished her work, she motioned for Anna to stay where she was, and began to tend her daughter's hair. She added an ornament similar to Anna's, but much smaller. Finally Standing Crane unrolled a buffalo hide to reveal an elaborate doeskin robe hidden in its folds. Although it was obviously far too large for a woman, Anna first thought that the chief's wife intended for her to wear it. Instead, she handed it to Blossom, who took the folded robe carefully, and holding it over her outstretched forearms, left the *wegiwa*.

"That robe must belong to Black Snake," Anna said aloud. Recognizing her husband's name, Standing Crane nodded. She pointed to herself, waved toward the *msi-kah-mi-qui*, gestured to Anna, then traced a wide circle in the air with her hands before she brought them together.

Standing Crane's gesture reminded Anna that she would be the focus of the feasting that evening. *But why?*

The answer that came to her momentarily stopped Anna's breath. *Perhaps the chief plans to give me to one of his warriors during this feast.*

Anna quickly rejected the idea. Like most of the Waccachalla villagers, the few unmarried warriors seemed almost afraid of her, and took care not to come close to where she worked. Only her captor had shown the slightest interest in Anna, and from the way the chief had treated that warrior, she'd thought herself free of him. Still, Anna often caught her captor staring at her, and she sensed he watched her every move. Could he have persuaded the chief to change his mind?

So absorbed was Anna in her speculations that she hadn't taken notice of the young girl's return. Now she saw that the girl and her mother were both putting on the same kind of richly ornamented robe that Blossom had just delivered to her father.

"*Oui-sah*," Anna said. She didn't have to feign admiration—their almost white shifts were beautifully fringed and adorned with delicate beading and finely wrought quilling. She watched Standing Crane put on a headdress similar to the medicine man's, only much smaller; then both mother and daughter stepped into beaded doeskin moccasins.

Standing Crane motioned to Anna. "*Wepetheh*," she said.

Anna stood and gazed down at the linen shift she still wore, then back at the woman. *Surely they don't expect me to go to a feast dressed in a man's shirt.* Anna pointed to the doeskin robe she had been wearing, but the chief's wife merely shook her head and repeated the command to come with her.

Anna was acutely aware of the contrast they made as she walked toward the council house between the elegantly attired mother and daughter. *At least my headdress is beautiful,* Anna reminded herself. She drew herself to her full height, lifted her chin, and walked with dignity.

As they approached the council lodge, Anna heard the sound of drums, the instruments that often regulated the pace of life in Waccachalla. Some half-dozen men sat in a semicircle outside the council lodge, beating in unison on skins stretched taut over hollowed wood. Anna had heard these drums beaten slowly for the warrior's funeral and much more rapidly for the feast that had honored the warriors' return. Now the drums' beat sounded somewhere between celebration and sorrow, almost as if in anticipation of some awaited event.

Everyone in the village must be here, Anna thought as they came to the *msi-kah-mi-qui.* The chief's immediate family and those of the medicine man and the elders of the village occupied places of honor inside the council lodge itself, while everyone outside crowded as near to the entrance as they could, so as not to miss anything that went on inside.

Anna noticed her captor sitting with several other men in an area near the drummers, dressed as they had been when they had danced in honor of their dead warrior. Opposite them sat a group of young women in fringed and beaded doeskin dresses, whose shell ankle bracelets suggested that they would dance later.

As soon as Anna set foot inside the council house, the drums abruptly stopped, leaving an almost palpable silence. Black Snake sat much as he had the first time Anna had seen him, but he was dressed far more splendidly in fringed buckskin trousers over a red breechclout, plus the elaborately beaded vest Anna had seen before. His ensemble was topped by a bearskin thrown across his shoulders.

Motioning for Anna to remain standing, Blossom and Standing Crane took their places behind the chief. Then Sits-in-Shadow came forward to chant and dance around Anna, much as he had done in the medicine lodge. When he stopped, he touched the gourd to the top of her head, down each of her arms and legs, and finally tapped the toes of her moccasin-clad feet before he stepped aside.

Immediately Black Snake came forward, raised both his arms, and began to speak in a loud voice.

I wish I knew what he was saying, Anna thought. She took comfort that neither his words nor his demeanor seemed threatening, nor had he called any warrior to come and stand beside her. She could make out only a few of his words, among them "Willow" and "An-na."

At length he finished speaking, and stepped back. Blossom and Standing Crane came forward to stand before Anna.

Standing Crane put both her palms on Anna's shoulders and looked into her eyes, her face expressionless. *"Nee dah-nai-tha An-na,"* she said, then stepped aside for Blossom to take her place.

Blossom smiled as she said, *"Nee the-tha An-na."*

Before Anna could consider what it all meant, Black Snake rose, put his palms on her shoulders, and repeated his wife's words: *"Nee dah-nai-tha An-na."* Then he added, *"Newe-canetepa, Wishemenetoo; weshe-catwelloo, keweshelawaypa."*

Standing Crane turned back to Sits-in-Shadow, who handed her a soft doeskin robe, beaded in the same design as the ones that she and Blossom wore. Standing Crane stepped forward and held Anna's headdress to one side as Blossom helped her put it on.

A group of older men who had silently watched the proceedings rose, and one by one, placed their hands on her shoulders and repeated Black Snake's words: *"Newe-canetepa, Wishemenetoo; weshecatwelloo, keweshelawaypa."*

Anna didn't know how she was supposed to

respond, so she merely made her expression as impassive as theirs, and slightly inclined her head to each man. When the last elder had passed before her, the chief took Anna's hand and led her to the door of the council house.

"Nee dah-nai-tha An-na!" he cried loudly.

Immediately a shout went up from the villagers. From the way they looked, Anna thought many of the villagers didn't seem particularly pleased with their chief's pronouncement.

Taking her arm, Black Snake then walked with Anna to the place of honor beside the central firestone. Standing Crane took her seat to her husband's right and motioned for Anna to sit on his left side, next to Blossom. When they were settled in their places, Black Snake raised his hand, and the drummers began a slow beat.

The fall twilight had faded into darkness during the ceremony in the council lodge. Now wood was added to the fire that always burned in the firestone, and flames leaped up, casting fantastic shadows among the dancers as they formed two lines opposite one another.

The dancers began murmuring, *"Ya ne no hoo wa no,"* a chant that gradually grew faster and louder with each repetition.

Anna found herself swaying in time with the beat of the drums and the sound of their voices. A strange rhythm vibrated inside her bones, and she closed her eyes and let herself be drawn into it. She had a fleeting sense that she had done this before, that she had sat in a circle of celebration, had even taken an active part in it. Part of her mind was always aware that such a thing was not possible, yet it all seemed somehow familiar.

This must be the way my mother felt when her people danced, Anna thought. Perhaps the lonely white trader Ian McKnight and the Indian maiden Silverwillow had first seen each other at just such a dance. Perhaps they had fallen in love at that very moment.

The beat of the drums and chanting of the villagers continued to a frenzied crescendo, then stopped abruptly. Anna opened her eyes to the realization that, whatever Silverwillow's situation might have been when she had met Ian McKnight, hers was now far different. She believed that the chief had adopted her as his own daughter, perhaps saving her from being given to her captor.

But Anna also wondered if being made the chief's daughter could mean that she was expected to stay in this village for the rest of her life.

Despite her warm robe and the heat emanating from the fire, Anna shivered. She realized she was fortunate to be so well treated, but no matter how good the chief was to her, he was not her father, this place was not her home, and—most important of all—her captor and the other warriors were not Stuart Martin.

Among the villagers who had taken an especially keen interest in the adoption ceremony were Gray Fawn and her eldest daughter. Before Stretching Cat took her place among the dancers, she and her mother speculated about the ritual's meaning.

Stretching Cat quoted the village talk. "It is said

that Black Snake has word that Bear's Daughter and Willow are dead. He takes this one who looks like the girl in her place."

Gray Fawn shook her head. "But did not Sits-in-Shadow himself believe that the *Shemanese* put an evil spirit in Willow and sent her back as this An-na? I do not trust this girl."

"Black Snake must soon make a match for her," she predicted.

As Anna had suspected he might, the chief came back to his own *wegiwa* the day after the feast. Blossom and Anna moved their beds to the lodge's most distant corner, an area screened from the rest of the dwelling by several blankets hung from the lodge-poles. Other-wise, Anna's adoption hadn't seemed to change any-thing. Blossom still shadowed her, and Anna knew that everywhere she went, she was watched closely.

At least this way, my captor has to keep his distance, Anna thought. Once when the girl's attention was diverted elsewhere, he had crept up behind Anna and grabbed her. Pinning her arms behind her, he had kissed her roughly and pressed himself against her before he let her go. He made a sign with his hands, which she did not understand, and ran away before anyone else saw him. After that, Anna was grateful that she was not left alone.

A few days after her adoption, Anna looked up from grinding corn to see a horseman entering the village. She shaded her eyes and stared as he walked his horse to the council lodge and dismounted. The short and somewhat stocky newcomer wore a standard linen hunting shirt with fringed buckskin trousers, and appeared to be in his middle years. But it was the color of his skin that drew Anna's excited attention. Tanned and leathery from exposure to the sun though it was, the man's skin was unmistakably *Shemanese*.

The word came instantly to Anna's mind. *I must have learned more from the people of Waccachalla than I knew, to think of him in that way.* Nevertheless, this was the first white man she'd seen since being taken from Kentucky, and she could scarcely wait to speak to him.

Anna dropped her grinding stone and started toward the council lodge, but she was quickly stayed by Blossom's restraining hand.

"*Mat-tah*, An-na."

Anna pointed to herself, then gestured toward the council lodge "I would see the *Shemanese*," she said.

Blossom shook her head and indicated the sky, then moved her hand to suggest the movement of the sun. She pointed to Anna, touched her own lips, then gestured toward the council lodge. Understanding that she could not interrupt the chief's talk with the *Shemanese*, Anna returned to her corn-grinding. As she worked, she allowed herself a cautious glimmer of hope. Even if this man didn't already know her father, perhaps she could persuade him to take a message to Bryan's Station.

At last the white man came out of the council lodge, accompanied by Black Snake. When Anna saw them heading toward her, she made herself continue working until Blossom motioned for her to stand.

Black Snake pointed to her. "*Nee dah-nai-tha* An-na," he said.

Up close, Anna saw that the white man's clean-shaven face bore deep smallpox scars, and the way his small, dark eyes stared at her made her uncomfortable.

The man spoke in a broad dialect that Anna recognized as British. "Yer father 'ere tells me ye speak English."

Anna nodded. "Yes, but my actual father is Colonel Ian McKnight, of Bryan's Station. One of the warriors kidnapped me from there."

"Colonel McKnight in Kentucky? Must be one of them rebel squatters. Since ye don't look all white, I reckon some squaw must of birthed ye."

The man's insolent tone and manner made Anna clench her fists, but she needed him too much to show her anger. Instead, Anna lifted her chin and spoke proudly. "My mother, Colonel McKnight's wife, was Delaware."

The man rubbed his chin and grinned as if he found her statement amusing. "Well, that ain't much 'elp 'ere in Shawnee country."

Anna struggled for a moment with the biblical adage that a soft answer turneth away wrath before she spoke again. "You have the advantage, sir. You know my name, but I don't know yours."

The man grinned again and made a rough bow. "Sorry. I never 'ad much manners to begin with, and livin' out 'ere amongst the savages has took away what I 'ad. Name's Edward Tucker, late of His Royal Majesty King George the Third's army."

Her heart sank as she realized that this same man could very well have been among the Redcoats that took the Indians' part against the people of Bryan's Station. Even so, she had to ask for his help.

Anna bobbed her head stiffly. "I'm glad to make your acquaintance, Mr. Tucker. I'd appreciate it if you would explain to the chief that I need to go back to Kentucky."

Edward Tucker threw back his head and laughed heartily. "Oooh, that's a good 'un, that is!"

Anna disliked this man more each moment, but she forced herself to speak calmly. "I don't think it's at all strange that I should want to go home. Perhaps if you'd just tell him—"

Edward Tucker made the cutoff sign. "No. The chief did ye a great thing by makin' ye Shawnee. Far's 'e's concerned, this is now yer 'ome."

It was what Anna had feared, but she wasn't yet ready to accept its finality.

"Please tell the chief that I appreciate the honor he has given me, but I must return to my father in Kentucky."

Edward Tucker laughed without humor. "Ye don't yet understand, do ye? The chief spared yer life, yet now ye beg t' be scalped."

Anna glanced past Edward Tucker to the chief. He watched them talking with his arms crossed on his chest, his expression impassive.

"The chief will not kill me." Anna's tone was far less certain than her words, a fact that Edward Tucker quickly noted.

He lowered his voice and leaned toward her. "Ye don't know these people like I do, missy. The chief 'as made ye 'is daughter. He'll not now let ye go."

Anna nodded that she understood. "All right. Don't tell the chief that I want to leave. But please find my father and tell him I'm all right."

Tucker frowned and shook his head. "I ain't 'zackly welcome acrost th' Ohio these days. I ain't about ter risk my neck fer nothin'."

For the promise of reward, this man can be persuaded to help me. Anna acted upon her insight at once.

"My father will make it well worth your while."

"An' 'ow do I know 'e's got the means? 'Tis well known that most Kentucky settlers ain't got one coin to rub agin' another."

His mention of coins reminded Anna of her own store. "I don't know how much hard money my father has, but I have several gold coins. You'll find them sewn into the bodice of a petticoat in my saddlebags in the lean-to of his cabin at Bryan's Station."

Edward Tucker looked doubtful. "Ye can't be sure it's still there."

"No one else knows of it. You can tell my father I said to give you that over and above whatever he might offer you."

"What else d' ye want me ter say?"

Anna felt a sense of relief. *He's greedy enough to do it,* she thought. "Just tell him that I'm safe and living in Waccachalla."

Edward Tucker sneered. "I s'pose ye think 'e'll come a-ridin' up ter git ye then?"

"What if he does?"

Tucker spoke with slow deliberation. "Missy, the minute any white man crosses the Ohio these days, 'e's as good as dead."

Anna didn't flinch. "By your hand, Mr. Tucker?"

The man spread his hands and shrugged. "Not me, missy. Bygones is bygones, and sleepin' dogs ort to be left to lie. I've nothin' personal agin any man who took arms agin th' Crown, myself. But things is in a flutter these days. Many warriors are lookin' t' lift a few scalps afore the winter sets in an' keeps 'em ter home. Yer father wouldn't 'ave a chance."

"Then when you see him, you may also add that warning," Anna said.

The man looked at her with grudging admiration. "I reckon ole chief got more'n 'e bargained fer when 'e took ye in."

"Find my father, Mr. Tucker. You'll be paid well for your trouble."

"Ye say 'e's at Bryan's Station?"

"Yes. Do you know the place?"

Edward Tucker looked amused. "I reckon ye might say as how I do. Now ye'd better think o' somethin' fer me ter tell the chief that we've been parleyin' about."

They both glanced at Chief Black Snake, who seemed impatient for their conversation to end.

"Tell him that I thank him for his kindness to me."

Tucker turned to address Black Snake, speaking with many gestures.

The chief's expression didn't change, but he glanced at Anna and nodded almost imperceptibly. When Edward Tucker finished, Black Snake spoke briefly, then bade Tucker farewell and returned, alone, to the council lodge.

"What did he say?" Anna asked.

"'E's glad ye like bein' his daughter."

"That's not what I said," Anna protested, then checked herself. "But I'm sure it was what he wants to hear. Now, about my father—"

"I'll think on it, but 'tis a long way to go fer nothin'. If I go an' don' git what it's worth, ye'll both be sorry."

With that vague threat, Edward Tucker left her. Anna brought her clasped hands to her chin as she watched him mount his horse and ride away. She well knew she probably couldn't trust this man and shouldn't allow herself too much hope. But he could be the key that would free her to return to Bryan's Station.

28

SCIOTO TRAIL

During the years he had lived among the Indians, Ian McKnight had learned many things that had stood him in good stead during his army days. From Indians Ian learned to travel light, live off the land, and depend only on himself. He could also blaze a trail for himself and track one made by others. When he and James Craig had ridden out of Bryan's Station in search of Anna, Ian had felt fairly confident in his ability to find her. True, it had been some time since she'd been taken, and it had been many years since his last sojourn in Indian territory. However, Ian had never forgotten the skills he'd learned there, nor the friends who had taught them to him. Now, riding north alone, he knew he would need all his skill—and a bit of luck, as well—to find and bring Anna home.

The weather had been unusually dry for several weeks, and when he reached his favorite fording place, he was thankful for the relatively low level of the Ohio River. His horse had to swim through the middle part of the channel, and Ian held his rifle, powder horn, and saddlebags at waist level. Even at that, it was a much easier crossing than some he'd made. *I hope that bodes well for the rest of my journey*, he thought.

Once he gained the north bank, Ian stopped to press as much water from his clothing as he could. He had worn his old moccasin packs; not only were they more comfortable than boots, but his tracks would scarcely be detectable. In the old days, Ian would have made a fire and dried himself thoroughly before continuing to travel, but now he dared not risk it. Sitting in the sun, he chewed on a pull of jerky and drank from his leather water bag. Although he remained alert for any indication that someone else might be near, he heard only the usual forest sounds.

Still, when he started out again, Ian stayed well away from the Indian trails that crisscrossed the area. Traveling northeast, he would eventually reach the village where he and Silverwillow had lived. Ian had heard that many Delaware had been killed and some of their towns had been destroyed, but he also knew that the Lenni-Lenape loved their land. No matter what happened, they always returned to the places that meant much to them. His old friends would know how to find Anna Willow; it might take some time and patience, but eventually he would find his daughter.

The rain, usual for that time of the year, began that night and continued for the next two days. Sleeping on the wet ground made Ian's joints ache, brought on a head cold, and reminded him that he wasn't the young man that he'd been when first he first came to the Ohio. Only once did he risk a fire, then had to flee a hunting party of Shawnee who spotted it and came to investigate. His escape took him far out of his way, and more than once he feared he might be lost.

Another time Ian stopped to drink from a clear stream, and a wild boar charged out of the woods and frightened away his horse. He spent several precious hours finding the animal. The search for food also slowed him. Although he had eaten sparingly, eventually all the food he'd brought was gone, and he had to stop to gather acorns and other nuts and edible grasses. He also managed to catch a few small fish using only his bare hands, but afraid to build another fire, he ate them raw.

Finally he reached the forks of the Muskingum and stood in the middle of what had been Silverwillow's home. However difficult the journey had been to that point, this was Ian's worst moment. The only remnant of the once prosperous village was its charred firestone. Ian had told Anna that he feared such a thing; and now he knew that it had, indeed, come to pass.

No one lives here now. The realization came with the force of a blow. *There is none left to help me.*

Ian rested for a long time as he considered his next move. He could continue on his rounds of the old Delaware villages, but from the destruction here, Ian knew it was unlikely that he'd find anyone to help him. There was still one other possibility, however. Years ago, Ian had traded with Shawnees in one of the three towns called Chillicothe, the one nearest the Scioto Trail.

Perhaps someone there will remember me, or at least be willing to hear me out.

Ian knew he was taking a great chance to ask help from a people who seldom showed mercy, even to their own, and who might even be among the very ones that had attacked Bryan's Station and taken Anna away. But he had come to the Ohio Territory to find Anna Willow, and he would not cross the Ohio again without her.

In the center of the ruined village where he had lived with Silverwillow, Ian vowed again to find their daughter.

His heart heavy with sorrow for what had come to pass in this place, he cast one last look around the ruins before he mounted his horse and headed southwest, toward Chillicothe. Already he felt that he had been traveling forever—he had lost all count of how many days had passed since he'd left Bryan's Station. The destruction he'd seen thus far in Indian country saddened him, and he feared for his newfound daughter Willow, that she might insist on returning to such an uncertain life.

At least she and Rebecca are safe and together. Ian took some comfort in that thought.

29

BRYAN'S STATION

Willow begrudged each and every day that she awoke to find herself still at Bryan's Station, away from White Eagle and the world that she'd always known. Yet Bear's Daughter had taught her to make the best of any situation, and once she began to work alongside the *Shemanese* women, the long hours seemed to pass more quickly. *Idleness becomes no woman,* Bear's Daughter had often told her.

As the days passed, Willow found some things to like about the *Shemanese* way of living. But even though in many ways she was far more comfortable than she'd ever been, Willow took no pleasure in it. She longed for White Eagle, and realized that her best chance of getting back home to him rested with her father, Ee-an M'night. Surely, after he returned with this Anna, he would let her go.

In the meantime, she worked around the Station and spent a part of every day with Stuart Martin, teaching him Shawnee words, while he helped her learn English.

One such afternoon, Stuart and Willow were in the McKnight cabin practicing each other's language while Rebecca sewed a baby garment. Betsy Craig came to the open door and called to them with excitement in her voice: "Miz McKnight, a man just rode into the Station looking for the colonel. He told Pa he's seen Anna."

Directing Willow to stay where she was, Stuart and Rebecca followed Betsy to the center of the Station, where a seedy-looking white man stood engaged in angry conversation with her father.

"What do ye mean, Colonel McKnight ain't 'ere?"

James Craig seemed relieved when Rebecca and Stuart joined them. "As I just tole you, the colonel rode out some weeks past in search of his daughter. This is his wife, Rebecca, and Stuart Martin, a friend."

"Edward Tucker," the man said, but he made no move to accept Stuart's extended hand. He stared hard at Rebecca. "I can see ye ain't her mother, but mebbe ye know the gal?"

Rebecca nodded curtly, returning him more courtesy than he had given. "Yes, of course. Her name is Anna Willow, and she was kidnapped by a Shawnee warrior when they besieged this Station. If you have any information at all about her, we'd like to know it."

Edward Tucker's mouth twisted sardonically. "I reckon ye would, ma'am. But I ain't sayin' another word 'less'n ye make it worth my while."

Stuart saw James Craig finger the hilt of his knife, and fearing that the men might come to blows before Tucker could tell them what he knew, he gestured for the man to come with him and Rebecca.

"We can discuss this at the colonel's cabin, Mr. Tucker. This way."

On the way to the cabin, Rebecca told the man she would provide some refreshment for him. "If you've come all the way from across the river, you must be pretty tired by now."

Edward Tucker scowled. "Ah, ye'll not trick me into tellin' ye nothin' fer free, Miz McKnight."

His first impression of dislike for the man now confirmed, Stuart suppressed what would have been an imprudent answer. "I'm sure Mrs. McKnight only meant to be hospitable," he said instead.

When they arrived at the cabin, Rebecca entered first, followed by Stuart and their visitor. Willow still sat where they had left her.

Rebecca and Stuart watched Edward Tucker's face when he saw her. His eyes widened, his mouth dropped open, and it took him a long moment to find his voice. It was the way most people who had seen Anna reacted when they first saw Willow, but Edward Tucker's astonishment exceeded most.

"Wha—who is she?" Tucker finally managed to say.

"She is called Willow," Rebecca replied.

Edward Tucker continued to stare at Willow, then he shook his head and turned to Rebecca. "What kind o' game do ye play 'ere?"

"It's no game, sir. This girl is a twin to the one you claim to have seen."

Edward Tucker frowned. "No claim about it, I seen th' girl not a week past—" Aware that he'd said more than he intended, Tucker stopped abruptly.

Stuart's heart leaped in his chest. "Where is Anna? Is she well?" he pressed the man.

"She was well enough then," Edward Tucker said sullenly. "She said 'er father'd pay me well for tellin' 'im 'er whereabouts, else I'd not a-come 'ere. I'll say no more 'less'n I see some hard money."

All except Willow had been standing, and now Rebecca indicated that Stuart and Edward Tucker should take seats. "I'll brew us some tea," she said calmly. "Then we will talk."

Willow couldn't put a name to this *Shemanese* who had seemed so surprised at the sight of her, but she thought she might have seen him around Waccachalla a few years past. Then he'd been one of the many soldiers who wore bright red coats with the shiny brass buttons that were so highly prized in trade. If this was the same man, he probably also spoke her language.

While Rebecca busied herself dipping hot water from the cooking pot, Willow rested her forearms on the table and leaned forward. Speaking in Shawnee, she addressed the man directly.

"Who are you? Where do you come from?"

Had she slapped him, Edward Tucker could hardly have looked more startled. In Shawnee he told Willow his name, and added that he was a trader who did business with Chief Black Snake.

Willow's reaction was immediate and intense. "The chief is my kinsman. You have seen him?"

Tucker nodded. "Yes. I come here to tell Colonel McKnight of this thing."

"What are you saying?" Stuart could make out a

few words and guess at the rest, but he didn't want to let Edward Tucker know he understood any of it.

"The girl asked who I was. I reckon she jes' wants t' talk 'er lingo agin."

On the table Rebecca set a china teapot—the only thing of value she still owned—and took four pewter mugs from a plank shelf on the nearby wall.

"I'm afraid you'll have to drink this tea plain, Mr. Tucker. We've not seen any sugar at the Station in many weeks."

"'Twill do," he said shortly. "Now, about my money—"

"As far as I can tell, you've done nothing to warrant any payment," Stuart put in. "What proof do we have that you even know where Anna is?"

Edward Tucker blew on his tea and took a noisy sip. He pointed to Willow. "Would I a-thought aught about this un 'ad I not seen t'other? I know where yer Anna is, an' without my 'elp, there she stays."

"Mr. Tucker, I believe you, but the fact is that my husband has no gold," Rebecca told him. "However, if you fancy any of our goods—"

"No!" He slapped the palm of his hand on the table for emphasis. "The girl tol' me that she'd some gold coins 'id in 'er petticoat. She said t' tell ye I was t' have 'em, above and beyond aught 'er father'd give me."

Rebecca and Stuart exchanged surprised glances. "I know nothin' about any money," Rebecca said. "Willow's been wearin' Anna's clothes. I'd know if there'd been any money in them."

Edward Tucker shook his head. "Mebbe not. I'll

wager the petticoat's in a saddlebag in the lean-to, like this Anna tol' me."

Rebecca started toward the lean-to, motioning Stuart and Tucker to stay behind. Willow, who wasn't sure what was happening but didn't want to miss anything, followed Rebecca. She watched, mystified, as Rebecca opened Anna's saddlebag and lifted out a long petticoat with an attached bodice.

"There's somethin' in here, all right." Rebecca reached into her apron pocket for her sewing scissors and quickly cut several large stitches, releasing a jingle of coins into her hand.

Willow gasped in awe, and Rebecca quickly tucked the gold into her pocket.

"Well?" Edward Tucker asked when they returned. "The girl was right about the money, warn't she?"

"If so, you've done nothing to earn it," Rebecca said.

The man's face flushed angrily. "I'll tell ye nothin' more 'til ye pay me what's my due."

"You agreed to tell Ian McKnight where to find his daughter. So far, you've not done it."

Tucker's cheeks reddened and he spoke sullenly. "I'd a-tol' Colonel McKnight if'n 'e'd a-been 'ere. That ain't my fault. As fer where the girl is—"

He broke off and looked at Willow, then back at Stuart. "She can take ye there if'n yer fool enough t' risk th' goin'."

Stuart had never been a violent man, but the knowledge that Edward Tucker knew where Anna was, yet would not tell them, tested his patience almost past the breaking point. He moved forward and gathered a fistful of the man's shirt. "That's enough riddle-speaking. Where is Anna?"

Edward Tucker glared balefully at Stuart. "In a Shawnee village called Waccachalla."

Stuart tightened his hold on Tucker's shirt. "Where is this place?"

"Off the Scioto Trail, near a Shawnee town named Chillicothe."

Stuart loosened his grip and Tucker backed away, still eyeing Stuart warily. "I tole ye, now give me my money." Although his voice was a bit less strident, it was obvious that Tucker's determination to have Anna's coins had not diminished.

Rebecca spoke before Stuart had the opportunity. "Let's all go have our tea. I believe we can reach a peaceful agreement in this matter."

30

CHILLICOTHE

White Eagle could not say how long he stayed in the lodge of the medicine woman at Chillicothe; he only knew it was far longer than he wanted. The bitter draughts she forced down his throat made him sleep for hours, even days, at a time, while she put one poultice after another on his wounded thigh. When her medicine took hold and the wound no longer threatened his life, White Eagle tried to stand—but found that he could not. The long period of inactivity, combined with the effects of the powerful brews the old woman gave him, had made White Eagle weak in a way he had never before known.

"You must give me a restorative," White Eagle told the medicine woman when he found he could not stand without aid. "Your medicine has taken away the strength I must have."

The old woman shook her head. "Ayee, you young warriors have no patience. Your sickness took away your strength. Only time brings it back."

"I have no time!" White Eagle exclaimed impatiently. "I must go to Waccachalla. Black Snake must know what happened to his kin."

The medicine woman raised her eyebrows. "This Willow is the chief's kin?"

White Eagle nodded. "The *Shemanese* who shot me took her away."

"So you have spoken many times these days past. I thought it was fever talk."

"No. I must get to Waccachalla right away. Have you no remedy to give me strength?"

"There is something, but it must be taken for three days. Each day you can do more."

"Then give it to me, *nik-yah*."

"Ayee, you young men are all alike. What will happen will happen, with you or without you. But this last thing I will do, if you promise to stay here and rest while you take it."

White Eagle nodded. His slight exertion had left him almost too weary to speak, but his determination to go on to Waccachalla remained strong. *Three days and I will go there*, he promised himself. *Chief Black Snake will know what to do about finding Willow.*

Thus resigned, White Eagle allowed the medicine woman to lead him back to his bed.

Days later, when White Eagle finally rode out of Chillicothe, he was accompanied by Red Pole, younger brother of Yellow Hawk, a warrior White Eagle had long known. The medicine woman had insisted that her younger son go along in case White Eagle suffered a spell of weakness and needed help, and reluctantly White Eagle had agreed.

For whatever reason—his youth and general good health, his own strength of will, or the vile-tasting brew that he'd taken for the past three days—White Eagle felt better than at any time since his encounter with the *Shemanese*. His thigh was still tender, and he favored the injured leg, but the medicine woman assured him that with time, his slight limp would go away. At any rate, White Eagle could now mount and ride his horse unaided.

Partly because of the nature of their errand, and in part to convince Black Snake that he dealt with able warriors, White Eagle and Red Pole had outfitted themselves in war paint and scarlet headbands, and White Eagle tied a feather in his hair. Thus attired, the men created something of a stir when they entered Waccachalla. They dismounted, and asked to speak to the chief of the village.

Black Snake had been warned by the lookout that two strange warriors approached, and he awaited them at the door of the council lodge.

"Peace, Chief Black Snake," White Eagle and Red Pole said together.

"Peace to you, warriors. Who are you, and on what errand come you to this place?"

White Eagle introduced himself and Red Pole. "Tall Oak, chief in Shawnee Town, sends his greetings. I bring you his gift." He paused for a moment, then added, "I also have news of your kinswomen, Bear's Daughter and Willow."

The chief's expression didn't change, but he moved aside and motioned for the visitors to enter. By custom, Black Snake brought out a tobacco-filled pipe and lighted it. Only when it had passed to each in turn three times did Black Snake nod to his guest to speak.

With great ceremony, White Eagle spread out before Black Snake the buffalo robe he had been carrying. "Tall Oak wishes to make treaty with the chief of Waccachalla. Our warriors fight beside yours. Your warriors fight beside ours."

Black Snake signaled for White Eagle to hand him the robe, which he immediately put around his shoulders. "It is good," he said. "Tell Tall Oak we will talk more of this thing." Then the chief laid the robe aside and leaned forward slightly. "Now I would hear of my kinswomen."

Forcing himself to speak slowly, White Eagle told the events in order, omitting nothing, for he knew he must convince Black Snake that he spoke the truth. He related how he had first met Bear's Daughter and Willow on the trail and returned to help them, and how the old woman had sickened and died before they could reach Shawnee Town.

"I promised Bear's Daughter that I would marry Willow, but even without her urging, I would gladly have done so."

White Eagle paused for a moment, and Black Snake frowned. "You say that you buried my kinswoman, and for that I thank you. But what of Willow?"

"We were riding to tell you the news of Bear's Daughter so she could be properly mourned. Then we met two *Shemanese*. I told Willow to hide in the woods, and I fought them and took a bullet here, in my thigh. The men took Willow. I followed their tracks to the O-hio-se-pe. By then I was too weak to go on. Red Pole found me on the Scioto Trail. His mother took me in and healed my wound. Only now am I able to come to tell you these things."

Black Snake listened attentively, not speaking until White Eagle finished his account. "We have known nothing of my kinswomen for some time. We thought that both Bear's Daughter and the girl were dead." The chief asked a few questions about times and places, then stood and motioned for White Eagle to follow him. "Red Pole stays in the council lodge. My daughter Blossom will bring him food."

White Eagle remained silent as he and Black Snake walked through the village, receiving the curious stares of many onlookers. When he reached a large *wegiwa,* which White Eagle guessed was the chief's, Black Snake motioned for White Eagle to wait while he went inside.

The chief emerged a moment later with a young girl he introduced to White Eagle as his daughter, Blossom. He directed her to take food to the council lodge, then turned back to White Eagle. "Come this way."

Becoming more mystified by the moment, White Eagle followed Black Snake to the banks of a stony creek, trying hard not to limp. Several of the village women had waded into the water and appeared to be washing their clothing. Most stood with their backs to Black Snake and White Eagle, but when the chief called out "An-na," one girl turned to face them.

White Eagle took a step forward almost involuntarily, so certain was he at first that his Willow had somehow made her escape from the *Shemanese* and returned to her village. Yet she looked at him with no sign of recognition, and White Eagle realized that he was mistaken. This An-na, as the chief called her, wore the same kind of doeskin shift as the other Shawnee women, and her chestnut hair had been dressed in a style similar to Willow's. But she was slightly taller, and the blank stare with which she regarded White Eagle confirmed that she didn't know him.

"Is this An-na like the girl Willow?" Black Snake asked, but White Eagle's stunned expression had already given him his answer.

White Eagle nodded, taken aback by the great resemblance between the two girls. "Willow did not say she had a sister," he finally managed.

"She could not say what she did not know. I adopted An-na as my daughter. One of our raiding warriors thought she was Willow and brought her back from a *Shemanese* settlement. She does not speak our tongue."

As Black Snake spoke, White Eagle felt a growing excitement. He was almost certain that she could help him find Willow.

"I have some English," White Eagle said.

"Then speak with her."

The girl An-na looked warily from Black Snake to White Eagle as if she thought she had reason to fear the young warrior. The other women had ceased their labors to watch them with great interest.

White Eagle gestured toward the women. "I would speak to this An-na in your lodge."

Black Snake nodded and gestured for Anna to come.

The girl inclined her head briefly to show that she understood. She waded from the water and followed the men, walking several paces behind them. When they reached the chief's *wegiwa*, Standing Crane was sitting cross-legged by the fire. Black Snake and White Eagle joined her, placing themselves around the fire, and the chief gestured to Anna to sit down also. She did not look at White Eagle until he spoke to her in English.

"An-na, my name White Eagle."

Startled, she raised her head to stare at him. From her first glimpse of him, Anna had thought the young warrior was much better-looking than those she had seen in Waccachalla. She had presumed from his limp that he had been wounded in some recent skirmish, perhaps even in the raid that had taken her from her Kentucky. She more than half feared that the chief had brought this man to her as a prospective husband. That she might be able to talk to him was a welcome surprise. "You speak English?" she asked.

"Yes. I come to tell Chief Black Snake of Willow. You look like Willow—my wife."

Anna felt a sudden rush of relief that he was already married.

"I know. The warrior who brought me here thought I was Willow. If you will tell the chief where she is, perhaps he will let me go."

When White Eagle frowned, Anna realized that she had probably spoken too rapidly for him to understand. She tried again. Pointing to herself, Anna leaned closer to White Eagle. "I am An-na. My mother was Silverwillow, a Delaware. My father is Ian McKnight. He lives at Bryan's Station in Kan-tuck-e. Black Snake's warrior took me from there. Do you understand these things?"

White Eagle frowned as if trying to remember something. "Fath-er Ee-an M'Night?"

Anna nodded. "Yes. Trader Ee-an M'night. Where is your Willow now?"

"*Shemanese* take her across O-hio-se-pe, to Kan-tuck-e," he replied. "I come Waccachalla, tell Black Snake."

As he spoke, Anna had a sudden thought. "What did those *Shemanese* look like?"

"One man short, hair like this." White Eagle pointed to his own head. "One old, tall." He touched his chin and cheeks. "Much hair here, red, white."

Anna clasped her hands in excitement. "My father!" Finally the pieces of the puzzle were beginning to come together. She spoke earnestly, adding gestures to her words to make her meaning clear. "My father is Ian McKnight. He thought Willow was me. That is why he took her to Kentucky."

White Eagle looked thoughtful as he considered her words.

"I don't know how it happened," Anna admitted. "My father lives at Bryan's Station in Kentucky. That is where he would take Willow."

White Eagle's voice was calm, but his eyes gleamed with excitement. "I go to that place. I get Willow."

"Take me with you," Anna pleaded.

Sensing that their conversation might be taking a

turn he didn't like, Black Snake asked White Eagle what the girl said. Briefly White Eagle summarized Anna's words.

"An-na thinks her father took Willow to Kantuck-e. She wants to go with me to help find her," he concluded.

Black Snake scowled his displeasure. "An-na not *Shemanese*. An-na now Shawnee, in place of Willow. Tell her this thing."

White Eagle translated Black Snake's words, then added a few of his own. "When he sees Willow, maybe Black Snake let you go."

"As soon as my father knows where I am, he will come after me," Anna said. "He could already be on the way. I want no fighting about this."

"I tell your father I see you, if he not shoot first."

"Take a white cloth with you. When you get to the Station, wave it on a stick as a flag of truce. Ask to see Ian McKnight. Tell him that Anna sent you. If he has your Willow and if she wants to go with you, he will let you leave in peace."

White Eagle thought for a moment. "This Ee-an M'night not know me. He say I try a Shawnee trick."

Given her father's normal caution, Anna thought, White Eagle had a good point. Instinctively she reached for her necklace. Then she realized that it could be the key to her freedom. Quickly she withdrew the necklace from beneath her shift and unclasped the chain.

"My father—Ian McKnight—gave me this. He will know it is from me."

White Eagle's eyes widened. He recognized that it was fine gold, worth much gunpowder and rifles and many warm blankets to *Shemanese* traders. It lay in Anna's outstretched palm for a long moment before White Eagle finally took it.

"What is this that you do?" Black Snake demanded when White Eagle took Anna's necklace.

"I take this to Kan-tuck-e to show her father. If he has Willow, I bring her here."

Black Snake looked away from White Eagle and stared hard at Anna. "An-na stays here," he said in Shawnee.

Anna inclined her head to show that she understood. *"Oui-sah,"* she said.

Now all Anna could do was pray that White Eagle would succeed in the quest for his mysterious Willow, and that this Willow's return would assure her own freedom.

White Eagle and Red Pole accepted Black Snake's offer of lodging for the night, but White Eagle slept fitfully. He did not understand all she had said about this Ee-an M'night, but he believed what this An-na said.

He arose before dawn to bathe in the creek and make preparations for his journey. With bear oil, he removed the last traces of his war paint, then larded his moccasins to repel snakes, which feared the scent of wild boars. Against the chill of the fall morning, White Eagle added a rawhide vest to his breechclout and fringed leggings. He tied a scarlet band around his forehead to keep his hair out of his face, but he wore no adornment in his hair.

When White Eagle had readied himself, he went

back to the council lodge, where Black Snake gave him a pouch filled with pemmican and venison jerky.

Red Pole watched White Eagle's preparations with a wary eye. "You have not yet recovered your full strength. Let me go across the O-hio-se-pe with you."

White Eagle shook his head. "No. I must do this thing as a lone hunter. It is a safer way."

"No way is safe these days," Red Pole muttered, disappointed that he would miss what promised to be a great adventure.

White Eagle removed his silver armband, a gift his father had bestowed on him when he had become a warrior. He handed it to Red Pole. "I owe you my life, my brother. You and your people have done much for me. If you want to help me now, go to Shawnee Town. Show this to Tall Oak and tell him all that has passed. Say that soon I bring Willow home."

"I will do this thing. My mother will want to see this Willow that you called for so often in your fever."

"Tell her that in good time I bring Willow to her at Chillicothe."

A fleeting smile crossed Red Pole's usually serious features. "She will be glad to hear of it."

Red Pole intended to circle his left bicep with White Eagle's gift, but to his chagrin, his arm was much smaller and he had to push on the armband to make it stay in place.

"Red Pole is yet young, as I was when first I tried to wear the silver band. You will grow to it," White Eagle assured him. "Come, it is time to go."

White Eagle took leave of Black Snake and went to his waiting horse. As he mounted, he looked back toward the chief's *wegiwa*. Anna stood outside, watching him. She lifted her hand briefly in a half wave, and once more the resemblance between her and Willow struck White Eagle with almost physical force. But no matter how much they looked alike, this one was not his Willow.

Soon I will bring my wife to this place, he thought. *When she and An-na meet, all who see them together will wonder.*

But all of that still lay ahead in a future that was not as certain as he might wish. White Eagle reminded himself that he had a long way to go before the thing would come to pass.

For the first part of his journey, White Eagle neither encountered nor heard another human being. From nearly every tree, squirrels chattered in noisy challenge, and at times the underbrush was so heavy that he had to dismount and lead Mishewa, but he continued to follow a small stream that would eventually bring him to the O-hio-se-o-pe, the river that he must cross to find Willow.

When the sun reached the top of the sky, White Eagle stopped to rest in an area rich with persimmon and oak trees. He gathered windfall persimmons and many acorns to supplement the fare Black Snake had given him. Even if he did not yet need more food himself, White Eagle would need provisions for Willow, and it wouldn't be safe to food-gather once he was in Kan-tuck-e.

At midafternoon, the creek White Eagle followed veered east, near the southern end of the Scioto Trail. He came out at what had been Lower Shawnee Town before the *Shemanese* had destroyed it. There began the Coschocton Trail, which ran north and west. White Eagle planned, when he returned with Willow, to take that trail until it crossed the Kanawha, and thus come to Waccachalla from the east. That way, they would avoid the more heavily traveled Scioto Trail.

Bypassing the ruins of Lower Shawnee Town, White Eagle had just skirted the edge of the trail when he heard distant hoofbeats. He jumped from his horse and crouched behind a screening bush and waited for the party to come into sight. From the sound, he guessed there were no more than three horses, probably only two. *A hunting party, most probably Shawnee,* White Eagle thought. It was unlikely to be *Shemanese*; except for an occasional trader and the men who had taken Willow, whites seldom dared to travel north of the O-hio-se-pe.

The horsemen rode at a deliberate pace, neither fast nor slow, but before they came near enough for him to see them, they stopped. *Maybe they're looking for the Coshocton Trail,* White Eagle thought. Curious to see who they were, he tied Mishewa to a sapling and made his way on foot toward the horsemen.

They were closer than he'd thought, and he was almost upon them before he realized it. He had judged well; there were only two horses. On one of them, a black stallion, sat a dark-haired *Shemanese* man that White Eagle knew by sight. A red-coat turned trader, he had often come to Shawnee Town, but not for some time. As White Eagle recalled, the man had cheated some village women, and Tall Oak had told him not to return.

The horse behind the trader sidestepped, allowing White Eagle to see the second *Shemanese,* a clean-shaven, slender young man with a great deal of light hair showing under his hat. He sat so high in the saddle that at first White Eagle didn't see that someone rode behind him—someone in fringed buckskin leggings, someone with long black hair—unmistakably, a young woman.

And not *Shemanese,* either. When the blond man turned in the saddle to speak to her, White Eagle had a glimpse of her face. He blinked and looked again, thinking that his eyes lied to him.

You see Willow everywhere you look, White Eagle told himself. But when the girl leaned forward and pointed a graceful finger straight ahead as if directing them toward the Scioto Trail, it was all he could do to stay where he was.

It is Willow, he realized. White Eagle's heart hammered in his chest. He wanted to run from his hiding place and lift Willow down from the *Shemanese* horse, hold her close, and never let her go again.

But White Eagle did not; he would be foolish to show himself now. The *Shemanese* were heavily armed, and with his wound not yet healed, he was not at his best. If these men held Willow against her will, he would have to fight them both. He well remembered how his first attempt to protect Willow from *Shemanese* had failed. He would not make the same mistake twice.

With his pulse pounding and every sense alert, White Eagle waited to see what would happen next. With relief he noted that Willow wasn't bound in any way, nor did she look distressed. In fact, even from the distance that separated them, he could see that she appeared to be animated and excited. When she continued to point toward the trail, White Eagle concluded that she must be directing the *Shemanese* toward Waccachalla.

When the blond man turned around again, White Eagle studied his face. He was positive that neither of the men who had taken Willow across the O-hio-se-pe had light hair. Their leader, the one who had probably shot White Eagle, was a bearded older man with once-red hair fading to white. That was the man described by An-na and named by Willow as their father, Ee-an M'night. White Eagle would recognize him on sight. He wondered briefly what had happened that Ee-an M'night was not with Willow now.

Who are these men? Where do they come from? Why is Willow with them? White Eagle wanted to stay there and fill his eyes with the sight of his beloved, but he feared that Mishewa would whinny when their horses passed. Even as White Eagle turned to retrace his steps, the *Shemanese* urged their mounts to a fast walk, and he had to hurry to reach his horse before they came to his hiding place.

White Eagle's leg throbbed as he got to Mishewa, barely in time. The horse understood White Eagle's hand on his muzzle, and he remained quiet and still while the riders passed only a short distance away. He could see their features clearly now. With a surge of joy, White Eagle confirmed that the girl riding behind the blond *Shemanese* was, indeed, his Willow.

He guessed they were taking her back to Waccachalla, and as long as they didn't harm her, he wouldn't interfere. If they had anything else in mind, he would fight them—but he would need help.

I shouldn't have sent Red Pole on to Shawnee Town, White Eagle thought. Although the boy was young and relatively unproved, the mere sight of a second warrior might make the *Shemanese* turn Willow over to them without bloodshed.

It wasn't too late to get help. If White Eagle rode hard, he could get back to Chillicothe long before dark. During his time there, White Eagle had met several of Red Pole's companions, young warriors who would ride with him. The *Shemanese* wouldn't risk traveling at night; soon they would stop and make camp. White Eagle knew a shorter path through the woods. He and his party would be waiting for them when they turned toward Waccachalla. With his plan thus formed, White Eagle mounted Mishewa and rode hard toward Chillicothe.

31

KANAWHA TRAIL

On his first day out of the destroyed Delaware village, Ian was seized with a chill that threatened to shake him from the saddle, forcing him to make a stop. Afraid to build a fire, he wrapped himself in his blanket and shivered through the rest of that day, then passed a bleak and miserable night. He tried to imagine that he and Rebecca sat before a roaring fire in their cabin. Although Ian saw the flames in great detail, they brought no warmth, and thinking of Rebecca made him miss his wife so keenly that he dismissed the vision.

The next morning, groggy from his head cold and weak from lack of food, Ian barely found the strength to pull himself onto his horse. Doggedly he rode on, stopping only when he had to. A day or two later—he wasn't sure how much time had passed—Ian took heart when he came upon a well-used north-south path.

The Kanawha Trail, he thought. From the angle of

the sun in the sky, he determined that he must cross this trail and head almost due south in order to reach Chillicothe.

When he'd first come to the Ohio Territory, Ian had ranged far to the west, setting traps and occasionally trading with scattered groups of Indians. In those days, all had been glad to see him, happy to get the iron pots, flints, and small trinkets he'd carried on his packhorse. In return, they'd given him their finest pelts. When his horse could hold no more, Ian would go to a trading post on the Ohio River, where he got a good price for the goods. He had traded with many Indians in those days, most as nameless and faceless to him as he was to them.

It was only after he met Silverwillow that Ian began to see the Indians he traded with as people. Now, to distract his attention from his aching joints and swimming head, he thought of those days— among the happiest in his life—and of the daughter that Silverwillow had given him.

No, he corrected himself. *Daughters*. For their sake, Ian knew he must remain alert and press on.

He neither saw nor heard anyone as he crossed the Kanawha Trail, but not far from it, he almost literally ran into a band of Indians coming from the other direction. Two rode, while three more traveled on foot. The Indians and Ian stopped about ten feet from each other.

In a hoarse voice, Ian addressed them in English. "I am a friend."

Their leader, an older man with a pockmarked face, looked dubious. "What business has a *Shemanese* here?"

"I seek friends in Chillicothe."

The men exchanged glances. "Which Chillicothe?" the older one asked.

Ian hesitated. He wished that his fever-clouded mind would think more clearly. He knew there were at least three Shawnee towns named Chillicothe, including the biggest one, the Shawnee capital. But it was not that one he sought. "Near the Scioto," he said.

The men exchanged glances, then their leader spoke again. "Who these friends?"

Ian felt a moment of panic when he could not recall a single name. "Men I traded with. They know me by sight."

The leader consulted with his companions, then turned back to Ian.

I don't like the look on his face. The thought had scarcely formed in Ian's mind before the men surged toward him. Quickly they pulled him from his horse, took his weapons, and tied his hands behind him. One of the men mounted Ian's horse, obviously pleased to have it, and the group once more resumed their journey.

"Where do you take me?" Ian asked, but his captors made no reply.

He raised his head to the sky in silent appeal. Now that he was in the hands of Shawnee who considered him their enemy, Ian had only one thought.

God help me.

The fall sunset gilded the western sky in shades of pink that gradually deepened to red. White Eagle noted the clouds, not for their beauty, but because they foretold that the next day would dawn fair.

It is good, White Eagle thought. He would welcome seeing Willow again in any sort of weather, but a clear sky was always a good omen. It would also make it easier to fight, if that proved to be necessary.

As he rode toward Chillicothe, White Eagle wondered where Willow had been living since he'd last seen her, and how the *Shemanese* had treated her. From what he had seen of Willow on the trail, she didn't seem to be harmed.

This Ee-an M'night, being Willow's father, might have seen to that, he thought. Even though the *Shemanese* had apparently never seen Willow until the day he had taken her from White Eagle, the man must have some tender feelings for his own kin.

Imagining the look that would be on Willow's face when she saw him again, White Eagle smiled to himself. Impatient to reach Chillicothe and find warriors to help him, he prodded his horse to go faster; then abruptly reined Mishewa to a stop when he heard horses coming his way.

Quickly White Eagle rode behind an outcropping of rocks and dismounted. To get a better view, he carefully, using his arms and his one good leg, climbed a nearby maple tree whose varicolored leaves of orange and yellow provided a good screen. Even if someone on the ground looked directly at the tree, White Eagle could not be seen. The muffled hoofbeats of several horses moving slowly grew louder as they approached. From the occasional snapping of twigs, White Eagle guessed that the horses were accompanied by several men on foot. As they neared, the murmur of their conversation also grew louder.

White Eagle held his breath as the party came into sight, then exhaled in relief as he recognized them. Red Pole's brother Yellow Hawk led the group on horseback, followed by Spotted Beaver and Lame Elk, who also rode. Several others unknown to him walked alongside. Since they wore no war paint, White Eagle assumed they were out to do some night hunting. Then he saw the man who walked between them—a *Shemanese*, with his hands tied behind him. His head was lowered, but as the group came closer, the *Shemanese* looked up. White Eagle saw the man's face, and gasped.

From his distinctive red hair, White Eagle recognized Ee-an M'night, the man both An-na and Willow named as father, the man who had taken Willow away from him and across the O-hio-se-pe.

This man is foolish if he crossed the river alone, White Eagle thought. And if he hadn't been alone, then his companions might be lying in ambush.

From his position in the tree, White Eagle cupped his hands around his mouth and gave a few notes of a peculiar call. To the uninitiated, it would seem only like another common forest sound, but to Shawnees everywhere, it was a useful way to identify one another.

At first the warriors didn't heed it, but when White Eagle repeated the call, Yellow Hawk stopped and signaled for silence. White Eagle called a third time, and this time Yellow Hawk returned it and added a single note to the end. When White Eagle exactly imitated him, Yellow Hawk spoke in a loud voice.

"Show yourself, Shawnee."

White Eagle emerged from his hiding place and carefully lowered himself to the ground only a few feet from the party. He raised his right hand with his palm facing them. "Greetings, Yellow Hawk."

Yellow Hawk stared at White Eagle in astonishment. "Can it be this warrior White Eagle, who my mother restored to his health?"

White Eagle nodded. "Ayee, the same."

Yellow Hawk looked around warily. "Where is my brother?"

"Red Pole is safe at Shawnee Town." He pointed to their prisoner. "Where do you go with this *Shemanese?*"

"To Chillicothe. Our chief will decide what to do with him. What about White Eagle? How come you alone in the forest?"

"In a way I have no time to tell now," White Eagle said. "I would take the *Shemanese* with me."

Yellow Hawk frowned. "I do not understand this thing. Better that White Eagle go with us to take him to our chief."

"No. This thing is between me and the *Shemanese.* It does not concern you or your chief."

"White Eagle, you are a brave warrior, but not yet strong. You cannot travel alone with this *Shemanese.*"

White Eagle impatiently made the cutoff sign. "We waste this daylight in talk. Untie the *Shemanese.*"

Yellow Hawk hesitated, then shrugged and shook his head, clearly conveying the message that if White

Eagle came to harm, it wouldn't be his fault. He unbound his prisoner, who rubbed his chafed wrists and looked warily at White Eagle.

"My rifle—" he began, but Yellow Hawk interrupted.

"We will return the horse," he said, looking up at Spotted Beaver, who reluctantly slid from the animal he had so recently acquired. "But we keep the *Shemanese* weapons," said Yellow Hawk.

White Eagle inclined his head. "It is good." While he thought that he could trust this man who was his Willow's father, he knew that his companions did not. They all knew *Shemanese* who had pretended to be friends to the Shawnee, only to turn on them and do terrible things.

White Eagle gestured to the *Shemanese*. "Let us go," he said in English.

"We would know more of this thing," Yellow Hawk said.

"Ayee. It will be done. Now there is no time."

Without another word, White Eagle mounted his horse, and with Ian McKnight following on his, headed toward Waccachalla. Soon the the hunting party was far behind.

Ian had recognized the young warrior the instant that he appeared, seemingly from nowhere, and his heart had beat faster at the sight of him. He had no doubt that this was the man who had been with Willow the day he had taken her away.

I don't wonder that Willow wanted to come back to him, Ian thought. The Shawnee was handsome, with the kind of commanding presence that could compel others to do his will, even against their own. His captors, who apparently knew the young warrior well, had called him White Eagle.

He's not a man you would want as your enemy. Ian realized that the Shawnee would blame him for Willow's abduction, and he knew that his punishment for taking her probably wouldn't be light.

I must find some way to make him understand that Willow is safe and that I'm Willow's father, he thought.

Ian spoke as forcefully as he could manage through his hoarseness, glad that this warrior understood English. "My name is Ian McKnight. I saw you with Willow on the trail. I am her father."

White Eagle looked at Ian without surprise. "I know this thing. Why come you here now without Willow?"

Once again, Ian wished that he didn't feel so lightheaded. He found it hard to frame the right words. "I came in peace to the O-hio to find my other daughter Anna, taken from Kan-tuck-e. When I took Willow, I thought she was Anna." When White Eagle said nothing, Ian added, "Willow is safe in Kan-tuck-e."

White Eagle glanced at Ian and shook his head. "This is not so."

Ian furrowed his brow and tried without success to make sense of the words. "What?"

White Eagle gestured expansively. "Willow here now."

"How could she get to Ohio?" Ian asked the question as much to himself as to White Eagle.

"*Shemanese* bring her."

"What *Shemanese?*" At the moment, Ian couldn't think of anyone at Bryan's Station who would likely undertake such a mission.

White Eagle shrugged. "You see. Come."

White Eagle turned into one of the deer traces that made mazes in the forest. He motioned for Ian to watch out for overhead branches, but Ian had already bent low, an automatic response from years of riding in forests.

I hope I can trust this White Eagle, Ian thought. If anyone could find Anna, it would be this young warrior. He only hoped he could believe that what he said was true: Willow had safely returned from Kentucky and was nearby.

Willow hadn't wanted to stop at all; she would gladly have traveled all night, if necessary, to get to Waccachalla. But when Stuart signaled that their horses needed a rest, she resigned herself to spending one more night away from the place she had always called home.

In the golden pink twilight, Edward Tucker led them to a place he knew, not on a main trail but reached by following a trace made years ago by thirsty deer and other animals. There, a stream of cold water ran from a limestone spring into a deep pool, before it formed a creek that would eventually find a larger stream before joining the O-hio-se-pe. From her first sight of the *Shemanese* Tucker, Willow had not liked him, but she realized that he seemed to know his way through this land.

If we must stop, this is a good place, Willow thought.

Her mind raced ahead to the next day, when they would reach Waccachalla. Willow imagined herself telling Black Snake about White Eagle and asking him to send word to Shawnee Town that Willow had returned home.

Then White Eagle will come to Waccachalla and we will be together again.

Rebecca McKnight had provided them with more than enough food to last for several days, and not wanting to draw unwanted attention, the men didn't make a campfire. Willow began to set out food for their supper. Stuart worked nearby, cutting branches to make their beds, while Edward Tucker tended the horses out of sight of the clearing.

Willow had just knelt by the stream to fill a water bag when a snapping twig made her instantly alert. In the twilight, she looked in the direction of the sound and saw the bulky shapes of two men on horseback, heading straight for their camp.

Before she had time to tell the others, the riders emerged from the underbrush in exactly the same place that Willow's party had ridden in. She watched as Stuart stood frozen in place, his eyes staring and his mouth agape at the sight of the riders.

Immediately Willow recognized the *Shemanese* Ee-an M'night, the man she now accepted as her father. But then she saw the other, and it was to him that she ran, even as White Eagle dismounted and started toward her.

Wordlessly they clung together, for the moment heedless of anything else but each other.

At the same time, Stuart Martin and Ian McKnight

stared at each other for a moment, then cried out the other's name. Still feeling weak and dizzy, Ian stumbled and would have fallen had not Stuart put out his arm to steady him. He helped Ian to a fallen log and sat down beside him. Both men started to speak at once, then laughed ruefully.

"Aye, Stuart, I never thought to see ye here in this place!" Ian finally managed to say.

"Nor I you, although I hoped to find you. I promised Rebecca I'd bring you home safely."

Ian looked bewildered. "Rebecca? Ye've been at Bryan's Station, then?"

Stuart nodded. "I came to Kentucky intending to ask for Anna's hand in marriage. Instead, I found her sister." His gesture took in Willow and White Eagle, who now stood apart, talking of all that had happened since their last meeting.

Ian raised his eyebrows in surprise. "Ye want to marry Anna? I'd no idea of any of this."

Stuart smiled wryly. "I presumed you wouldn't object, but I'm not too sure how Anna feels. Now I wonder if I'll ever have the chance to ask her."

Ian clasped Stuart's hand. "Aye, we maun believe that we'll find her. Did ye know that Anna turned down several proposals of marriage at the Station?"

"So Rebecca told me. She said you didn't know that Anna was coming to Kentucky until she got there. You must have been quite surprised."

"Aye, and at first 'twas quite pleasant. But many's the time since the siege that I've wished I'd taken Anna Willow back to Pennsylvania. I don't know what I'll do if any harm has come to her."

White Eagle and Willow had started toward Ian and Stuart, and overheard Ian's last words.

"An-na not hurt," White Eagle said matter-of-factly. "This one at Waccachalla."

Ian gaped in wonder. "Ye have seen her?" he asked hoarsely.

White Eagle nodded. "This An-na daughter to Chief Black Snake."

Ian regarded White Eagle blankly. *Anna an Indian chief's daughter? Surely White Eagle must have seen someone else. Or perhaps he's making it all up to punish me for taking Willow.*

"My Anna is no chief's daughter," Ian declared.

White Eagle reached into his shot pouch and withdrew a delicate gold necklace, which he handed to Ian. "An-na say give Ee-an M'night."

The sight of the necklace filled Ian with such strong emotion that for a moment he could only stare at it through eyes damp with tears. "I sent this to Anna before she left Philadelphia."

Stuart nodded. "I saw it—she wore it constantly." With renewed hope, he looked inquiringly at White Eagle. "You say that Anna is at the same place where we take Willow?"

White Eagle nodded. "Waccachalla."

"How far is it?" Stuart asked.

"A half day—" White Eagle began, then stopped abruptly at the sight of another *Shemanese* emerging from the forest with his rifle leveled and his finger on the trigger.

"Why didn't ye call me?" the man growled to Stuart.

"Put that down," Stuart said quickly. "These men are friends."

Edward Tucker reluctantly lowered his rifle, and Stuart made the necessary introductions.

Tucker looked at Ian with interest. "McKnight, is it? Yer gal promised ye'd give me gold for tellin' ye where she was."

"He already knows," Stuart said shortly.

At the sight of Tucker, Ian had instinctively thrust Anna's necklace inside his shirt; now he shrugged and showed empty palms. "I have no gold to give ye," he managed to say before being seized by a racking cough.

"You're not well. When did you last eat?" Stuart asked.

Ian shook his head. "I don't rightly know. The last few days have been a bit hazy."

"Well, don't take too much at once, but here's some fresh johnnycake. Rebecca made it just before we left."

At the mention of Rebecca's name, Ian looked anxious. "Is all well with my wife?"

"Very well," Stuart assured him. "Apart from her concern about you, of course."

"I reckon she never thought when she made this johnnycake that I'd be eatin' it." Ian finished the bread and a bit of venison jerky, and drank a few welcome draughts of water.

"You look better already," Stuart said.

"Aye, hearin' that Anna lives is the best medicine I could have."

Stuart agreed. He still didn't understand all that

had come to pass to bring Willow's father and White
Eagle together, but he took heart that they would
soon find Anna.

Suddenly Ian looked around. "Where's Willow
and White Eagle? I want to know more about this
Waccachalla."

Stuart had seen them slip into the woods, and he
had a fair notion why. "You can ask tomorrow. I
doubt we'll see them again tonight."

While the others talked and ate, White Eagle quietly
untied his horse and motioned for Willow to follow
him. A safe distance from the camp, he stopped in a
small clearing, unsaddled Mishewa, and took something from the saddlebag.

In the deepening shadows of the approaching
night, he held it out to Willow.

"Our wedding blanket." She touched it almost rev-
erently. "I never thought to see this again."

Her heart was full, remembering the moment
when Tall Oak had put it around their shoulders. She
had been proud then that White Eagle would be her
husband, and so full of love she could scarcely speak.
Her memories of the time, brief as it was, that she and
White Eagle had shared on this same blanket had sus-
tained her through the many long nights when she
had lain alone, desperately hoping that they would
both live to share that love again.

Only once in all those weeks had Willow cried, but
now that their long separation was over and her man
once more stood before her, the dam of her pent-up
emotions burst, producing a torrent of tears.

White Eagle's puzzled distress showed in his voice. "Why do you weep? Are we not together now?"

Willow raised her chin. "You have much to learn, my husband. I do not weep because we are together now, but because we were so long apart. I cry because you look so thin and I see that the wound in your leg gives you pain."

White Eagle took the blanket from her and spread it on the ground, then turned back and kissed Willow's cheeks, tasting her salty tears. He did not understand all of her words, but his heart knew their meaning. The woman he loved still loved him, and that was all that mattered.

"You are also thin, *neewa*." His fingers traced the planes of her face, then traveled down her torso, outlining bones that before had been covered with flesh.

She shivered beneath his touch, and when they again embraced, her taut nipples pressed into his chest, feeding the growing fire in his loins. But when her own thigh pressed against the wound in his, he winced and groaned.

Immediately she drew back. "I will not hurt you."

He pulled her to him once more, his lips stopping any further talk from hers. "Not loving you—that would hurt more."

A moment later, Willow pulled back from the growing ardor of his embrace. "Lie down. You must not stand so long."

"I can stand as long as I like," he said, but the ache in his leg told him that Willow spoke the truth. He joined her on their wedding blanket and lay on his side, facing her.

She lifted his hunting shirt and bent her head to his chest. He closed his eyes and shuddered as she kissed the hollow above his breast bone and each nipple in turn, then probed his navel with her tongue. He groaned and pulled up her shift, touching the secret places that for so long he had felt only in his dreams.

She sat up and pulled the garment off over her head, and he let her remove his shirt the same way. When he took off his breechclout, he heard the sharp intake of breath when her hands brushed against his manhood.

"You have not grown thin there," she said.

He had not heard her laugh for too long, and it pleased him that she could still make a jest, after all she had been through among the *Shemanese*. The night had grown too dark for him to see her face, but his hands could read the message in her warm, pliant flesh as she came into his arms.

Perhaps he was not as strong as when they had first shared this wedding blanket, White Eagle thought, but he could still give his wife pleasure. Her legs spread wide to welcome him inside her, and her hands played over his body as he urged her toward the next peak of their love.

Finally spent, they rolled on their sides and lay face to face, panting from their pleasant exertion. Aware of the chill night air, he pulled the edges of the wedding blanket over their bodies. With their arms entwined and their bodies pressed seamlessly together from head to foot, they finally slept.

*   *   *

In her bed in the chief's *wegiwa*, Anna awoke early from a confused dream in which she had seemed to be getting a scolding from Miss Martin for bringing the chief's daughter into the school. She lay there for a moment, puzzling over what could have influenced her to dream about Philadelphia. As much as she wanted to see Stuart Martin, Anna had no desire to go back to his aunt's house. She sighed. If nothing else, her dream had served to remind her that her future was still uncertain.

She heard Standing Crane moving around outside and smelled the unpleasant odor of game being fried in bear grease. The day before, Otter had brought the chief two gifts, a huge turkey and a fat rabbit. The way he had looked at Anna made her know that he hadn't given up on taking her into his lodge. But so far, the chief had shown no sign that he wanted to give her to any warrior, and from that she continued to take heart that he would not.

Yesterday Anna had helped Blossom and Standing Crane pluck and clean the turkey and hang it to ripen. Then Blossom showed Anna how to skin the rabbit, which was left to soak overnight; she presumed that Standing Crane now fried it for their breakfast.

Anna continued to hope that either the trader Edward Tucker or the young warrior White Eagle would reach her father, who would then come to Waccachalla to take her back to Kentucky. She still doubted their ability to help her, however. She didn't trust the trader Tucker, and she found it somewhat hard to believe the warrior's story that the Willow she had been mistaken for had herself been kidnapped by Anna's father.

"An-na? Come eat."

Anna arose and went outside, pausing at the water bucket to wash her face and hands. The fried rabbit lay elevated on a slab of wood so the village dogs couldn't get to it. The meat didn't smell at all appealing, but Anna ate her portion, along with pumpkin slices flavored with a sweet syrup the Shawnee called *melassa*. In her weeks with the Shawnee, she had not grown accustomed to their food or to the way they ate it, dipping their fingers from a common pot. She had lost some weight, but she had eaten enough to keep up her strength.

The task that Standing Crane set for the girls this day was more tedious than arduous. Anna and Blossom were to take all the feathers that had accumulated in the past few months and separate them by size, color, and their eventual use.

The girls had almost finished their work when the village dogs barked, a signal of approaching visitors.

The trader, perhaps, or even White Eagle. Anna's heart beat faster in anticipation, and she longed to go see for herself. But she had learned that she must wait to be sought out; a chief's daughter, even one only by adoption, did not lower herself to seek out visitors.

From where she sat, Anna could see little, and it seemed that a long time passed before Sits-in-Shadow called to her.

"Come to the *msi-kah-mi-qui*," he said. When Blossom started to follow them, he shook his head. "*Mattah*. An-na come alone."

With her heart racing, Anna followed the medicine man. She alternately hoped and feared what she would find.

Edward Tucker has brought my father here, she hoped. *The trader brings bad news,* she feared.

Approaching the council house, Anna saw four horses tethered nearby. The villagers who had gathered outside the *msi-kah-mi-qui* murmured excitedly among themselves. When they saw Anna and Sits-in-Shadow, they fell silent and moved aside to let them pass.

Anna paused at the door of the *msi-kah-mi-qui* and took a deep breath, gathering strength to face whatever awaited her.

Then, holding her head high, she stepped inside.

32

WACCACHALLA

If Black Snake was at all surprised at the sight of the oddly assorted group of men who returned Willow to Waccachalla, he didn't show it. The chief remained impassive as he greeted each man with his customary ceremony. When at last Willow stood before him, he spoke to her only briefly, and with no more feeling than he showed the others.

"It is good that our Willow has returned. We sorrow for our kinswoman, Bear's Daughter. Later, I will hear more of this thing."

Willow nodded. "It will be as you wish, my chief."

Black Snake turned to Sits-in-Shadow, who had hurried to the lodge the moment someone told him that Willow had returned. The medicine man had insisted that the girl was still alive, and he could scarcely contain his pleasure that his words had come true.

"Bring An-na here," Black Snake ordered, and the medicine man left.

The chief fastened his gaze on Edward Tucker. "Black Snake has no business with the trader Tuck-er today," he said.

Tucker's face flushed angrily, and he looked to Ian and White Eagle as if he expected them to come to his defense.

"The chief bids you to leave," Ian said.

Tucker glared at Ian. "I'll go, but hear this, Mc-Knight. Ye owe me gold, an' I'll not fergit it. One day I'll have my due."

With a final malevolent glare, the trader left the lodge.

Stuart shook his head. "I fear the man will get his due, all right, but not in a way he will like."

Ian scarcely noticed Tucker's departure. "Can it really be true that Anna is here?" he asked.

"Black Snake has sent the medicine man for An-na," Willow said.

"I thank God for this day," Ian said fervently.

White Eagle glanced at Ian. "Thank also Black Snake. He take her as daughter."

"Tell the chief that I am Anna's father. Now that he has Willow back, I would take my daughter home with me."

White Eagle shook his head. "I cannot say this thing. An-na comes soon."

"Not soon enough for me," Stuart muttered. Now that the moment he had imagined for so many months was almost at hand, and he would once more be with Anna, his mouth felt dry and his head seemed suddenly light.

Black Snake gestured toward the door and addressed

Willow. "Look that way. My daughter comes."

Willow watched the lodge entrance as Black Snake had told her, curious to see this strange An-na. She had accepted the fact that she had a sister who resembled her, but she was totally unprepared to be gazing into her own face when she saw An-na in the doorway.

"Ahh."

Willow didn't know whether she had uttered the sound, or if it came from somewhere behind her. For a long moment, Willow and Anna stood still and stared at each other, while everyone else gazed at them, astonished at their uncanny resemblance. It was the first time that anyone then present had seen the girls together in the same place at the same time, and even Sits-in-Shadow shivered at the sight.

With her eyes still fixed on Anna's face, Willow walked toward her sister with a slow, deliberate pace. She stopped at the lodge door, and the girls continued to regard one another in silence, stunned to see how much they did, indeed, resemble one other. Anna stood slightly taller, and Willow's skin was somewhat darker, but otherwise the girls' appearance was identical.

"An-na?" Willow put out a tentative hand to Anna's cheek, as if to make sure that what she saw was real.

In return, Anna gently touched Willow's hair, the only like her own she had ever seen. Without taking conscious thought, Anna spoke to Willow in Shawnee. "*Neetanetha,*" she said, and added in English, "My sister."

"My sis-ter An-na," Willow said.

Almost overcome with emotion over a reunion neither had ever expected, the girls spontaneously embraced one another. When at last they drew apart, Black Snake gestured to the girls to come to the center of the lodge.

Anna had been so occupied with Willow that she had not noticed anyone else, but when her father called her name, she turned to him.

Unashamed of the tears that ran unchecked down his bearded cheeks, Ian McKnight put an arm around each of his daughters and hugged them close.

Anna's tears mixed with his as she kissed Ian's cheek. "Oh, Father! I never gave up hope that you'd find me."

"I reckon God heard us all, lass. But there's somebody else here's who's been doin' a lot of hopin'."

Ian stepped back to Stuart and handed him Anna's necklace. "Tell her she can have it back now."

"Stuart!" Anna's tone revealed her astonishment, while her expression silently told Stuart that all he had hoped for had come true. He held out his arms to Anna, and with a cry of joy, she came into them.

"Oh, Anna—I thought I'd lost you," Stuart murmured. "Thank God you're all right."

"I always dreamed that we'd be together again. But I never thought it would be in this place."

"The same with me." Stuart spoke softly into her ear. "*Amo te,* Anna Willow."

"Oh, Stuart! I love you, too," Anna whispered back.

Behind them, Ian cleared his throat.

Thus reminded that they were not alone, and had

no doubt exceeded all the bounds of propriety, both white and Indian, Stuart and Anna broke off their embrace, but stood close together, holding hands. Near them, Willow stood with White Eagle and smiled at Anna as if to say she was glad that her sister also had found a man who loved her.

"I think the chief wants our attention," Ian said.

Willow and White Eagle stood on Black Snake's right and Anna and Stuart on his left. Ian took his place between his daughters and took each of their free hands in his. Thus finally joined, the twin Willows, their father, and their men stood before Black Snake.

The chief addressed Willow first. "This warrior White Eagle has taken you as his wife?"

Willow nodded, somewhat embarrassed that she had allowed the chief to see the depth of her feelings for White Eagle. Such a thing was unseemly; even though Bear's Daughter had made the match herself, she would probably frown at the way Willow's eyes openly adored White Eagle.

Black Snake then turned his attention to Anna. "You are my kinswoman, even as this Willow. These *Shemanese* would take you with them. Is it your will to go?"

Anna looked to White Eagle, who quickly translated Black Snake's words. With her head high, Anna nodded. "Yes. I thank my father Black Snake for all he has done for me. I can never forget him or the people of Waccachalla. But I must stay with the father that I have always known."

Black Snake sat silent for a moment after White

Eagle supplied Anna's words, then he nodded slowly. "Then An-na goes when she will. But she is my kinswoman. She will always be welcome in this lodge."

Anna's eyes thanked Black Snake when White Eagle translated his words.

Willow laid an imploring hand on Ian's arm. "Do not take An-na back to Kan-tuck-e."

"Ye will have some time together, but then I maun return to Rebecca."

"And Anna and I must make some plans of our own," Stuart said.

Ian smiled ruefully. "Aye, to think that I finally found both my daughters, only to lose them again."

Anna shook her had. "No, that will never happen. The ties that bind us all"—her gesture included Willow and White Eagle—"can never be severed."

Black Snake looked to Sits-in-Shadow. "Prepare a *psai-wi oyi-eluh*," he ordered.

"He will give us a feast." Anna recognized the words and said them before White Eagle had the chance.

Anna nodded to the chief. *"Oui-sah."*

"It is good," echoed Willow, proud she knew those English words.

Despite the short notice, that evening's *psai-wi oyi-eluh* went well. In this time of harvest, food was abundant, and Otter had just brought in a fine, freshly killed venison.

As it roasted over the fire, Blossom made Anna understand that Otter had intended it as a marriage gift. If Anna would have accepted him, then Black Snake had agreed to give his permission.

"I do not like him," Blossom concluded in something of an understatement.

Otter sat apart from the others with the corners of his thin mouth turned down and his forehead wrinkled in displeasure. He had lost Willow twice, once when she left with Bear's Daughter, and now to this warrior White Eagle she called her husband. She looked at that Shawnee as he had long wanted her to look at him. He had then planned to marry An-na, who should rightly be his, but now he knew that was not to be, either. Before the *psai-wi oyi-eluh*, Black Snake told the village that his daughter An-na would soon be leaving Waccachalla with the same yellow-haired *Shemanese* who had returned Willow to Waccachalla.

These things should not be, Otter told himself. Tomorrow he would leave Waccachalla. He would not return until he had found a wife. Then they would have his own *psai-wi oyi-eluh*.

Anna paid no heed to Otter. Too excited to eat, she feasted her eyes on Stuart instead, with occasional glances at Willow and her father as if to reassure herself they were still there. She admired the healthy, ruddy glow of his skin. Stuart's recent hard physical labor was evident in his muscular arms, which Anna longed to have embrace her once more.

She smiled at Stuart's clumsy attempts to eat the Shawnee way. When she put her hand on his to show him how to use a shell to dip a portion of baked squash, she felt her whole body tremble in anticipation of a more intimate touch. The brief time they had spent in his aunt's carriage house had been etched in her memory for months. She longed to be alone with him, to repeat the kisses and caresses that her heart treasured. And from the way his violet eyes held hers, Anna knew he must share the same desire.

When the feast ended and the dance drums began to beat, Stuart leaned closer. "How long will this go on?"

"Two hours, maybe more."

"Is there a place we can be alone?"

Anna glanced around and saw that no one watched them. She and Stuart could slip away without being missed, especially if they went singly.

"Mind where I go, then wait a moment before following."

Stuart nodded, and Anna walked away without haste.

"This puts to mind the trouble we had being alone at my aunt's house," he said when he joined her.

"Yes, but the chief's lodge in Waccachalla is not at all like Miss Martin's in Philadelphia. Here, if I tie the door flap closed, no one will disturb us."

Stuart looked around the lodge while Anna brought the door-skins together and secured them with a strip of leather. The only light came from the smoldering fire pit in the center of the lodge. A thin plume of smoke rose toward the open smoke-hole at the top of the dwelling. Clothing, animal skins, storage vessels, and a variety of other implements lay scattered about the large single room. His nose wrinkled at a smell he couldn't identify.

"Bear grease," Anna said before he could ask. "They use a lot of it.

"The chief's wife made a place for me on the other side of that blanket," she added. "There are no chairs, but we can sit on my bed."

Stuart looked puzzled when they reached the partitioned-off area. "What bed?"

Anna pointed to the buffalo robes piled against the wall in the far corner. She lifted them, revealing a stack of fresh-cut, fragrant cedar boughs underneath. "Sit down and try it. It's more comfortable than it looks."

"This is quite pleasant," Stuart commented when he had settled himself beside her. They sat, leaning against the lodge wall with their legs stretched out before them. "No wonder Willow wouldn't sleep on your pallet at the Station."

"You must have been surprised when you saw her for the first time," Anna said.

Stuart groaned at the memory. "Not nearly as surprised as she was. I thought she was you, and started kissing her. She thought a wild man was attacking her, and started screaming and hitting me."

Imagining the scene, Anna smiled. "That must have been quite a sight."

"I'm sure it was. After that, it took a while for Willow to trust me."

"It must have seemed strange to be around someone who looks so much like me, but is so different."

"Strange is not the word I would use. At times, it was torture. Looking at Willow only made me want you more."

In the semidark, Stuart turned and took Anna's face between his hands, reading it as a blind man might. His thumbs traced her high cheekbones and straight nose and brushed the indentation above her mouth, then moved on to outline her full lips before he bent his head to kiss them. Anna put her arms around his neck and eagerly returned his kiss. One hand pressed the hollow in the back of his neck and the other tangled in his thick hair, urging him even closer.

"Oh, Anna, you don't know how many times I've dreamed of this moment."

Without letting her go, he moved to face her, and knelt with his legs astraddle her. Each point where their bodies touched produced a heat that spread through them like a wildfire. She was aware of the beating of their hearts, his strong and steady, hers becoming more rapid with every passing moment.

Without warning, he leaned back on his heels, then sat back beside her, so that their bodies no longer touched.

"What's wrong?" she asked.

"I was about to forget myself again. I love you, Anna, and I know you love me. But I want to do the right thing by you."

His words did nothing to lessen the growing ache she sensed that only his love could ease. "And what is that?"

"As my aunt would say, we should wait to be together until we can get back to Kentucky and find someone to marry us."

Anna sighed. "If it had been left up to Miss Martin, you wouldn't ever be with me, anytime or anyplace."

He nodded. "That is true. Besides, we will be married as soon as we get back to Kentucky. What difference will a few days make?"

"None," she said firmly. "We've waited long enough. Let's start where we left off in the carriage house."

"Oh, Anna—"

"Shh! We didn't talk much then, remember?"

He took her into his arms, just as he had that day so many months ago, and kissed her the same way he had then, with a tender, growing passion.

"*Amo te,*" he whispered against her cheek. "I love you."

"Then show me," she whispered back.

He needed no further urging. Gently he guided Anna to lie down on her side, and stretched out beside her. Holding her close, he kissed her forehead and her cheeks, her eyelids and the tip of her nose. She shivered when he nibbled her earlobe, and her head fell back almost reflexively as his tongue probed the hollow of her neck and traced her collarbone. His hands moved lower, pressing in slow circles against her breasts, teasing her nipples to become pebble-hard. She strained against him, longing to feel his hands against her bare flesh.

Knowing her need, he plucked at the drawstring on her shift until it fell open, freeing her full breasts. Even in the dim light he could make out the puffy duskiness that surrounded each nipple. With her breasts cupped in his hands, he pressed his thumbs against their taut center. His mouth covered one erect nipple, and his tongue first circled, then sucked the sweetness there before repeating his movements on the other breast.

He eased her shift the rest of the way off, then

quickly removed his own clothing. She didn't have enough time to take in all the wonder of his naked body before he lowered it to cover hers. She felt as if every bit of her flesh strained toward every fiber of his body, seeking union.

Closing her eyes, she sighed softly and concentrated all her senses on the pleasures of his touch. While his head remained at her breasts, his fingers brushed the small of her back, then his hands moved to the curve of her buttocks. When he pulled them toward him, she shuddered at the sensation when his unexpected hardness pressed against her tender womanhood. He continued to kiss her face and her breasts while his hands caressed her thighs and his fingers lightly probed her most private part.

Sensations she had never known could exist flooded over her as her body urged her to seek the center of the most intense feelings she had ever experienced. She writhed under his touch, and her body arched toward his, wanting something more, something stronger, but not knowing what.

Her legs, already half-parted, opened wider at the gentle urging of his hands against her knees. She felt his probing hand being replaced by something more, something much heavier, that reached deep inside her, where nothing had ever before invaded. Eagerly she rose to meet him, crying out in pain and wonder when he broke through her maiden body's last barrier.

He heard her, but continued moving inside her, unable to stop and aware that her temporary hurt was the necessary prelude to their future pleasure. His shaft was hard and hot and felt tight inside her. He cupped her buttocks and urged her to meet each thrust. She wrapped her legs around his back and continued to cling to him. After a moment she found the silent rhythm to which his body moved and answered it with her own. The beat was similar to the insistent sound of the nearby drums. It moved like a sea tide, ebbing and flowing toward an inevitable destination.

With one final stroke, he groaned and pitched forward. With his head resting on her breasts, she still trembled from the experience. With the evidence of his fulfillment warm inside her body, she lay in quiet contentment.

For a long while, she thought, she had feared she might never see him again. But now, coming together in this most unlikely place that neither would have chosen, their bodies had sealed their love.

After a moment, Stuart rolled over on his side and drew her close again, lying as they had in Miss Martin's parlor. Only this time, they would not be interrupted. They snuggled close together, their bodies touching at the hips and knees. She pressed the palm of her hand on his still rapidly beating heart and exulted that their blood at last could course together. Before their pulses had time to calm, they kissed again, quietly at first, then with rekindled ardor.

This time, she needed no urging to open her body to him again, as she had long since opened her heart. Without the haste of their first coming together, the sensations she felt were even more powerful. This time, the strange cry from her throat told him that she shared his ecstacy, and when he kissed her, he was surprised to taste the salty tears on her cheeks.

Stuart pulled back, suddenly concerned. "Are you all right?"

She nodded and wiped her eyes with the back of one hand. "Until now, I never thought anybody could cry about being happy."

"In that case, I ought to be sobbing out loud."

She heard the smile in his voice, but she spoke seriously. "I will never forget this night as long as I live. Surely nothing can ever be as wonderful."

"Except for the next million nights we'll be together."

They embraced again, then reluctantly she pulled away. "I wish we could go to sleep now and wake in each other's arms, but we mustn't stay here any longer. Soon the dancing will end and the chief and his family will return."

Stuart looked around the lodge. "Not much place to hide around here, is there?"

"I'm afraid not. Put on your clothes and follow me."

"Anywhere, my love," he murmured, and would have gone on kissing her for a long time, had she let him.

No one saw Anna take Stuart to the creek, where they stripped again in the darkness. Shivering in the cold water, they washed away the evidence of their lovemaking and came dangerously close to repeating the performance before Anna thrust a blanket at him.

"Dry off with this and put on your clothes. Hurry! The drums have stopped."

They dressed themselves and walked together to the council lodge, where Stuart and Ian would spread their blankets for the night. "It will be hard to sleep beside your father tonight," he said glumly.

"Yes, I know that he sometimes snores."

"You know that's not what I meant," Stuart said.

"This separation won't last long. Tomorrow I want to spend some time with Willow, but the day after that, Father and you and I will be on our way back to Kentucky."

"And the day after that, we'll be officially married."

Anna smiled faintly. "Us married—I can scarcely believe how this has all worked out."

Stuart looked over at the firestone, where Willow and White Eagle stood conversing with Ian.

"That Shawnee warrior and I are the most fortunate of men," he declared.

"Oh? Why do you say that?"

"Because he has Willow and I have Anna Willow."

Anna lifted her chin proudly. "And we twin Willows have you."

Silverwillow would be pleased, she thought.

The early history of Kentucky and the Northwest Territory contains many actual events that rival any fiction writer's powers of invention. *Twin Willows* draws on several such true stories, unusual circumstances, and real people.

One such occurrence is the siege of Bryan's Station (often incorrectly called Bryant's Station) in August of 1782. Many of the residents mentioned in *Twin Willows* actually lived there at the time. Also surviving the siege were my great-great-great-great-grandparents, who had come there from the Yadkin River area of North Carolina with Daniel Boone and other neighbors.

Among the several dozen books, periodicals, videotapes and microfilm resources used in recreating this period, the most valuable were Allan W. Eckert's *The Frontiersmen* and *A Sorrow in My Heart,* and James Alexander Thom's *Follow the River* and *Panther in the Sky.*

History has always been made by ordinary people,

and each of us now living has been preceded by thousands of history-making ancestors. We should never forget that in meeting the challenges of their own times, these men and women made it possible for us to have the same opportunity today.